AND
SO I
ROAR

**ALSO BY ABI DARÉ
AVAILABLE FROM RANDOM
HOUSE LARGE PRINT**

The Girl with the Louding Voice

AND SO I ROAR

A Novel

ABI DARÉ

RANDOM HOUSE
LARGE PRINT

Copyright © 2024 by Abi Daré

All rights reserved. Published in the United States of America by Random House Large Print in association with Dutton, an imprint of Penguin Random House LLC.

Original cover design by Dominique Jones
Design adapted for Large Print
Cover illustration by Vikki Chu

The Library of Congress has established a Cataloging-in-Publication record for this title.

ISBN: 978-0-593-91539-4

www.penguinrandomhouse.com/large-print-format-books

FIRST LARGE PRINT EDITION

Printed in the United States of America

1st Printing

To girls like Adunni, who face daily struggles for life's basic necessities: May the world listen, learn, and be transformed by your unwavering courage, strength, and resilience. May you roar, always, with the indomitable spirit of a lion, and may the legacies of the unsung heroes who stand by you inspire generations to come.

And to A & D, who are the guiding lights behind every dream I pursue: May you always know the immeasurable depth of your worth.

AND
SO I
ROAR

A good education can never be good
enough when you have a bad name.

—THE VERY IMPORTANT SMALL BOOK OF
LIFE'S LITTLE WISDOMS BY ADUNNI
(THE ONLY EDITION, WRITTEN INSIDE
LOCKUP IN IKATI VILLAGE)

THURSDAY
JANUARY 2015

||||||||||||
TIA
||||||||||||
PORT HARCOURT

I used to tell people my mother gave birth to a thousand books and one girl.

They would chuckle, believing I was attempting to be humorous. I wish I were. Now that she's dying, I find myself clinging to a particular childhood memory: I am six years old, and my scalp is pulsating from a headache triggered by taut cornrows. I am sitting on the cool floor tiles outside of my mother's home library and, desperate for comfort, I knock, pleading for her to let me in, but she is too engrossed in a one-sided, animated conversation with the author of the book she's reading to hear me. She has imagined this author, as she often does, and for the time being, he is her beloved child, my phantom sibling. I fall asleep waiting and dream of her pulling me into a deep hug and pressing my head into her bosom, into her scent of fresh basil, and together, we sway to the rhythm of her laughter until I startle awake and realize it's been hours. I knock again, and this time, there is a pause from inside, a brief consideration of my persistence, before the resumption of her occupation. Eventually, our housemaid, Ada, discovers me huddled on the floor and sends me to my room.

It's been nearly thirty years, and I'm still haunted by this memory.

My mother was readmitted last week to a private ward in a hospital in Port Harcourt and has been sleeping since I arrived. I must admit that sitting this close feels unnatural, difficult. I can smell her breath, and every expulsion from her partly slackened mouth warms the air between us with the odor of antibiotics and sulfur. I used to take refuge in that green padded chair by the door of her hospital room, in filling the chasm between us with practiced smiles and delicately rehearsed responses. It was a pragmatic choice, easier than sitting close enough for her to see the pain of her childhood rejection still etched on my face.

But today is different.

Today I'd like for her to witness the scars stinging my face, to (and this seems unfair in the face of her distress) afflict her with some of the trauma I've recently suffered. I fear it's the only way she'll understand why I must pry the relics of my buried past out of her grip.

She stirs, and I pitch forward.

"Mum?" I whisper. "Are you awake?" Her bald scalp reminds me of the small retractable head of an aged tortoise. Her fists huddle the bedsheet at the sides, but she says nothing. I suspect she knows I am here; that she is, as usual, taking her time.

Her eyes snap open. "Your face," she says, her own gaunt, weathered face austere with the silent analysis of recollection as she considers the lines etched under my chin like a signature, the cruel Y-shaped welt crawling along my jaw. "Dad said you had an . . . accident," she says. "What happened?"

"I lied," I say. "It wasn't an accident." A pause. The lacerations are slowly disappearing, but the memory of being whipped in a fertility ritual my mother-in-law organized continues to torment me. I couldn't look in the mirror for days after. Sometimes I still can't. Sometimes, in the night's stillness, when my husband, Ken, is asleep, I hear a whip, a vicious crack in the air, and I startle, catch myself.

I ball my fists to control the shaking in my hands. "I've been thinking," I say haltingly, "about—"

"That's a stack of bloody good books." She nods at the pile of novels on the wooden table beside me. "Pass that blue-covered one, will you? The one with the bookmark?"

She's expecting me to deflect, to bow under the weight of her gaze, but I hitch my chair nearer, back straight. "I realize it may be uncomfortable, me asking about a sixteen-year-old document, but I need it." I bring my hands together, a forced plea. "I wouldn't have flown over if you'd replied to my emails or texts."

She presses a finger to the control panel on the handle of her bed so that it tilts upward with a whirring sound, and when her face is level with mine, she licks her lips, the tip of her tongue tinged yellow and textured like aged cheddar.

"Tia," she says, voice soft. "Your dad is around. I can't talk about this now. Give me some time. I just recovered from another infection. My novel?"

"I need a moment," I say, rising and hurrying out of her room, past a woman retching in the next ward, past the line of nurses' stations. It's not until the elevator pings open that I realize I forgot my handbag. I dash back and halt at the cracked-open door. My mother is speaking to my aunty on the phone, on a video call, as they often do, and in a voice so serious and penetrating that I am compelled to eavesdrop.

"You are asking me not to tell her?" my mother is saying. "To carry this secret to my grave? No, Beatrice. Let me die in peace. Let me explain why she can't have the documentation she's—" My aunty interrupts, her voice high-pitched and garbled like a cassette tape on fast-forward.

I listen, eyes on my distorted silhouette reflected in the foil-tinted window of the opposite ward, a hot tingle filling every crevice of my body. I am struggling to grasp on to their fragmented conversation, to slot piece after piece in to make an entire portrait of my past, but they carry on back and forth, piercing me afresh with the sharp edge of each discovery until my aunty's voice falls to a mumble that no longer rises and I can no longer wait in this excruciating anticipation for the glue that binds the fragments of the words—"it's too late" and "she will never forgive you"—together.

So I push the door open and walk in.

My mother immediately ends the call with a feeble jab of her finger, her face contorting into a strange, anguished expression. We stare at each other: both of us trapped on this island fenced with decades of bitterness and spite, with the thorns of this fresh revelation sprouting around its barbed edges.

"You lied to me." My mouth forms the words, but I am not sure I utter them or if I am merely thinking of speaking. "You told me—"

"Not here, Tia," she says. "Give me time to be ready."

"How could you?" I yell, feeling stuffed with shattered things.

"**How could I?** Tia, please." She has the audacity to blink back tears, to look away. "Everything was to protect you," she says. "Your future was—"

"Stop it!" The shattered things in me accumulate, filling me with a strident noise. It rides up my throat and into my mouth, and I am forced to stuff a fist in, to choke on it. In the silence, my breathing aligns.

My mother turns to look at me. "Sometimes, Tia," she says, "we toss ourselves the lifeboat of lies to save us from drowning. You were drowning. You're still struggling to keep your head above water after all these years. Does your husband know about your relationship with Boma?"

Silence. Cowering beneath the intermittent beeping of a machine and my thudding heart.

"Don't think I haven't noticed that you stop by to visit him before coming here."

"My marriage is none of your business," I say when I find my voice.

She closes her eyes, shutting me out. "Your father will be away at a business meeting next Wednesday. We can talk then."

My father materializes from the doorway as if summoned, a paper bag full of meds scrunched up in his grasp. He stops at the foot of my mother's bed, catching his breath. "Is everything all right with my girls?" He peers at the book my mother was reading as though we inscribed the condition of our collective state of mind on its fancy blue cover. "How are you both?"

"I need to get back to Lagos," I say, my pulse thumping in my ears.

"Now?" my father asks.

"She will be back on Wednesday," my mother says, her miserable smile an unstable curve digging into the gaunt hollowness of her cheek. She has arranged her face into a controlled recalcitrance because she knows I have no choice. That she's right makes me want to scream. Something acrid rises in me, and as I walk away, I decide to return one last time to hear what she has to say, and afterward, I will conduct a wretched funeral for her in the graveyard of my heart.

Wednesday will be the end of us.

TUESDAY

|||||||||||
TIA
|||||||||||
LAGOS

At eight o'clock, Adunni waltzes into my living room, drenched in morning sunlight and the scent of mint bodywash.

Adunni is a brilliant fourteen-year-old I met while she was working as a housemaid for a neighbor down our street in Lagos. The faded ankara dress she first wore from her village hangs loosely around her neck, and her calloused toes—the evidence of a year of punishing labor—protrude out of the worn shoes she inherited from the maid who served before her. Her matted, tangled hair is sleek with cheap grease, a pen sticking out of her month-old cornrow, but her eyes, like her smile, are liquid with the thrill of expectation, hope.

"Hey!" I tilt my laptop closed, averting my eyes so that the sun does not illuminate their swollen red state. "Did you sleep well?"

"I didn't able to sleep one eye," she says, squinting at the sunbeams lancing through the partially drawn blinds over our bifold doors. "Did you really text me this text message, or was I dreaming of it?"

She produces her phone from the pocket of her dress and holds it up for me to read my own words:

Adunni!! you got in!!
You won a place in the scheme!
I am not waiting ONE MORE DAY!
I will fight Florence if I have to.
I am coming to get you now!!
Pack your stuff.
xx

I sent the text and picked up Adunni yesterday, but it's been nearly a week since I was notified of Adunni's long-awaited scholarship offer, since I walked out on my mum in hospital and returned to a thankfully empty home (my husband is away at a conference).

The visit had left me feeling disintegrated, and I'd used the time alone to train my emotions into a semblance of normalcy. Then, finally, I'd felt ready to go and do what I'd been wanting to do for months: liberate Adunni from my neighbor Florence, who had used her as an unpaid servant.

"It's not a dream," I say. "You won a scholarship. You did that, Adunni. You wrote that essay and got yourself a place, and I am so proud of you."

She grins. "You know, I was looking at the long hand of the clock chasing the short one, ticking-tock-tick from yesternight till seven in the morning because I am too full of excitement! Ms. Tia, why is a clock so slow to run fast when you are in a hurry? What is the time now?"

"Five past eight?" I motion toward the dining chair opposite me, the plate of buttered toast and the steaming mug of chocolate next to it. "I made you some toast and hot chocolate."

She glances at the food and covers her mouth. "Ah! Sorry! I keep forgetting myself to greet you good morning! Good morning, Ms. Tia." She bends her knees in a curtsy, offering her greeting with a gesture of respect I can't get used to. "Is today or tomorrow the day I am going to school true-true?"

My mouth gives way into a lopsided smile. "Today we'll go pick up your uniform, buy some more books, get your hair done. **Tomorrow** I'll drop you at school."

"What are you doing on the computer machine? Why didn't you drink your good-morning coffee?"

It surprised me when Florence agreed to release her. I had expected some resistance, but I sensed Florence was tired of combating our relentless fight for her freedom. Adunni spent last night in our guest room—and I can tell, from the energetic bounce in her step, that it's the best night she's had since she arrived in Lagos.

"I am trying to find a flight for Wednesday," I say. "I need to return to my mother."

"Tomorrow? But we are going to school?"

"She wants to talk to me tomorrow, but I'll leave after I drop you off at school. I can catch the last flight back."

Sleeping pills haven't stopped the cruel loop of that conversation replaying in my mind. I've been rolling off my bed, stuffing the edge of my pillow into my mouth, and screaming silently into it until my voice becomes hoarse.

Why this ache pulsating in my bones now, at the thought of returning to Port Harcourt? Why didn't I insist at the time on hearing what she had to say? Could I call Aunty Beatrice instead? I have a feeling she'd simply refer me back to Mum.

"Ms. Tia?"

"I am good, thanks," I say in response to a comment or question that has lost its precise form and shape. "Eat."

I am careful not to watch her eat, focusing instead on sorting out my flight timings, but she's gnashing her teeth, swallowing with rapid gulps, burping and offering apologies for disturbing me with the noise. It's as if there is a timer somewhere, ticking a warning toward some punishment should she eat any slower.

When last did she eat proper food?

"Don't rush," I say, glancing at her. "You'll choke. And then we can't go shopping."

She stops chewing abruptly, holding out a piece of her toast, staring at the teeth marks indented on the soggy edges as if transfixed by this very act of eating a piece of toast. Her eyes fill with tears, one sliding gracefully down each cheek, which she swipes away quickly with the back of her buttered hand, streaking grease across her face.

"Sorry, Ms. Tia," she says. "I am just too very hungry."

As I watch her, the ache in my heart expands with fresh guilt. I want to spend a lifetime making up for all she's suffered, as though I am personally responsible for her misfortunes. Perhaps I am. Partly. I could have done more for Adunni from the first day I saw Florence nearly dent her scalp with the heel of her left shoe, but I returned to this comfortable house instead, with my constant electricity and minimalist-by-choice furniture and organic diet. I closed my eyes and sobbed myself to sleep; not just because of how helpless I felt, but because I felt paralyzed by my helplessness, by the haunted, pleading look I saw in Adunni's eyes, by this child who had, unknown to me, lived down the road for months, slaving away from dawn till midnight.

Adunni opened my eyes to true compassion. She was there for me when my husband's mother took me for the baby-making ritual bath that left me with scars along my chin, arms, and shoulders.

"There's more bread," I add gently. "The butter is in the fridge. Adunni, there's a lot of food here."

She blows a path through the milk froth in her cup, watching me over the chocolate-tainted rim. "Who throw the flight away?"

"Sorry?"

"The flight you want to catch. Who throw it? How will you reach far up to catch it?"

"Oh, my love," I say. "It means you'll board, get on, a plane."

"Is there a mat on the plane?" A frown puzzles her face. "For people to sleep?"

"There are chairs. And windows. It's quite nice."

She is mute for a moment. Then: "I want to catch a plane one day. But not to see my mother, because she is in heaven. But maybe with you?"

"Maybe with me," I say, but she's already eating and talking about how excited she is to go shopping.

I jiggle my mouse to wake my computer, complete my flight booking, and slam the laptop shut. For now, I'll concentrate on getting Adunni to school. And when I finish with my mother, I'll find the strength to return home to tell my husband about Boma.

And that I'm not who he thinks I am.

❀

We are in the school uniform shop behind Ocean Academy's admin block, and I cannot stop thinking of him. Boma. Or **Bow-Mar**, as I often used to say, with a false American drawl.

I have resisted the urge to say his name aloud until now, to sound it on my lips; the bubble of spit that forms on the first syllable, the release of breath on the last, like a tired sigh. I don't enjoy thinking about him when I am not alone, for fear that the heat flushing my face will warm the room, that my thumping heart will be visible underneath my t-shirt or blouse, that people will stop and stare in wonder.

The seamstress, a cherry-faced Ms. Somebody with a tapered gray afro, who has a safety pin tucked into the corner of her mouth and a yellow measuring tape hanging around her neck, is motioning to Adunni to pull up her school skirt. There is an electric Singer sewing machine on the wooden desk next to me; beside it, a used ice cream container filled with spools of red, blue, white, and green thread. On the floor, a mound of clothes: school skirts and blouses and berets, perhaps awaiting mending. There is a headless polystyrene mannequin on a wooden tripod projecting out of the mountain of clothes like a flag on a hill, cut pieces of the blue uniform fabric pinned to its foam breasts.

I've got my AirPods in so that I can pretend to listen to music. I want to be lost in my thoughts, but I can hear and feel everything around me: the throaty laughter from the seamstress, Adunni's chirpy voice riding high and low with tales of how her essay won

her a place in this school, the click from the button
on Adunni's skirt as she fastens it, the flutter when
she twirls around so that a mint-scented breeze
caresses my knees.

"What you think, Ms. Tia? How I look?"

I turn, but I am distracted, briefly, by the framed
photo of thirty-six girls in their uniforms on the
wall, the edge of the folded ironing board covering
half their faces. I noticed the same photo behind
the principal in the admin office, but now I have
an urge to inspect it.

"Ms. Tia?"

I fix my gaze on Adunni, nodding with what I
hope is a keen smile. "Amazing!"

She laughs, clapping, saluting. She keeps doing
that: saluting when she has the school beret on, perhaps because she thinks she looks like a soldier.

"Where next?" The seamstress's voice is kind
and patient. "Busy day ahead?" She wedges herself
between the desk and the wall to sit. Picks up a
pen, scribbles into a booklet, and tears out a leaf for
Adunni. "Please hand that over to your . . ." The
seamstress trails off, giving me a hesitant smile. She's
aware I am not Adunni's mother. This is a school for
girls born into extreme poverty, girls whose mothers
do not own iPhones or wear AirPods, girls whose
only hope is what they are given on these grounds:
a sound education and a solid mindset to prepare
them for the future. But she's unsure of what to call
me and I am not in a mood to clarify who I am to

Adunni, so I smile back and take the paper out of Adunni's hands.

"It's the receipt for the uniforms," she adds. "More shopping?"

I wish she'd move that damn ironing board out of the way or shut up and tidy up. Her name comes to me then, Ms. Erinle. I wonder if she has children of her own. Why, of all things I could think about, is this what comes to mind?

"No more shopping," Adunni declares, shaking her head in an emphatic no. "Ms. Tia been so kind to me. She already take me to the ice cream shop to lick ice cream and eat **choc-late** and cake, she buy me new school shoe and new schoolbag from Shoprite supermarket shop, then she buy me this new yellow dress, and after, she take me to a hair salon with mirror-mirror on all over the wall, where they plait my hair this fine all-back style. See it, Ms. Erinle. See the hair!" Adunni yanks off the beret and runs her fingers along each line of freshly braided hair on her scalp so that the seamstress is forced to admire the feed-in cornrows.

Adunni slaps the beret back on, salutes. "When we leave here, we go home, we sleep, we wake up early tomorrow and come back here to this fine-fine school." She's stepping out of her school skirt and folding it now, gingerly, as if it's baby skin she's careful not to bruise. "Me, I stay here and learn, and Ms. Tia will run to catch her flight. The end."

"We will see you tomorrow." Ms. Erinle nods.

The safety pin is back in her mouth, and she talks through it. "I am certain Adunni will enjoy Ocean Academy."

I mumble an agreement, pick up the bag of uniforms, tell Adunni to change into her normal clothes and meet me outside. I step out into the faint chatter of schoolgirls and reprimanding teachers and ringing bells.

It's a nice school: a neat building within a large compound in Apapa; three blocks of residential flats converted by the owner, which sit behind a large garden bordered with pink and blue flowers.

There is a tree in the middle of the spacious garden, the top of which is a gargantuan crown of twigs and leaves, and I think of the tree in the garden of my childhood home; of how, before it became my meeting point with Boma, I would sit under it and watch the speckled darkness of the night sky through tiny slits in the canopy of its leaves, hoping my mother would feel the anguish of my absence at dinner and come out herself to invite me to eat with her.

The boardinghouse at the back of this red brick building is a tidy dorm of four rooms named and painted after precious gems: Amethyst, Ruby, Sapphire, and Topaz. The rooms are furnished with metal bunk beds enough for thirty-six girls. Adunni will share Amethyst with two other girls. Her roommates were in an English lesson when we went round, and when I asked if we could peep into the lesson, the matron, a woman with thinning hair dyed blue-black, raised her eyebrows at me and asked if I understood that this was a "highly secure school environment," as if I'd asked permission to kidnap one girl.

I put the bag of uniforms down and lean against a red brick column.

My phone jiggles against the back pocket of my denims. Ken. I let it ring off. Later, I'll send him a text, and when he's home tonight, I'll be ready with a lie for why I must return to Port Harcourt.

Two girls walk past me, laughing at a shared private joke, gripping exercise books in their hands, and something about their uninhibited laughter, the carefree youthfulness of their chatter, sends a surge of tension through me. I try to parcel it, to look out for Adunni, who is taking longer than expected.

The smaller of the girls stops abruptly and turns to ask if I am lost, if I need directions back to the reception. She has a small hook nose and buckteeth, and her English is stilted, like Adunni's, and I am drawn to her in inexplicable ways so that my legs move of their own accord toward her, my arms contracting as the distance between us narrows. Before I can help myself, I am grabbing her by her shoulder, my fingers clawing into her flesh so that she drops her notebook and yells, "Excuse me, ma!" rubbing her shoulder, eyes wide with shock. "You pinch me!"

"I am sorry!" I crouch to pick up and shake the

dust out of her notebook. Her name, Ebun Obuke, is scribbled across the top of the cover, her handwriting neat and spaced out.

"I am so sorry, Ebun," I say, rising, unable to stop trembling. "I was . . . I thought I saw something on your shoulder and I . . ." I trail off. My explanation is as useless as my understanding of what just happened. What is wrong with me?

Adunni appears, a ply of toilet paper stuck to her heel. She hurries to join us, glancing at me and the two girls. "Sorry, I keep you waiting! I was doing piss. You okay, Ms. Tia?" She waves at the girl, offering a huge smile. "Adunni is the name. Sorry for that!"

The upset girl curtsies and scuttles off with her friend.

I watch them run off, feeling lightheaded, unhinged. Is it me, or is the air in this school, this environment, toxic?

It's me.

The visit to my mother changed me.

It changed everything.

"Ms. Tia?" Adunni peers at me. "You okay?"

I force a laugh and joke that I am going mad, but I wonder if it's true, and if returning to Port Harcourt tomorrow would cure me of this aberrant lunacy.

❧

My husband isn't due back home for another hour, and so after I tuck Adunni into bed and set the alarm in her room for seven a.m., I make my way to the storage shed behind our kitchen. I don't know what compels me to go there now.

It is more than the conversation I overheard: The familiar pulls me in to the one who understands me without words.

A rush of noise fills my head as I turn the key in the lock and flick the light on. A naked bulb buzzes from the ceiling, illuminating the room with the washed-out amber of a sullen sunset, and it stinks faintly of stale rodent urine, of cockroaches and mothballs, the tiles cold underfoot, the air humid and dense. I put my phone torch on, holding it up to the neat stack of wedding gifts that have remained untouched since we moved in: a box of stainless steel food flasks; a carton of an oversized facial steamer apparatus that came with a manual written in Chinese; two professional, standing hooded hair dryers that do not belong in a home; ten sets of (ugly) patterned fish-shaped mugs with matching plates; twenty vacuum-sealed bags stuffed with bundles of Swiss lace fabrics and **geles**, which I might have worn if I knew how to tie the bloody things.

I shuffle in, a gentle wind rattling the glass louvers, rustling twigs and debris trapped between the partly open slats. The box I am looking for is behind the bag of fabrics, a solid wood chest with a flat lid swathed in thick cobwebs I am forced to ignore because I don't want to draw my husband's attention to this box, and to the padlock that keeps it secure. I buried the key under a heap of copper coins and rusty keys at the bottom of a clay pot behind the box. The key opens the padlock easily, expectantly—a homeowner returning to a not-quite-abandoned house—with barely a hiss and a click. The air fills with a ringing silence as I pick up the envelope stuffed fat with letters.

It's a haphazard pile, the letters flimsy, delicate. The most recent of the bunch is not what I am after, but I pull it out and unfold it under the torchlight. There is still the faint smell of the ink: fruity, like bubble gum, the words crammed together, the letter unfinished after Ken nearly caught me writing it.

I don't feel the tears forming, but I watch them drop on the paper, diluting the ink to a greenish blue. The words in this letter, like the others, are still vivid in my memory:

December 2014

Dear Boma,

I am sorry I left without saying goodbye: my husband called, and I didn't want to lie to him (again) about being with my mom. I know I promised not to do this anymore because the burden of deceit and guilt is heavy on me and unfair to you, but Bow, I've just found out my husband is infertile!!

I feel like I need to tell him about us.

"Ms. Tia?" I hear her stumbling in, knocking into a carton. "Why is the light not bright?"

I don't have time to hide the envelope and lock the box, so I tuck it underneath my armpit and find Adunni outside, with Ken standing behind her, his arms folded, their backs turned to a crepuscular spray of light across the sky.

He looks tired but pleased to see me.

"Oh . . . hey," I say to Ken, hoping my shock, the catch of my breath, isn't obvious. I close the storage shed door and turn the key in the lock, sweat soaking the edges of the envelope in my armpit.

"I tell the good doctor you are here," Adunni says. "He says you don't like coming to this place because it is smelling of rat piss inside."

"I've missed you." Ken gives me a tender but worried glance. "You were not picking up your phone. And now we find you here? What's up? Come here."

He holds his arms out for a hug, and I trudge into his embrace, my arms pressed to my sides like pins, the envelope trapped underneath.

"I bought dinner," Ken says. I sense him scrutinizing me as I wiggle out of his grip. "Sushi. Adunni says you ate out."

"We eat FKC and chickens!" Adunni proudly announces.

"Adunni had a chicken burger from KFC," I say. "I am not hungry, but thanks."

"What were you doing in there?"

"I was searching for old newspapers for research,"

I say, observing Adunni still wearing the school uniform. "I thought you'd changed?"

"I keep changing from my nightdress to my uniform to my nightdress," she says. "Sleep was running from me, so when I heard the good doctor calling your name in the parlor, I ran down to tell him you are in the outside. Want me to carry that envelope for you? You keep pinching it tight to yourself."

"I'm good, thanks," I say. "Let's go."

We begin the short walk to the kitchen.

"And your mum?" Ken says. "How is she?"

"Mum's . . ." My windpipe closes in on me, and I am grateful that he cannot see my face. "She's good."

I yank the screen door open, and we step into the warmth of the kitchen, the smell of rice wine, vinegar, and fresh salmon. Adunni does not linger. She darts through the kitchen and shoots up the stairs with a promise to get changed and "truly sleep a deep sleep."

I lean against the fridge door, the sharp edges of holiday magnets probing into the small of my back, my biceps aching from the strain of holding the envelope. "Are you not going up to shower or something?"

"Think you can put your . . . research down?" Ken goes to the sink, washes his hands, shakes them dry. He pulls out a bar stool and perches on the edge of its seat. "I'm going nowhere until I understand what's bugging you. So come sit." He pats the empty stool beside him. "There's scrumptious sushi in the fridge. Turn around and grab it, will you? We have some chilled wine in the wine cooler." He lowers his voice. "Is it Adunni? She is a bit much, isn't she? Is her school stuff stressing you out? It costs a fortune, doesn't it?"

I let out a slow breath and peel myself away from the fridge door. I'll wait until after midnight to hide the letters. Or write one more, or maybe destroy them all. I won't know until I am alone with him again, with Boma.

"Tia?" Ken's eyes follow me across the kitchen. "Can we at least talk?"

I reach the door. "I need to lie down," I say. "Maybe later?"

He nods. "Florence called to ask about Adunni's school."

"And?" I briefly wonder if I ought to be concerned by this, if, given Florence's erratic nature, I ought to panic, but my arm is throbbing and Adunni's admission is secure, and Florence was okay with me taking Adunni away yesterday. "What did she want?"

"Nothing really," Ken says, hopping off the stool and heading toward the fridge. He opens the door, ducks his head in, and rummages about. "She was brief: She asked, and I said Adunni starts school first thing in the morning, and she said she wishes her well." He emerges, armed with his box of sushi and a bottle of soy sauce, and shuts the fridge door with his shoulder. "Where was I? Yeah. Florence.

She said she hopes Adunni does well in school, and she said thanks and hung up. You appear exhausted. Go lie down."

"Good night," I say, letting the door slam shut behind me.

ADUNNI

The time is exactly ten minutes to twelve in the midnight and I cannot sleep.

I am lying down in Ms. Tia's chewing-gum-smelling guest room on a bed with a soft-breast mattress and wearing my school uniform on my body and my school shoe on my feet and my school cap on my head, and I don't know of anybody who ever been able to sleep comfortable like that.

But I am not just anybody.

I am Adunni, a person important enough, and tomorrow I will go to school.

I have been waiting for this moment since before I was winning a scholarship with my essay, since before Ms. Tia came and collected me from the hand of Big Madam and brought me here to her too-sparkling-clean and too-quiet house, so that I can go to learn all the schooling and books I didn't able to learn all my life and become a teacher and be helping the girls inside Ikati, my village.

I sit up. Swing my legs from the bed, put my feet down. The silver shining buckle of my brand-new shoes makes a **jing** noise, like a tiny bell ringing. I stamp my feet again just to hear it—**jing!**—before I stand and go to the window.

Outside, the night is yawning, stretching itself to sleep, dripping moonlight from its tongue. Soon it will empty itself of darkness, and the sun will climb up on top of it and wave us all good morning from the balcony of the sky, and the tomorrow I have been waiting for since I was around five years of age, since before my mama was dead, since before I was working housemaid for Big Madam in this Lagos, who is having a brain sickness because of how she was always flogging me for no reason, **that tomorrow** will come.

It is very nearly here.

There is a pinch of green light blinking on the bedside table like half a dot of an eyeball in the chin area of the clock. Ms. Tia says this clock has a special name of Alarm Clock. Why a clock needs to be alarming people? Anyway, she set the time on the clock for seven in the morning. It will make a **shree-shree** noise and cause me to alarm myself and jump out of bed so that I don't sleep and forget myself. How can I forget myself and sleep when I have been waiting for this all my life?

It is because of Ms. Tia that I will finally be free. Free from all the worrying and crying in Big Madam's house, from doing the everyday washing of Big Madam's pant and bra, which is the wide of the gray waterproof cloth they are using to cover her Jeep car.

I turn from the window and find my way in the near-dark to the bedroom door and switch on the light on the wall, blinking from the too-bright of it.

I close my eyes, facing the long mirror hanging behind the door. I have peeped this same mirror maybe thirty times since we picked up the uniform from the Ms. Erinle tailor woman in the school this afternoon, but I will take another look now—just one more—and then I will take off the uniform and fold it and wear the t-shirt nightgown Ms. Tia bought for me so that I can try to sleep.

I open my eyes. My breathing cuts.

I press my hand flat on my stomach, where the blouse is tucking inside the band of the skirt, and feel my heart there, feel it jumping with joy.

I honest never seen anything so beautiful. It looks to me like a wedding dress and birthday dress and everything dress all at once. The skirt is blue, long to just under my knees, spread out like an open umbrella hanging around my waist. I pinch the edge and hold it up. I don't want to rough it because I ironed it until there was not one wrinkle on the skin of it. I sprayed it with iron-water too, and it is smelling now of the flowers of a morning field.

I shift my feet left, right, in a dance to the quiet **jing** of my shoe buckle. And look! Look at the shining white of this blouse! I don't think I will ever let it dirty, ever. I will remove it before I eat food so I don't stain it. I will wash it every thirty, thirty-five minutes to keep it forever clean. I gentle-touch the collar, the edge like two small plates resting on the bone of my neck.

I look more close at the photo on the right pocket-breast. What it mean? Ms. Tia calls it a **low-go**. Is a photo of a tiny eagle sitting in the middle of an open book and the words **OCEAN OIL ACADEMY FOR GIRLS: EXCELLENCE FOR ALL** in red and orange stitching of thread curving around the book. I touch the eagle, feeling its power, a shock from the touch climbing up my legs like electric, so that I push myself up on my feet, as if to fly.

I breathe out. Set my feet down. Look at my face. Step back.

This morning, Ms. Tia took me to the hairdresser, and after the hairdresser tickle-scrub my head clean, she put me under a glass upside-down bowl that blows out hot heat from its mouth like a breathing fire-devil. I shouted **ye!**, running out from under it, my hair bouncing wet and dripping water down my shoulders.

Ms. Tia, who was reading a magazine in the salon basket-chair, looked up and smiled and said, "Oh,

Adunni! It's just a hair dryer. It won't hurt you."
I tell her maybe it won't hurt me, but it sure will
fry up all the brain I want to use for learning in
school, and Ms. Tia and that nonsense hairdresser,
they laugh and laugh. Well, the hairdresser laughed;
Ms. Tia just made a sound like a sad puppy bark.

Ms. Tia been sad since when she came back from
visiting her mama in Port Harcourt. I asked her just
this morning, when I seen her trying to hide the red
of her eyes from me, about what is deep troubling
her, but she said nothing. Maybe tomorrow, before
she takes me to school, I can ask her why, for example, she pinched that girl in the Ocean Academy
school like that? And why is she been looking at me
as if she wants to say sorry but doesn't know how
to say it or what to say sorry for? And why did she
go and hide herself inside the storeroom at the back
of her house today? What is inside that research of
envelope she was holding tight stiff under her arm?

I like Ms. Tia too much and I don't want her to
be sad, but I also want to be happy for myself, so I
turn myself around and around, trapping my happy
noise in my mouth because Ms. Tia likes to sleep
at the same o'clock every night and I don't want to
wake her and make her more sad. The cap flies off
my head and lands on the bed with a soft slap. I
stop spinning. Pick it up. Set it on my head. It sits
stiff, like a crown of cloth on the head of a queen.

I touch my hair, running my finger on one line of
plaiting. I honest never seen my hair like this, in a

neat all-back weaving style, so shiny and clean and smelling the fresh of rose hair pomade.

I tilt the cap a little to the left. Like a soldier-queen and make a salute at myself.

In the mirror, my eyes catches my books on the bed behind. Five new-learning books. All of them have the word "Introduction" on the cover. **Introduction to Science. To Handwriting, Grammar & Spelling. To Math. To French.** How can I have Introduction to another language when I am still struggling to finish my introduction to English?

What a plenty Introductions! I promise with all my heart that I will never get tired of making intro-ductions to all of them. I promise to learn and learn until my teacher in school is tired of me.

I met one of the teacher today (Ms. Tia call her Principal)—she said her name is Mrs. Catherine Sola-Something. She was wearing a too-thick glasses that pinch on her nose too-tight, I have a fear of how she can be able to breathe. She gave me a handshake in the school reception office as if she wants to uproot my hand and smiled a wide smile and said: "We loved your essay, Adunni. It made us laugh and cry. We'll see you tomorrow. Your roommates, Halima and Fisayo, cannot wait to meet you."

I saw the sleeping room which they named after things like gold and silver, with the iron ladder bed in the corner and the reading table and chair, but we didn't see the girls or the whole school because the matron with hair which is the color of a smelling leg wound say they are inside class. So, Ms. Tia said we must go home before "traffic gets insane."

Halima and Fisayo. I test their names on my lips now, rolling them around my tongue. **I cannot wait to meet you too! I hope you will have sense! I hope we learn together and be friends together forever!**

There are another five books on the bed, full of lines on the white pages of it. This evening, after eating the FKC chickens, I sat myself down in the dining table and wrote my name on top each of the cover, joining the **n** to the **n** to the **i** the same way I seen Ms. Tia write.

Me. Adunni. I am going to school. Eh! I want to shout it out loud to the ears of the walls and trees and green grass outside and the solar electric surrounding us in Ms. Tia's white house! I want to say, **Listen, all of you! Adunni is going to school!**

The tick-tick of the alarm clock is a drumming music inside of my belly now as it is nearing itself to midnight. It is a dancing and tapping of feet on my back, a calling to my legs to jump up on the soft mattress bed and dance, but I know Ms. Tia doesn't like noise—

There is a sudden banging **bam** sound.

It jumps inside my thinking, snatching away my mind. It is coming from the outside-downstairs of Ms. Tia's house, sounding like an impatient somebody is knocking the head of the front gate of the house, **ko-ko-ko**. What is that? I don't like it, this angry-bitter-cracking-banging noise. I switch off the light and run into the bed and climb inside, pulling the bedsheet up to my neck. I tell myself maybe it is a dog from the next-door house, finding food, kicking the gate. Or the air conditioner box in the wall up to the left of me, breathing out ice-block air from the inside of its rectangle nostrils.

Another **bam** sound.

There is no mistaking it this time. **Bam. Bam-bam.** Like a very vexing somebody is slamming a car door, stamping the floor with the leg of wood. Who is visiting Ms. Tia?

The alarm clock sounds the twice clicking of its plastic tongue behind its square throat: twelve o'clock midnight.

This noise is near the mouth of the gate, a finger of iron plucking the loose teeth of the gate out.

What is it? Who is it? What or who are they finding or fighting?

TIA

Ken came up at a quarter to midnight with his nightly cup of tea.

I listened to him brush his teeth, the tuneless humming under his breath as he changed into his PJs, the fluffing sound as he bolstered up his pillow and climbed into bed beside me, the yawn, the flick after flick of the pages of the book he's been reading for three weeks: an A3-sized hardback with a giant pink-fleshed, pear-shaped uterus on its cover, an image that brings to mind the head of a mountain goat with curved horns and a deformed, featureless face.

Outside, the night is calm, ethereal. A blue-black bored-faced sky. Fallen petals from the jacaranda tree rest on the windowsill, but the coolness of the air-conditioning in our bedroom feels raw, brittle, and my neck aches from my stiff posture, from trying not to move because the envelope underneath my pillow rustles every time I adjust. I suspect Ken knows I am awake. I sense him watching me now over his book. He takes a sip of his chamomile tea, a slow slurp. I hear the mug hitting the side table.

"Is it Adunni?" he says, after a moment. "Because I have been thinking about . . ." His phone vibrates next to his mug. I hear the soft clap of the book as he sets it down, the swipe of his finger against the phone screen to silence it. "About your involvement in her schooling and all. Shouldn't her parents be looped in on such decisions?"

I turn around. "Maybe it's because there's no way to reach dead parents?"

That's not the absolute truth. Adunni's mother is dead, but her father, who married her off to a filthy old man with no teeth called Mo-Something, is alive in her village.

"She's going to school in less than . . ." I glance at the neon clock blinking at the edge of the A/C box. "In less than eight hours. Think you can live with her in the same house until then, and if it's a bother, I could, I don't know, find us a hotel?"

"Don't be ridiculous," he says. Exhales. His breath smells of fishy toothpaste. "I like Adunni. I don't mind that she's here. I just think . . . you shouldn't wade into family issues."

"Florence is not her family." My words come out strained, stretched through clenched teeth. "That woman was physically abusing her." I squint at him. "Are you sure she didn't say anything else when she called you today?"

"We spoke for barely a minute. I feel a little uneasy with how you took her away. Do you understand the legal implications of . . ." He trails off, his words lengthening in a yawn. "Taking her away to school? Do you know why she left her village to become a maid? Did you investigate?"

"Did I investigate? Seriously, Ken?" A hiss of irritation slithers out of me. "If I—" I stop talking. There's a sound, a car door being slammed, voices from outside our gate. Or is it the A/C compressor? "Do you mind if I turn off the A/C? Awesome. Thanks." I snatch the A/C remote from my side table and switch the thing off. The room falls silent with a shudder. The air grows warm, stale.

"I am sorry," Ken says. "You've been a rock to Adunni. I think I am just . . ." There is faint despair in his voice. "A little jealous? I feel like I am losing you. Like everyone—your mum, your dad, me?— we've all lost you to Adunni." A pained cough. "It's hard competing with a fourteen-year-old who has been through so much, and it seems unfair to want to take your attention and affection away from her, but it seems like she's all you think about these days. Or maybe it's me. Maybe I'm being a selfish idiot. I don't know. You've seemed to disappear a little from me with each passing day ever since you learned about my infertility. And then my mother with the ritual, the scars . . . I feel like I brought all of this on you, and I don't know how to help you. Tia, please." His searching gaze feels like fingers, slowly tapping the frown off my face, my heart. "Tell me. What's wrong with you?"

I sigh, looking away.

We'd been "trying for a baby" for a few months when I discovered Ken was infertile.

This was after I thought we **both** wanted and were actively **trying** for a child, after his mother invited **me** for a ritual bath she believed would wash away the stain of our childlessness, a harrowing event that resulted in the scars I now carry.

The discovery of Ken's infertility rocked the core of our already fragile relationship, and sometimes I want to punish him for not disclosing his truth, but how can I do that when it's **me**, not him, who's keeping the biggest secret?

"Tia?" Ken says, touching my cheek and then tilting my chin gently, to look at him. There is a puzzled expression on his face. "Are you all right?"

I should tell Ken that I have just unearthed one half of this . . . this thing that feels like a wild raging fire compared to the tiny spark that was his own revelation. But how? How do I begin to find the words to explain without the second half to make sense of everything?

Breathing feels like a struggle.

"I am sorry," I mutter, an easy way out. "There is so much going on, stuff my mother and I have to iron out. I must return to Port Harcourt tomorrow evening on the last flight. Will head out after I drop Adunni off. Sorry I didn't tell you earlier." I immediately felt less burdened after I booked the flight, as if the process had stripped me of many murky, turbid layers.

He nods. Sighs. "That's . . . fine. Whatever makes you happy."

Tears fill my eyes.

Ken leans forward and kisses me, his lips warm and moist on mine, trailing my tears across my cheeks, along the tip of my nose, down my neck, growing in intensity. As he reaches my collarbone, the curved arch of my breasts beneath my nightdress, the envelope under my pillow crunches.

"The hell's that?" he whispers into my skin. "Under your pillow?"

I am considering how to respond when something strikes our front gate.

Ken pushes himself away from me and looks up with a perplexed frown toward the window, beyond the vast garden of freshly cut grass to the front gate. I think I hear feet crunching on the graveled pavement outside our gate. And are those voices? A car whizzes past, drowning the sounds for a moment.

What's that? his eyes say.

Yes, voices. Deep, grating, rising over the night air. It comes again: a banging, urgent, startling.

Ken climbs out of bed, a look of bewilderment on his face.

The voices are stronger now, more aggressive. There must be at least two men. **Who are they?** I remember then what Ken said earlier, about Florence calling. **She knows Adunni leaves for school in the morning.** Are the men here for Adunni? Did Florence direct them to our house? No, I think, refusing to give in to fear, dread. Adunni is safe. Adunni starts school in—

"ADUNNI!" one of the men bellows. "COME OUT-O!"

"Ken?" I whisper, sitting up, clutching the edge of the duvet to my chest. "Who are they?" I recognize a tremor in my voice, the memory of helplessness.

"I think it's Adunni's family," my husband says, pulling on a shirt and twisting a button or two in place. "If it is, then we've got to let them in before they cause a scene. Come on!"

I watch him backing out of the room before I throw the duvet off and follow him down the stairs and into the dew-soaked air of the night, through to where my husband is fiddling with the gate to let in two figures who barge into my garden with the smell of something decayed, one holding a stick and limping, the other charging toward my front door, yelling, "Adunni! Killer!"

ADUNNI

When I climbed down from the bed and went to the window to look outside, I saw two men afar, behind the trees, behind the gates. I saw Ms. Tia running, nearly falling herself on the shine-shine stones on the floor, her husband pressing his finger into the gate automatic-padlock so that the gate was automatic-grinding open, and the two men was rushing to enter, marching in like an angry lion to the kitchen back door. I only see the faraway face of one man, and I know from the deep black marks vexing up and down his two cheeks like a hot knife carving that it is Mr. Kola. It was the idiot of him that brought me to Lagos from Ikati, my village, to be doing wicked housemaid work for Big Madam in this big shining Lagos.

What is he looking for here? Who shows him the way to get here? Why is Mr. Kola shouting "Adunni! Killer!"?

Who is the killer? Me?

And who is the other man with him? The one wearing white cloth like a bedsheet and walking as if something clip off his leg at the ankles area?

My heart is fighting karate-fight with my chest now as I run back into my bed in my uniform and school shoes and school hat and lie stiff like a dead person inside a dead-people fridge. They are downstairs in the parlor. I hear the **chink-chink** of feet wearing a necklace of clapping cowries; voices talking, rising in argument; Ms. Tia asking questions; her husband, the good doctor, giving her answers. Then her husband is calling the phone and I can hear the microphone speaker ringing, **griiin-griin**. A voice, like a quaking thunder, is talking now inside the phone, saying: "Mr. Dada? Don't make me walk down to your house at this ungodly hour. Have you let them in, or do you need me to call the police to arrest that murderer?"

Big Madam.

I know her voice like I know how my own shit smell.

I honest can even almost smell her perfume-bleach smell from inside the phone. Why is she calling me a murderer to the good doctor? What is "murderer"? Is it the same as "killer"?

Now Big Madam is saying Mr. Kola is owing Refund all the money she was paying me—who is Refund? Why did this Refund want to collect money for the work I was doing? Did Big Madam call him after we were leaving her house early this morning? Why?

Mr. Kola is now talking about me, saying how I was leaving Ikati, telling lies I was running away after killing Khadija, who was the second wife of the man I married. It was because she died that I was running to Lagos, to save myself from troubles. Yes, I ran because I was one of the last persons to be seeing Khadija before she was dead, but I didn't kill her! She was my friend! It was not me! They must find Bamidele, her love-boy-man-friend, because he knows the truth! He knows she was pregnant for him and she died after waiting for him to come and help her. I hear another voice and my soul escapes from my body. The voice of Oloye, one chief of our village. What is he doing inside Ms. Tia's parlor?

I listen, holding the pillow tight to my chest, pressing my heart in, to keep it from falling as the good doctor is making explanations of words in English for Ms. Tia, as Ms. Tia is shouting, "No! Adunni cannot go back tonight!" As Mr. Kola is saying how they want me to return for killing Khadija, because the blood of Khadija is weeping from the earth after they found her body swelling up by the river in Kere village, and that the weeping blood is staining all our rivers and causing all our water in Ikati to dry up small-small. They want me to by force come back to Ikati to beg. To make a sacrifice.

No.

I throw the bedsheet from my chest, push myself up. I am innocent of this. I can run. I can run far and hide, and in the morning, when Mr. Kola and chief have gone back to Ikati, I can come back here, and Ms. Tia will take me to school and keep me there forever. I can take my mobile phone too, find a place near to call Ms. Tia, tell her to come find me. I can . . . I look around.

Where can I hide? If I open the window and jump, I will crash-land, and all my bones and blood will scatter and mash up. I cannot go downstairs inside the parlor or climb up the roof or disappear to become air and evaporate myself into the shadows. And even if I run, will I be running forever with a stain on my name? If I don't go back, what will happen to my people, our land? If I finish all my education and become a teacher, will I be happy knowing I've been running all my life? I look up at the ceiling through the window of the tears in my eyes.

Can I maybe try to go back?

But what will happen when I get to Ikati? Will they stone me dead? Keep me in prison?

No. I shake my head left, right, left until I hear

a buzzing buzz inside of my ears, until the school cap is sliding down the back of my head. Not now. I cannot go now.

But. I bite my lip, tasting the blood and salt of it. If not now, when? I slap myself to stop my tears. Can I try to maybe drag myself from this bed and march to the wall-switch to slap on the light and pick up my nylon bag of belongings and open the door and climb down the stairs to meet my people and tell them I am ready?

Yes, I can. I will. I must. But why I cannot move? Why are my legs not listening to the commanding of my brain?

I hear the **tink-tink** of a ring-wearing finger gripping the glass handle of the staircase; the wood under the feet sighing as somebody is climbing up slowly, as if to leave the pinch of a shadow on the face of the stairs.

Now the door handle is twisting left, right.

I bury myself under the coffin of my cover-cloth and squeeze my eyes close.

ADUNNI

The door opens.

I shiver, wanting to melt myself, to curl until I can hide my whole body in between my knees. Darkness breathes ice-cold air through the mouth of the air conditioner in the wall, and I feel myself rising, falling. I breathe in and out, wanting to slow the rushing of air from my chest, to don't let anybody see or hear me, but my body is stubborn to reach out and collect the air, and I cannot stop it.

"It's me," Ms. Tia whispers. "I am going to turn the lights on, okay? Don't scream." She jams her elbow to the wall, and the whole room fills with light.

Air rushes out of my nostrils, trembling the cover-cloth like the cloth of a flag in a fast wind.

I sit up holding tight my nylon bag of belongings to my chest, my eyes growing big in my head. "Ms. Tia!" She presses a finger to her lips, closes the door, locking it two times. I nod. I won't talk one word.

She pins her head back to the door, closes her eyes. Breathes deep. In. Out. When she opens her eyes, she focuses on the school cap sliding down my head, the top of my black school shoes under the cover-cloth, my white blouse. As if she didn't too sure if I am still Adunni or if I magic to become somebody else.

"Oh, Adunni. Was your sleep tee uncomfortable?" She nods to the long t-shirt dress on the cupboard door. "I could have found you something else to wear."

"I want to wear my uniform forever, Ms. Tia." There is a ball of tears in my throat. What did they really tell her about me? "I didn't do it," I say, my voice shaking. "I didn't kill Khadija."

"We'll talk about that later," she says, talking fast, whispering still. "Listen, Adunni, there's a ladder inside that closet. We need to get it out." She points a finger at the cupboard-inside-the-wall and slides the two doors apart so that the new travel-box we bought for school yesterday comes tumbling out and lands itself by Ms. Tia's feet. She looks down, as if the box too is a strange thing, like she doesn't understand how it arrived inside her house, what it is doing here.

She enters the cupboard, drags out a ladder, the type one our palm-wine tappers in the village will set on the tree and climb up it to cut fruit. Only this one is silver in color, folded up into two around the waist.

"What are you doing, Ms. Tia?" I ask. Is she wanting me to climb down it? And run to where?

"It's a foldable ladder," Ms. Tia says, dragging it near the window, breathing hard. "I hope it can reach. Come over here, Adunni." She makes a beckon, trying to straight up the ladder, but the bones of it are full of a dusting of sand and clay.

She pulls it twice, but the thing is stubborn; it refuses to stand up straight. "Come help me," she says. "Let's try to open this out. Get this down."

I hear Mr. Kola and the good doctor. In no time now, one of them will climb upstairs, see us, and then Ms. Tia will enter inside a big pot of cooking trouble. I don't want Ms. Tia inside trouble.

"No," I say. "No."

Ms. Tia puts the ladder down, gently resting it on the wall. "No?"

"No," I say again. "If I run, it means I am full of guilty of it. I am innocent." The word "innocent" flies out like an arrow from my mouth.

"You understand me, Ms. Tia?" I raise my head, feeling more and more sure of myself as I talk. "Kayus, my brother, is suffering. My people are suffering. I made a promise to my mama, before she was dead, that I must take care of Kayus all my life. If I run, it is only my body that will run. My mind will keep itself as a slave, locked up in fear. Maybe it time to make proof of my innocent. That is what it means to be freely free, Ms. Tia. To have a good name is better than a thousand and one educations. You know that?"

"No, Adunni." Her eyes are filling with tears as she twists her fingers inside of each other as if she is trying to plait it like hair. "There has to be another way out of this!"

"No another way." I shift down the bed with my buttocks, dragging the pink bedsheet along with me. "For how long I keep running?"

I stand, the bedsheet a swelling sea wave of cloth around my feet.

"We planned like fools," she says, talking to herself, "without a clue of its looming tragic end." When I come to stand in front of her, she takes my two hands.

"Gosh, I can't cry." She waits a moment, looking away, her lips shaking. "They are talking about . . . a sacrifice . . . like a trial. I don't even . . . It sounds ludicrous, outrageously senseless. Adunni, going back means returning to a life of marriage to an older man, to your village, to a life devoid of the precious education you are desperate to get."

I look her in the eye. "I did not do this. I am going to face them and tell them it was not me!"

"Adunni, you silly goose! You are so naïve. It's insane!" She drops my hands, and I see the fire of annoyed in her eyes. "Look, I know you don't want to keep running, but you are not responsible for rain in your village."

"That you don't believe in something doesn't mean it is crap," I say. I take off my cap, place it gentle on the edge of the bed. "Whether you believe in the sun, it will still shine. See, me and you are a—" I try to find the word of my thinking, but I can't, so I press my two fingers close.

"A speck?" she says.

"A speck," I say. "That's what all of us are in the whole science of life of this world. What you believe or don't believe doesn't change a thing about how the world runs itself. The only thing that makes a different? You. You fight back, you speak up, you refuse to sit down and look when—"

"I am coming up, okay?" the good doctor calls. "These men are getting agitated."

I focus my eyes on the door, thinking maybe to listen to Ms. Tia, to climb down the ladder. Is it too late?

"Please, Adunni," Ms. Tia says. "Let's get this ladder down—"

The door makes a **jig-jig** shaking sound. I press my palms on top of my two ears.

"Tia." It's the good doctor. He sounds afraid. "Open up!"

"We're getting changed!" Ms. Tia shouts, then

keeps low her voice. "Adunni! I can delay Ken a bit. Just run. Go. Keep your uniform on, take your phone, and—"

"No," I say. "It is too late." I use the edge of my thumb to rub my cheeks, as if to twist the tears back inside my eyes, keeping it locked in there. Still, they slide down the street of my face, into my mouth. The door handle turns harder. A knock. Two knocks. "Tia?" the good doctor says. "Open up."

"Adunni?" Ms. Tia says. "Please."

"I must . . ." My voice is playing hide-and-seek with my tongue. "I must fight for my innocent. To be freely free. Please open the door."

"Are you sure?" Ms. Tia is looking at me as if her heart is slicing into two, as if she cannot remember how to breathe.

"Wait," I say, slow-dragging off my blouse and pulling down my school skirt. I kick off my brand-new shoes, closing my ears to the muffle sound of tears Ms. Tia is making. I find the rag of my ankara dress, my old shoes in my nylon bag, the ones I wore from when I was first coming to Ikati this time last year, and wear them.

I fold the uniform slowly, slow, taking my time so it doesn't ever, ever wrinkle; press the folded clothes to my nose and sniff up the smell of the rose iron-water, and in that one sniff, I sniff up all the memory of my school, all the Introduction books, the strong handshake from the principal, the imaginations of how Fisayo and Halima, my roommates, will be, until my heart is full of the smell of that memory, the imaginations. I will forever remember the smell, and it will be a reminding of all that I must fight for when I get to Ikati so that I can come back.

I give the clothes to Ms. Tia, but she shakes her head and staggers herself away from me as if the clothes contain a firebomb, and so I lay them gentle on the bed, set the cap on top. "Please tell the school I will come back," I say. "Please beg them to keep my space."

I stiff my back and hold my head high. "Open the door, Ms. Tia. Please."

Dr. Ken doesn't enter at first.

He stands there, wearing a night-trouser-dress for men, black in color, the trouser falling down his buttocks so that he grips it tight with one hand and holds the door handle with the other hand. "What took you so long?" His eyes run around the whole room on tired legs and stop on the ladder resting itself on the wall. "Tia, where are you thinking—"

"Oh, shut up, Ken," Ms. Tia says. "You let those bastards in here. We could have saved her!"

"I did not know they were coming!" The good doctor looks at Ms. Tia as if she knife him with her angry words. "I had no choice!"

Ms. Tia grabs a pack of her twists and pulls her hair as if she wants to uproot her brain. "Shit. This is messed up. What can we do?"

"Calm down," the good doctor says, his voice quiet, tired. "Please."

"I cannot calm down, Ken!"

I feel bad that I am the fault of much fighting troubles between the two husband and wife. They have already been having troubles since before I came here, fighting over having a baby or having no baby, and the whole thing was a matter of confusing pain for Ms. Tia, and now me and my trouble is making things worse.

I grip my nylon bag close, taking one step near the chief priest. I must face my life, leave Ms. Tia to face her own. If God wishes it, then we will see each other again. If not, then—what? I cannot think it, of a life where I will not see Ms. Tia, or where my getting education will be killed dead because of what happened with Khadija.

But.

I cannot imagine it too, a life full of education and living in a good house and enjoying sweet things, when my name is stained deep with lies that I killed Khadija, when my family is suffering because I ran away, when my baby brother is hungry for me, crying for me, wondering why I forgot him to suffer.

"I am ready," I say.

Ms. Tia jumps in front of me, stopping me in my

march to the door. "No," she says, holding her arms out, spread wide as if to take off and fly. "No. Ken. Please. Do something. Call someone."

"I will, if you just give me a moment to think!"

Ms. Tia looks around, facing me, gripping my hands, holding it tight. "Adunni," she says, falling on her knees. "I am sorry I delayed saving you. If I had acted from day one . . . if I had . . . gosh, I don't have a clue of what to do. Ken and I . . ." She looks at the good doctor. "We want to make a few phone calls to see if anyone can help us, but that might take a few hours, and the men downstairs insist you have to come with them first. Or else things could turn hostile. We want you to be safe. They've promised to not harm you, but I don't believe them. Oh, God . . ." she whisper-cries, rocking on her knees.

I climb to the floor. Me and Ms. Tia hold each ourselves and cry.

"Adunni," she says, sniff.

I look at her. Rise. "Yes, Ms. Tia. I am listening, Ms. Tia."

"Go. If that's what you want to do."

"Is what I need to do," I say, pushing out my chest. But when I take a step forward, Ms. Tia runs to block my path with her whole trembling body, making it tough for me to reach the door.

The good doctor's jaw is hanging slack as he looks from me to Ms. Tia. He says, "Come here, hon, come here."

"Fine," Ms. Tia says, shifting for me to pass

through. "Go, Adunni. Tell your . . . those men I'm bringing the money." She wants to give them money. For why and for what?

"Please," she says, touching my shoulder, as if she can sense the bitter anger growing inside of me. "Just tell them to wait for me in the car. I'll bring the money."

"I am sorry, Adunni," Dr. Ken says, his eyes red, tired too, like he didn't sleep one wink since 1992. "Try to be strong and hold on until we can get help."

I want to nod, but my head cannot move, so I shift my feet, inch by inch, until I reach the door. When I turn around, Dr. Ken is holding his wife, her face to his chest, her shoulders moving up and down.

I take one more look at my uniform folded on the bed, and with my heart sinking to the bottom of my stomach, I wave the good doctor a slow bye-bye and tip my toes across the hallway and down the stairs.

The lights in the parlor are switched on, shining on Mr. Kola and the chief.

"You . . . look different." Mr. Kola nods at me, looking behind me as if finding the rest of my flesh. I know I am even more thin than when I left Ikati because Big Madam didn't use to give me on-time food. "How are you?"

What type of nonsense question is he asking me? How he thinks I am?

"You didn't change," I say, talking inside my breath. "Still looking like a frog that didn't able to poo-poo for one year." I kneel quick, bending my head to bow low at the feet of the chief who is sitting on Ms. Tia's soft sofa. I greet him with the greeting-respect of a chief, keeping my head tucked inside my laps.

"Adunni." The chief shifts his leg back. The left of his feet is missing the small toe on the end. Be as if something saw it in half, leaving a full-stop of brown flesh.

"Sir," I say, "it is me, sir."

I wait for him to touch my head with the stick of feathers, to give me a greeting-blessing, but when he lifts his stick, he breathes a deep sigh and touches the stick to the left and right of me. And my spirit sinks low. He doesn't think I am supposed to collect any blessing from him. I wonder too, as I kneel there, what my friends in the village will think. Will they turn their back on me? Will they think I am a bringer of bad luck? A thief of rain?

"Let us go," he says, rising from the chair with much struggle maybe because he didn't ever sink himself inside a sofa this soft in his life: The poor man keeps falling, fighting to push himself up.

Mr. Kola pulls the chief up. They march out of the parlor, and as I follow behind, I hear the doctor from upstairs, saying, "Tia, do you know how ridiculously unsafe it is out there?"

I don't wait to hear Ms. Tia's response.

Outside, the night is wide awake, watching me with blinking eyes as I walk to Mr. Kola's car, the big-mansion houses on her street surrounding us like a string of strange, giant triangle hats; the light in all their windows off, curtains drawn together. The heat is a stiff hard thing, with a soft whistle breeze blowing every often. As I reach Mr. Kola's car, a dog in a cage outside gives two, three mournful cries of sorrow, and it plays like the quiet **wow-wow** of an ambulance speeding pass in my ears.

I climb inside Mr. Kola's car.

The car is even worse off than I remember. The cushion pinches me with wire fingers, and through a small hole in the floor of the car, I see the shiny black street blinking like diamond eyes on the road.

Mr. Kola adjusts the looking-glass above his head. The dark road ahead feels like I am peeping inside the throat of a crocodile through its wide-open mouth.

"The woman is bringing us money," Mr. Kola says in Yoruba. "Should we wait, or we go?"

"We go," the chief says, lifting his stick of feathers up in the air, pushing it out of the window, to maybe give a warning to any arm-robber that they must not come near us. I watch as a feather collects itself from the stick and sails in the wind, blending inside the shadows, and I wonder, truly, which arm-robber with sense will want to steal the metal box of Mr. Kola's car?

Mr. Kola starts his car engine. The thing makes

a noise as if it is about to explode, burst us all into a fire flame, burn us until we are a charcoal powder.

I look behind my back. The small black gate is swinging soft, in a dance to a whistle tune from the mouth of the wind.

Ikati.

My village.

Ikati is the place that doesn't answer yes when I call it home.

The place where I was running away and leaving my baby brother, Kayus, all alone, abandon him by himself and come to Lagos to work as a housemaid. Where my friends Enitan and Ruka and Kike were always making me happy.

The car settles itself with a coughing-grumble.

Mr. Kola pulls the changing gear stick back as if he wants to uproot it and clears his throat.

I feel a slow drag under, a heavy sorrow on my spirit. The tears come. They come in a big crashing wave, like rain falling fast, climbing down the floor of my face. I hear my mama replying to my crying with her own whisper, saying, **Don't cry, my sweet child Adunni, don't cry. Everything will be okay.** Everything will be okay, even if Ms. Tia is not coming outside to say bye-bye to me with a big embrace. My mama is here, always living in my mind-parlor and mind-kitchen and mind-bedroom. She lives here, here with me in my heart.

"If we drive now," Mr. Kola says, shifting the

mirror in his car this way and that, "we can get to Ikati in—"

"WAIT!"

I look up.

Ms. Tia is running to us, holding a box of her belongings, looking like she is about to fly to the Abroad of the UK, shouting, "Wait for me!"

"Ms. Tia! Ms. Tia!" I jump up and down in my seat, calling her name.

"What is all this?" Mr. Kola says, looking at her in the mirror of his car as if she is thiefing something from her own house and wants to run away.

Her husband comes running behind her, shouting at her to wait too—"to think this through, Tia, understand the implications of this decision."

But Ms. Tia keeps running until she reaches the car and pulls open the door so hard, I am fearing the door will fly off and reach Ikati before all of us. She climbs inside, throws her bag to the floor, panting hard. "Let's go," she shouts. "I'll pay you double! Just go now! Hurry!"

Mr. Kola jams his foot to zoom the car forward, and Mr. Ken jumps and stands back on the roadside before the car will clear him dead under its tires. There is a shock and pity and confuse inside his eyes, as he watches the car shaking down the road, like a can full of coins money.

When I look back again, his two hands are now resting on top of his head, his mouth dropping wide open, as if he cannot believe it true that his wife of two years, the woman he met on Facebook of the internet and fall inside love with her, a woman with Abroad education and a rich mama and papa in Port Harcourt, a woman who have a moneymaking work in Lagos and who speaks big English about change of climate and layer of the ozone, will just leave all what she knows—her fine house with shining roofs and coughing air-con and good doctor husband—and just follow this Adunni, the strange girl who was once a housemaid, back to her village, which is far at the bottom of Nigeria.

WEDNESDAY

TIA

Predawn

I am sitting on the edge of the car seat, the only position that provides relief from the stabbing in my tailbone.

The air feels viscous, stifling. Adunni sits beside me, with her head tipped back and with her eyes closed and arms wrapped around herself, as if to protect her secret thoughts. We are now trawling along on a sepia-toned dusty road, a bed of gravel under the car tires. Mr. Kola, a man with tribal marks, a charcoal-black incision under each eye trailing a path toward his jawline, is gripping the steering wheel, trying to navigate around another pothole. While he was in my home, I told him I thought he was vile to bring Adunni to Lagos to work without pay. He nodded solemnly and touched a hand to his chest as if I'd acknowledged something elegant, deeply reverential about him.

The chief is asleep, the feathered cloth draped across his left arm soaking up his saliva. The tip of the handwoven Aso-Oke cap on his head remains upright, pointing upward like the pricked ears of a startled dog. White cowrie shells outlining the embroidered brim click and clack, his head swaying back and forth. Both men reek of camphor and decay. And Adunni—I watch her chewing on the insides of her cheeks. What is she thinking?

I regret letting them in. Ken thought we could reason with them if we were hospitable, but there was no changing their unyielding determination. At one point, Ken and I huddled behind the dining table and pressed our heads together, whispering furiously, debating whom to call for help. I thought of my father . . . He knows influential people. He could get them to wade in, stop this . . . this sickening injustice, but my father is sixty-five and my mother is dying, and they are both in Port Harcourt, and neither of them knows Adunni.

We called Florence, the bitch, and put her on speaker, hoping she'd help talk to them—horrid mistake. Turns out she gave them our address and had known all along that they'd be coming to pick Adunni up. At one point, she yelled that Mr. Kola owed her the money she spent hiring Adunni, a murderer; that the men could accuse us of kidnapping:

Did we have any legally binding documents to keep her with us? She warned us that if we called the police or tried to stop them, they'd deny everything about Adunni working as a housemaid and the resulting abuse, about Adunni needing to go back for a sacrifice or whatever crap this is, and insist that she's needed back in the village because her father is unwell. I felt utterly and completely helpless, and it breaks me to watch Adunni now, knowing she's facing this sickening reality on the precipice of freedom, of a much-desired education.

My bag is heavy on my lap, my phone battery slowly draining with each text Ken sends. He has called every hour since we left Lagos, and every time, I hit the call-end button and reply with a text: **I am okay. We are safe. Call u when I can.**

It's past three a.m., and I wonder if I should call my dad, let him know I might need to delay my flight to— **Shit.** The envelope with my letters is still underneath my pillow, forgotten in the manic dash to catch the car that was taking Adunni away. I twist my phone in my lap, fresh panic expanding in my throat. What if Ken finds them? How do I explain Boma, my visits, the letters, the years of deceit, what we had? **No.** Not "had." What we **have.**

I glance over at Mr. Kola, his expression stoic as he grasps the steering wheel. Can we turn back to Lagos now? Would it be insane to ask?

"Ms. Tia?" I sense the burden of Adunni's gaze on me. "Are you afraid, Ms. Tia?"

Ken will not find the letters. He's too busy trying to help Adunni, us. He'll be downstairs making
frantic phone calls, and we'll get the help we need
and be back in Lagos way before lunch. I'll have
time to get home and get changed and hide them
before I head to Port Harcourt.

Shit.

I tuck my phone into my bag, exhaling the panic.
"I am not scared," I say to Adunni. "Are you?"

"I didn't kill Khadija," she says with a shudder in
her voice. "Do you believe me, Ms. Tia?"

Do I believe her? What do I know about Adunni?
We met at Florence's house. We became friends,
despite the difference in our educational and socio-
economic backgrounds—not that any of that stuff
should ever matter. Adunni helped me through
confusing times. I know her to be kindhearted and
compassionate and funny and determined. I know
she loves me like she loved her mother. But what
about her past? This crime she's accused of?

Everyone's past is a pocket of untruths. Mine is. I
am choosing to believe what I know of her.

I close my eyes, wedging my chin on the brim
of the window, wind thumping my face when the
car hurtles down a portion of a newly tarred road.
Adunni is no killer. She might be anything else, but
she cannot hurt another human.

I open my eyes. "I believe you," I say. "With
everything in me."

"I am sorry," Adunni says. "For causing trouble with you and the good doctor."

The car slows down to join traffic.

"Ken will be fine. He'll call around to help us."

My husband couldn't have stopped me if he'd wanted to. I think he knows just how much Adunni means to me. He doesn't understand it, but he accepts us with equal measures of grace and grudge, and after today, I'll tell him everything about the past, my relationship with Boma, the secret visits, the cord that binds Boma and me together, and how Ken's infertility, the bath, and the resulting scars led me into this tangled mess, why Adunni matters more than anything else right now, and why it's a complicated knot I need my mother to help unravel.

Our car is sandwiched now between trailers and petrol tankers, long transport lorries and buses filled with night-travelers who press weary noses against windows, looking desperate, exhausted.

"Are you sure?" Adunni says. "That the good doctor can help us?" Her eyes are on a woman on the side of the road, stirring a thick wooden pestle around a pot of burning oil, gray steam billowing, the fragrance of peppered **akara** and yam filling the air.

"He promised to call around for a sound lawyer," I say, leaning in so that Mr. Kola doesn't hear us. "Do you know if there's someone, anyone we can speak to in Ikati? About the process?"

"I don't know much of it myself," she whispers. "The last sacrifice like this was when my mama was not dead. I think if they judge us and I am free, they release me and go."

"But why tonight?" I raise my voice, hoping the man in front will at least say something meaningful. "I've got some more money in my bag, Mr. Kola . . . please. I just need to understand the urgency."

Mr. Kola clears his throat. "There is a full moon this night." He pauses as if trying to decrypt a word. "On a full moon, when there is a problem in the villages, we gather to make sacrifices and beg the spirits for rain, for blessings, for mercy for our wickedness . . . Then we will judge the women who are causing offending. We judge the men too, but not today."

I swallow. "Right. How bad is the rain issue?"

"It is getting worst," Mr. Kola says. "They were having very small rain in Ikati for many months. Even in some areas surrounding Ikati, the rivers are reducing, and they are afraid everything will dry up soon."

The wheels spin in my head. If farming is the main economic activity of the community, surely these regions will be more prone to drought and desertification? It is relevant given the current global climate issues, but this is not the time to investigate, especially with a snoring chief in the front seat. "Did you say judgment for those accused of murder is imprisonment?" I ask.

"I am not from Ikati," Mr. Kola says, sounding cross. "But I hear they will kill those who kill. When we get to Ikati, we will know the rest."

Panic surges through me, a sluice of adrenaline, hysteria, taking hold. I look out the window and stare at the moon, a ghostly, blue-eyed witness in the sky, so Adunni won't see the tears leaking from my eyes.

"Ms. Tia?"

"Yes, my love?" I turn.

"Thank you," Adunni whispers. "For following me."

Something inside of me ruptures.

The traffic eases.

Mr. Kola turns into a cave-like opening on the road, a narrow road framed by a canopy of thick branches leaning into each other. The drive twists down a ribbon of mud, around a lumpy hill underneath the arch of trees. There are gaps in the curved ceiling of the multitudinous leaves above, where slivers of moonlight glint through slim gaps, and it feels as though I am being watched by hundreds of sleepy silver-eyed foxes, a chorus of chirps and howls. We continue down this winding alcove, an endless blue-black horizon, with Mr. Kola swearing, and I look on, terrified, indebted to the dense darkness ahead that protects me from seeing beyond the windscreen.

"Maybe try to keep closed your eyes?" Adunni says. She, perhaps sensing my fear, the rigidness of my tensed-up body against hers, rubs my hands as if to knead the tension out of me.

She starts to sing in Yoruba, words that, when I crack open an eyelid to check, appear to have a calming effect on Mr. Kola: The perplexed frown on his face has dissolved into the crevice of his neck, and his mouth drops open languidly, as though he has suffered a partial but relaxing stroke.

EIGHTEEN HOURS
TO MIDNIGHT

‖‖‖‖‖‖‖‖‖‖‖‖‖‖‖‖‖‖‖‖‖‖‖

ADUNNI
‖‖‖‖‖‖‖‖‖‖‖‖‖‖‖‖‖‖‖‖‖‖‖
IKATI

Agan waterfalls is no more full.

Before, it was a wide-open mouth with no teeth, from which the tongue of crashing waters, a hundred tiny shine-shine horses, come galloping down to the river below. The sound of it now is the noise of a throat with a wound along its fleshy walls, a scratching sound. It looks to me, in the darkness of this morning, like a head once full of hair now shedding, falling out around the edges, hanging limp and tired. Is it because of the small rain that the waterfalls are looking malnourish? Hope drops from my chest, rolls under my feet.

We pass the forest road leading to Agan, where Iya, the friend of my mother, was living. She was the one who helped me to run away from Ikati around this time last year, when Khadija first died and when I was afraid for my village chief to catch me. Sadness is a big block in my heart now, as I imagine that Iya must be already dead by now. When she was helping me last year, she was too old, her eyes going blind, her mouth making conversations with spirits. We pass women walking slowly, no tray of plantain or firewood on their head, nothing in their hands except maybe the baby with malnourish necks hanging limp on their backs. Why are the women not carrying a tray of food? Where are the farmers who use to pass this road, with chickens and dogs and goats running in front of them?

When we near the market square, I sigh, shifting in the car seat, my heart jumping in my chest. Will Papa be waiting for me near the market square, or will he be waiting in my house? Will they take me home? Will I see Kayus? I smile a little, thinking of Kayus, the only thing of hope in my returning back to Ikati.

But Papa is not waiting by the market square. Nobody is waiting for me anywhere. Not even early-morning birds or lizards or chickens. Except maybe the statue of our village king, and the welcome sign that is saying **Welcome to IKATI, THE VILLAGE OF HAPPYNESS.** The chief is still sleeping as if he suffers a curse of sleeping. I tell you true, even if our car tumble now and fall inside a deep hole and a crocodile is eating our bones and we are all dying dead, I don't think the chief will wake up. Mr. Kola parks his car to near a mango tree and tries to turn off the car engine, but the engine keeps itself on, hissing and shaking.

The chief jump awake, wiping spit from his mouth, looking as if someone bang his head with a pot-pan and push him, without warning, out of the darkness of a sweet sleep and inside the white-hot light of a bitter waking-up.

We climb down and slam the door of the car, and maybe the slamming somehow resets the car-brain because the engine coughs twice and die dead.

Dawn peeps from the orange bed of the sky, and all around me is the picture of empty houses which the feet of fire have trampled on. Everything looks burned. Thirsty. The tall coconut and palm trees, which use to have a tent of leaves, like a cap perching high on top of it, is now looking dull, the once shining green leaves now dry and crusty and dropping, landing to the floor with the cracking sound of crunching eggshells. The ground under my feet feels like hard bread, and if I raise my leg and stamp on it, I am sure the floor will crack open, vomit a tiny earthquake. There is silence too, a quiet, afraid kind of silence, when before, around this time, some women will already awake, iron buckets clanging by their side, with their children holding clay pots on their heads as they dance their way to the stream. I don't hear the sawing of cutlasses and axes slash-slash-slashing the buttocks of the tree from the farms and forests in the afar. I don't hear the **coo-koo-roo-koo** of the cocks which use to wake us up, the singing birds up in the trees, the voices of one of the church-women, Mama's friend, who use to always sing "Good morning, Jesus" at the front of her market shop. It crushes my spirit to see it so.

"Is this . . . ?" Ms. Tia whispers near me, a tremble in her voice, as she leans her back under a mango tree with mangoes as hard as a coconut shell, so green it looks like it doesn't ever have any plans to be ripe. "Is this Ikati? Your home?"

Is it?

I lift my head. Ikati. The home of my mama and papa and friends and enemies, but is it **my** home? Why is it bending low at the sight of me, like somebody finding a treasure lost under the table of the world?

"It's . . . stunning," Ms. Tia whispers, making her eyes big, bigger than almost her head.

I wonder why Ms. Tia sometimes likes to say things that don't always make sense. "Nothing's turning about this, Ms. Tia. Everything is standing up straight and dry."

Ms. Tia makes a clicking sound in her throat, gives me a tender, soft look.

The chief climbs out of the car. He pushes two fingers into his lips and makes a loud whistle: **Wooooo!**

Why is it so quiet? Where is everybody? And then I remember.

My mama told me the story of when they last made a sacrifice like this. She said that around that same time, a too-hot sun was punishing our village, killing our crops and plantations and animals. This whipping-hot sun lasted about six months, and everybody was wondering, questioning what is causing this problem, until the chiefs say all women must beg and make sacrifices for rain.

The day before the sacrifice, the chiefs and the king made an announcement that the whole village must keep silent. Everything and everybody must keep quiet at the first peep of the early-morning sun for fifteen minutes. They say we must make pretend to be dead. One of our old dogs, he barked a sharp bark of hunger in that fifteen minute of quiet, and my big brother, Born-boy—Mama say she never seen him look so angry—he yanked off his left shoe, stone the dog in his buttocks for making that stupid noise.

The chief pushes up his stick of feathers and begins to make a incantation of words: calling the spirits of the earth and the water and the sky to come and make a witness of my coming back, to be ready to climb inside a seat of judging, to be ready to accept my blood or to reject it. He says all this with a shouting voice, while turning around himself, around and around, until he nearly daze and bangs his head on the car-bonnet of Mr. Kola's car.

Two women come out from afar and walk to meet us, looking like two devil-masquerades. They have slashed their faces left and right, up and down, with charcoal and chalk and pink clay and dragged a circle of eyeshadows around their eyes like eyeglasses, along with a baking of lipstick as pink and as swelling round as a baboon's buttocks. It cuts across their lips and points nearly to their chin like an arrow. They very much resemble Big Madam on her way to a party.

I am trying to hide myself behind Ms. Tia, to crawl inside her and curl myself in the bottom of her belly, to go back to a time when the only thing that mattered to me was my education.

Ms. Tia grabs my hand, says, "What now? Where do we go?"

I know one of the women. Or are my eyes joking me? I squint, press my eyelids close to measure her as she is marching down like a soldier going to war. Is it who I am thinking it is? Even though she is no longer having a small frame and her stomach is now swelling with pregnant, and her eyes are no longer having the spark of a dream of one time becoming a tailor, I know her.

Me and this girl, we use to live in the same house. Her name is Kike, and it was she who taught me to become a teacher in my mind. Her mother, Labake, is the first wife of Morufu, the man my papa married me for.

The second woman with Kike, I don't know her

name, she falls first to her knees in front of the chief, and as she raises up her hand in a worship-greeting, I see the round top of a local-gun, the color of copper, the type of one Thembu, the hunter, is using to kill the bush-rats that run around in the forest. Why is she hiding a gun? Is she a hunter? Kike climbs to her knees too, one by one, because of her stomach.

The chief is still chanting and spinning around like an empty bottle of Coke. Now he is lifting his stick of feathers, sweeping it around the women's heads, seven times. I hold Ms. Tia even more tight.

The chief stops turning. He puts his hand on his legs and pants as if he's about to collapse of a very sudden heart failure problem. He stabs the soil with his stick, striking the stomach of an already dead mango seed, sending it twisting around to near the tire of Mr. Kola's car.

"Kike," I call her name and she looks at me first, before she and the other woman rise and march to where I am standing.

"Ms. Tia . . ." I say, "help me."

Ms. Tia steps in front of me, pushing her hands out. "Excuse me. Listen. My name is Tia Dada. I am from Lagos, and I—"

The second woman shifts Ms. Tia and her plenty-English introductions to one side and snatches my hand so that my nylon of belongings crashes to the floor. Ms. Tia rushes back, trying to fight the two both women, to pull me away, but the other woman is so strong, she somehow manages to push Ms. Tia to the floor. I watch, afraid, as Ms. Tia lands on her buttocks as if a rock flied out from the sky and knocked her down, burying her under the rain of sand and dirt.

She blinks, says "shit," and jumps to her feet and comes charging back. Never seen Ms. Tia look so full of rage, anger. "This is illegal!" Ms. Tia shouts. "Let her go!"

I look to Mr. Kola for help, but the idiot man is leaning back on his car and crossing his hand in front of his chest as if he is watching a TV show. "Madam," he says, a grumble of a warning in his voice, "you better leave them alone before they shoot you!"

Ms. Tia keeps on her stubborn rushing at the woman. Kike tries to stop Ms. Tia too, to stop me. Soon all four of us are in a tangle of pushing and pulling and slapping and blowing. But the other woman—I think she was a boxer in another life, she's so strong—she shocks Ms. Tia with a hot slap, sending her staggering to collapse herself by the mango tree. She faces me, twisting my hands behind my back as if to uproot it from the socket of my shoulders, tying up my wrists tight with a rope. In all of this, she does not speak one word. Just grunting and panting and grunting. I stand with my head bent, too tired to keep fighting, with my bones aching as Kike pulls out a thick black scarf from inside her bra and cover my eyes with it.

Darkness.

They begin to drag me across the square.

Ms. Tia shouts, "No! Please! Hear us out!"

She is running behind us, breathing fast, her canvas-shoe making **dum-dum-dum** on the ground. Now she is trying to tear the sleeve of my dress, scratching my arms, to save me. The strong woman releases her grip on me for a moment. I stand there, panting, looking left and right in the prison of my covered eyes, hoping maybe they will let me go, release me to run to Ms. Tia, to clean all the dirty on her body.

Suddenly, the **pra-pra** of a firing gunshot like a bomb. Like a thousand thunders. The air fills with the stink of powder of gun, like a children's Christmas banger, burning wire.

"Ms. Tia!" I shout, trying to snatch myself from the padlock of Kike's hands, the strong woman's grip. "Ms. Tia!"

Ms. Tia groans a sick groan. I hear her crashing to the ground, the slap of her body hitting a rock, the bash of something—a piece of wood—knifing the bone of my ankles.

The ground under my feet swells and falls, and as the two women drag me away, I keep screaming and screaming.

TIA

I stagger to the trunk of the mango tree and sag onto a flat-topped boulder, with Adunni's screams resounding in the swarm of dust swirling around my head.

What the hell just happened?

I draw in deep breaths, pressing a hand to my sternum. When that woman dug a hand into her wrapper and produced a gun and pointed it at me, I stood, glaring at her, eyes wide, expecting death. Then she thrust her gun up in the air and fired. I crumbled and lay down from the crack's force, the ground pulsating under me.

The space in front of me is a blur.

I inhale, holding air, my lungs aching on breathing

out. There's a stinging pain in my ankle, rips in my denim above my knees, gashes of blood from where the exposed skin scraped the rocky ground.

A sob erupts: part laughter, part fury, part pain. I nearly died. In Ikati. Unfulfilled, resentful, hollow. My throat shrinks. Warm dappled sunlight falls through the canopy of leaves, hitting the rough ground with shadows that appear to usurp the light.

My phone gives a warning beep. I groan, wiping its smudged surface against my trousers and stopping to stare at the lock screen image of Ken and me in Vegas before my world crashed.

Pain hammers my forehead.

A pack of gray speckled pigeons swoop down on a mango. They peck aggressively at it, peeling back its skin, wriggling chunks of yellow pulp away from the kernel. The battery glows amber: 30 percent. Ken is calling. I let it ring off. I need a moment to stop panting. For the throbbing in my joints to ease, for something to say to keep him away from my pillow.

I am surrounded by mud-brick houses with thatched palm-frond roofs, but there is a house perched on the edge of the red hill above, eclipsing the rest. An ostentatious structure with giant gates in front and an aqua-colored roof embellished with a DStv satellite dish. Who lives there? Is it a country home for someone who lives away from Ikati? Can they help? I wipe the sweat off my temple with the hem of my t-shirt. Hit the call button. Ken snatches the phone on the first ring.

"Tiana, you are safe. Thank God!" Relief pulses through his voice, and I swallow. He's not seen the letters. My envelope is safe. Still safe. "Where the hell are you?" The relief explodes out of his voice, and in its place, a quivering, simmering rage. "I've been going crazy!"

"I'm in Ikati," I say calmly. "Adunni is in major trouble. Some women came and took her away, and I fell and hurt myself, but I'll be okay. Did we get—"

"Are you hurt?"

"I am fine. There is nothing wrong—"

The raucous laughter of a group of children interrupts me. It's three girls walking behind their mother, plastic buckets in their hands, strings of beads around their waists, ankles, and slender necks. They rattle and tattle like musical instruments, and as they approach, one of them stops, pointing at me like she's spotted something foreign. Their mother bellows instructions in her language, forcing the girl to turn away.

"How far away from Lagos?" Ken says. "Is there an airport nearby?"

The line sizzles. "Not sure. We drove for about six hours. Can you check if there's one? Maybe I'll fly from there to see Mum?"

"Just checking," Ken says, fingers clacking on his phone screen. "Let's see. Nope. There isn't. Tia, your flight is at five."

I close my eyes. If we leave Ikati in a few hours . . .

"Do you want me to move it?" Ken asks.

My eyes flick open. I hesitate. "No. Not yet. I've got to get Adunni out of here before I decide. I need to speak to Dad. It's too early to call. Did you call around? Are we getting any help?"

"I called a few people," he says in a softer, more controlled tone. "A high court judge, a friend who knows a top guy in the force. They . . ." He sighs. "They are saying it's not within their jurisdiction. A few have stopped picking up my calls. Can you tell me where exactly you are so I can come get you?"

My phone produces a cautionary bleep. "They've taken her away to prepare her for whatever the heck it is, and I can't . . ." My voice breaks. I pause. Inhale. Let it out. "I am not leaving without her."

"I am not asking you to leave without her," Ken says. "Send me a location so I can . . ." His other phone trills in the background. "One sec. Let me get this."

I wait, the sun blazing down, searing my face. Ken comes back.

"That was another friend. He says he cannot influence things, but he's willing to send two police officers, personal security guards of some sort, to come with me to Ikati. But I've got to pay for them and go pick them up! The insanity! I wonder if Florence said something to dissuade folks, because the reticence is baffling, Tia. Absolutely baffling." He sighs. "I'll keep calling around. In the meantime, send me—" Twin alarms blare off at the same time, cutting him off. I realize with a sickening dread that it's both my bedside alarm and the spare in the guest room. There's a clatter, and I sense he's in our room, leaning across my side of the bed, perhaps against the pillow, as he reaches for mine and hits the snooze button. The clock in the guest room carries on, a muffled screech. "Shit. I'm going to need to turn that thing off. I'll jump off now. Send me your location and I'll come get you. Okay?"

"Think you can turn the alarm in Adunni's room off and go downstairs? You know, to wait for help?" **Don't look under my pillow.**

"I love you, Tia," Ken says.

Is it me, or do I hear a crunch? I feel myself swaying, the world slowly spinning in a haze of dust.

"Love you too," I say.

"Good. Keep your phone on. Don't make yourself obvious. Call you in fifteen minutes with an update."

I hang up, raising my eyes into the distance, the desert-sanded chasm between me and the houses, the narrow path through which Adunni disappeared. What if I'm left here by myself, looking over this parcel of land that separates us for the next month? What if no one comes out to meet me and take me to her? What if something terrible happens to Adunni?

What if Ken finds the envelope?

I draw in deep breaths.

Everything will be all right. Adunni will be safe.

They need her alive, at least until midnight. I blink the grittiness from my eyes and breathe in another lungful of dusty air.

I stand, grabbing our stuff and jogging across the expanse—the air so arid it cracks my lips—and stop on a path that leads into the cluster of mud-brick houses. There is a reddish-brown stump on its edge, of an acacia tree felled long ago. I stare at the intricate lines of black zigzagging its ringed brown surface. Beside it, an umbrella-shaped acacia, as ancient as the village itself, with gnarled roots and contorted branches snaking out of it, the tentacles of an octopus encased in a leaf-patterned cloth. A young pregnant woman waddles down the path, dragging her bare feet along the route, hauling along a bald toddler with skinny legs. Up close, I realize how young, how fresh-faced she is, and I almost envy how her bump sits, easily, like a hardened, well-sculpted ball of wrapped clay on her hips. She sighs, massaging her lower back, and the envy oozes away, a deep sorrow replacing it.

There is a patch of dry skin at the base of the child's bald head: hyperpigmentation caused by ringworm?

"Hi!" I say to the child, crouching, wiggling my fingers. She gapes at me as if in wonder, reaching out, tentatively at first, to trace my jawline with lean fingers. I smile, and something in my smile frightens her—my braces? She squeals, burying her face between her mother's legs.

"Hey." I touch my chest, a sign of solidarity, friendship. A demonstration of my harmlessness. "My name is Tia. I am Adunni's friend."

The woman eyes the black Air Maxes on my feet, my torn jeans, the smudge of blood around my knees, my pink-flowered t-shirt smeared with ocher dust, fragments of dried leaves. She rolls herself away, clinging to her daughter's arm, pausing at a bend in the path, to give me a long look, before disappearing with her half-naked child.

I sit on the stump and glance around, pushing my tongue under my lip, exploring the brackets on my braces, a snag in the wire holding them in place. My phone glows neon—blue with an email from Ken.

I click it open, a bubble of fresh panic whirling in my belly. An image, slowly loading, shedding its layers like an animal, across the drag on the network. Before the image fills the screen, I already know it's a photo of a letter I wrote to Boma.

10th April 2012

Dear Boma,

I've met the man I am going to marry.

We met on the Facebook thing I told you about in my last letter, and we kind of clicked. Sorry it's taken me a few weeks to find the courage to tell you about him, I guess I didn't want to make you feel like I was moving on without you.

A few things:

1) His name is Ken Dada and he's a gynecologist. I can't get past that: I'm marrying a man who specializes in vulvas and uteruses and all. It makes me a bit insecure: I can't stop thinking, what does he see when he's examining another woman? When he's eating pounded yam (his fave Nigerian dish), I often find myself staring at his fingers as he carves and molds a morsel and dunks it into a bowl of vegetable stew, thinking, where the hell have those fingers been today?

   My mother said, "Thank God you got it right this time."
   That hurt. A lot.

2) He's nice. Good-looking (the tall, dark, etc. type). Plus, he's borderline-OCD neat, which means he'll take extra care to scrub his fingers and skin after work.

3) I am not in love with him. Yet. I guess I am hovering around love with him, if that makes sense.

4) He doesn't want kids. Now this should be point one, but I wanted to ease in gently. It's virtually unheard of, Boma: a Nigerian man who doesn't want kids. But we share this desire to remain childless in this marriage and to be ready to

battle the onslaught of questions and opinions and concerns and probing that will come— because they will.

5) He lives in Lagos. Yep, I am relocating. England no longer feels like home. I guess it never was. It's time to come back home—to be closer to you and to find pieces of my heart and try to mend. I will be in Port Harcourt a week before my wedding in July, and I think it makes perfect sense to spend the day with you—just because, right?

It was always meant to be you, Boma. Not Ken, not whoever else.

We were going to wear matching t-shirts with the words BOW-TIE 4EVER on our wedding day, remember? We were going to damn the consequences and love each other hard.

But life has a way of throwing shit your way, right?

xx
Tia

PS: It's 2012 and no one writes letters anymore (except us!), but I have, as always, sprayed this letter, so . . . smell after you read, and guess the fragrance. xx

ADUNNI

I am still screaming.

My feet are sweeping up rocks and sands and sharp stones, the skin of my toes peeling back, my toenails bleeding, my eyes dizzy. Did the gunshot fire her legs? Or her head? Is she dead? Can she just die dead like that?

"Gbe enu e dake!" Kike hisses, pinching my arms. "Keep your mouth quiet!"

My head is swinging left and right in a no-no-no. I will not stop screaming. Never. I will slice my throat with the knife of my sorrow and pluck the box of my voice out and throw it all over Ikati! I will send my screaming on a rage of errand, to go back to that square and pick up my Ms. Tia and clean her wounds and wipe her blood and breathe life inside of her. I will give her bread to eat and sing her a song and tell her a joke and tickle her armpit so she can pluck her hair out from her face and laugh her shining-teeth laugh and say: **Oh, Adunni! You silly goose!**

"Adunni!" Kike pinches my arms. "**Kai!** Keep quiet! Keep your mind strong."

Which mind?

My mind is full up to the top with the **crack-crack** of that gunshot, with the **bang** of Ms. Tia's body falling to the floor, with slashing and stabbing things. My heart is stucked between my wide-open mouth. I want to push it out, force it out into the dark circle of a world without no Ms. Tia. A world with no meaning.

Kike hisses, says: "**Dake!** Quiet! She didn't dead!"

What?

I stop walking. Stop screaming. "You say what?"

"She did not dead," Kike says, the air from her throat hot in my ears. Something yanks the cloth from my eyes so that it hangs like a shirt collar on my neck.

I look at Kike, my eyes pinching from the biting sun.

She nods, lowers her chin to her chest, and says: "Your friend didn't dead. She only wound herself small. Stop your screaming."

My legs curve, nearly falling me down, but I catch myself quick, straight up my back. Through a sheet of sunlight and dust, I see that we are in another compound, that people are starting to come out of their houses to peep at me, some from behind the ankara-curtain cloth they pin up over their windows, others from under a basket of skinny peppers and tomatoes on their heads. I see that another strong woman, the one that gunshot Ms. Tia, is far ahead, marching in front.

Kike pulls the cloth up to cover my eyes, hands gentle. "Let's go, Adunni," she says, voice soft, speaking English. Her voice is full of kindness too, and for the first time since we arrived in Ikati, I hope Kike will help me.

This time, our walk is slow, like an evening stroll from one family compound to the other family compound, from road to road. I sense the wonder of eyes on me as doors creak open, close. I feel the rain of their heavy whispers falling upon me, the hissing and clapping and sighing, the questions, the answers.

But I don't have a care for them all.

My Ms. Tia is not dead.

Kike takes off my eye-cloth when we reach her husband's house.

His name is Baba Ogun, and his compound is having three houses, a well in the corner with an outside kitchen and bathroom, and a shrine which is like a dining table for the spirits to be eating free food. We walk to the last of the three mud-brick, square-shape houses, painted with the dirty of years that have passed, with sleeping grass growing up to the wall to the roof, with a door of iron-metal cage in front, a bottle of red oil hanging on it to keep off evil spirits.

We stop at the door, and Kike breathes out loud, rubbing her pregnant stomach and leaning against the wall with a sigh. Fourteen and pregnant as a wife of a medicine man priest must be very hard work. Her husband's job is to take instruction from the spirits and make explanations to us here on earth. I think he is the one who will give the instructions for the preparations of the sacrifice, and now that Kike is his wife, she will maybe help him.

The second woman stands back and scratches her throat with her tongue, as Kike looses her wrapper and finds the padlock-key sleeping inside the bed of her hair. With it, she opens the padlock on the door.

"Kike," I say.

It takes a moment, but when she speaks, she puts her head down, as if to hide her mouth, to tuck her words inside of her chin. "Sorry, Adunni, sorry you are coming back . . . like—" She falls silent.

I keep my eyes on her. **Like what? Say it, Kike. Say it. A thief? A killer . . . ?**

She raises her head. "I open this door and keep you lock up here until it is time."

Time for what?

"Okay," I say. I have been through many troubles,

and I come out of them all. I will come out of this one too. Because Ms. Tia didn't die. Because I am Adunni. A person important enough because my tomorrow will be better than today.

"Enter," Kike says. "Your room is first. Right."

I take a step, pause.

"Kike?"

She lifts her head. Answers **Yes?** with her eyes.

There is the sudden cry of a mosque calling to prayer, the chanting of Allah-Akbar, from speakers in the mosque behind the market square. It is so loud, is as if someone planted the speakers inside the soil of my brain. I wait for the prayer call to quiet a moment before I ask her the question that has been heavy on my mind for the last one year:

"Where is Kayus? Where is my baby brother?"

I want to see Kayus. I want to soak him up with my eyes and hold his head and tell him that yes, I have come back to face this trial, but I will be okay, and he will be okay and me and him and Ms. Tia, who is here in Ikati; we will everybody be okay.

But Kike does not answer me when I ask her about my brother. She pushes the door wide open so that it bangs against the wall and a voice inside the corridor makes a scream **waah** so loud. It is the voice of a girl from a stubborn lung and chest, a voice that comes flying out and causing Kike to jump and rub her stomach to keep calm her baby.

And this second woman with Kike, who gun-fire the gunshot to almost kill Ms. Tia, who is not talking, who is she? She is older than Kike, but I make the very wise assumption that she must be the second wife of Kike's husband. What type of a madness is this, that a second wife can be thirty-something years of age and the first wife can be fourteen? Crazy mental.

I remember this time last year, when Kike was still living with Morufu, her father, the man they married me to. She told me how she didn't mind marrying an old medicine man. I am sure that Baba Ogun must be at least 250 years old because he was alive when my mama's mama was alive. The second woman doesn't make any response to the scream or to the banging on the door. She just keeps looking at me with that wicked-fire burning in her eyes.

"Kike? Is Kayus okay?" I ask again. "Can you find him and tell him to see me?"

Kike puts her head to her chest. Why she keeps doing that? Am I hiding between her breasts? Why she keeps putting her head down to answer me?

"I will try," Kike says, talking soft. "Please enter inside and wait for me."

The second woman makes a noise like a hungry puppy bark, points a soaked red finger at my bleeding left foot, my scattered shoe, and makes another noise, as if fifty-two bees are buzzing inside her throat, dancing under her tongue, trying to help her form words that we can understand. She hisses, pointing a finger to Kike, to Kike's lips, to my feet.

"Ah," Kike says, lifting her head. "I will tell her.

Adunni, this is my **Iyawo**, the second wife of my husband. Her name is Shaki. I am her **Iyale**, the first wife, but she is more old than me, so I give her that respect. She says you must off your shoe before you enter the room of power."

Which room of power? The room in front of me doesn't look like it has the power to even light half a bulb.

And now, as I watch Shaki tie and retie her wrapper around her chest, I think that Shaki is not able to talk or to hear. But maybe she can be able to read lips, which must be why Kike is hiding her mouth to give me communications.

"Okay, I'll do that." I say in English. "The shoes are useless now, anyway." I didn't bring the new shoes Ms. Tia bought with me. I didn't bring anything she bought for me, except the mobile phone, but even that one is inside my nylon bag back in the market square. Now I wish I had a small part of Ms. Tia to hold.

"Your English," Kike says, talking to her chest with something marvel in her voice. "Did you go to the Abroad?"

My head swells a little with pride. My English is not the best, but it is better. Better plus better will one day equals to the best.

"I went to Lagos," I say, lowering my head too. Shaki hisses. I think she knows what me and Kike are doing.

"Lagos is a big shining city with cars and bright

lights," I say, smiling at the memory. "Ms. Tia, the woman in the square, with teeth that shine like a spoon under a hot sun. The English people call it **brazes**. That woman is my friend, my second mama. She has a good spirit. Please help her! Please don't let your husband or any of the chiefs see her."

Kike sighs, says, "Miss Tee-Yah with Shining Teeth."

I don't tell her about Big Madam beating and suffering me, maybe because sometimes all of us want other people to wish they were like us. Even for five minutes. So, I carry on talking about the good things. "In Lagos, there are people living well, eating well, traveling to the London and the America, and there are even people making money selling cloths and writing in magazines and sewing clothes and making money as a tailor. Lagos is a very wonderful place!"

I look up and see that my words sting Kike in the eyes, the reminding her of her dead dream of becoming a tailor.

"Sorry," I say, not just to herself, but to myself too, for cutting the only one slice of truth from the big cake of my time in Lagos and giving it to Kike.

Kike sighs, says, "Adunni, you are so very having lucky to live in Lagos and taste a rich life there."

"Yes," I mumble. "Very rich life. And you too? You been enjoying life as a wife?"

"Yes," she says. "Is a good life."

Which nonsense good life? By the time Kike's new-born baby is five years of age, Baba Ogun will be around 255 years of age with one teeth in his mouth. How is that a good life? But how is my own life a good life? So, we look each other in the eye, and both laugh a laugh that is dragged down by the weight of the lies we tell each other.

Shaki pushes me down the thin corridor into the room, banging the door shut behind me. There is a window up in the wall, from which a patch of sunlight tips its toes around the room. It takes a moment, but my eyes soon learn the room around me, my feet feeling the roughness of the floor under a thin mat, my nose taking in the scent of incense mosquito coil burning.

I pick up the cup beside me, drink up all the sandy water, until there is not one drop left inside, and set it down.

I pull my knees up to my chest, give myself a close embrace. **Everything will be okay, Adunni. Everything.**

Where is Ms. Tia now?

I wonder if it is seven o'clock. If my alarm in Ms. Tia's house is alarming itself.

I smile, remembering the very mystery square bottle beside the alarm clock in Ms. Tia's guest room, the size of two boxes of matches join-up together. There was a chewing-gum-smelling perfume water, the color of watery blood, with six short broomsticks digging inside of it, like a spoon stirring a pot of red beans-stew. I remember picking it up, sniffing it, and how, just like that, I began to cough and sneeze so I put it down quick before it will cause me to die dead of a chest collapse. When I asked Ms. Tia what this bottle was, she made a chuckling sound and said, "Oh, Adunni, that's a reed diffuser. It's handmade by Tolani's Apothecary in Falomo. Amazing fragrance, this. All calming and relaxing. It's meant to help you sleep like a baby. Did you inhale it?"

I smile at how rich people like Ms. Tia always say special and costly things are handmade. Ms. Tia will say, **The shoe is handmade, Adunni!** or **The bag is hand-stitched!** As if anybody will ever stitch up a bag with their nostrils.

Oh, Ms. Tia, you silly goose! Thank God you are safe.

When I see her again, I will tell her to bring thirty bottles of reed diffusers to my nose and I will sniff it all up to make her happy, laugh. I hope she didn't wound bad. I hope she will find a way to call the good doctor for help.

Honest.

Tomorrow is a big fat liar. Did it not tell me it will be better than today? I relaxed myself and believed it, and just like that, it came and pulled the rope out from under my feet and caused me to fall splash inside a river full of sorrow-fishes. How do I swim out?

I lift my face to the window high up in the wall, blinking back my tears. Morning is no longer peeping like a stranger over the earth. The sun is awake now with all its chest, blazing like a fire, burning up all my dreams of going to school, of freedom.

SEVENTEEN HOURS
TO MIDNIGHT

‖‖‖‖‖‖‖‖‖
TIA
‖‖‖‖‖‖‖‖‖

I stare at the phone trembling in my hands.

Ken knows. He would have found out regardless, but it shouldn't have happened like this. How do I begin to explain? My phone rings, the screen a white blur, and at first, I am unsure of how to pick up, what button to press.

"Are you having an affair?" There is a sharp coldness to his tone, an accusation underscoring every syllable. "With this Boma dude? You saw him last month. You told me you were going to see your mother."

I swallow. "I can explain." Phone static crackles, snaps in my ears. "If you can—"

"You told him you are 'hovering around love'

with me? Tia?" He sounds tortured. "That I was infertile?"

A flock of birds soar above the trees with a loud trill to form a distorted letter **M** in the sky. "I am sorry," I whisper hoarsely, uselessly.

"This thing started in 1997?" he says, a muffled whisper against the quiet rustle of paper. Is he crying? "With this Boma? You've loved this bastard since 1997?"

A shell cracks open in my mind.

"Ken," I manage, blinking into the distance, my eyelids achy, heavy. "Now is not the time. If you haven't read them all, please can you . . . can you not? Can you leave them until I can explain? Please?"

"Where is Adunni?" He sniffs. "Where are you?"

"Ken, please." A sob shudders out of me. "You need to trust me. It's not what you think."

"Send me your location," he growls, and hangs up before I can reply.

I feel like I am crashing through a spiral tunnel. I close my eyes, the scathing phosphorescence of the sun assaulting my eyelids, and bright red dots dance along the fleshy insides. I can smell the acrid earth, the vinegarish, aromatic scent of a dying African basil plant, and I think of my childhood home, of the pink flowers with petals as long and as slender as fingers, growing in intricately patterned clay pots in our garden. They formed a queue along a path opposite our kitchen wall. In the evenings, my mother would sing as she watered her plants, tilting her purple watering can just so, as if to admire the steady stream from its spout, but she'd stop the moment I skipped along, often to point a finger at the house, top lip curling.

Boma's face hovers on the brim of memory, his smile, the shape of his fingers, his smell. He deserves to know what my mother did, what I heard her say, all of what she's been hiding. I'll finish up here and return to Port Harcourt, and on my way home, I'll stop by to see him, maybe for the last time. Maybe not. But I need to talk to him first, before I deal with Ken, because everything else will be aftershock.

My head pounds. I rub my eye, swipe sand from my jawline. I should call Dad. Ask him to tell Mum I'm running late. It's the way we often communicate, my mother and I, through the medium of the man we share.

I fire up Google Maps, type in my home address, click directions. The network lags, and it takes minutes for the directions to come up. I record my surroundings, send the video and directions to Ken. There's one tick, and I don't know if it's because he's blocked me, or because of the network. Still, I give the phone a wave in the air, hoping to catch a signal, trying not to panic at the amber bar on my battery icon. A muezzin calls for prayer in the distance. A minute later, and there's still one tick. I turn the phone off, count thirty seconds, turn it back on. The long warning beep rips through the silence like an alarm. Life surges out of it. The screen turns black.

I remember Adunni's phone. I rummage through her bag, and my heart sinks as I retrieve the basic phone. There's no internet access. It's only useful for calls and texts. I turn it off, deciding to conserve the battery. There's a bellow in the distance, the squeak of backyard taps, pots and pans banging in narrow kitchens at the backs of these outbuildings.

I flip my wrist over and check my watch. 7:15 a.m.

That's it. I am going to find Adunni.

❀

I trace the sound of a saw slicing through wood, past a blue motorcycle beneath a tall tree with a piece of red fabric on one of its branches. I pause briefly to catch my breath, to observe. The tree trunk fascinates me; the large slits carved into it make me think, weirdly, of a calcified labia, two thick lips delineating the opening that leads to its sacred hollow core, tickled pink by the sun.

I stand facing a rural cul-de-sac, five houses built with mud-cement, separated by slender acacias and low shrubs, encircling a large communal yard. Across it, a wide path lined with trees.

It leads to a cluster of mud-brick houses fenced by tawny and limp savannah grass and with rows of plowed, parched earth. I follow the path, stopping only when I hear footsteps pattering down or the sputter of a machine coming to life. I pause often, leaning on tree trunks to rest, to regain strength from the biting sun, from the effort of the inclined landscape, my hand muscles pulsing from holding my bag over my head to hide my face.

There are two women sauntering toward me. I duck beside a young paw-paw tree, eyes on the line of red ants briskly marching off in a queue that disappears under the thinning and deformed roots of the tree.

The older woman with creases lining her weathered forehead leads, her thick, tremulous head swinging left and right as she gesticulates widely, as if to prove a point, speaking in a language that is a proliferation of sh's and o's with a curious hissing sound.

The younger girl lags. She is carrying a scantily filled basket from which bruised red peppers and globe-shaped tomatoes leak yellow- seeded water onto her bare shoulders. When she notices me, she stops walking; the gap in her upper lip extending slightly into her nose twitches as she observes me through hooded eyes.

The older woman turns and sees me. Her eyes broaden.

I hold my breath, legs quivering, as she raises a hand, her mouth slackening in the launch of a scream. The girl plunges the basket on her head to the ground, spilling seeded tomato juice out of the thin, perforated skins. Her mother slaps her, hurling out what sounds like a string of curses. The girl falls to her knees, crying, pleading, crawling farther away, obliging her mother to run after her, to pluck one of the damaged tomatoes from the ground, hurl it at her. I can't help feeling like she did this on purpose, to distract her mother. To help me.

I count thirty seconds and run in the opposite direction, blending into shadows of trees behind a bamboo fence covered with large banana leaves, with wrappers and wired lace bras hanging across it to dry.

I sag against it, panting.

The pregnant girl who took Adunni away emerges. I think Adunni called her Kike. She is pulling along a young boy of about eight by his skinny left arm. He is wearing a faded gray t-shirt, loosened at the neck so that it looks almost like a stylish off-shoulder top. His shirtsleeve bears marks of rodent-like bites.

I squint into the distance, sunlight searing a path along my scalp. Adunni's brother? I sit up, eyes on Kike, fingers curling around a small rock, and when she's near enough, I aim. It thumps the boy's dust-patterned khaki shorts. Startled, he halts, clutching his backside with a yowl. I watch him with my heart drumming as he turns to look. At me. I raise an arm and wave, manically. He frowns, tugging the pregnant girl's wrapper. He points at me. The girl stops to look. Her eyes spring wide.

I stiffen, my gaze zipping across the yard, sourcing

the nearest exit. There isn't one. If she draws attention to me, I am colossally ruined. But she beckons, dashing behind the fence with the boy.

I half jog and half run across.

"Hi," I say when I reach the girl, whose eyes have lost their initial blazing determination. The boy digs his bare feet under the sand as if to hide his toes from me. I notice a greenish-brown stick, the stem of a flower nestled in his uneven afro. He self-consciously reaches out to pluck it while stealing a glance at me.

"We. Met. Earlier," I say. "Me. Tia. Friend. Of. Adunni."

"Adunni," the young boy says, looking up at me, his brown eyes filling with tears. Why is he crying?

"Yes? You know her?" I ask the boy. "I am sorry I hit you with the stone," I add, noticing a pair of tribal marks, short dashes under each cheek, the line faint as if someone buffed out each scar with sandpaper. "Are you Adunni's brother?"

"Talk your mind quick," the pregnant girl snaps, scolding the boy in Yoruba until he bites his lips and stops crying. She peeks over my shoulder. "You are Miss Tee-Yah with Shining Teeth?"

"Yes," I say, in an exhale. "Me. Tia. How is she?"

"Adunni? Save. Very save."

"Safe? Great, that's . . . great. Thanks." I thrust Adunni's bag at her, but she lets it drop to the floor. I snatch it, shaking a cascade of sand from it. "Sorry. This bag. It is Adunni's. Can you?" I gesture the bag toward her chest without letting go. "Give. To. Her? Please. Can you also please take me to her?"

"Run, go back . . . Lagos," she says, making a shooing motion. Her bitten nails leave small indents in the skin around her fingers. "Adunni save. Go!" She snatches the boy by the hand. "**Oya!**"

Sunlight stuns my eyes as they amble off, turning into a muddy alleyway. I let out a breath and bolt after them, trailing behind, giving them distance, although I suspect she knows I'm following. She ambles along pathways that appear deserted, as though deliberately selected with me in mind.

The boy glances behind often, to look at me, to wave, and I press my fingers to my lips and wave back, until they reach a trio of houses sitting at the end of a broad yard of slightly elevated earth, like a three-headed monster crouching on a bench. There is a mud-brick fence, as tall as me, around the house; a thick forest behind it; canopies of tall indigenous timber trees with tops like open palms carrying floating white clouds. The trees are shaped, almost by design, around a baked hollow space in the middle. The girl and boy walk across the yard, and I follow, but the girl breaks her stride and turns.

She thrusts a hand up in the air, gesturing for me to stop.

I obey.

She jerks a finger toward the mud-brick fence to my left, to the broom leaning against it. "Hide."

I retreat. Obey.

The girl hauls the boy furtively toward the third door, fumbles with the lock, twisting it open. They enter. The door slams. I turn my phone on, and it stutters awake and immediately lets out a beep. There are two emails waiting in my inbox. Another letter. I click it open, and it unfurls like a scroll rolled back:

December 1997

Dear Boma,

I am sorry my mother thinks you don't belong in our house, that she thinks you are beneath me. Your lovely mum seemed so sad (I think she was crying silently) when my mum picked up that disgusting kitchen broom yesterday and made a sweeping motion at you—as if you were dirt. Thank you though for not talking back to her, for walking out of the kitchen without a word.

I hate her.

But you already know that.

I'm taking your advice, trying to be better at expressing my feelings, but I haven't gotten to the point where I can verbally express myself to my mother. Each time I try, I feel a tightening in my larynx, a seizing of my voice.

I never told you this, but I wrote to my mother the night Princess Diana died. I felt such an acute sense of loss, maybe because she touched my

life with the hope she gave to the world with
her kindness.

It didn't make a lot of sense though, my letter.
I think I sounded very whiny, with a lot of whys:
Why don't you love me, etc., etc.

I sprayed a mist of Dior and slipped it under the
door of her library. It's been six months, and the
only reference she made to the letter was last
night, after she sent you out of the kitchen. She
called me to her cold, cold library (the A/C there
is always on full blast because apparently books
are better preserved in the cold, but I think it's
because my mother is a vampire and needs to live
in the freezer, ha ha ha).

So, she called me in and asked me to stand
by her reading desk. I obeyed. She looked
up from her novel, and said that I needed to
improve my writing skills, and was I not smart
enough to know that spraying perfume on ink
would invariably dilute the ink and render the
letter illegible?

She pointed at this tattered novel at the foot of
her office chair, I forget the author and title now,
and said, "if you want to learn to write better,
learn from the greats."

She shooed me away like I'm this bug, but
before I stepped out of her library, she said, "Stay
away from that Boma boy, Tia. You hear me? You

have your whole life ahead of you, and he's not the kind of boy you should be seen with."

The old me might have cried, but this new me has swallowed a dozen I-don't-care pills of what she thinks of me, what she feels, whatever. I nearly gave her a talk-to-the hand-cos-the-face-ain't-listening gesture, but that would earn me a week's worth of grounding and I cannot imagine not seeing you for a whole week, so I stepped away from her and quietly shut the door in her face. Please disregard her feelings about you. All that matters is what I think of you, how you make me feel, and the forever love we share.

I cannot wait to see you at our usual spot behind the pond!

Sleep tight and don't let the bedbugs bite.

Tia

PS: The imprint at the bottom of this page is of my lips, slathered in lipstick, a wet kiss from me to you.

ADUNNI

There is a girl living inside the wall of this room.
She has been screaming for the last two, three minutes nonstop since they locked me up here, and her voice is a rough tangle, as if she wrapped up her voice in a nylon bag and shoved it down the hole of my ears.

I sit with my shoulders tilting to the side, pressing my ears to the wall. Yes. She is in there, or maybe in a room on the opposite of me. What is troubling her? I try to make sense of her shouting. All I can hear is a language like a mix-up of another language like the peoples that is in the Telemundo movie channel in Big Madam's house.

I use my elbow to knock the wall to make the girl

stop. She stops. Starts up again, adding a drumming to the music of her screaming and banging
something on the wall, **ko-ko-ko**. An empty can of
milk? She scratches the wall too, making her nails
a shovel, digging something hidden deep inside the
chest of the wall. It is making me to want to run
mad, this nonsense noise. Making it hard to think
until I shout, "STOP!"

Silent.

Why did I come back to Ikati? Why am I sometimes so stubborn and thinking I can be bold to
face any troubles? Why didn't I collect the ladder
in Ms. Tia's house?

The girl resumes her screaming, and this time, it
is a whole commotions of her digging and screaming plus including the morning noises of the village:
the blenders blending beans; the shouting of hurrying mothers calling to children; the flies buzzing
up in the wall; the goats bleating **meh-meh** outside
Baba Ogun's compound; the cutlass cutting and
saw-chain machine hitting and slicing of the buttocks of thick trees, the creaking and twisting of
the tree as it is falling, down, then boom, crack,
crashing to the floor. I imagine it in my mind how
all chickens and lizards and goats will run-scatter
for their life as the tree is coming down.

These woodcutters been cutting the trees since
before I was born. They cut down the iroko and
ma-ogani and shea nut and mango and palm and
cashew and neem trees. They cut them, as far Kere

and Goma and Ikati forests, and use it for charcoal wood, for making bench and table and chair, for roofing house, for selling to big-men in Lagos and the Abroad, for building boats, and I use to wonder it, when I was young, if the trees are not feeling pain when these woodcutters are cutting their tree-hands and tree-legs and tree-necks with axes and cutlass. The cutters, they cut and cut and don't ever remember to grow a new one back.

I remember one tree, the body white as a toilet tissue and lean like a neck with tribal marks along it so that it looks as if the neck is wearing bangles. The leaf of which is the most beautiful I ever seen in our forests. It is the red of a flaming fire, so bright you can see it from far, lighting up the dark forest. It use to make me think of a beautiful church-hat with millions of red bows, perching on the head on the bangled neck of a slender woman, tilting a little to the left.

When the woodcutters cut down that tree, I cried. The tree cried too, leaking tears and bleeding blood from the woodcut in its wood flesh, from the gap in one of the neck bangles. Even now, sometimes, when you walk into the forest early in the morning, you see trees with big thick bodies and deep wounds inside their back, and now, as I think of it, I imagine the tree crying and begging the woodcutters not to slash them, the way I was begging those women to not flog Ms. Tia that long time ago. Trees, they die dead like people too. They need care too. The earth around us needs care. We come from earth, we eat from earth, and one day we must go back to earth, so why are we treating it so bad?

What time is it now? Where is Ms. Tia?

I have another memory: a sweet one of my life before in the past, of how I use to laugh as a small girl of maybe five, six years of age, when my mama will take me with her to go and beg some of the woodcutters for wood chips for us to make a charcoal for toothbrushing.

I remember too our visits to Labake, my mother's friend, who is Kike's mother, who is the first wife of Morufu, the man I married. She and my mother were best of friends since they were two years of age. When we were small, Labake will call me and Kike and Enitan and make us to be gathering the shea nuts as they are falling from the shea tree and give it to Labake, and we will watch her as she will cook and dry it and pound it with a stick, and we will be laughing because Labake didn't use to wear a bra, and her breasts will be swinging up and down like a car wiper, as she is pounding the nuts. The shea cream, a yellow toothpaste milk, is what Labake will mix with coconut oil and give it to my mama for body and hair cream.

Because of Labake, we growed up with shining smooth skin and smooth hair.

One day, Mama and Labake stop befriending

themselves. Labake will shift to one side when she sees Mama coming, and Mama will drop her head, sad, as if she cannot look at Labake's face.

The day Mama was dead, I ran to Labake to tell her. I can never forget how Labake turned her back to me and cried a silent cry with the shaking of her shoulders. "Go," she said, after a long moment. "Give her . . . good burial."

She did not even come to Mama's burial.

Till today, I don't know why my mama and Labake stop befriending each other. I tried to ask Mama, but all she said was, "Don't worry. Everything be okay one day."

Anyway, this cream, the one Labake makes, is the very same cream Ms. Tia is paying plenty money for in Lagos, calling it organic handmade lotion this and that. What is it meaning anyway when something is organic?

I think if Labake had found a way to learn more education about her shea butter business, she maybe would have packaged it, drawed a small picture of one of her organs on top of the package paper, maybe her kidney or her liver, make it Organic, and sell it to Ms. Tia for plenty money. I picture it in my mind, imagine a block of shea butter wrapped up in a yellow nylon bag, with a beans-shaped kidney picture on top, the words **Labake's** (swinging breasts) **ORGANIC Hand Made Shea Butter** on the face of it.

An ant is crawling around my toes and climbing up my left leg and marching its tiny self toward my private under. I slap the thing off with a hiss, and the girl in the wall stops screaming.

I tell you true, sometimes I talk too much and think too much and in the middle of the too-much thinking and talking, I will lost and find myself in a roundabout of my thoughts, confuse of where to go next. My thinking is tired of me. Maybe I can close my eyes and— Listen. What is that outside the door? Is somebody coming?

The door opens and light enters the room, bringing along with it Kike's stomach first. She is holding a swinging lantern with a low flame in its glass, and who is that small boy with her?

Is it . . . Kayus?

I sweep the cobwebs from my eyes with my fingers and push myself up. Kayus?

"KAYUS!" I scream, but Kike slaps my mouth with her hand so quick, it automatic killed dead my happy noise.

"Ah, Adunni," she says, looking behind her shoulder. "You know what will happen if my husband catch me with Kayus here?"

I don't care if her husband plucks out her eyelashes and uses it to make medicines for curing madness. I don't care if he uproots her **shuku** hairstyle and wears it like a wig to cover his own shining head with no hair. I don't care if the roof falls and the sea swells and the rains refuses to come for the next three years. Nothing matters to me right now except my Kayus.

I look at him, my heart growing big in my chest as I gather him in my hands and hold him close and press his head to my chest. My Kayus. He smells of shoe-polish and washing soap and motor engine oil. My Kayus, his ribs are like the teeth of a comb in my hands, his head of hair so full, it makes me wonder when last he barb it. When last did anyone care for my Kayus? I push his chest back, look at him up and down, drink up his face with the cup of my eyes. My Kayus, he is now so tall, but why is his neck now so thin? And his eyeballs, why are they pushing deep inside his forehead? And what is that sharp edge on his cheekbones?

"What happened?" I ask, my voice breaking with sorrow as I pull him close again. "Why are you so thin?"

"Food is small," Kike says in a whisper. "We are managing food in the village. Your papa sometimes drink so much, he forget to give Kayus food. Kayus been working as a shoemaker and mechanic, but I hear they didn't pay him one naira for one day of his work."

My soul cracks. I went to Lagos to slave, but Kayus was here, slaving too. Slaving is maybe the curse of children with a dead mama and no education. How can my papa forget to give his own son food? What kind of a useless somebody is my papa? "Eh, Kayus? Is it true? Did Papa forget to give you food?"

But Kayus doesn't answer. He staggers back, leaning against the wall and looking at me with thick fat tears running down his rough, thin face.

I tell you true, even if the darkness is ten times thick more than this, I can see my brother in the bright light of my soul-eyes, the way his shoulders tense up. I sense the stiffness of his legs, the tears standing in his eyes. I see the sorrow sitting on top of him, and I sense anger too, breathing fire in and out of him, cooking his soul, making a sizzle inside of the pot of the darkness of this room.

"Kayus," I say, talking gentle. "What is heavy on your mind? You didn't even greet me hello. You didn't say one word since morning. How are you? How is Papa and Born-boy? What happened since I left our village?"

My baby brother shifts closer to me, so that we are sitting shoulder to shoulder; then he presses his head close to my chest and wraps his hand tight around my neck and cries. I parcel up my sorrow in my chest, trying to be strong.

Kike leaves us in a thick darkness, shutting the door with a quiet click on the back of her.

|||||||||||
TIA
|||||||||||

I t's true.

I hovered around love with Ken for a while after we met, until something inside of him sucked me into his center and kept me glued there. And now I love Ken and I love Boma and I hate myself, and that is the summary of my reality.

I feel a throbbing relief that he's reading the letters, that somehow I can explain it all when he gets to the end. Maybe it's a form of comfort amid chaos. **No.** There is no comfort in knowing that I carried a lie into our marriage, that Boma has always nestled on the brim of my union with Ken, that our marriage feels like a sham.

So yes. I'm in a shitstorm, but I am not facing death. Adunni is. Where the hell is she?

I train my ears to the faint whirr and rumble of a chain saw in the distance, the sound of cutlasses hacking at the base of a tree trunk, the tilt and groan of a tree being felled, the resounding **thwack** that follows as it hits the mangled shrubs on the ground in the forest, the flock of birds it sends surging into the sky.

It sounds like there are illegal loggers at work in this forest, felling trees that should be protected, and it reminds me of the slide deck I had to create at work with data derived from research papers on deforestation, published by the Forestry Research Institute of Nigeria. I recall sitting at my laptop, back hunched, my nearly empty cup of latte in my hand as I read that Nigeria has lost over one million hectares of tree cover since the year 2000 to illegal tree logging.

"That's a staggering five hundred million tons of carbon dioxide emissions," I said as Ken pried the mug out of my hands and gave me a glass of water to drink.

"You look stricken," he said with a side smile. "It's not that serious."

"We are destroying ourselves," I said in a panicked voice. I couldn't believe how clueless he was, how clueless we all are. "We are dying, and we don't even know it. It's alarming, the shrinkage of our forests,

Ken. Between 1990 and 2005, the world lost a forest the size of Turkey. Can you imagine that?"

He'd chuckled to himself when I said that, and suggested I write a blog post about it. I did. I furiously typed it up that night, and in it, I lamented the statistics, carefully highlighting the importance of trees in food production, their absorption of carbon dioxide, their contribution to the slowing down of the horrendous effects of climate change. Two people commented, one of which was a website advertising increased followership.

Could I text Ken?— A ferocious hen bursts in front of me and I leap backward, nearly knocking over an upturned wooden stool. It squawks, flapping its brown feathered wings in a frenzied chase after an orange-necked lizard.

I wait until my pounding heart slows, count to ten, and tiptoe across the compound, eyes trailing the tidy procession along the track of about ten wooden figurines of pregnant women with pointed breasts and two bronze-like statue heads of women with oblong-shaped headgear.

I stop when I am close to the three houses. Is Adunni in one of them?

A hiss.

It's Kike. She's holding a paraffin lamp and pressing a finger on her lips, a gesture of silence.

She beckons, and I follow her around the side to the second house, the one just before the chamber, to another door covered with a curtain of cowrie shells. She leads us into a tidy, fragrant room and closes the door, lifting the lamp.

My eyes adjust. There is a raffia sleeping mat on the floor close to the wall, a pillow of folded clothes, a green kerosene stove, clay pots filled with plants that smell of mint and bitter leaf, a pair of leather slippers, four round baskets. The basket closest to the door appears to be filled with junk. I look closely. Are those vintage sewing machine parts? I spot a hand crank, spools of red, yellow, blue, pink thread, scraps of fabric. Why is she collecting these? The two other baskets are full of clothes—hers? A bra or two, folded cotton panties. My heart melts. This is her version of a wardrobe. The basket closest to the sleeping mat is padded with folded clothes, the severed head of a white doll with blond matted hair resting in it. The doll blinks incessantly, its thick lashes fluttering.

"Is that where your baby will sleep?" I ask, softly. "And is that . . . doll for your . . . child?"

"Dolly. Yes. For baby coming." She gives a terse smile as she shakes out a piece of cloth, nodding approvingly at the doll. "Baby likes dolly. I find it in dustbin, bring it."

My mother never bought me a single toy. It comes extemporaneously, this thought, barging into my consciousness without warning or consent, and I find myself transported to when I'd sit with the dolls my **father** brought back from his trips, on the marble-hemmed edge of our abandoned fishpond

from midday till a purple mist descended over the
garden, dipping my toes into the blue-black caligi-
nous water, trying to break its dense opaque surface,
to see if a school of fish would hurtle toward my
feet, to gnaw on my toenails. I'd wonder if they'd
bite, if it'd get so badly infected that I'd fall sick
and my mother would be forced to sit by my side,
to take care of me.

"I think it's wonderful," I say to the girl. "That
you got your child a toy. Were you . . . were you
born in Lagos?" She couldn't have been, I think.
She's from here. They all are. I hope.

"Off your cloth," she snaps, ignoring my question. "Quick."

"Sorry? What?"

"Off it now. Quick." She tugs at my jeans
and pulls.

"Whoa." I grab her hand, forcing her to stop dragging my jeans down my butt. "I've got this. Thanks."

"You do quick before Shaki is coming."

"What or who's that?"

She ignores me, eyes on the door. I step out of
my jeans. Fold them. She reaches into her basket
of clothes, finds an ankara wrapper, shakes it loose,
and it smells fresh, of lavender. She presses it to my
chest, says, "Off shirt, wear this. Tie."

I yank off my t-shirt.

She turns to say something, but halts. Gasps.
Covers her mouth with her palms, eyes roving the
length of my arms, my chest. At first, I think she

knows. That she can see it, my past, tucked into the rough folds of my skin, but her eyes flicker over to my shoulder and I realize she's staring at the fading scars.

"It was an accident," I explain. "I'll be okay."

"Dress quick," she says. "Tie the cloth."

I haven't got a bloody clue how to tie this thing. I fumble with the cloth as she folds her arms around her chest, watching me with a slight tilt of her lip. I sigh, draping the cloth around my shoulder with a shrug. She makes a clucking sound with her tongue, removes the cloth, and holds it out. "Open your hand. Like fly."

I spread my arms.

She wraps the cloth around my chest and tucks it in at the edges under my armpit. Considers me for a moment. Nods. "Good. Off shoe. Quick."

I kick off my trainers.

She reaches for a pot resting on the windowsill and opens it. It is full of white talcum powder. I start to query what it's for when she, with the speed of light, licks her thumb, dips the wet thumb into the pot, and presses a dot of powder on my forehead and on my cheeks. If I weren't so pissed at this transfer of body fluids from her person onto my forehead (not even Ken is allowed to lick his thumb and touch my face with it), I'd have attempted a smile because I am sure I look like a clown with sister locks.

She nods. "Good. Follow me, come like this."

"But I need my phone," I say. "To help Adunni. Please." And to ask Ken to stop sending me the letters. I know he's read them all, and there's nothing I can do about the knowledge he's acquired until I can explain what happened with Boma and me.

She clucks her tongue. "Take," she says. "Hide inside breast."

I unzip my bag, grab my phone and Adunni's phone, and slide them into my bra. Now I look like a clown with misshapen boobs.

"Now come," she says, grabbing my arm and a lantern. "Quick."

Back outside, I yelp as I step on the scorching, sanded floor.

She gives me a stern look.

The other woman, the shooter, appears. She's wiped off her facial makeup and still looks sinister. Kike whispers, "Bend head, quick."

I give the semblance of a nod and hold my breath, folding my arms across my chest to cover my protruding, angular boobs, and focus on my sanded toes.

Shaki makes a sound in her throat, and Kike responds, talking in very slow, deliberate tones, carving her mouth around the words and gesticulating. Finally, Shaki walks away, her hips rolling behind her.

I exhale.

"She is the second wife of my husband," Kike explains. "But she have a hearing and talking problem. I tell her you are from other village. That you are one of the girls for sacrifice. Follow me, come this way."

I halt. What? "But the chief knows me," I say.

She turns around. "They don't be coming out again until the sun is sleep. By then, you find yourself to your Lagos."

We don't stop walking until we reach a padlocked metal door. There, she produces a key from her hair, opens the padlock, and shoves me and the lantern into the room.

ADUNNI

Ms. Tia enters.

I jump up with joy. She didn't die, and she didn't leave me abandon and go! She even allowed Kike put powder with spit on her forehead and cheeks. Ms. Tia, who is very sparkling clean and don't even sometimes like her own spit, allow Kike to do this? I hold her tight, pressing my head to her chest to tell her thank you for staying with me, but I think her chest is having a weapon inside. It knocks me on my head so that I jump back and shout ye!

"Sorry, gosh!" Ms. Tia says. "It's the phone! Mine and yours. Well, mine's practically dead." She digs her hand inside her chest, plucks out the phones. Gives to me my own. I feel the eyes of Kayus growing wide as I collect the phone and press it on. It sings a ding-dong and come alive with a blue dancing light.

"Can we call Ken?" Ms. Tia asks.

"We can try." I punch the number of my PIN password, 1234. She gives me the number to the good doctor, and I punch it inside the phone too and press it to my ear. "Hello?" I say, talking to the phone, my eyes on Kayus, who is looking like I am a magic, as if he has never seen this kind of a wonderful, beautiful thing in his life before. I know the understanding of how he feels. He didn't ever think Adunni will one day have a mobile phone. Me too, I didn't ever think it. I didn't ever think of all the things that have happened to me, both the good and the bad things. It is why I say life is sometimes like a rope over a water full of sorrow-fishes and happy-fishes.

"Any luck?" Ms. Tia asks, coming close. She is walking so stiff inside the wrapper, as if it gums her whole body tight. "Is it ringing?"

"Silent." I give her the phone.

She holds it up, mutters "Damn the bloody network," and faces it to the window as if it is a flower that needs to collect sunlight to wake up.

"This place is a dungeon. We've got no reception." After one minute of holding the phone to collect the sun, Ms. Tia sighs. Gives it to me, blinking as she makes a notice of Kayus. "Hey," she says. "I saw you out there with Kike. You were so brave! Are you—"

"Kayus," I say.

Kayus climbs himself up to his feet. I hold him close and rub his plenty hair. "This is my brother, Kayus, Ms. Tia. I been taking care of him since our mama was dead. I taught him all the English he knows. Kayus, greet Ms. Tia English greeting."

Kayus says, "Good afternoon, Miss Tee-Yah. My name is Kayus. How are you? Fine, thank you, and you?"

I laugh, rubbing his head up and down, happy that my brother did not forget all I was teaching him. "But you don't say 'Fine, thank you' to the 'How are you' question you asked her," I say, using my teacher voice, which I miss so much because I didn't able to use it at all in Lagos. "You ask the question, Kayus. Wait a moment for her to say, 'Fine.'"

"My name is Tia," Ms. Tia says. "Nice to meet you, Kayus." She hooks her eyes on my own in the lantern light. "What now?"

I sit on the floor, and she and Kayus sit to the left and right side of me as Kike enters, carrying a basket of cloths, her pot of powder is in her other hand. She sets the basket and pot of powder down, peels back the cloth covering the basket, brings out a bottle and a bowl. "Water," she says, giving Ms. Tia the bottle. "Drink. Your eyes is showing the crack of dryness."

"Is it . . . clean?" Ms. Tia asks, eyeing the bottle like as if Kike is holding a cobra. "Sterilized?"

"It don't use to kill me or my baby," Kike says. "Take it."

Ms. Tia collects the bottle, tips it to her lips, and drinks it like she didn't drink water since she was first growing breast. Even Kayus looks shock at how she is swallowing, her throat riding up and down the curved road of her neck, until she finishes and wipes her mouth with the back of her hand and smiles. "Damn, I needed that," she says, giving Kike the bottle. "Thank you."

Kike gives me and Kayus one bottle each. Kayus drinks it all. I don't finish my own. My throat is not able to open well to collect the water because of fear.

Kike brings out a hot rectangle of bread, the top of it sweating from the too-early covering under a cloth. She tears the bread into three, give to each one of us. Ms. Tia, who don't use to eat bread because it didn't have organic, snatch it up and push the whole bread inside her mouth and swallows the thing before she even chews on it. When she sees me looking at her with concern, she covers her mouth with her hand and shrugs her shoulder as if to say, **What?**

I don't feel able eat the bread, so I fold it inside the pocket of my dress.

Kayus bites a pinch, presses the rest into my hand, and says, "You eat it. You need it to be strong for later." I use my head to kiss his own, say thank you to him for ever thinking of me.

"Thank you," I say to Kike too as she loads up her basket with the bottles. "Thank you for helping Ms. Tia. Can you please make the explanation for what will happen? Please speak English for Ms. Tia to hear."

Kike takes her time to arrange the bottles and cover it with a cloth before she lowers herself to the floor near her basket and tells us that there are two steps to the sacrifices of me. But not just only me. Tonight, on the dot of twelve in the midnight, under the big eye of the full moon, they will arrange about six of us girls for the sacrifice. All of us are having one offense or the other. We are all from different communities around Ikati, but tonight we come together for this sacrifice. I try to ask her what the other girls are accuse of, but she waves away my question with her hand and says I should face my own matter.

Kike rubs her stomach, shifts herself. "Shaki, the other wife of my husband, is collecting the other girls. She will bring them come. After, all of you will dance around the village, then baff in the stream."

"Even me?"

"Yes."

"Then what?" Ms. Tia asks. "What next? When's the sacrifice? What does it entail?"

Honest, Ms. Tia can like to confuse somebody with her English. How will Kike know what "entail" is meaning? The poor girl is frowning; I am too sure she is thinking maybe the word "entail" is something to do with the tail of an animal.

I help her. "What is deep inside the sacrifice, Kike? What it really meaning for me? Tell us step by step. Please."

"First, they stay inside the Circle of Forest at the back until nearing midnight. Then they go for the baff at the tall rock where my husband will cut your hand here and there." She makes a slicing around her arm, near to the elbow as if it is new yam. "Your blood will drop. One. Two. Three bloods to the ground."

I feel Kayus tense up by my side when she says that. What is wrong with him? We all know it is not a too-big cut. "We seen it before in the past," I tell Ms. Tia, because I sense her fear too. "It is just a small pinch to drop a blood or two, finish."

"Right," Ms. Tia says. "And the sacrifice?"

"They kill a chickens, and cook it sweet with Maggi and onion and salt and serve some for the fathers to eat and be full—"

"Chicken?" Ms. Tia says. "Are you for real?"

Kike continues her talk. "The rest of the chicken—the bleeding heart of blood, the liver, the head—we put it all inside a bowl, mix with gin and other things, give to your papa to take to the middle of the back of my husband's house. The other girls too, their father or husband will help them. If they didn't have a father or husband living, then a man of their family that is more than eighteen years can help them."

"If they don't have a brother or husband or father over eighteen?" Ms. Tia asks.

"We lock her up until her mother find a man from the family."

"That's barbaric," Ms. Tia mutters.

Kike shrugs. "Not one girl is having a father that is doing barbing work," she says with a thick frown, giving me a look. "Is your Miss Tee-Yah having hearing problem?"

Me myself, I am not too sure what "barbaric" is meaning, but I know it is not barber work.

"Carry on, Kike," Ms. Tia says, waving her hand in the air. "Keep going."

"To where?" Kike asks. "Shaki is going to bring the other girls, not me."

Honest, I cannot give Kike fault. English is a language of confusions. You say one thing, you mean another thing. "Keep on talking," I say. "Is the girl screaming under lockup because she didn't have a father or brother?"

"No!" Kike says. "That girl screaming is not from among of us. Her mama bring her here for another thing, but she will follow all of us to the Circle of Forest."

"I don't understand?" I say, but Kike keeps talking.

"No time for story," Kike says. "Now listen well, Adunni, after your papa put down the . . ." She curves her two hands in the air, trying to make her brain connect to the correct English word for what she is thinking. "The, erm . . . **ikoko** of the sacrifice—"

"**Ikoko** is pot," I say to Ms. Tia. "Clay pot with dolly-baby legs."

Ms. Tia says, "Yep. Seen them in art galleries."

Kike says, "Your papa is your father, your same blood, he will beg the spirits to collect the sacrifice, to not be angry with our land, to bless us. Now listen well. Are you listening? Good. Adunni, don't look so full of fear. Is not you that kill Khadija. I know it. My mama know it too. We know Bamidele have a hand in it. We know him and Khadija was doing love."

Ms. Tia throws her confused look around the room. "Wait. The Khadija who died, whom Adunni is accused of killing, did she have an affair with this Bamidele? And—"

"Not affair," I say. "Love. They were doing love-boy and love-girl. Like you and the good doctor, only they didn't marry."

"That's kind of what an affair means," Ms. Tia says. "Well, one of the meanings. Never mind. 'Love-boy and love-girl' works in this context."

See what I been always saying about English?

"So, who is he? Where is he?"

"He is a welder in Kere village," I say. "The day Khadija died, she was going to see him, to ask him to give her a soap to wash off a curse, so she can born her boy safe. He took us to the edge of Kere river, and he told us he will bring us the soap. He leave us there until she died dead."

Ms. Tia shakes her head. "Wow. That's so . . . I am sorry she died that way. I am sorry she died at all."

"Khadija was a good woman. She helped me so much." Tears leak from my eyes.

Kike says, "Adunni, you have no fear. My husband will do the correct thing. He will give you a good judging to be free to go." She unhooks her wrapper, fold the edge to sniff up her nose.

"Right," Ms. Tia says. "What if . . . What if her father's sacrifice is not accepted? Or if he refuses to carry it for her? Can her brother help?"

"Kayus is too small," Kike says, "and Born-boy, her big brother, been living in another village. We didn't see him for since-since."

"Born-boy has been living in another village?" I ask. "Why?"

"To find work and food," Kayus says. "He is too far from here."

Ms. Tia says, "So . . . what happens to Adunni if her dad doesn't help?" Ms. Tia looks at me. "Because he married you off, right? And I keep hearing how he has issues with alcohol. I guess I am just concerned he won't help us now when we need him to."

"He will," I say. "He will think of how I been a good child, how I was cooking and cleaning for all of us in the house before I went to marry Morufu. He will think too of my mama in heaven and all her suffering. Papa will help us."

I hope. I very hope.

"Kike," Ms. Tia says, "what happens if Adunni's father is not able to help us?"

"What happen is . . . ?" Kike sighs a deep sigh. "If

her papa didn't carry the sacrifice this night, they take Adunni and tie her hand and leg with the rope of blood and lock her up."

"The rope of blood?" Ms. Tia asks. "What's that?"

"The rope of blood is a rope we are dipping inside a blood of a chicken," Kike says. "When we tied it around of a person after my husband is finish judging the person, then it means that person must enter lockup. They lock up the person and suffer the person with a beating until it is time to take the person to the big . . . **ile-ejo**."

"What's that?" Ms. Tia asks.

"The Big Court," I say, "of the Area."

"What, like a proper trial in court? For murder?"

"Something like that," I say. "This court can say yes to killing peoples by stoning or hanging."

Ms. Tia says "fork."

Kayus makes a noise as if something pinch him.

"But that's bullshit," Ms. Tia says.

"But they are cooking chicken," I say. "So chickenshit."

Not one single laugh.

"And the others not accused of murder?" Ms. Tia asks. "What happens to them tonight?"

"Nothing. They do the sacrifice and go. We already seen their papa and brothers. Everybody is here. I didn't have too much worry for those ones. I worry for Adunni. Because they think she kill Khadija. Her own is the worst."

"So, is tonight"—Ms. Tia spreads her arms

out—"essentially to appease the, uh, spirits of the land for rain and then bully Adunni into confessing so that she can then be charged for murder?" Her eyes grow wide. "Could they maybe stone her tonight too? I mean, if they believe she killed Khadija, could they stone her before she even gets locked up? Is that a possibility?"

"I seen it," I say, a whisper. "I seen them stone peoples before. One time, they burn a man for raping the wife of a chief who died after the raping. I seen them put tire on people's heads and stone them dead for stealing things or the cursing of the gods or giving the baby of another man to another husband."

Kike nods. "The true is this: If I tie Adunni with the rope of blood, and the people are very vex, they can begins to stoning her or beating her or anything." Kike looks at me with big-wide eyes, speaking in Yoruba, "Adunni, because I am carrying this pregnant, if my husband says I must to tie you up with the rope of blood, then I must to do it. And if I tie you with the rope of blood, I don't know how you ever be able to escape yourself."

She pushes herself forward, and I can see she is wanting to cry. "Please, Adunni," Kike says. "Keep safe yourself from me."

TIA

What this . . . pregnant child-bride of a senile narcissistic man is telling me, with deep conviction, is that Adunni's father first gets served chicken casserole—it takes a moment to get past that—before she's judged.

If Adunni is found guilty, Kike—because she's the wife of the chief priest and because she is pregnant, perhaps the embodiment of female fertility and whatnot—would be the first to tie the rope of blood around Adunni? And if that happens, Adunni would be locked up and probably beaten or worse, until she's formally charged with murder?

I remember reading a newspaper article about a thirteen-year-old girl from an area not too far from

Ikati who was accused of murdering her older husband. There was a two-year wait before charges were brought against her, another three-year wait for her death sentence to be appealed. All this while the child was locked up in a cramped, dirty cell with five other women.

I checked a few months back and was horrified to learn that she was still in prison. In spite of the ruling, the appeal, the involvement of international human rights organizations. It hurts to imagine what could happen to Adunni after tonight. The scale of the trauma, the tragedy.

There must be a way out of this dreaded sacrifice and judgment and its aftermath.

If we find Bamidele and he's able to explain what happened that night, would Adunni be freed? I ask Kike, and she nods as if impressed by this suggestion. She explains that Adunni's father still needs to carry the sacrifice to make atonement for Adunni running away, but that she'd be released immediately after.

But.

If Bamidele is not found, and if her father doesn't carry the sacrifice, we're screwed.

"So where is Bamidele?" I ask.

Kayus bursts into sudden tears and grabs his sister's neck. Adunni is stiff in his embrace, as if stunned by her brother's outburst.

"Come here," I say to the weeping boy, disentangling his arms from his sister's neck and pulling him into my arms. "Stop crying, okay? Shush . . . That's it. Calm down, my love."

I tilt Kayus's chin up with a finger so I can peer into his brown eyes. I've never seen so much desperation, bleakness in a gaze. "Listen, Kayus, we have to be strong for Adunni."

"Can you promise me something?" he says in a tiny voice. "Promise you keep her save for me? To don't let her dead like my mama. If Adunni is dying, I don't have nobody."

He searches my face, as if expecting me to speak, to nod.

But I can't. I cannot say yes to fighting the unseen enemy of tradition and cultural beliefs. But tradition is made by people, and culture is an intricate basket of behaviors and beliefs woven by human hands, by humans with feelings and thoughts and opinions. If I can find someone to talk to, we could negotiate without harming Adunni and the other girls. But where to start from? Who to speak to?

"What about the other girls? What did they do?" I turn to Adunni, and the question is a diversion from what it would take to promise a lie to the young boy looking up at me. The question is a Band-Aid around my fractured, fearful mind.

"There is a girl, twelve years of age," Kike starts, and as she carries on, and I find myself repulsed by the details and unable to keep listening.

"Enough," I cut in, feeling a surge of nausea. Sweat pools in my armpits, prickling my skin. The bread I hurriedly ate is a lump of undigested flour at the base of my belly, and it rises now, swelling along my throat. "I'm sorry, I can't. I might just throw up."

Adunni glances at the ceiling when I say that, touching my shoulder. "Ms. Tia. Don't block your ears. Please listen . . . so that you can be full of thank-you that you are born in a part of the Nigeria where a girl-child is not a curse. Be full of thank-you that your papa can pay money to send you to school."

Her voice takes a dip, like she's plunged her head into something hollow, buried. "Please listen, Ms. Tia—so that you can count how many lucky you have in this life. Know this, your lucky is not because you are better than any one of us, or because you have more intelligence, but because life make a choice for you to be born in another place at another time. So, to not listen to our stories is to believe that you are better than us."

She's right.

But also wrong.

We, the city-born-and-raised Nigerian women from middle-class and wealthy families, might be free of some harmful traditions and customs, but we still get the short end of the stick. Deola, my former boss, who is successful and well traveled, was raped by her ex. She got examined forensically after subjecting herself to the torture of reporting it. The police opened an investigation and closed it a week later. The suspect was not even interviewed. The statistics are shockingly grim: Only a minute percentage of rapes reported worldwide end up in conviction.

I have faced injustices as a Black woman living in England, microaggressions from some work colleagues and lecturers, internalized racism that at first made me nearly resent myself, and then forced me to return to Nigeria, not just because I wanted to be near Boma, or because I met Ken, but because I needed to find myself so I could know and love myself.

But.

Being a girl-child in a poor, remote, rural village like Adunni's presents unique, often unconquerable challenges spanning generations. Stuff I can't even comprehend. Stuff that lacerates me with guilt beyond understanding. I feel like I did this to them, that I have failed each one of them. I am compelled to listen, as Kike carries on in a tortured, fractured voice. When she finishes speaking, I release a throttled breath.

"Is there a chance," I say slowly, "that . . . uh, that any of these girls were born in Lagos?"

Kike shrugs.

I ignore Adunni's confused glance. "So, Adunni's father is going to carry the sacrifice, right?" I ask, looking round at each frightened face.

"No."

It is Kayus, a whisper.

"No?" Adunni whips her head around. "He won't carry it for me?"

Kayus shrugs, picks at the cuticle on his toenail. He's hiding something.

Adunni unfolds herself and stands, placing her hands on her hips. "My papa refused to wear his brain inside his skull and get a working job when my mama was alive. He refused to get the job when she was dying dead. He refused to send me to school. He said I must marry"—she slaps her chest hard, and we all blink from the impact—"when I was fourteen years of age. I obeyed him and married Morufu, an old man with no sense—sorry, Kike, I know he is your father, but his brain is full of spoiling rice. When I was there, I saw how his second wife, Khadija, because she was so very much wanting a boy, went to meet her former lover and carry pregnant for him and died dead with the pregnant stomach.

"I ran away to Lagos, and what happened in the end? I became housemaid for one crazy stupid Big Madam because I didn't want them to stone me for the dead of Khadija. Now, after nearly one year of living in Lagos, on the day before I was supposed to be starting school after winning a scholarship, Mr. Kola came to Lagos to bring me back here. I followed them because I gave myself the hard talk that a good education can never be good enough when you have a bad name."

Tears roll down her face in fast, furious drops. "I

ran away to save myself," Adunni yells. "Because nobody will save me. Why is my papa blinding to all of that?" Now her voice drops, and she exhales. "By now, me and Ms. Tia should be on my way to school! I already have a uniform! Blue skirt with white blouse. Did you know, Kike?" she whispers. "Did you know I was winning a scholarship?"

"You can drive it?" Kike asks with wide eyes. "Who teach you?"

"Drive what?" Adunni hisses, slapping her face with the back of her hand, as if she's irritated by her own vulnerability.

"A ship. You say you win it?"

Adunni smiles sadly at me. "Ms. Tia, is this how my English use to give you frustrations before I learn it better? Sorry."

I am baffled at how she can find a sliver of humor in this heartbreaking reality.

"Can I speak to the chiefs?" I say, after a moment of silence. "About Bamidele. See if they can get the word out to get him here to confess?" Can I maybe convince them to release the other girls? My head is spinning with ideas, thoughts. I could try to reach someone in Lagos, an NGO dedicated to rescuing girls like Adunni, see if they can get down here and stop this madness? Do I have time to do that with a now dead phone and no shoes?

"Ms. Tia," Adunni says, "this thing has been in our land for years and years. You cannot just come from Lagos with your big English and talk

spree-spree to them and expect to change everything. Today the chiefs don't come out until midnight. Not so, Kike?"

"Has anyone tried? In the history of your village, has anyone tried to talk to them about these practices?"

They look at each other blankly and so I take that as a no.

"Your state governor can help, right? He—" I stop talking because it's a useless suggestion. There's no way I can get to see a state governor without a connection to his office, an appointment, my name on a waiting list. But I could, after tonight, raise awareness about Adunni's plight. I cannot leave Adunni in Ikati. What if she's harmed while in captivity? Or raped? Tortured? **No.** We absolutely must leave **together.** Today.

"What we need now is my papa," Adunni says. "We need to ask him if he will carry the sacrifice because I am not understanding why Kayus is thinking he will say no. Unless he wants me to die? Is he so very angry with me for running that he wants his only daughter to suffer and die?"

Kayus whimpers. I stay silent, thinking. Agitated.

Adunni continues. "If we can find Bamidele to make confess, I can leave Ikati, and maybe Kayus can come with me."

A pulsating silence congests the room.

"I take you, Miss Tee-Yah." It's Kayus. He's barely holding up his hand. "Me. I take you."

"Take me?"

"To my papa. Beg him for Adunni. If we go now, we catch him before is he going to out."

"But who will help us find Bamidele?" Adunni asks. "He will never come by himself, and he will never make confess."

Kike clucks her tongue and looks up at me. "Miss Tee-Yah, stand up on your feets of two."

"Me? Why?"

"You go out there with that white dot-dot on your face, and everybody will be saying a sacrifice girl is running away. Since the time Adunni . . ." She trails off, glancing at Adunni, deciding to say whatever it is she wants to say. "Since Adunni was running, they tell the whole village to always be keeping eye on girls like her. Girls that are thinking to run."

I rise, trying not to writhe as Kike licks the backs of her five sticky fingers, wipes the white dots on my face with them, and unfastens her coral beaded necklace and hangs it around my neck.

Adunni's bottom lip wobbles. I walk up to her, wiggling in the wrapper that makes me feel like squashed minced meat in a sausage casing, and push her chin up with my fingers. "It's okay to cry some more if you want to," I whisper. "Tears release emotions, it's not a weakness."

Adunni twists her jaw out of my grip and faces the wall. "Go, Ms. Tia," she says. "If you sense trouble, find your way back to Lagos. There is a bus garage in near Agan. I don't want anything bad to do you. I will not never forgive myself if anything bad happen to you. You hear me, Ms. Tia?"

"I won't leave you here by yourself," I say. "That's a promise. Come on, Kayus. Let's go speak to your dad."

❦

Kayus drags me to the back of the house, where a colony of caterpillars are gnawing holes into the leaves of ivy plants climbing up the rocky wall.

There is a sea of slimy green moss at its base, like egg white spilled over a bed of flattened grass. A queue of geckos with translucent skin lies on the moss, bleary-eyed and lethargic, as if sedated by the morning sun. My feet have grown used to the warmth of the earth. Even my skin no longer feels sticky, sweaty. We curve around a naked thorny bush, a densely packed set of tiny antlers around the wall, and I wonder if it was put there to discourage escape through the window. He lets go of my arm when we get to the acacia tree with scanty flowers like patches of golden-yellow cotton balls. A tapestry of brittle brown flowers covers the ground, around the tree roots like tiny, scrunched-up pieces of carton. I can hear the shrill voice of a girl in agony, and it sounds as though she stuffed her throat with rolled socks. I wonder who she is, what torments her so much. She's lamenting an injustice, and her voice pricks at my conscience.

Two girls, sitting on a stone beside a rocky well, are shelling groundnuts into a bowl in between their feet, and behind them, the sun-crested forest inclines forward, as if to break off a piece of the bronzed sky. Each has tied a matching fabric around her flat chest—a stunning batik wrapper, intricate swirls of blue and purple bleeding into each other—and it makes me miss home, the comfort of my living room.

It's a waiting game for these girls, I think. In a few years, it might be their turn to face punishment for making choices that, according to the rulers of this village, would be defined as a rebellion. A sadness shudders through me.

"What's the plan?" I ask when Kayus perches on a knobbly tree root extending out of the ground like an arm bent out of shape. He picks up a stone and draws spirals in the sand, as if to communicate his state of mind, the tumultuous intricacies of his next move. He drops the stone and looks up, terrified eyes searching mine. "We go to Goma village," he says. "Now."

ADUNNI

The girl picks up her crazy screaming again the second Ms. Tia bangs shut the door.

"Why she keeps on screaming?" I ask Kike. "My heart cuts a wound for her." I honest don't even mind her screaming because I think my ears been grown use to it, so it just sound like a bee buzzing inside the bowl of my ears, but I ask because I need something to catch my mind, drag it from all the too-much thinking of the troubles waiting for me this midnight, the big question of if I will ever go to school, if Ms. Tia will be safe, if my papa will carry the sacrifice for me.

Kike picks up her basket, sets it on her head, leaves it to balance by itself. The girls in our village

learn how to do this from when they are first growing two teeth. They know how to use every part of
their body to work so that their hand can be free to
do even more work.

"The girl screaming is from one of the afar village," Kike says, speaking Yoruba now that it is just
me and her. I watch her, the skin of her stomach
lifting itself under the white cloth and rolling to
one side like a tennis ball under a blanket, and I
think maybe the baby, the little devil, is stretching his leg and hand, trying to find a good place
to sleep in her belly. I wonder if she feels as if she
will born a part of her soul out with the baby, if her
hopes and dreams will swim out of her as the baby
is swimming out.

"Her mama bring her here," Kike says when her
baby settles itself. "But she is full of plenty English.
She keeps asking us for **wai-fai** and telephone."

For a moment, I am confused of who she is talking of. Then I remember: the girl in the next door.

"Why are they locking her up?"

"We are hiding her," Kike says. "We don't want
anybody to be seeing her until we reach the Circle
of Forest. But the girl is having a too-very-strong
mind. What is English word for it?"

"Stubborn?"

Kike gives me a long look with no blink. "It is
soon time to prepare you. Adunni?"

"Yes?"

"I don't want to do it."

"You be strong for me, and I be strong for you."

She nods. Turns to go and pulls the door, and just before she steps out, Papa appears in the front of the door.

I rub my eyes, check it sure I am seeing it well. It is my papa. My heart rolls around in my chest, knocking into memories into thoughts and feelings, making me dizzy a moment, confused. From where he is standing, the sweat on his head and chest smells of the same palm-wine drink he been drinking since my mama was dead. His left eyeball has a dot of blood inside like he prick it with a pin, let it bleed a little. His chin area is full of so much beard, as if he grow the thick curly hairs to the shape of a hanging sack so he can tuck his anger inside of it until the day I will return back to Ikati.

For eight and a half seconds, I count every second with my beating heart, and me and Kike and my papa, we stand there, looking at each other as my papa's eyes run up and down the road of my thin neck, the neat lines of weaving of my hair, curving a circle around the zigzag of the fabric of my tired ankara dress, the cracks of my dusty feet.

I think he is both sorry and angry, and he's not too sure which to show first, the sorry or the angry.

The very last time I saw my papa, the sky cracked itself open and stoned the ground of Ikati with rain. That night, the moon was high up in the sky, peeping over the earth with a single eyeball of yellow as I ran home from Kere village, sweating and crying, and came to my knees in front of my father and made a true confess of what happened to Khadija.

My papa promised to help me if I wait for him to go to the village chief to tell him what happened. I wanted to wait, God knows I wanted to wait, but I remembered how my papa promised to my mama not to marry me to Morufu, and how he crushed that promise. I did not wait. I ran, under a grumbling cloud, under a booming thunder to where Iya, my mama's friend, helped me to connect to Mr. Kola, who slave-traded me to Big Madam. The last time I saw my papa, he didn't have a growing sack of hairs on his chin.

"Adunni," he says to me now, and I automatic climb to my knees, bend down my head.

"Papa."

I keep my eyes on the ground, on the shadow of Kike, which is growing smaller and smaller, and the shadow of Papa is growing longer, covering my own kneeling shadow. He enters the room and closes the door so that the only light around us is the blinking orange and brown of the lantern.

"Good morning, sir." I make my hands a shovel, dig a hole in the middle of my closed-tight laps. **Did he see Kayus and Ms. Tia? Where are they now?**

"You speak different," he says in Yoruba. "You went to Lagos? The city?"

"Yes, sir."

"You go school? **Suhr.** What is 'Yes, **suhr**'?"

"No, sir. I didn't go to school."

"How you learn to speak so . . . pure?"

"I listen, sir. I listen and learn."

"You listen, eh? Tell me, what work did you do in Lagos?"

I focus on his feet, the big toe curling like the left claw of a mud-crab, the toenail like the clipped shell of it.

"Housemaid. Sir. I was doing work for a woman—"

He grunts, slapping himself on his left thigh, **pa**. "Eh. You run away from Ikati as the wife of a rich man and go to Lagos as a slave. Ordinary **omo-odo**. A housemaid? You leave a life of glory," he says this in hard Yoruba, and everyone word like a shovel packing the sand from the floor, burying me with it. "You leave a good husband, Morufu. A good house, with good car, and you run go to Lagos to be housemaid?" Papa spits, and it lands by my knee with the sound of a drop of water on hot oil. "Shame," Papa says. "Shame on you."

My heart is running ten times fast. But I want to make correction to my papa for just one thing, which is this: Morufu didn't have a good car. First of all, the window of his car is a sheet of a nylon bag. The door jams shut three times a day, so he drive about with a spoon and knife like it is a plate of cow-foot he need to slice open to climb out of it.

And Morufu is not seeing any good of education. He thinks a boy-child is more better than a girl-child. He, like many of the men in our village, see us girls as toilet tissue you use to wipe buttocks and flush inside toilet. Pity my papa thinks he is rich. Pity, for his poorness of the mind, the empty of his thinking, because when you don't have money, you can manage. But when you have poorness of mind, you are finished, killed dead even if you are still breathing and people are still shining teeth with you.

"You didn't learn one thing in Lagos," Papa says. "You leave with nothing, and you come back with nothing but shame and disgrace of my name, your dead mama's name."

I didn't learn nothing in Lagos, Papa, I shout in my mind, with my mouth zip tight shut. **I learn how to scrub the square of a bathroom tile until I see the curve of my nose inside of it. I learn how to wash pant the size of a bedsheet and bra as round as a wide-open umbrella. I learn how to read more better than now, how to use the Collins. I learn words like "communication" and "extermination" and "independence" and "frustration." I learn facts of the Nigeria, Papa. I learn when Nigeria collect independent from the British, when they make a law that the slave-trading of the peoples must stop and how the law was just a scratch on paper because slave-trading is continuing here in Nigeria and in the Abroad in many different ways.**

I learn about life, how even with your plenty primary, secondary, university, professor education

as a woman, you will still face troubles in this world, all because of one stubborn man Ms. Tia is calling Pay-trah-Kee.

And most of all, Papa, did you know, that I learn how to write an essay? Me, Adunni, I wrote an essay all by myself with no help, and I got a high mark and won a scholarship to go to school?

But Papa is somehow correct. I ran away and came back with a empty hand and a full head, which is now hanging down with shame. Papa touches my bent head, his palm warm, oily on my head. When he calls my name, his voice is soft, so full of pity. "Look up."

I raise my head. Blink. Look again. My papa's eyes are leaking tears. Why?

Papa bends low, wipes his tears. "The rains have been small. The throat of the land is drying, and the chiefs think it is time to beg the spirits."

"Yes," I mutter. "I am the fault of all the rain problems because the rain zip itself inside my dress and followed me to Lagos."

"Adunni, listen," Papa says. "Your sharp mouth will only put you inside more trouble. Tonight they will do a judging for you, which means tonight one thing must surely happen. You will leave Ikati free—if you want—or they lock you up and killed you dead. You know, after this tonight, me and you may never see ourselves again." He stops talking to wipe his eyes. "This is your chance, Adunni," Papa says. "Tell me true. Swear it on the grave of your mama that you didn't have a hand in the dead of Khadija."

I hear a slow song from the wind. It carries me in its arms, swaying me left, right.

"I didn't . . ." My voice breaks, packs some sorrow between the cracks of it. "It was Bamidele. He didn't use his hand to kill her, but he promised he will come back for her and give her a special soap to wash off a family curse. He didn't come back, and because of that, Khadija died. He was living in Kere. A welder." I squeeze tight my eyes, trying to remember what he looked like. "Tall. His wife's stomach was swelling. That child must be nearly one years old now. His house is facing a tree, a shop . . . a woman selling sweet things." I open my eyes, and Papa is nodding yes, yes, as if he wants me to keep memorying.

"Anything else you remember? Think, Adunni. Think it well."

Is Papa going to find Bamidele? Will he come back in time for the chicken-eating and the sacrifice preparations? Even if he didn't want to do the sacrifice for me, surely he will do it for the chicken? Eat a good night-food for once in his whole life?

"Think, Adunni," Papa says, his voice pressing. "Look back-back and tell me what you know?"

I turn upside down the cupboard of my mind, pulling the doors of it open, searching inside, closing the ones that bring up memories that don't make sense, opening another door, slamming it close, until I find what I am looking for, folded like a tiny baby cloth at the bottom of my mind-cupboard. "Yes, Papa," I say, opening my eyes. "He said one very important thing. That his family have plenty boys. His mama born only boys. The boys also born boys. Boys are gold, Papa. Everybody will know his family once you make mention of this."

Papa climbs to his feet, slaps off a fly from his shirtfront. "I go." Where is he going? My eyes crawl behind, following him until he reaches the door.

"Papa," I whisper. "Are you going to find Bamidele? Will you come back for the sacrifice?"

My papa's answer is the closed door, a tiny pop of air. It sounds in my head like the crashing of my world into a thousand pieces.

SIXTEEN HOURS
TO MIDNIGHT

‖‖‖‖‖‖‖‖‖‖
TIA
‖‖‖‖‖‖‖‖‖‖

"Wait, what?" I ask, checking my watch. "Goma? I thought we were going to your father."

"No." Kayus sniffs, wiping his nose with the back of his hand. "But me and you, we must talk alone by ourselfs. We must very now-now, go to Goma. To see Iya."

"Iya?" The dust in the air scrapes my lungs. "Why do we have to go to this Iya now? Who is she?"

"Is a very old woman who was before-before living in Agan village," Kayus says. "She is now in Goma. She is the very best friend of my mama."

"An old woman was your mother's best friend?"

"No," he says, nodding. "I mean to say yes. But before Iya, Labake—Kike's mama—and my mama was best of friends. One day, they fight a big fight, and they both say no more friending. So, my mama turn to Iya. This Iya is knowing a very something that can help us, but Miss Tee-Yah, there is no time to talk too much now, let's just be going."

"What does she know?" I ask. A generator whirrs somewhere afield, and I think of charging my phone.

"Something very deep. Something only she can say."

"Can you tell me so I can understand how best to help you? How far away is Goma? That's where she is now, right?"

He wipes his palms against his shorts, and there is a tremor in his hands. What's wrong with him?

The phones probe into my chest like I've grown a cracked rib there. Mine's still dead, but I twist Adunni's phone out, hold it up. There are three dots where the signal bars should be. I tuck the phone back in, slap it into a position that doesn't feel like I'm being stabbed.

"Goma is plenty-plenty minutes of walking," he says, glancing right, toward a parcel of farmland bordered by tall, leaning maize plants, the linear leaf blades like skinny arms linking each other.

"If we walk quick-quick," Kayus says, "or you bring motorcar?"

"I don't drive," I say.

Kayus stares off into the distance, at a couple of goats butting heads, locking horns. We both watch as one of the girls picks up a stone, flings it in the air, and a short, stocky man appears, catches the stone, and appears to scold the girls.

"Papa!" Kayus whispers. "That is our papa." He shuffles backward with his buttocks against the ground, blending into the shadows of the wilting acacia, pulling me along with him.

"Is it?" I half squint against the sun, shading my eyes with my palm. The man appears middle-aged, and his beard hangs, thick and full, from his chin, nearly touching his collarbone. He's got no shoes, and walks with a stagger, a halting tilt in his skinny legs, which are encased in faded khaki shorts. That's Adunni's father? "So that's a good thing?" I say, relieved. "He is going to help her, right?"

"He cannot help Adunni," he insists. "My papa knows it, and me too, I know it. But Adunni does not know."

The earth around me sways, settles. I take his hand. "Calm down, Kayus. You are shaking so hard."

"Miss Tee-Yah." Kayus starts to cry, silent tears sliding down his face. He makes no attempt to wipe them off. "I will tell you what I know, but first we must go quick before Iya is crossing to the spirit world."

"Why her, and why now?" I hear the slight raise of panic in my voice. He's projecting his terror on to me, and I must not let him. I've got to be calm enough to make rational decisions. "If we go now"—I glance at my watch—"we also have

to ensure someone can find Bamidele before midnight." I still nurse the intention of speaking to the
village chief or one of his wives—but I don't tell
Kayus that.

He nods, eyes curtained with desperation, terror.
"Hear this, Miss Tee-Yah. The sacrifice is the number one thing. The first leg. Adunni's father must
carry it for her. Nothing can change that. But my
papa cannot do it. He cannot. He just didn't able to.
Do you very understand?"

I have no idea what he means, but I nod to
encourage him. "If you give me an idea of why we
have to go now. Please."

"It is a secret," he pleads. "Something about my
papa there. Something me and you must find . . .
I tell you if you follow me. I cannot talk it here. In
the open here. Please."

It breaks my heart to see him so flustered, anxious, and I realize he is unwilling to reveal why we
must go there right now. Whatever is in Goma must
be important to Adunni's life, and so I say, "Fine,
Kayus. Let's go."

We cut through to a farmland full of ridges and
cone-shaped heaps of dry earth like shallow graves
covering the entire plot.

Kayus nods at a bald and shirtless farmer who
is kneeling in front of one of the heaps, holding a

yam seedling with skinny purple tendrils swimming out of its bottom like curly hair. The man slices the tendrils off with the blunt edge of a machete and pushes the seed into the heaped earth with a concentrated frown as if to drown it. I wonder how long it'd take to become a tuber. I think, randomly, about one of life's mysteries: the finality of death and how it intricately links with the miracle of life. A seed cannot germinate, bear fruit, until it dies and is buried. Life often demands that we die, drown, so that we can rise, become.

Kayus hurries along, past another farmer, the surrounding farmland sparse, empty, void of crops. The farmer hacks hard at the ground with a hoe, the haze around him smoldering with heat.

"That farmer," Kayus says, leading the way, and I limp behind him on blistered feet. He takes giant leaps down the path, feet snapping and crunching on shrubs and sticks, left arm swinging up and down. "His land was very full of plenty foods, but everything is smalling now."

Often, Kayus pauses to look back with screwed-up eyes as if concerned by my pace, or with a nod of encouragement, before promptly resuming his hurried walk and occasional talk. He tells me about the landslide that nearly buried a Muslim scholar's family home, about the increasing number of girls getting attacked for the water they've fetched from neighboring areas several kilometers away, about the spitting rain—the sky turning blue, the flash of lightning, the rumble of thunder, the dashed expectations of the people at the trickle that falls from the sky.

I slow to a trot at a circular patch of weeds, a mini roundabout of some sort, to check Adunni's phone for reception. The signal bar is now an erratic blinking dot. I hold Adunni's phone like I need it to breathe, jutting it out, desperate to locate a cell phone mast buried somewhere in the dense center of the surrounding forest, but the bars remain an erratic dot, and now the battery gives its first warning beep.

The landscape on this side of the forest is blighted, a V-shaped hole in the canopy of flowers from which the sun burns down with a furious intensity. The sky is littered with gold-rimmed clouds like the plucked feathers of a swan dispersing and coming together, the swash and backwash of a sea wave.

"Quick!" Kayus urges, quickening his pace.

A whirring fills the air with a grating noise. I press ahead, trying not to focus on the grove of timber trees about fifty yards to my left, the mouth of which is stuffed with tree stumps, like gravestones in a cemetery. Behind it, rows of felled timber floating on a sea of sawdust and shrubs and mud. There is a lorry with a broken headlight and dented alloys perching on the edge of the cleared path. I count four men behind the truck, their voices drowned by the rumble of machinery.

"What's up?" I say when I catch up with Kayus. "Who are those guys?"

He slows down, glancing up at the sky. "What's up where?"

"The men?" I nod toward the parked lorry. A distant creak and crack fills the air, and the bushes quaver. I hear the tree fall with a groan, wincing at the reverberating **thwack** it hits the ground with.

"Woodcutters," he says. "They been cutting trees for years. They come from afar and cut to sell for the yellow mens from the big Abroad companies."

"Really?" I am sickened by the thought of foreign countries leaving their land and economies intact and coming to areas like this to rape the land.

Kayus scratches a spot behind his neck. "Yes," he says. "They sell to make chair and table and things. Is good money. One day, I buy my own saw, cut down the rubber and iroko tree, sell it for plenty money, put Adunni in school, build us new house." He nods as if this future is determined, decided. "Why asking?"

"It's illegal, right?" I run my teeth over my lip. "It is . . . not right. To cut trees everywhere. Kill the forest. The wildlife."

He shrugs, squinting at the distance, his mind already on other things. "We go that way." He points at a mossy hill on an elevated parcel of land behind the timber grove. "When we reach, we cut a small stream, take a shortcut to Goma. You can swim?"

"Why?"

"If you fall inside when we cross the water, you must quick off your wrapper and swim fast. If you don't off it, it drag you down under."

He's kidding, right? "Is there another route?" I ask. "Another way?"

"It take us long," he says. "We need quick way." He squints at me. "Everything all right?"

I yank up my wrapper, clutch it tight in my fist. "Come on."

I hear the gurgle of water the moment we reach the path that leads to the stream. The buzzing and chirping of insects. The raucous laughter of boys and girls, the plunk of metal buckets hitting the surface of the stream. The air here is at first soothing, and then a shiver travels through me, stiffening my spine. I grit my teeth, wishing I had a cardigan, shoes. My feet dip into a puddle of prickly semi-solidness that feels like a giant jar of chilled honey mixed with a thousand fingernail clippings rotating underfoot, until we reach the stream where green algae clings on to sediment and rocks underneath, snapped tree branches like detached arms floating across its frothy edges.

Kayus stops at the edge of a narrow wooden plank cutting across one ragged shoreline to the other. "First I go over," he says. "Is not so deep because of no-rain. Before, it was very more deep than this."

I swallow. Nod. I can do this, right? I've got

this. Actually, no. I haven't got this because I cannot swim.

I drag the hem of my wrapper higher up to my knees and watch him take one tentative step forward, touching the tip of his toes first, resting the ball of his foot a moment later.

I should have thought hard about this. What if I fall into this phytoplankton-riddled water and drown?

Kayus darts across in two giant leaps, lands on the other side with a stagger. He steadies himself, stands tall. Grins for the first time in hours and beckons. **Your turn**, his eyes say.

The forest bristles. A black egret swoops down, landing on a rock, and, spreading its wings like a triangular umbrella, it dunks its head into the water, hunting fish.

I glance behind, and through a curtain of thick vegetation, a car whizzes by, its brake lights flashing in the corner of my eye.

"Miss Tee-Yah!" Kayus yells. "Come!"

I shake my head. "I cannot swim!" I shout my confession into the wind. "I cannot do this."

Despair seeps into Kayus's face. "Just try," he urges. "Don't look. Just run. Run fast."

"Just run," I mutter. As if he's asking me to stroll across bloody Freedom Park.

"Iya is dying," Kayus pleads, his voice tiny and desperate. "Come." He makes a praying gesture, prancing left, right, as if he's pressed for the loo. "Please. Don't leave me and Adunni by ourselfs. Adunni say you are good person."

I exhale. Focus. Take a step. Pushing my foot up to the tip of my toes and lowering my feet. Gradually. Spreading my arms out, teetering until I find my balance.

But I find that I cannot move, and so I hold my breath, praying that I don't fall, that the phones don't slip down the tunnel of my wrapper into the water.

"Think of something bad, something that afraid and angry you so much, you want to just crush it," Kayus urges, lifting his leg and stomping on the ground. He looks like a frail little soldier, marching on the same spot. "Think of it like that. Like the head of your enemy under your feet! Stamp and run!"

My mother's face swims to my vision. I see her again on that hospital bed, frail and skeletal, the gaunt cheekbones, the sunken eyes, dry lips blistered with sores, the skin over her bones like cling film wrapped around a comb. The image clears, and the thing I want to crush takes shape. It's the partially formed memory of her betrayal, of the moment that precious thing was taken from me.

"Miss Tee-Yah!" Kayus's shrill cry cuts into my thoughts. "Crush it and keep on coming!"

I leap—wrapper slipping out of my grip, the bonk and crack of the plank flapping from the pressure of my weight—and collapse against Kayus into moist savannah grass.

"Well done, Miss Tee-Yah," Kayus says. "No time to rest. We keep moving."

We start to move, but I find myself wondering if I'll ever hear from Ken, if he's read any more, if what he's discovering will make him abandon Adunni and me.

June 1998

Dear Boma,

How did I not get it last night when you called me Tie instead of Tia?

It only just hit me now as I got into bed: Bow + Tie = Bow-Tie. Oh my!!!

You asked me to ponder it. This is what I think you mean: We are Bow-Tie. We are no longer two but one string, two ends of a ribbon becoming one. Our love is eternal, a thing of elegance and beauty, a timeless adornment.

So, here's me saying thank you, Boma, for listening to me. For loving me. For teaching me virtues wise beyond your years. For making me smile.

Oh, and what you suggested about you and I breaking up so my mum would let you be? That is NEVER going to happen! You and I will be

together forever, and there's nothing my mum can
do about that.

Love you till eternity,
Tie

PS: What we did last night was . . . incredible.
Thanks for being my first. It will always only
be you. That's a promise with my body, soul,
and spirit.

ADUNNI

Outside the high window, I see two girls sitting on the ground and fanning a tray of ground-nuts, red peels flying in the air like floating paper, brown nuts settling back on the tray with a **shraaa** noise, like beads breaking off its strings and falling like rain into a metal bowl.

I see black goats around a tree, eating flowers of weeds; chickens with brown feathers scratching the ground with their feet of scales; a dog lying under the shade of a tree, its ribs like broomsticks. I see the maize farm in the afar standing on thin legs in between the cracks in the ground, the leaves the color of sand.

But I don't see Kayus or Ms. Tia. Where did they go?

I slide down, rest my buttocks on my feet, and press my head to the wall.

I want my mama. I want to take my life, pour it inside the stained-glass bowl of this lantern, and wind the winding stick to reverse back, back to before I was born, so I can try to make a choice to not be born inside this kind of hardness of life. Then I feel a sickness at the thought. Why am I feeling bad to be born into this land? Maybe I was born for a special reason. To make a change, open people's eyes and minds for the better. But how?

I thumb-drag the tears down my cheeks, and sniff.

Dear God.

I raise my eyes to the ceiling.

Keep Ms. Tia and Kayus safe. Make Your eye big over them. Change the mind of the peoples of this land from their foolishness and wickedness because they somehow think we and the spirits is the problem of small rain. (Ever hear anything so stupid?)

You hear me, God? I know You hear me . . .
"Amen."

"Uh . . . amen?"

Who say "amen" just now? My own "amen" is a amen of sureness. This one is a question amen. A check-if-God-will-answer amen plus the "uh" in front of it. And it come from inside the wall. I tear open my eyes, turn my face to the wall. Something or someone near my buttocks say "amen," but it is not me or my buttocks. What is that? A hole? Yes. There is a hole in the wall at the bottom of the wall, right under the window, a T-shaped hole, the edges of it a zigzag of cement and mud as if a rat use that very edge to sharp his teeth. I climb to my knees, press my cheeks to the floor, and wink one eye to look.

One eye is looking at me from the hole. One very white eye with brush eyelashes.

I draw back. Shake my head. Put my head down again. Look at the eye. The eye looks at me back. I wink. The eye winks.

"Well, hi," the eye says. "Name's Zenab?"

"Names Zenab?" I say. "Are you asking me question of if your names are Zenab?"

"I'm telling you my name's Zenab."

"How many names did you have? The. Name. Is. Zenab." I say. "That's how you speak it correct."

"Whatever." She blows out air from her mouth, scatters floor dust into my eyes so that I sneeze once. "I need a mobile phone. Like, it doesn't even have to be an iPhone 6 plus or whatever as long as it's got Google Maps or Siri or some sort of thingy that can guide me out of here like ASAP?"

I squeeze my nose, thinking. "I don't know of Siri," I say. "But I know Sidi very well. She is helping her mother with plaiting hair near the roundabout. But she didn't have a phone to guide you out of here like Hay-Sap."

"Duh," she says. I don't see her face, but I'm almost hearing her eyes rolling and knocking around the wall of her brain with how she is vexing.

"Siri," she says, talking slow, "is a voice-activated virtual assistant developed by Apple."

"Ah," I say. "But why a apple is developing a what-you-call-it?"

"Oh, crap. I am so doomed."

"Why so doom?"

"BECAUSE!" she shouts.

I blink. Why is she vexing? "Because of what?"

She slaps her hand on something. "Just because!" A pause. A sigh. "It's you. Me. Us. This entire convo, this entire situation, everything is pretty much doomed because I didn't listen! And you are clearly clueless as to how to help me." She grunts and I don't see the white of her eyes again. Then, from afar: "I've got to think. Focus. Make a plan B because clearly, my plan A to scream down the damn village isn't working. Hey, listen. You just stay there. Sit tight. Be right back."

I hiss and drag myself away from the stupid non-sense girl and her stupid nonsense talk.

‖‖‖‖‖‖‖‖
TIA
‖‖‖‖‖‖‖

October 2005

Dear Boma,

   I cannot believe I've let six months go by without writing you.

   Right now, it's bloody cold (my flatmate thinks the weather is "rather pleasant, innit?" and gives me some strange look when she sees me wearing a sweater in autumn). Thing is, I could never get used to the cold! It's punishing and I miss home, and I think this winter will be particularly gloomy. I want to come home for Christmas, to spend the day with you, but my mother has refused to let me. She keeps asking me to forget you like you aren't a part of my life, but that's never going to happen.

Tia

||||||||||||||||||||||||||
ADUNNI
||||||||||||||||||||||||||

Feet.
Like sandpaper scraping the wall from behind the window, the small **ko** of a small stone dropping near my feet. I look up, seen it come from the window. Another stone, flying inside my room, nearly clipping my right ear before it knock itself on the lantern glass.

I push myself up on my tipping toe to look out of the window, but all I see is a long line of girls afar with white wrapper around each their chest, walking to near the back of Baba Ogun's house. I sense the sadness of their souls in the bags of their dragging feet, their voices and tears sealed tight shut in the dark well of their closed-tight throats.

Are they the girls for sacrifice?

The sun is slicing the air with a heat that boiling my anger and pushing me to want to shout,
to beg the village elders to let these girls go free to
live their lives, but I know my voice is useless to
the ears of the one who is not here. I watch as they
walk pass, their stick-thin arms dancing beside their
body. One of the girls—the last one on the line—
slides her eyes to me in a welcome-greeting of sorrow as if she knows they are coming for me, that it
will soon be my turn.

The fingers of cold air grabs tight the bones in
my back.

I turn away from the window. **Ko**, another stone.
This time, it knocked the door of my brain and
pushed it open.

"Who is throwing stone?" I shout now, turning
around and pressing my mouth to the window.
"Who is there?"

"Adunni!" A whisper. From outside the window. "Adunni?"

I push myself up more and through the iron cage
in the window, I see her smiling, her lips bending a
little. "Enitan!"

She was my best friend since I was two years
of age, the very first to know when I started my
monthly visitor, who knew the very moment when
I made up my mind to become a teacher and to not
marry any man until my mind and body is ready
for it. She was always giving me beans and rice and

plantain and corn from her mama's farm and will tell Papa lies to cover for me when I was running to teach the village children ABC and 123.

She curves herself out from behind a tree, runs to the wall, with her basket of makeups pressed to her chest. She sets her basket down and climbs on a short stone, her feet shaking a little until it stable itself. "Did my stone wound you?"

"It didn't wound me," I say. "It reset my brain to zero."

"Sorry, I didn't want to be shouting your name."

"If the chiefs catch you here, they will cook you in hot soup." I can smell her, her same-same smell of nail polish and red pepper and fresh tomato, and it makes me want to cry.

Enitan scrubs my whole face with the sponge of her eyes, her fingers gripping the black iron cage covering the window. "I know you come back to wash your name clean." She sounds broken by my coming back, but she smiles. "I know you will always do a good thing, so I say, let me find my Adunni and paint her a fine face, make her beautiful for this night. Wait!"

She climbs down from the stone and holds up her basket and gives it a little shake so that the yellow, red, pink, purple eye-pencils and lipsticks inside jump up and down in a rattle-dance. "You see it?"

"Makeup?" I look down at her, hiss a small hiss. "So, with all the troubles and problems I am facing now, is it makeup that will help me?"

She curves her bent lip a little to one side. "Eh. See you. You cannot face your problems with a ugly face. Bring your lips, let me paint it this fine green for you?" She plucks out one green paint from the basket, holds it up.

"Why not paint it white and green so I go about looking like I gum the flag of the Nigeria on my lips, eh?" I crack a pinch of a smile. "Oh, Enitan," I say, feeling my heart swell.

"Ha!" She laughs, bending to put down her basket. "I am happy to see you smile," she says, now back up on the stone, her eyes the same level with my own, her voice serious. "I was so very afraid when you run away. I am so afraid now you are back."

"I'll be okay," I say. "You don't worry for me."

"Your English is . . . pure. Something about you shift in Lagos."

A black goat marches to the well behind one of the trees and dips his head inside of the iron buckets on a long line of about fifty other buckets in front of it, all of them dry and empty.

"You didn't marry." I am not asking a question. I can see her finger is not having a bead of ring on the third of her left hand.

"I very want to marry. But nobody is coming. I paint my face many colors and put beads here and there, but not one single man is looking at me to say, hello, how are you. Not even Benbo."

"You will marry Benbo?" I sniff a laugh. Benbo

is one young man in the village that if you ask him what time of the day it is, he will smile with all his teeth and say, **Purple.**

"My mama says I will never find a man. I am afraid because I am growing more old."

I want to take Enitan's hand, squeeze it. "Your mama, and many women in this village, thinks all that makes a woman good is marriage. They forget that God gave us a brain and a mind and a soul for big things that can change the world. You keep focus on doing big things and love will find you, but before love find you, you find yourself first."

"Adunni," Enitan says, starting to cough-cry, "you have too much gift of wise things inside of you to give the world. I know I cannot make up your face, but I can give you something?"

I nod.

She steps down from the stone, and I hear her shifting things inside her basket. When she climbs back up, she is holding a blue pencil with a long gold line along of it. Never seen anything like it. Sharp on the tip too, shining new, like a pin. "This pencil," she says, "is a special pencil. I didn't pick it from the dustbin of town hair salon." She turns it around in her hand like it can do magic. "This pencil, I buy it with the money from my sweat of makeup work. It is the first thing I ever buy. Take it, Adunni. Take it and think of me. I will be there this midnight. I will be there among of the crowd of women, and we will all stand and gather and pray with all our sweat that they don't make a wicked judging."

I collect the pencil through a small gap in the window-cage, sniff up my tears.

"No matter what happen this night," Enitan says, "I will take all what you been teaching me and keep it in my heart like a book, and when I am alone and sad, and not sure of things, I can check inside my heart and find the book and open the page and read your words."

Now the stupid girl will make me to start to cry too. I close eyes and drag my breath. "You must go," I say when I open my eyes. "Go before someone catches you and gives you a punishing."

I watch her climb down and pick up her basket before I run off and set my feet down and sit on the floor, with the lantern blinking a slow light of orange into the room. I think hard of what Enitan said. What Kike has been saying but not saying. The truth of the matter is this, I may die this night. I may close my eyes on this side of our world and wake up in heaven with Mama. Am I fearing to die? Small. A small pinch of fear.

Mama tell me heaven is full of angels and plenty food. I like food, and I think angels have a beautiful shining wing. Nothing to fear there. But I mind dying before I live my dreams of helping girls and of becoming a teacher. It makes me mad, to think of how the village chiefs, the people of our land, want to silent my louding voice before I can make myself great. I turn Enitan's makeup pencil around in my hand and open my bag of belongings and peep inside. I look at all the books of grammar; the Oxford Dictionary Ms. Tia bought for me; the two rectangles of paper there; my mama's Bible; the beads belonging to Rebecca, the girl that worked as housemaid before me and who was missing in Big Madam's house; and the nine hundred naira I been carrying around with me.

Of all the things inside here, only the books have been able last forever, passing from one hand and mind to another, from age to age, city to city. Books have a special gift of not ever dying. The words in a book have wings that can travel far, reach minds and hearts of people in countries and cities in the world. Books can speak a million billion of languages, telling forever stories and truths with a forever pen and forever ink, more than the writer of the book.

The only way I can keep on living, to make sure my voice will not die with me, is to find a way to write something like a book.

But how I can do that? With what? I don't have a pen or pencil. Only two rectangles of paper.

I bring out one rectangle of paper, put it on the grammar book, and balance it on my lap. I exhale deep. What do I want to write? A letter? A story? Enitan thinks I am full of wise things. Maybe I can write some of the lessons and understandings I been learning in my life. Snapshot it like a photograph and put it on paper, write it and give it to Enitan this midnight before the judging and tell her to make a copy of it in the printing shop in the town and share it to all the girls in our village. That way, I can be teaching them, make them hear my voice, even if I am buried deep inside a grave.

Yes, I think, my heart tumbling in my chest. I can have a louding voice even if I buried in the silent of the dead. I think up a title that will resemble the **Book of Nigerian Facts** I saw in Lagos, and with my blue eye-pencil, I write along the top of the page:

**The Very Important Small Book of Life's
Little Wisdoms by Adunni (the only edition,
written inside lockup in Ikati village)**

I look at the title. Measure it up and down, left and right. Is it a good title? Or is it too long? It is too long, but who cares? I crack a smile and close my eyes and think back to all the lessons I have been collecting in my brain, learning since I was born.

I decide to start with what I learned around the middle of yesternight:

**A good education can never be good
enough when you have a bad name.**

FIFTEEN HOURS
TO MIDNIGHT

Oh, I know!"

It's the girl from behind the wall.

I keep down my writing paper and pencil and put my eye in the hole. "What is it again? You keep saying you know! You know! What you exactly know?"

"I'm thinking to, like, start a fire to send an SOS signal or something? How about a laptop? Surely someone's got to have that, right? Think you can find us a laptop and hook it up to Wi-Fi and I can, I don't know, maybe log on to Facebook and connect with my dad and let him know where I am?"

"No computer laptop. No nothing. Sorry. Why are you here? Kike said your mama brought you here. Why?"

"My mother literally dragged me here," she says. "All because I am refusing to be treated like a second-class citizen just because I am a girl. And I won't let that happen to anyone. Have you seen Hauwa? She's a tiny frail thing? Seen her? No? I need to find her and protect her! You. Why are **you** here? Are you part of the sacrifice thing going on tonight? Hauwa is, and I guess a bunch of girls are, but I'm not. I mean I kind of am but not exactly. I've got to figure out a plan right this minute. But first, I need a drink."

"Excuse?" I say.

"Yeah?"

"Keep shut for one seconds," I say.

"That's rude."

"When Kike come back, I tell her to bring you water."

"There's no way I am touching that parasite-infested liquid."

"Then you die of thirsty," I say.

"I'll tell you what I'll die for right now? A chance to kill the idiot that came for Hauwa!" She sighs loud. "Life out here seems brutal. How the hell do people live here with all these traditional rules?"

Who is Hauwa? Why she keeps mentioning things that don't make sense?

I hear her scratching something, as if she is sweeping the floor under her chin with the broom of her fingers. She sneezes two times, and I fear she breathe in enough dust to fill up her whole chest with enough sand to build a small house.

"So. My dad's majorly pissed off at me because I could have spent the week skiing in Switzerland or something, but my mum called, and I thought, I'll spend time with her, doing girlie stuff and soaking in some country air. I thought I was doing the right thing at the time, but look what that got me. A very pissed-off dad and incarceration in some matchbox-sized clay room that stinks literally of shit."

She is not making plenty sense about her papa pissing on her, so I say, "Did you come from Ikati or where? Which family?"

"Oh, no! I'm not from anywhere around here. Wait. This right here is Ikati? I think that's what Hauwa called it. Is this Ikati village?"

"No," I say. "This is the middle of the America. What kind of nonsense question are you asking me? Who is Hauwa, and did they bring you here with your eyes folding?"

"I was literally blindfolded, yes."

I am not understanding why she keeps saying everything is **lit-ruh-lee** this and that, so I keep my words to myself and let her keep talking her mind.

She sighs a loud sigh. "And Hauwa is my friend." A pause. "There's no Wi-Fi . . . or laptop or, oh, I know! Do you think I could maybe get black coffee? Because I have to find a way to stay awake! I can't risk falling asleep and letting them harm me. Hey, is your dad pissed off at you too?" she says. "I thought I heard you guys arguing a while back. I am not sure: The walls here are so thick, plus he speaks mostly in Yoruba, which is like, I don't know, Greek to me. Actually, not Greek cos I studied a bit of Greek in summer school a few years back, so maybe another super-tough language like Mandarin or Basque? Listen, uh, what did you say your name was again? Ah-What-Knee?"

"Dear Father Lord in up heaven," I say, looking up at the ceiling. "When You were creating this Zenab, did You somehow forget to put a sense inside of her brain?" I try to look at her, to bend my neck like a doctor looking a patient up and down for signs of madness, but all I can see is her one large white eye.

"Not funny," she says, a mutter. "All I asked for was coffee. You don't have to be such a meanie."

"Okay. Sorry," I say. "When you come out from here, you walk small to the left by the shrine of Baba Ogun, then turn right down-down the road of maize, in the left of it, you will see Okuta farm. In the left of that farm, next to one short tree, you will see the plant that is having the coffee beans seed. Cut the plant, pack the seeds, roast it under a fire, put inside cup, add water, drink as coffee. You hear? And Adunni is the name. Bye. Bye." I push myself off the floor, wipe off the sand from my knees.

"Well, my dad drinks his coffee black!" she shouts as I stand. "My dad says it makes him super-focused!" Her voice breaks a little. "You're so lucky your dad came to see you! My dad hates me! He's never going to speak to me ever again! I am such an idiot!"

She breaks off to cry, and all I want to do is scratch her two eyes with the sharp pencil in my hand.

The handle of the door turns, creaking open.

It's Kike.

She is standing stiff like electric shock her back, the sun shining a triangle of golden light over her head. Her whole face is a painting of freeze-up terror, fear. "My people tell me that Miss Tee-Yah and Kayus is going to see Iya in Goma," she says. "They save."

To see Iya? That means Iya is not dead? Good! "Is Iya no more living in Agan?"

"She move to Goma six months back. For nearer water."

"Goma is far! And Papa, what about him?"

"Your papa . . ." She steps inside the room. "He try his very best. Honest. He was able to fight Bamidele and drag him here, but . . . Adunni. Don't be happy yet. Him and Bamidele fight a big fight and . . ." Kike rubs her stomach. "Your papa is bleeding so much blood." She takes one step inside the room so that I can really see the fear crisscrossing all over her face. "It is time to be going to the Circle of Forest, but your papa is in your house, and he been begging of me to bring you."

I nod. Feel my heart thick with fear. "Where is Bamidele?"

"They tie him up and lock him until this midnight. Hear me, Adunni. We soon going to the Circle of Forest. We going to dance and pass the front of your house. When we reach there, me, I will drag my feet and change our singing song. When I do like this to you"—she nods—"you cut from the singing line and go quick to see your papa and come back."

Kike gives me a square of white cloth. "Wear this, Adunni."

She keeps her eye on me as I climb out of my dress, let it drop to the floor. I wrap myself in the wrapper, tie it under my armpit. "Can I take my paper and pencil?"

She nods.

"After I see my papa, what?"

"We go to the Circle of Forest," she says. "We keep all of you girls there until it is time for the sacrifice."

TIA

We are now flanked by tall grasses, the full-throated, resonant cry of forest animals and collective snorting of what sounds like antelopes, but it is the coarseness underfoot gradually giving way to a gritty moisture that drags my stride to an unbearable pace.

"I've noticed there is more rain on this side," I say, hopping behind Kayus, afraid to step on a slippery frog or on the head of a snake. "Why is it dry in Ikati and getting wetter toward Goma?"

"Drying season in our side is more worst," Kayus says. "This one this year, the hot is plenty-plenty. It burn everything like a fire. But in the last raining season, we have plenty rain in just two days.

It sweep everything away. Then everything dry up again. In the state near the back of Goma, they suffer a flooding not too long now and the water wash inside Goma and kill peoples. Is why the chiefs are very sure we need the sacrifice before everything will just dry up finish or water will swallow everything."

It appears that flooding and drought have historically coexisted in these regions, but I wonder if climate change has cranked up the intensity, exacerbating the frequency and severity of disrupted rainfall patterns to dangerous levels.

I've seen, in case studies at work, cases of intense rainfall leading to flash floods and rising sea levels, followed by crippling drought in the dry season. The people have a right to worry: The next proper rainfall might be torrential and lead to flooding and displacement. Or it might be a trickle, leading to drought.

I wonder if there's a case here for my company to consult with partner agencies that can work with these communities, to ensure there is a reliable supply of water that pumps through flood and drought. I wonder if the deforestation I've seen around here has exacerbated things, because trees and forests act as a buffer against extreme floods and drought.

There's a rustle, a disturbance in the wilderness.

Kayus holds up his stick. Touches his lips. I stop walking. Nod. **What is it?** I ask with a frenetic movement of my eyes. **What?**

He makes a loud clicking noise in his throat. Then a snarling, like a pit bull growling at an intruder.

The rustling stops. Retreats.

Kayus tilts his neck and cups a hand over his ear, to listen.

"You hear that?" he asks.

I hear my heart palpitating along my ear canal.

"Is gone," he says. "Maybe is a lion?" He smirks at the clench of terror on my face. "Just joking you, Miss Tee-Yah. Not a one single lion in this forest. But sometimes a small baboon, or maybe a **buffah-low**. If it come like that, we make that noise, and it run away, leave us alone. Let's go."

"No," I say. Enough of this eight-, nine-, whatever-year-old boy dictating where we go, while delightfully insisting there are baboons, not lions, surrounding us, as if he's suggesting there's going to be pepperoni, not mushrooms, on our pizza order.

This is my life, his life, on the line here.

"No?" he repeats, his eyebrow lifting. "No, what?"

"No, I am not going. I don't think it's fair for you to make me walk, jump, run in a dark forest without shoes . . ." I pause, injecting calmness into my voice. "I've been patient enough until we got far away from Ikati. There's no one here now, right? Tell me, Kayus, why we need to see this . . . woman Iya. Why are we not in Ikati, helping Adunni?"

"We must go," he says in a cautious tone, "because if we don't go—"

"Adunni would be in trouble. I know that. You've said that. Many times. What exactly does Iya know that can save Adunni?"

Kayus turns his back to me, snaps a leaning branch out of his path, and, pushing it back, he disentangles intertwined twigs to clear the way for me. When he senses I'm not following, he throws a glance behind his shoulder. "Okay, I tell you. But you don't tell another somebody. Promise it."

"I promise."

He squeezes his eyes shut. Opens them. Stares at a spot behind my head. "Iya knows the man that will carry the sacrifice for Adunni this midnight."

"What man? I thought your papa—"

"My papa is not Adunni's papa." He hollers the words into the wind, as if they'd been heavy on his tongue for too long, causing insane discomfort, tension. "You hear me?" He rushes on. "That man, the man we keep calling Papa? My mama's husband. Is not the same-blood papa for Adunni."

"Whoa. Let me get this right. Your papa is not your father?"

"He is my . . . me. And Born-boy. Not Adunni."

I blink. Stunned. "He's not Adunni's father, but he's your father? Damn. That's . . ." I trail off, unsure of what to say.

"Papa know it, and me too, I know it. But Adunni didn't know this, and Born-boy, my big brother, didn't know it. Is a big-big secret in the middle of me, Papa, my dead mama, and Iya."

Kayus watches me as I struggle to process what he just said.

How's he so sure? How did he find out?

"I know," he says, answering the yet unuttered question on my lips. "I catch the truth when Mama was telling Iya, many years back. I was maybe five years, small for my body, thin like a stick. That day, my mama climb me on her back . . ." He trails off. "And carry me to give Iya food—yam and palm oil soup. See? I still remember it, the yam was soft, breaking, the palm oil fresh from the market, sweet with salt. After Iya finish her eating, my mama turn her neck to check it if I am sleeping inside the wrapper, before she cry and tell Iya how my papa is not Adunni's father. I don't remember the everything, but I remember that one true thing."

So, who the hell is Adunni's biological father?

The trodden grass path continues to thaw, slosh under my feet. Cold water purls around my ankles, riding up my calves.

"We must find the man," Kayus says. "Adunni's real papa, we must bring him here and beg him to help us carry sacrifice. You hear me, Miss Tee-Yah? If not, then my sister die." He shakes his head firmly. "And my sister cannot—" He thrusts the broken twig toward my chest. "She cannot die. Now take my shirt," he says. "Hold it. Another five, ten minutes or so, and we get to the main road of Goma.

"Pull your wrapper, Miss Tee-Yah. Up. Up."

Kayus pauses at a water plant with white fringe-petaled flowers, tears off a handful, and crushes them in his fingers. He smears the extract across his forehead, behind his neck, down his stomach, around the exposed flesh of his thighs and knees. He goes for another bunch and holds it out for me. "Rub it the flower everywhere. It chase off the biting water fish or ants or scorpion."

I do as I am told. The flowers emit a peppermint-and-cinnamon aroma that causes my eyes to sting, water.

"It smell very more strong in the nose of the water animals," he explains. I roll my wrapper under my butt, furrows of fabric sagging around my stomach like a postpartum belly with a bad case of diastasis recti.

Our walk descends into a downward sluggish wade, and Kayus glides along, using a broken twig to sweep debris out of the way, while explaining that when rain falls in the coastal states beyond Goma, everyone from his own village would rush over to Goma, with buckets and basins and bowls and plastic bottles to collect and store water. "Sometimes the water from there will fill up our river and help us. Good thing you don't need to knock on the door of water before it enter your house. It just flow when it want and stop to flow when it want."

I am amused at how like Adunni he sounds. How much time did she dedicate to teaching him the English he knows, to sharing her own nuggets of wisdom?

"Did you ever go to school?" I ask.

He nods without looking back. "Small. I learn small English with Teacher Sola. I go to the school of Adunni. She was teaching me since I was able to say good morning."

"Who is Teacher Sola?"

"She come from Lagos to do her Youth Service work. She have no money, but she keep teaching because she has love for learning childrens. But the no-rain drive her go back to Lagos last year."

"Would you like to finish school, Kayus?"

He shrugs. "Adunni say it is a good thing, but I don't see how it is good. How will learning books give you money to build house? Me, I just want to make plenty money to help my sister. Keep her happy."

I want to give him a mini lecture on how life-changing education is, how it would help him be more confident, make informed choices, get better jobs, improve his life and Adunni's, but the ridges of my wrapper are starting to get soaked.

"Is the water rising?" I ask.

Kayus turns to look at me. "Yes. It keep getting higher."

"What . . . does that mean?" My voice is a thorn, poking into the stiffness of the air, the verdant thicket of trees. "You know I can't swim."

"Ah," he says, scratching his head with his twig. "I make a whistle?"

Is he asking or telling? "A whistle?"

"I make it. Call it so my friend who is doing canoe-taxi can come and help us. If he hear us, he help us. If not, maybe you can climb up on my—" He taps his right shoulder with the twig.

"Whistle," I say. "Make it. Whatever it. Just do it."

He nods. Shoves two fingers into his mouth, lets out an earsplitting hoot. And another. I look down at the unreflecting water, as black as asphalt, as it forms a whorl of concentrical loops around my legs.

What if his friend doesn't hear us? What if we get stuck here?

"If he don't hear us, I can leave you here and go and come back with boat?"

"No bloody way," I say. "I'm not staying here by myself."

Kayus hoots again, pitching his neck forward, cupping the palm of his other hand over his ear, a deep frown on his face.

"I hear something," he says. "You hear it? Bend your head like this."

I incline my head, listening. There is a resonant hoot from the distance.

"He is coming," Kayus says. "Bala is his name. My friend."

Finally, the pointed deck of a wooden canoe comes into view. The young boy—shirtless and bald—is sitting on the stern and steering the canoe toward us with a wooden paddle. When he's near enough for us to climb in, Kayus gives me a push, and I flounder my way into the back of the seesawing canoe and perch, shivering and soaked, on a wooden slat.

Bala tilts his head in a greeting and starts to chat in Yoruba with Kayus, gesturing often at the sludge of black water with his free hand. The canoe gently swirls, and I grip the edges as it starts to float along water that soon turns brownish green with water hyacinths and other vegetation until we ease out of the cover of the forest and into the brightness of a sky that fills suddenly with hundreds of black birds. They fly in a whirl, changing patterns so that the sky appears as if painted with innumerable tiny strokes of black paint. An airplane roars past, and Kayus looks up at it in wonder before he says, "We soon reach."

We sail past a building nearly submerged in water, where three or four kids sit with their legs dangling from an open veranda on the top floor; past a sunken church with a megaphone hanging from its thatched roof; past another canoe filled with women standing in a short queue along the length of their boat, dressed in long, flowing white robes with blue and purple and red belts around their waists. Another woman wades along the waist-high water, a plastic tray loaded with sweets and baked goods on her head. Where the hell is she heading to, drenched like that? A shirtless man swims past her, dark, muscular arms pulling and pushing the water in fast and furious strokes. I am shattered by the reality of these people, and by the salient optimism with which they navigate this reality.

Why are disasters like this not covered on TV? Where is the governor of this state? What's he done with the millions he received in funding from the federal government? I bet his kids are all over social media, showing off trips in private jets abroad and brandishing super-luxury monogrammed bags. The bastard.

The water tapers and the canoe grinds to a halt on a bed of gravel. There is a wooden sign in the sand, battered by wind and rain, tilting toward the ground. It reads: **GOMA**.

I nearly weep with relief.

FOURTEEN HOURS
TO MIDNIGHT

ADUNNI

They wrapped us all up like a Christmas gift of girl-bodies for the spirits: Our uniform of sacrifice is a thin white fabric, tied around our chest, down to our legs. So different from my school uniform. I join the line of girls, the very last at the back because Kike arrange it so that I can cut from the line and go and see my papa, but I cannot see each their faces; I cannot tell which one of us is the Zenab that was talking to me in the room.

Shaki is holding a **shekere** in front of the line. It is a round of wood with plenty beads around its neck. She lifts it up in her right hand, and with her left, she fires a gunshot—**pow!**—up in the air so that some of the girls scream and cry, others cover their ears with their hands. A bird or two takes off from the forest behind Baba Ogun's shrine. A dog begins to bark. Shaki shakes her **shekere**, **pa-pa-pa-pa**, and dances, her feet tapping the floor left, right, left.

"We dance to the forest!" Kike shouts. "**Ijo-ya!**" She sings a song in Yoruba, her voice rising up and down like the hills that surround us, and there is a trembling in her voice, from the forcing of joy into it:

> **The daughters of the moon and sun**
>   **are coming!**
> **Dance! Dance! Dance!**
> **The daughters of the moon and sun**
>   **are coming!**
> **Dance! Dance! Dance!**

We shift this way and that, as if fingers from the wind is pulling each our hand, left, right. I am thinking of Papa as I keep my eyes on my feet as it appears and disappears under my wrapper, the white edge of the wrapper like a paintbrush dipping into the watercolor of the earth, turning the brown of sand, the red of spilled peppers.

As we walk pass, women stop everything they are doing: They stop sitting on stones, feeding crying babies, grinding peppers on grinding stones, milking milk from the breast under the bellies of thin goats. They stop scattering seeds of corn for the chickens, they put down bundles of firewood from their backs and heads. They stop. To look at us, to shake their heads, to smile, to wave.

I keep my head down, lifting it up only when a wind wraps dust around my nose and face, or to walk around the burned mouth of a drying clay well baked deep inside the oven of the earth.

In front of the house of Morufu, the man I married, I see the children of Khadija, Alafia and the one I can never remember her name, standing under the door. The two both girls are wearing yellow pant with no bra, their necks long and thin, their eyes almost the wide of the empty iron cup in their hands, breasts like groundnut shells. I feel a stinging of tears in my eyes at the memorying of how Khadija showed me around this house the first time I married, how she took me as a friend, a sister. I want to run to her children, to tell them I did not kill their mama, that I am so very sorry for how everything happened, but we keep moving and singing, from house to house.

We reach my papa's compound. My singing dies. The air feels like it grown up thick and wide, the shape of a mud-brick. I feel as if I need to catch this brick and crush it to breathe as Kike changes the song to a more loud one and starts to dance in front of Shaki, who looks very confused. Kike holds Shaki with her hands and turns her back to me, making a beckon to the girls to form a circle around of her so that all of them are backing our house. I drag my feet, my dancing, with my eyes on Kike.

When she nods, I turn around and run, past the back of our house, past the green plastic bucket that I use to fetch water with at the river, past Papa's bicycle on the ground, the flat tire spinning, his brown cap on the edge of the seat, and to our parlor.

I see Labake, Kike's mother, holding a bowl of water, a cloth of blood swimming inside the water, a bottle of medicine leaves in her other hand.

"Adunni," she says, nodding her head at me in a greeting. What is she finding here? Is she wanting to beat me like before when I was the wife of her husband? I swear if she takes one step close to me, or stop me from seeing my papa, I will bite off her black-brown breast, chew the flesh of it, and use it to draw mad-people makeup on her face.

"Be quick, Adunni," she says, speaking Yoruba because her English always sounds like she cut it with knife, into small-small pieces. "Talk to your papa, tell him to not leave his body." Her voice soft, heavy, different from the Labake of before. "He is inside. Go. Quick. I stand here and keep eye on the rest girls."

I push the cloth covering the door and enter inside the stomach-twisting smell of sweat and blood wound that punches my face. The parlor is still the same as how I left it last year—the TV that is not working in the corner, the sofa-chair with no cushion pushed to one side—and in the center of the small parlor, Papa is lying on a mat, his head on the pillow of a folding cloth, his eyes swollen and gum shut, his chest covered with a cloth soaking up his blood.

I kneel on the floor near the mat. "Papa?" I whisper.

The singing of the girls outside changes to a faint clapping.

Papa turns his head a little and try to open his swollen-up eye.

"Oh, Papa," I say, tears pinching my eyes, sliding down my face. "I am so sorry, Papa. I bring all this bad luck to our family! If I didn't run away, maybe you will not wound like this." I wipe my face. "Is it paining you here? Near your under-hand? Is it still swelling? Sorry, Papa. Thank you, Papa, for finding Bamidele, for saving me."

"I didn't find him to save you," Papa says in Yoruba, and he sounds like he is climbing up a mountain with his voice, a mountain that is hard to climb. If he didn't wound bad, I think he will slap his chest as he is talking, make high his voice.

"I find him to show him I am a man, that I am three men." He swallows spit, closing his eyes as if it is a rock inside his throat. "I find him to cover the name of our family. The name of Akala."

I nod, feeling my heart crack a little. But that tiny crack in my heart is filling up with thank-you, so I say thank you again and again until Papa says, "That Bamidele?" His voice is sudden soft now, more slow, his breathing like he needs to dig inside his stomach to find the air, to push it out of a too-thin nose.

"What happened to him?" I ask.

"He was begging me to leave him as I was tying up his hand tight with rope. Then he say something about you."

My nose catches fire, burns. "About me?"

Papa nods—feels like two minutes before his head climbs up and down. "That Khadija say speak good of you. That you did not for one day talk bad about me."

"Papa, I can never talk bad about you! Never!" The true thing is this: Many times, I was wanting to slap sense into Papa, to open his eyes and see me as Adunni, a girl important enough, but now is not the time to be saying all sorts of foolish stupid things.

"So Bamidele say that if I leave him to run free, he will find a way to come back here today, before this midnight, and free you too because of your good heart."

"Papa, that is not true!" I shake my head no, sniffing, looking at his chest climbing and falling. "Bamidele is a big liar! There is no how he will come back! He made a promise to Khadija too. He didn't ever come back."

"I know," Papa say, coughs. Sounds like an eggshell cracking under feet. A line of blood falls down his nose, and I swipe it with the edge of my wrapper, stain it red.

"That is why I fight him with my last of everything to drag him back to Ikati," Papa says, his voice so tired, so quiet, that I have to stretch my ear around it to trap what he is saying.

"Everything be all right, Papa," I say, talking through my tears, trying to keep it back so I can make sense. "Labake is bringing medicine to help you. Bamidele will confess this night and I will be free. See, Papa, I didn't run away from Ikati to make you or Kayus to suffer. I ran away to try and find my future. I found it, Papa! I am starting school in Lagos, and if after this night I am free, I will go back to Lagos and go to school and become a teacher and make money and buy you a fine car, Papa. A fine motorcar. A Benz, maybe. I will take you to Lagos too. You will see it, Papa, a very fine noisemaking place. If I had married Morufu, I will be only that: a girl who married a man, the end. Nothing more to my story. But my story is bigger than that! I chose my journey of life and I will take you along with me, Papa. It's a matter of small time before I will be able to take care of you and Kayus, even Born-boy. I promise I will do very well in school. I will read my books morning, afternoon, night, every waking second. I promise it."

"Adunni," Papa says slowly, quietly.

"Papa?"

Labake enters. "It is time."

I look at Labake. "Please, ma, give him all the medicine. Everything. Keep him alive for me."

Labake nods, her eyes sad. "Go before Shaki sees you are not dancing."

I kiss the floor near Papa and touch my hand to his forehead. It is a little cold, like a stone sitting at the edge of a river. "Be strong, Papa. Be strong for the sacrifice this night, and even if you will not do the sacrifice to save me, do it because you are three men."

There is no answer from Papa, so I stand and turn around.

"You are so full of dreams," Papa says, sudden, just as I push the ankara cloth covering the door. "Your mind . . ." He sniffs and gives a sad, slow laugh, a mix of water and blood climbing down the skin growing out of his cheeks, his chin area. "Your mind is hard to bend, to break. You want to be a teacher?"

His voice is having more strong now. I turn to nod, to smile. Once. Twice. "Yes, sir. So that I care for you and Kayus."

"If life didn't do me bad, you know what I have dream of? What I wish to become?"

I shake my head no. Didn't ever even think somebody like my papa can have a dream or even talk to me about it. Why didn't us two talk like this all our lives? Why didn't we ever have one single conversations about me wanting to become a teacher?

He bends his lip in a slant of a smile that seems like it knife him to even try. "When I was seven years of age, I wanted to be caring for sick peoples. What you call them?"

"Doctor," I say thinking of Ms. Tia's husband. "I know one. He lives in a fine house in Lagos."

Papa is quiet again, his breathing like a hissing-song.

Outside, the clapping, dancing is slowly dying.

"Quick," Labake whispers. "Kike is tired to be keeping Shaki in one place."

"I didn't able to follow my dream," Papa says in a force of power through his mouth. "So I forget it and face my drink and marry a wife. But you? You keep your dream and hold it tight. And you don't let anybody stop it. You teach me a lesson, Adunni. A lesson of how to don't never give up on good things." He stays silent a moment, and I sense something thick slip outside of him and float away. "Me, I didn't get chance to live a good life, but maybe you can. Go, Adunni. Go."

I wipe my eyes and step out of the room and run to join the girls, who are now bending low and rising in another dance. Kike sees me, nods, makes a hand sign to Shaki.

Shaki stops marching. Chanting. She lifts her gun, shoots another gunshot.

The air makes a flutter with the wind of angry whispers from the trees.

A thick silence.

I look back at our house. Semi, one of the small-chiefs, is entering into our parlor, the black mat for dead-body burial rolled up under his armpit. He stops to look at us, to wave like a bye-bye at one of the girls in the front of the lineup with something like a dying fire in his eyes, before he turns to the room where Papa is. How he knows one of us? And why is he holding that black mat?

I force my legs to keep moving, to stop worrying for Papa.

After that, I stop taking observe, just keep dragging my heart under my feet until we reach the forest backing the hills, the back of Baba Ogun's compound.

Shaki turns into the forest, and we follow her behind, our feet crunching on dry grass and sticks and stones.

THIRTEEN HOURS
TO MIDNIGHT

########################

ADUNNI
########################

THE CIRCLE OF FOREST

The Circle of Forest is a basin of pink sand in the ground, be like a tongue pushed back in the wide-open mouth of the bushes. Around us is a embrace of tall trees with leaves dropping down like a half-closing umbrella, the sharp red nose of the hills, the edge of a cliff beside of a sharp teeth of rocks.

In the middle of the circle of sand: seven short wooden benches. Behind each bench, a clay pot filled little of water, a stick of green plantain on the side, the skin black and wounded, filled with holes where birds been picking at the white flesh of it.

The air whistles. It smells too. Of the body of us girls, of sweat from our armpits and head, of the space in the middle of our press-together thighs, of the blood we bleed under and on top our skin, of chickenshit, flowers, forest, coal. It smells of shame. Fear.

Shaki claps. Once. Two times. Sweat pours from the side of her head as she nod to Kike.

"I greet all of you!" Kike says, stepping into the middle of the circle, wiping her hands on her wrapper. Her voice is loud, slicing like a blade in the forest. "My name is Kike. **Aya** Baba Ogun. The wife of the chief priest of the Ikati. I speak first in English, which many of you are learning; after, I speak Yoruba. The one you didn't learn, please ask me and I try to my best to easy it for you.

"Our land is no more the land of plenty. Our land is crying in some places and in some other places, it is cracking. This very middle of night, the village of Ikati, Ekiri, Milega, Okunsi, Shanta, and Fuyetu is doing something we never do before. We joining as one to beg for the problems to stop."

Someone sniffs.

"But how is that the fault of us girls, **na?**" one of the girls says. I raise my head. She has low-cut hair, the color of early-morning sun. Hips like she gum two calabashes to the side of each her waist, round and hard, a thing you can crack. Her wide teeth has a space in the bottom that can hold a pencil. Eyebrows make me think she pluck the number 7 from a ruler and hook it around eyes that can spark a fire. "This is madness-o!" she says, her voice rough, hurrying. "Madness with a capital M! My mother begged me do this, I swear! If not for my mother, I won't be here!"

Shaki, who seems to only know how to grunt and fire a gun, plucks out her gun from her chest and points it at the girl, her teeth like a dog about to bite.

"She won't shoot me," the girl says, stepping back, touching her hand to her chest. "Will she?"

"She very will," I say with a low hiss. "With a happy smile too. Shaki can be happy to fire a gunshot and killed us all dead and nobody will do anything. So, keep quiet and let Kike talk."

Kike nods at me. "So, after this very midnight, many of you be free to go. We do sacrifice, you collect judgment, small punishing. We dance and sing, we go and wait for blessing. Some of you free to go marry. Some free to go born, to go back to the city, but"—she sighs—"some of you, if you kill a person, you don't free."

I drop my head as Kike is repeating everything she just said in Yoruba.

"Nothing to fear," she continues. "Keep yourself quiet. You stay here. The spirits of the forest keep big eyes on you. You don't run. Shaki is at front of forest with her . . ." Kike presses two fingers to form the shape of a firing gun. "Nobody can run. We don't want anybody wound themself. Please. Stay here until is nearing time for baff."

We cannot run.

This forest is too thick, and the end of it is a cliff that leads to the rocks below.

"One of the small-chiefs," Kike says, "his name is Semi. We soon bring him come to talk to his coming-soon wife."

Who among of us is the coming-soon wife of a small-chief? I throw my eyes around, settle on one tiny girl with no hair on her egg-shape head. I keep my eyes on the small girl, her bottom lip, which is shaking, tears climbing down her face. Can it be her? Is it her that Semi was waving bye-bye to near my house? No. It cannot be. This small child? She don't look like one minute pass the age of ten.

I wonder too which one of us is Zenab. Can it be this small child? I don't think so. She don't look like someone that will be saying **Oh, I know!** every one seconds. Or is it that girl over there with a blue scarf covering her head, making it hard to see her face? Or that one with the face like a wound and with beads around each her thick legs like a neck-chain? Or that one with yellow skin that keep talking to her chest? Or which one?

It is hard to pick. I will sharp-up my ears to listen well so that when they speak, I will be able to catch which one is Zenab. Unless maybe Zenab is not among of us. Maybe she already gone back to her mama, or was it papa?

Why it matters anyway? The girl is full of troubles.

"When the small-chief is come," Kike says, "please don't shout. Just give him small time to talk to his coming-soon wife. She going to marry him in one month. But me and Shaki, we come back with the man." She nods her head at the clay pot of water. "Drink small water but keep rest for baffing. I go!"

Kike leaves the circle, walking slow. Shaki follows her behind.

We are sudden alone. Six of us. Strangers. Girls. Alone in a forest. One by one, we sit on the ground, turn our backs to each other, and wrap ourselves in the pocket of our waiting.

After about thirty, thirty-five minutes of sitting on the ground, with some of us crying, others keeping their head down and crying with no noise, plucking the grass from around their feet or talking quiet among of ourselves, I see Labake standing on the entering place of the circle and calling my name. There is load in her eyes. Did something bad happen again? I sit stiff until she makes a silent beckon. I follow her outside of the circle, where she begins to walk fast, until we reach to almost the mouth of the forest.

She stops and turns.

"Well done, Adunni," she says, her Yoruba soft. "Is a good thing you came to see your papa."

I blink at her, not sure whether to say something or keep looking.

"Your papa . . ." She kicks something with her

feet, shifting her wrapper, making it tight. "Your papa is gone."

"Is gone to where?" I look at the first wife of the man I married, the before best friend of my mother, and try very hard to make full sense of what she means by **Your papa is gone**.

"To where?" I throw my eyes around the forest as if Papa hiding himself in the spray of sunlight falling through the roof of leaves above us. "My papa is gone to exactly where?"

Labake bends, puts her hands on her knees as if to think, to gather the strong to say what I already know. When she finally straights up herself and looks at me, there are tears, standing like tiny knives of glass, in her wide-open eyes. "Akala, your father," she says, coming to the side of me, to catch my falling self, "he is gone far to the Land of the Spirits. To join your mama. Sorry, Adunni. So very sorry."

I cushion my head on top of Labake's breast, sniffing up the spoiling-pepper smell of her wrapper. Papa is dead. I don't sure how to feel, what to feel.

She grips me tight, and her touch is the mix of a shock and a comfort.

"The Spirits of the Dead will carry him," Labake says to my bent head. "Don't be too sad—"

"I don't want to hear!" I shout the words out loud, struggling to free myself from the tight rope of Labake's hands. I twist around, slapping Labake to free me. "How can he die today? How can he die just when I was just learning of him? When I was peeling back the skin of his hard heart to find the true him? I want to see my father! I want to—"

"Shut up your mouth!" Labake shouts, and her voice is a punch on the remaining rest of my words back inside my mouth. "Stop shouting, **jo**! Me and Kike, we want to help you before everybody knows."

My eyes climb all over her face, searching for what she is trying to say. "Help me how?"

"He is not your father," Labake says, lowering her voice so that her words climb down the dark steps of my already full ears and sit like a ball at the bottom of my stomach. "Your papa—Akala—he is not your real papa! This is a secret. Him and I and your mama known it since before she died dead."

The forest is a sea with thousands of stabbing sunlight twisting and turning like little fishes of light in the air. I sway on my feet, my legs becoming water, flowing down the thick wall of Labake's body. "You say what? That Papa is not my father?"

"No." She releases me to breathe. "Be strong of yourself, Adunni! Be strong. We must find your blood father before midnight. Or else . . ."

"Who is my father?" Who owns the voice that is asking this question? Why is the voice calm like this?

Because the voice is tired of fighting. To die sudden don't seem so bad now. Maybe Mama will be waiting on the other side; Papa too, maybe. Only poor Kayus I feel sorry for. Who will take care of him? Ms. Tia? Since Ms. Tia very much wants to be a mother, maybe I can beg her to make a promise to care of Kayus for me because I think to be a mother is more than the science of body. It is the true deepness of heart, the filling of love that Ms. Tia carries with her to everywhere that will help her. I know she can do it. She can take Kayus; give him the gift of toast bread and choco-tea in the morning, of a sandal-shoe to cover his burned feet, of a barber to barb his hair every once in two weeks.

Labake sniffs. "I never seen your blood father with my two eyes. You know the house on top of the hill? Blue roof? That is the house of his grandma. Your father, he was living in the land of the white man for many years. Your mother, Idowu, always talk of the man, says he have a good head. She never tell you of him?"

"No." I raise my wet eyes to Labake. Is her brain full up with ice-block? How will my mama tell me that the papa I known all my life is not my papa? In our village, any woman that give her child to another man will die dead with stoning, so my mama will never talk that secret. She will carry it to her graveside. Use it as the sand to cover her dead body.

Labake twists the corner of her wrapper, use it to wipe her eyes. "Sorry, Adunni. I am the fault of all the troubles in your life. But"—she lifts up her head—"the chiefs and Baba Ogun know the truth. They will not make a noise of it tonight. Nobody in the village will know if you keep it quiet yourself."

Why is she saying sorry? Did she kill Mama and Papa? I shake my head, wipe my eyes.

"This is not your sorry," I say, in a voice that is not at all my own, that sounds like I drag it across the rough road from Lagos. "What will happen to me now? The sacrifice? We don't have time to find Born-boy." But even if we find Born-boy, are we of the same blood father?

"We keep up hope," Labake says. "We hope that before this very midnight, Kayus and the woman from Lagos? Maybe they come back with a message of where your blood father is. Born-boy and Kayus, they don't have the same father blood like you. Only you is different."

Only me is different. Only me is fighting. Only me will die.

"If we find your real papa, we tell the village he is the brother of Akala, to cover the shame of Akala." Labake slaps a flying ant from her shoulder, catches it in the fold of her palms, releases it to fly away. "So, pray that we find your blood father before midnight. That he will help you. Adunni, this is too much for you, eh!" She sighs deep, looking around and lowing her voice even more. "The senior chiefs are burying your papa now-now at the east side of the forest. I can take you near there so you can see them, say bye-bye from afar? Maybe it help you to not feel sad?"

No.

I don't want to see the chiefs throw the body of
Papa inside a hole in this forest.

I want the last memory of Papa to leave a sweet
taste in my tongue; for my heart to dance from the
beat of the first real-deep talk we ever shared, to
swell too with the pregnant of the dreams he was
carrying inside of his heart.

Even if he was not my blood father. Even if he
married me to Morufu at fourteen and didn't give
me a chance for education. Even if he spent his
whole life drinking until he drunk and daze and
waste off all my mama's money on nonsense. I
understand now that an empty hand can only give
the gift of air. And air is the greatest of gift for those
who struggle to breathe.

I know Papa failed a thousand times as a father,
but I will never forget how he died trying to help
me, by bringing Bamidele, even if he thought it was
his own way of showing himself as a man. To me,
he was trying to give me air to breathe.

I look up at the sky, and I think it is a mystery,
how the sky divides the earth and covers this side
of the world with a bowl as if to keep sorrow closed
tight on us down here, protecting the heavens above
from tasting of it, from staining it with the wickedness of men like Bamidele.

I think I peep a smile up, up there, a curving
swoop like the wing of an eagle turning a bend, and
I know it is the slanting lips of my smiling mother.

She and Khadija are waiting in the sky, calling me to come.

I am not afraid.

|||||||||||||||||||

ON DYING
We are all going to die one day.
To know this is a gift, a curse tied with a
bowstring of a blessing.
No any number of education, science, prayer,
money can change that.
Is a fact of life, so take every chance to
live a fully full life.

—THE VERY IMPORTANT SMALL BOOK OF
LIFE'S LITTLE WISDOMS BY ADUNNI

TIA

GOMA VILLAGE

Kayus leads me to a compound where a man is pulling along a scraggy white goat with red markings running down the patchy fur on its distended stomach.

The man drags the goat to the back of the tree, produces a glinting knife from a pouch on his side, and slits open the goat's throat in one single swipe. The goat's eyes widen in a sickening, final bleat, blood weeping from the gash, as it crumbles like a feeble tree struck with an axe. It lies on the ground, teeth bared in a death grin clamped over the turgid tongue, hind legs twitching. The man raises his eyes in that moment, catches me looking at him. I glance away and jog up to Kayus.

"I go talk to him," he says. "Wait in front of that house." He points at a modern house built with cement, the bottom half painted in gentian violet-blue and top half unpainted, as if the task became too tedious, too costly to complete. There are six or seven rooms facing each other, and I climb up a pair of steps to a narrow corridor and lean on a wall opposite the first room, which stinks of stale urine and shit and bleach. I watch Kayus through a haze of muggy heat, chatting with the man, gesticulating vaguely in my direction.

I dig out Adunni's phone, tasting the bleach on my tongue. Three bars. Finally. I hit Adunni's password in and call Ken. He doesn't pick up at first, so I send him a text:

Please call Ocean Academy and let them know what's happening.

I nearly drop the phone when it rings.

"I already did," he says, voice curt. "They are concerned but have assured me they'll keep her space until next week. They have a waiting list, and the cutoff age for fresh applications is fifteen."

"Thank you," I say, relieved but only just. What will happen next week? Will Adunni be here? Or— My eyes slide to the slaughtered dead goat on the floor, and a spasm lacerates my body. I force myself to focus, be positive. "My phone's dead. Please call me on Adunni's phone if you need me."

Silence. I hear voices in the background. A car honk. He's outside.

"Where are you?" I look down at my hands; they are twitching.

"Your father called," he says. "He's asking if and when to pick you up from the airport."

"Can you please . . . please tell him I'll have to move my flight? I'll see them first thing tomorrow."

"Fine."

"Ken?"

I want to ask if he got the location I sent earlier, if he will come down, if he should come down, but I am afraid to ask, to lose him. Adunni's phone gives another quiet buzz, the battery bar flickering against the dark, gray screen.

"I am sorry," I say.

"Yeah, sure, Bow-Tie," he mutters. "Listen, there's insane traffic and I've got to go—"

"Wait. Ken. Please." I exhale, gripping the phone, my voice wavering. "Did you, did you read all the letters?"

"I'm not going to discuss—"

"Fine. Listen. There's been a development. About Adunni. We need . . . to find her biological father to help her with the sacrifice. I know you think I am . . . Please. Let's put aside whatever is happening with us now and help Adunni. I haven't got a phone, and this one is on its last legs. Can you help me find Adunni's father?"

He lets out a sigh but says nothing else.

"Ken? Can we please help Adunni? Just this once?"

"Who the hell is he?" He slaps what I assume is a hand against the steering wheel.

"I am about to find out." I rush my words out. "I just got to this older woman who will give us the info we—"

"Save your battery. Call me with something solid."

He hangs up.

I pinch my eyes shut. Open them. Kayus is jogging up to me with a glint in his eyes.

"Iya is living alive," he says. "Come let's go."

At first I don't move. I stare at the phone screen, half expecting Ken to have sent me another Boma letter perhaps in a string of text messages. He doesn't, but still, I feel like my words are slowly filling the screen, that Ken is getting closer to the truth I couldn't bring myself to share:

January 1999

Dear Bow,
    This evening my mother found me waiting for you by our spot in the garden and told me she'd sent Ada (and you, by extension) away to work in our village home??? That's insane!!! She says there is a lot of work that needs doing (roofing, gardening, plumbing, etc.), but I've only been there once and remember a blur of a building so vast, it could have been a cathedral.

She says she put you and your mum in a taxi late last night. I am surprised: When did she make that decision???? Why didn't you wait to speak to me, to say goodbye? When will you be back? Does she think this will break us up? She better wake up and smell the coffee! We are 2geda 4eva!

She did say she's increased your mum's salary, that it's a great change for your family. That's a good thing, I guess? I can't help feeling she sent you and Ada away because of me.

Anyhoo, I'll keep our letters till you return!

Roses are red, violets are blue (are they? I thought they were purple?), here's me sending all of my love to you!

Tie

ADUNNI

I come back to find the girls still sitting quietly, some on the bench, others on the ground across the circle, nobody saying much. We all have reached the end of the journey of words and all we can do is wait.

I fold up my sorrow and shock and keep it in the cupboard of my soul. Maybe, one day, I will take it and the rest of the cloths of my life out of the cupboard and wash it and spread it to dry so that I can join the happy cloths to the shock cloths and sorrow cloths, sew it with different color threads, and make it a pretty dress to wear. Or maybe it won't make a pretty dress.

Maybe it will make a rag.

Or a burial cloth for a dead body.

I lean my back on a tree and put my head in my knees, thinking of how just midnight yesterday I was wearing my new school uniform, and how today I am in the middle of a forest and Papa is already dead and my blood father is a tiny football, rolling around in the middle of the earth, and where will anybody find him for the sacrifice?

Funny how life just like to push his tongue in your face and laugh ha-ha at your stupid plans. But. I can choose to cry, or I can keep up hope. I am thinking about this, biting my pencil, when a low whistle comes from somewhere near the back of me, from the mouth of one of the plants.

I turn around, see nothing but thick trees joining hands with other trees. I look at the girls, but it seems nobody but me hear a low whistle, so I think maybe it is the air and slide out my papers and start to write another lesson.

There is another whistle. It is not the air. There is the sound of feet too, snapping the branches that fell on the ground. I put my paper down and turn, facing the forest behind me. Somebody is walking fast, breaking sticks on the ground. I nearly shout of shock when the person jumps over a tree log and lands beside me.

"It is me, Adunni," he says in Yoruba, eyes wide. "Don't shout!"

It is Semi, the small-chief that I saw entering my house with a bury-mat, which I now know is for my father. He has grown even more tall and handsome in the one year since I been in Lagos. There is a chain of red beads on his neck, reaching down to his knees, a stick of black feathers in his left hand, a wicked smile on his thin lips.

"Did my papa not die?" I ask, keeping my voice low, because the girls are now turning to look at us, to look at him.

He shakes his head no. "He died already. They are burying him now, at the east of that place—" He points to somewhere behind his head. "So, I say, let me take the chance to quick come here to greet you sorry for your father. The gods will carry him."

Semi says the prayer to me, but his eyes is running around each of the girls scattered around the circle until he sees the small girl, who is keeping her head down, as if she is afraid to look up at him. The girl with the blue scarf is beside her, but she is knifing Semi with her eyes, her lips curling as if she wants to say something wicked to him. How he knows the two both of them? I think "one of us" is this small girl but who is the girl in the scarf?

"Hauwa?" Semi lifts his stick of feathers and points it to the small girl. I stand back, watching the small girl push her head more down, to bury it like a seed in the ground, her shoulders shaking. Semi starts to speak in another language that I don't understand. I remember now that his mother, Talatu, was a friend of my mama. Talatu use to plait wood to make very fine baskets to sell in the market, and she was from a village in the north, where they use to speak this very same language Semi is speaking now. So how he and Hauwa knows themselves?

I watch, feeling more confuse, his voice a low rough, as if he wants to shout but is afraid of shouting.

The girl with the scarf climbs to her knees and crawls so that she is in front of Hauwa like a fence, shouting something in the same language Semi was speaking, her voice pure, sweet like the sound of music, but also sharp with a warning.

Semi listens for a moment, spits on the floor. It lands by my feet. The girl in the scarf looks at the spit, at his feet, at her own feet, her toenails brown with paint, making a sound like an animal.

The two both of them, they look each other from across the circle, Semi's eyes thinning and the girl in the scarf looking at Semi, her hands tight up beside her, like she wants to box something and crush it. Semi grunts, turns away, and runs back into the forest. The girl sits and holds Hauwa and begins to rub her shoulders.

"What happened just now?" I ask, but everybody is already minding their own matter. I wait a moment, looking around, before I shrug, pick up my pencil and paper, and begin to write my next Life Lesson.

Life is not too much about what happened to you, I write after a moment of thinking deep, but about how you answer the question of what happened to you. "True!" I say, reading out the line, breaking the silence. I pause from my writing, holding my pencil in the air.

"That is deep," the girl in the scarf says. She's standing to her feet and walking across the circle, shifting the edge of her scarf behind her ears, to clear her face to very well see me.

Now close and with no scarf covering all her face, her skin is a shining blackness that seems to breathe in and out; her lips are the pink of a flower; eyes wide and bright; the bones of her cheeks like she sharp it with a knife. When she pushes her scarf away even more back, her hair falls to her face in a bounce, tapping the tip of her nose, the deep of her lean neck, and coming to rest as a curve around her shoulder. She is honest the most beautiful I ever seen of girls.

"Sorry about what happened with that idiot," she says. "He's a bully, that's all. It's, like, the second time I've had to scare him off Hauwa. First time was when we arrived, right at the what's-it-called-now? The town-center space? Uh . . ." She eyes me from up to down. "I'm pretty sure you are the girl I met earlier? Name's Ah-Something-Knee? I couldn't recognize you because of that wall separating us. Did you by any chance grab a mobile phone on the way here? Does anyone have a phone? I need to call my dad! Anyone?"

No one answers her. Not even me. I keep looking at her like she is something wonder. And now that there is no wall in the middle of us, her English-speaking is sounding two times more polish than Ms. Tia's English. What is **she** doing here?

"Well," she sighs, "since no one is saying anything, I might as well introduce myself. Name's Zenab, and I am fifteen." She touches her hand to her chest, a drawing of lines and circles on her palm in brown paint.

"What are you writing?" She tilts her head, reading my paper. "A book of 'Life's Little Wisdoms'? That is **really** clever!" Honest. Her English sounds as if she salted it with salt and peppered it with pepper and oiled it with Ms. Tia's organic coconut oil before she spread it on her tongue to speak it.

"Adunni is the name," I say. "Remember?"

Her eyes bright up. "Well, hello, nice to finally meet face-to-face! We met," she says to the rest girls, "like a few hours ago, and she was just . . ." She claps her four fingers to her thumb, like a mouth open-close-open-close. "Chatting all sorts? I know I am chatty, but Adunni is a bit mad!" She smiles. "So. Adunni. Did I get it right this time? Why are you writing all this stuff?"

"Because . . . I want to leave a part of me for the world to remember. The only way I can keep on living is to find a way to write something like a book. I don't have much time or paper, so I am writing a short book of lessons." I push up my chest, slap my tears away. "But I will not let them just kill me like a chicken! Tonight I will fight! I will fight to live."

One by one, the girls turn around to look at me, their faces dropping with the heaviness of our heart.

"We must not let them break our hope," I say. "We must not let them take away from us the only thing we have. If they break our mind, we are finished. We must not let them finish us. Please don't waste one minute feeling bad or sad."

I make a beckon for all the girls to come close, to turn around and sit facing me, forming a embrace round the basin, every eyes, except of one, shining like stones.

I touch my hand to my pounding heart, waving my papers in the air. "I am writing this small, tiny book, but my dream is more big than this. Can you tell me your own dream? If you have just this night to live, what will you spend it doing?"

I smile at Hauwa next to Zenab. "Maybe you start. Tell me your name and your dream?" I know her name, but I want her to talk. To tell herself her dream. Something powerful about saying your dream to yourself, to force your own ears to hear it loud.

But it is the girl with the gap in her teeth, the one with low-cut orange hair, who speaks first: "My name is Efe." She makes a hand sign of two fingers up in the air like a V. "I am sixteen and mad because I run away from Middle Belt because I am carrying the baby of two men. **No shakings!**"

Two men? I blink. Shock.

"Wait," Zenab says. "Hold up. You literally just told us you are pregnant for two men. At the same time? And you say 'no shakings'? As in 'no worries'? Are you nuts?"

Efe shines her teeth like she is making a joke, before shrugging her shoulder.

"My name is not your business," the girl with the beads on her legs says next. Her voice is sharp, angry. She is the only one that did not look at me when I was speaking, and now that I see her more close, I can see she is much old than us, her eyes tired. "Mind you, I am not a girl. I am a woman, a mummy of twins—boys—and my dream is not the business of anybody." She hisses, stands, and rolls her buttocks away to sit even more away from us, her stomach bouncing like she is pregnant of water, the beads jumping and slapping the bones of her ankles. Those beads . . . I thin my eyes, trying to look, to see if I seen them from somewhere, but Efe pinches the flesh of my arm and shifts close.

"That Madam No-Name over there," Efe spits into my ears. "She thinks she is more better than us because she is older? Some Nigerian women can like to behave like old age is a special prize. Rubbish!"

The yellow girl beside Efe lifts her head. "Me, I am Chichi," she says, her words like she is blowing air, not words, through her teeth. She is truly ripe-looking, like a too-sweet yellow fruit, and when she looks at me, I see her one eyeball is pointing left, the other one pointing right. "I didn't supposed to be here. Excuse me, but I am not like all of you. I did not wronged anybody. I am a wife. A happily marry wife. To Zuke. My husband, the apple of my eyes. He is on his way to save me." She puts her head down and starts to pinch the thread of her cloth.

"Well, I am not meant to be here either," Zenab says. "I, like, keep thinking I'll wake up from this . . . this nightmare! This has. Literally. Turned out. To be the most inconceivably catastrophic turn of events. EVER! What the hell was I thinking?"

I blink at Zenab and her big English, look again at Hauwa. She been too quiet since. Why is she so quiet? Afraid?

"What is your name?" I ask her again.

She looks at me as if she is seeing me for the very first time.

"That's Hauwa," Zenab says, more calm-down now. "She is twelve. Our . . . How should I say this? Communities? Yeah. Our communities are literally next to each other in the north, but we met shortly after we got here. So, we, like, got here in two different cars, right? And that idiot Semi comes out of nowhere and comes to grab Hauwa's hand, and no one—I mean no one, not even Hauwa's dad, who brought her—says nothing. So, I started to scream

at him and kick and basically make a scene, and
he's like giving me this look like he thinks I'm disgusting, and the other guys with him, the chiefs or
whatever, they ended up dragging me to that room
and locking me up just so I'd shut up and I didn't. I
was just screaming the whole place down for hours."
She blows out air, fanning the scarf around her
cheeks. "I don't care! I won't let him touch her, no
way. Oh! And she does not speak any English. Or
Yoruba." She winks at me. "Or Greek or Basque."

I smile. I think I like Zenab. How she can
jump from happy to sad in less than one seconds.
"I am from Ikati," I say. "I speak Yoruba well, so I
can help you people to make sense of everything
this night."

Efe stands and points at me. "You. I will call you
Wisdom from now because I cannot remember
your name. You just talked a very wise thing." She
smacks her lips, licks it. "Why don't we each make
introduce . . . Introduction, I mean. Excuse me. My
English sometimes suffers malaria. We each introduce a more happy introduction of ourselves. With
a song because I like to sing because I am going
to one day enter TV and be a star inside movie.
Big star!"

She starts to swing her waist, snapping her fingers, dancing around a stone.

"Who is the fine girl in this forest?"

She swings herself to my front, tries to pull me
up to my feet, but I snatch my hand and give her

a look like she is having the problem-brain of a vexing chicken.

"It's me, Efe," she sings.

"I am going to be a TV star!

"I am—"

She stops. Looks down. "Why are you all looking at me like a dunce? Wisdom, you are not dancing? Come on!"

We all keep looking at her, except the girl who seems much old than us. She is frowning and peeling the skin of the green plantain on her clay pot. Efe keeps singing, not minding anybody, and when she finishes her song, she turns around and bows. "Thank you! Thank you!"

Efe folds herself to the floor, humming.

The air whistles. Something trembles the tall trees.

I shiver, thinking about my real father. Who is he? Where he been all my life? What happened to him and my mama? I think of Papa. Can I still call him my papa? If only we can have one more moment to talk a little more.

Zenab slaps the ground with her hand, **pa**. "Wait? Hang on! I am sorry, I can't seem to get past this. Are you really pregnant for two men?"

I look up.

Efe is lifting herself up, sniffing. "You want me to tell you the story?" She crawls herself on her knees until she is close enough to Zenab. "I want to talk about it."

"Actually"—Zenab pushes herself up—"you said

something in your song? Something about being on
TV, like a star? You want to be on TV?"

"I want to act inside film," Efe says, eyes closing
as if she is traveling far behind her eyes, into the
land of her dream. "To be big like the biggest actor
in the whole world." She opens her eyes. "Wisdom,
you are writing a film?" She nods at the paper in
my lap.

"I said a book of the things I learn," I say. "My
true dream is to become a teacher."

Efe squeezes her nose like the word is a smelling
word. "See why I call you Wisdom?"

I smile.

We all stay quiet again.

Zenab stretches out her leg, starts to pick the edge
of her toenail. "One of my absolute favorite shows
is the Oprah Winfrey show? I know it's old now,
reruns and stuff, but it's incredible! It shows on satellite TV? Anyone of you know it?"

"Oprah Win-what? What she win?" I ask.

Zenab laughs. "I don't know if you are funny on
purpose or just ignorant? Anyway, Oprah? She is
this Black American talk show host? She's so cool!
Like. I love how, despite a tough childhood, she
made something of herself out of literally nothing.
Plus, she's, like, so giving and inspiring?"

I yawn, not caring for this Oprah this or that. I
just want to write my book.

"So . . ." Zenab plucks her hair out of her face,
eyes shining like Ms. Tia's teeth. "On the journey

here, I kept thinking that if I don't end up becoming a computer scientist—that's what my father wants—then I could like have my own talk show one day? Does anyone have a phone? I keep asking as if that would somehow make a phone appear. I, like, really need to call my dad. He needs to know how sorry I am."

I sense her spirit sinking, so I ask: "What is a talking show?"

Zenab smiles a sad smile, biting her bottom lip as if she needs to think. "I really need to tell my dad I am sorry. He doesn't know I am here and I wish I could call him. I promised never to disappoint him." Before I can ask her why her father didn't know why she is here, she claps her hands. "Oh, I know! We can do it now! I will be like Oprah!" She points at me. "Adunni. You, you can transcribe the show!"

"I can what?"

"Write down what happens! That way, the transcript can be sort of my own book!" She points at Efe. "You? You could film the show, but you can literally also be the music director and producer and also be a guest?" She turns to Hauwa, says something, and Hauwa nods, standing to her feet like a robot, and begins to shift the wooden benches and arrange it in a line-by-line like we are in a classroom: five benches at the back, two in front for the teacher.

"Chichi?" Zenab says.

"I am waiting for my husband," Chichi whispers, without looking up from plucking her wrapper.

"Fine," Zenab says. "Will you tell us about him? Will you be the first guest on my show?"

It takes a moment, but when Chichi looks up, her eyes are bright. "I can tell our love story?"

"You can! Er . . . Older Woman?" Zenab points at the woman with no name and shouts at her: "Will you . . . ?"

"I am not interested," the woman shouts back, biting into her plantain. "I have nothing to say to you children."

"Oh, but you've got to be a part of us!" Zenab puts her hands together like as if to beg. "Pretty please with a chewy cherry on top? Come on! It'd be fun! Plus, we literally have hours until the judgment thing, so we might as well, like, make the best of our time together? Please?"

The woman puts her plantain down. Nods. "I will spare my time to be the watcher of you children. Finish."

"The audience?" Zenab nods. "We're good with that, right? We are! Great! Awesome! Now everybody take your position. Adunni! You sit there in front of Hauwa and transcribe for the book?" She laughs a tinkle of a laugh, and my heart grows more warm, happy. "You have enough paper? No? Shame. Well. Use a leaf, then. Pretense is literally the next best thing to reality. And you, ma'am? You won't give us a name, so can I call you, uh, Lady Grumps? Why, because you sure are grumpy! Happy with that? No? Well, you do need a name, so Lady G it is. Can you, like, maybe sit behind Adunni?"

I am surprised when Lady G smiles a little before picking herself up and coming to sit behind me, but the bench is too small for her buttocks, it rolls away, and she laughs a shock of a laugh as her buttocks hits the floor.

"Actually, Efe," Zenab says. "Pick up that stone, will you? Awesome! Now hold it like a camera. Why are you frowning? No frowns allowed out here, folks! Only smiles! And, Efe, you will be the star of the show, so do smile! Okay? Everybody set? I will be Oprah. No, actually, there is only one Oprah, but I can be like her! What will be the name of my show?" She taps a finger on her chin, thinking. "How about **The Zee-Zee Show**?"

Me and Efe, we clap, and burst into another laugh at how we are both clapping at the same time. "**The Zee-Zee Show** of Ikati Forest TV," I say. "I like it!"

I am so happy at how the focus is shifting from fear and worry, at the cloud of small joy that is filling us instead of sorrow.

Zenab nods. "Good! When it is my turn to tell my story, one of you will interview me? Okay? Okay!" She arranges her hair, her scarf, making pretend to paint her lips with her fingers, to pat powder on her cheeks. She walks back to near the

trees, then walks forward into the top of the circle of sand, tipping on her toes, as if she is having
one leg instead of two.

"Music please!" Zenab shouts, looking all at once
very serious.

Efe cups a palm over her mouth like a speaker:
"Dum-dum-dum! Ladies and ladies! This is Ikati
Forest TV! Welcome to **The Zee-Zee Show!**"

Zenab bows and waves as if she is waving to five
hundred of us and not just five of us sitting on a
forest bench. She sits on the first bench in front,
crossing her legs under her wrapper and pressing her
fist to her lips like a microphone.

She begins to speak: "Tonight, on this special edition of **The Zee-Zee Show**, we have
many special guests! Please join me in welcoming Efe! And Chichi! And Hauwa! And Adunni!
And . . . Lady G!"

We all clap, making a hoot, drumming our hands
on our thighs.

"And the very first guest is Chichi! Come up here,
Chichi!" Zenab pats a hand on the bench next to
her. Chichi struggles to stand, to sit.

I pick up a stick, twist a sleepy paw-paw leaf from
the branch of it, and pretend it is a paper and the
stick is the pen, and with it, I begin to pretend to do
the transcript work for **The Zee-Zee Show.**

||||||||||||||||||

ON WHAT HAPPENED TO YOU

Life is not too much about what happened to
you, but about how you answer the question of
what happened to you.
There is a simple English word for
this thing: re-action.
How do you re-action to what happened to you?

—THE VERY IMPORTANT SMALL BOOK OF
LIFE'S LITTLE WISDOMS BY ADUNNI

TWELVE HOURS TO MIDNIGHT

CHICHI

Transcript of The Zee-Zee Show on Ikati Forest TV

Zee-Zee: Welcome, everybody! I've already told you how special tonight's show is!

I literally cannot wait because at the end of the show, you'll find a special box under your seats. Do not look at it or open it until after the show! This is going to be very exciting. Our first guest is Chichi! Chichi, welcome to the show. Are you comfortable?

Chichi: I don't want this talk to be long. My husband is coming to take me away.

Zee-Zee: Of course, Chichi. We'll keep it short. Can you tell the audience a little bit about yourself?

Chichi: My name is . . . Chioma. Which is Chichi for short. They born me in the east. I went to primary school. Saint Agnes Ekiri. I did small secondary school. Government College Ekiri. I met my husband, Zuke, a farmer in the—

Zee-Zee: An incredible introduction, Chichi! But you are running ahead here. We will get to your husband, I promise. Tell us first? About your family? The audience would like to hear it. Right, audience? They are nodding! They are dying to know! Well, not literally!

Chichi: My father has seven girls and two boys. We did not have plenty money. My father send the girls to secondary school and stop. The boys, he send them to polytechnic. After I stop schooling in my final year of secondary school, I started selling groundnuts to help my parents. At first, I was sad. I wanted to go to hairdressing school or to find apprentice work. Maybe become something great, I don't know what. But I met my husband, Zuke, when I was nineteen. The day I met him, I knew what I wanted out of life: to become his wife.

Zee-Zee: That is, like, so romantic, Chichi. How old are you now?

Chichi: My age? Twenty-one. Me and Zuke, we been in our marriage now for two years. Two years of joy and plenty happiness. He . . . Please! Don't hold your hand up to stop me from talking of Zuke! He likes it when I talk of him. What time is it? He will soon reach here. I am not meaning to cry.
He does not like it when I cry. He said he will get here before midnight to stop this sacrifice. We have plenty of time till then. I know he is on his way.
The travel from Ekiri, our village, is just two hours from here.

He is very handsome, Zuke. He is thirty years and a pig-farmer with two small lands in Ekiri. After me and him we married, he said I can relax myself from selling groundnuts in the hot sun. He started to take care of me. He will wash my hair and my cloths and cook for me. You see this color-yellow nail paint on my legs? My Zuke paint it for me. He cooks and cleans and works very hard. Zuke, my husband, he has many dreams for us! He said we should take our time to born children so that we have enough money to send them to school. He—

Zee-Zee: All right! I am, like, **so** sorry to interrupt, Chichi. All of this sounds like a lovely love story! Very lovely! Can I, like, ask exactly why you are here? I mean for the sacrifice tonight?

Chichi: Why I am here? Excuse me. I don't know.
I just find myself in a bus this morning, coming

here. Someone said we must sacrifice. I did not do anything wrong. Excuse me, but I am not a part of all of you. Zuke is on his way. He would have come with me, but he went to buy meat pie for me. It is my best food: the meat pie from Mimi Foods on Obote Road in Ekiri with extra potato. Zuke went to buy some for me because I was hungry for it. Did I tell you about when Zuke plaited my hair in Ghana weave **shuku** style? Nobody taught him to—

Zee-Zee: Chichi. You, like, don't know why you are here? Or you don't want to share with us?

Chichi: I don't know why I am here.

Zee-Zee: Oh . . . Okay. Fine. On to my next question: What are your dreams, Chichi? What would you love to become in life? Like, if nothing, absolutely nothing, could stop you, where would you be right now? Or in five, ten years? Share it with our audience! They want to know, right? Right!

Chichi: Please. Excuse me. I already been become what I want to become: Zuke's wife. Excuse me. I am tired of talking. I need to sit down and wait for my husband. Excuse me. Bye-bye.

Zee-Zee: Uh, sure. Of course. Can we clap for the wonderful Chichi? What an incredibly enthusiastic

guest! Who do we have next? Efe! Can we stand
up to welcome Efe to the show? She's Efe, the
Superstar Oscar-Winning Actress-to-Be! Just take
a look at her cat-walking? She's hot! She's fire!
Here she comes!

TIA

Iya lives in a dark, dank bedroom flung to the far
end of a corridor.

There is no door. Inside is a square space with a
hole carved into the wall for a window, from which
the arched back of the man who killed the goat
comes to view, his arms moving up and down in a
sinister slicing motion. Kayus shuffles in. I tiptoe
in behind him, noticing that the room is swathed
in the scent of menthol, fermented yeast, moldy
clothes, stuffed secrets, death.

There are rows of clothes hanging across a pole
that runs from wall to wall, a door handle peeking from behind. An open, tattered suitcase with a

broken zip sits on the floor, beside a polythene bag stuffed with empty cans of Peak tinned milk, Milo hot chocolate, tomato puree, Geisha sardines. The woman, Iya, wizened and balding and atrophied from disease, is lying on a yellow foam mattress as thin as a slipper sole, a wooden walking stick with a curved handle beside her like an extra leg. She is staring through us, muttering incoherently. Every breath is a protracted, tremulous effort. Her eyes are glued shut with green mucus, feet with overlapping toes twisting toward each other, peeking from underneath the faded ankara fabric covering the rest of her body. The fan blowing at her feet struggles to oscillate, sputtering as it makes its rounds, circulating humid, recycled air.

Kayus lies flat with his arms spread out, touching his forehead to the concrete floor in a greeting, and without rising, he says something in Yoruba.

Iya makes a slapping sound with her mouth. "She can sense you," Kayus says. "She say you smell of stranger. Iya, Miss Tee-Yah, who is the friend of Adunni from Lagos, is not able to speaking Yoruba." He switches to Yoruba, while Iya keeps her head tilted toward him, listening intently, saying nothing. Finally, he falls silent and pushes himself up to his knees.

"I been waiting," the woman says in English, and I startle. "For you. I was going gone. But. The spirit of her mama is not letting me enter the gate.

She keep saying I wait for the woman and the child. To tell the story I been keeping in my mind for plenty years."

Happy carefree laugher drifts in from outside.

"Tell her Adunni can't come," I whisper. "That we are here to help Adunni. That it's urgent." I ought to have asked how unwell Iya is, if she's taking medication, what the nature of her illness is.

"We are here," Kayus says, dusting the smudge of sand from his forehead. "This Miss Tee-Yah, she will collect the story, help us find the real-blood father of my sister." He's looking at me, as if this information is for my benefit. He turns to look at the woman. Bows his head toward her and speaks what I assume is profound gratitude for her patience, for struggling to hold on, for not dying. I'm assuming. For all I know, he could be telling her what an absolute idiot I've been.

"She will tell us the story," Kayus says. "She will give us the name of the man when she finish telling the story. I will tell her to make it hurry because we don't have plenty time."

Iya says more stuff, slurring her speech in parts like something's triggered the slow-motion functionality in her voice box. She looks at me, and I stand with my arms behind my back, feeling trapped, ensnared by the attention of her sightless gaze.

"Sit down," she says. A command. She tilts her head to where Kayus is crouching. "Kayus, look the back of my head. You see a cup of **agbo**. Bring, let me drink for power. I need power for this talk."

Kayus crawls to a spot behind her mattress and picks up a metal cup full of brown water, floating leaves dancing at the surface. He tenderly places a hand behind her bald head and puts the cup to her lips. She bends her head, slurps, closing her eyes in a gradual swallow. She repeats the act twice, settles her head back on the pillow. Her eyes remain closed.

I rest my back to the wall and listen to raised voices in the corridor, arguing, in pidgin English, over a bucket of water, whose turn it is to fill a water tank. There is the subtle sound of some-one else sweeping the floor, a song of gratitude in mezzo-soprano.

Finally, Iya coughs. "Open the door of your ears wide and listen well-well," she says, speaking slowly, every word squeezed through the narrow crevice between breath and memory. "The story is starting from the year of 1992. The year Idowu was **fit-teen** years of age."

"Idowu?" I say in a barely audible voice.

"My mama," Kayus says, coming to sit beside me. "That's my mama's name."

She pushes herself up a little, folds her pillow under her head, to prop herself up. There's more strength in her voice, countenance. That stuff must be Red Bull on stilts.

"Now," she says, coughing, clearing her throat. "Kayus. Come here and drink all of this water." She nods at an opaque metallic bottle by her feet. It's hard to tell what's inside. Kayus looks at me askance. I shrug.

"Drink it," she says, "or else I don't say one word."

Kayus crawls to the bottle, twists the cover open, and takes a sip. He makes a face like he's tasting something putrid, decayed, and knocks the rest back. I half expect him to drop dead, but he crawls back to sit beside me and nods at Iya.

Iya raises her head in my direction. "The two both of you, close your eyes a moment. You closing it? Good. I sense it from here, the curtain of your eyes closing. Take my hand in your hand, hold it tight, and come with me, let us walk back-back to the year when Idowu, the most beautiful **pickin** you ever see on the face of the earth, was just turning **fit-teen** years."

IYA

You see her in the looking-glass of your mind?
   Good. I see her too.

See her skin.

Feel it.

Feel it in your hand like the buttocks of a new-born, the soft, party-cloth satin, the color of the sand around the mouth of a beach.

She's smiling.

You see her teeths? The shape of a cowrie. The too-white color of the beads roundabout the neck of a queen.

Her name is Idowu, the last born of five, the only girl-**pickin** in her family. They live in a house the **sliver** color of the hair on my head, set back from the river of Dende, like a stone hanging around the neck of the river. She have four brothers. Those four boys have the curse of a angry madness and of the hard heart of Yeye, their mother.

But Idowu? **Oti o.** Not her. Idowu take up her father's quiet spirit. She rather eat up her words and swallow it than to talk it. Her heart and mind be ever afraid to say what she think. Not like Adunni with her quick mouth. Not like Yeye, Adunni's . . . what is English word for **iya'ya?** Or **iya agba?** Gran— What you call it? Ah. Gran. Ma.

Thank you.

Idowu is not like Yeye, Adunni's granma, who have the kind of anger, the words of fire from a mouth so wide, it can roast up a **elefant** when she vex.

Now her father? Hmm. You ever meet a man that will just be looking you like **mumu** if you slap his face? Smash him with a branch of a tree or rub pepper on his back, and the man will not answer you one word. **Lai-lai.** Never.

Yeye and me, we are good of friends even though she is more old than me by a few years of age. Me and her been selling side by side for years. She sell puff-puff, hot and sweet, and I sell my **zobo** drink and other leaf drinks for medicines.

Around that time, Akin, my husband, a good man, he die of a blood-boiling sickness. I think you English people call it pressure high blood? High blood pressure? Ah. Thank you.

The pressure slap him in the heart, strike him

dead in the middle of the night. The people of his village want to make me suffer for him dying, so I run to Dende, a small village not too far from Ikati.

I hide myself in Yeye's house, and she—bless her sharp-mouth soul—she give me a place to sleep, food to eat. I share a room with Idowu, her girl-**pickin**, after her four boys were going away to live with a— What is English for **babalawo**? Medicine man? Healer? A man to make better their sick, angry mind?

Idowu was the beating heart of her baba.

I never seen a father love his girl-**pickin** like that. But since she was a small **pickin**, he be always saying it, talking in his quiet voice, saying that the beauti-fulness of Idowu is both a blessing and a curse. He didn't tell a lie. Idowu, back then, was so beautiful, she always be pulling all sorts of mens to her like houseflies to shits. But her baba was always quick to say no. He didn't—

❀

TIA

"Why?" I cut in, wishing I had a pen and paper to write this stuff down, capture the story in its most accurate, raw form. "Why did her father not want her to get married? I assume it was a thing back then, right? I mean, it still is, in many parts of the world. Adunni's own father married her off to

Morufu last year, so child marriage, as vile as it is, as flawed as the rationale behind it is, is not a big deal for some people, right? So why did her father not want it at that time?"

Iya glares at me through her sealed-shut eyes like I've pissed her off with the interruption.

"**Wo . . . Wo bi**," she says. "Look a-here this way. You keep shut your mouth and listen well until I finish. You hear me now? The drink inside of me is running fast, and soon I have no power to keep talking. I am tired of this world. The fighting each other, the everyday killing, the no-love and wicked things we share, the way we suffer other peoples. I want to off the load of this story so I can journey with no load. You keep shut your questions and let me talk finish. Now. Where I was before you bring your pencil-mouth to cut my thinking?"

||||||||||||||

ON LIFE
Life is a mess—it comes at you how it wants
to, when it wants to, and as loud or as quiet as
it wants . . . Even if you squeeze your buttocks
to keep it quiet, it can still disgrace you and
loud itself.
So, mess freely and laugh freely, live freely.
Hold nothing back.

—THE VERY IMPORTANT SMALL BOOK OF
LIFE'S LITTLE WISDOMS BY ADUNNI

IIIIIIIIIIIIII
EFE
IIIIIIIIIIIIII

Transcript of The Zee-Zee Show on Ikati Forest TV

Zee-Zee: I tell you, the first time I saw our next guest? With her dyed-blond hair and the whole feisty look thing going, I knew she was so special! Efe. Please can you stop dancing and come up here to take a seat? Oh. I think we have someone else joining us in the circle? Who is it? Kike? I am sorry, Kike, but is it okay for us to do this? Can we carry on? We literally need to do this to keep our minds occupied? Oh. You'll sit with us and listen? Great! This is great! You are awesome, Kike! Awesome! Can we all clap for you joining us? Thank you, Kike.

Could you maybe translate for some of the girls? Perfect, thank you. Right. Back to you, Efe. So. You had the most fascinating introduction earlier on. You said you are pregnant for two men. How is that so? Why are you here?

Efe: I need to smoke **ciga**. Anybody have two Benson? Why are you all looking at me wicked? Is **ciga** not good for baby? No **ciga**? No shakings! Any whiskey? **Ogogoro?** No? This place is dry **abeg**! In that case, can I rap?

> **Yo!**
> **My name is Efe, and I am a popping pop!**
> **I'm sitting on this rock!**
> **Flexing like a flock!**

Zee-Zee: Efe, please. Can you answer my questions? Wait. Are you . . . crying? Efe? Are you okay? Do you need a moment by yourself?

Efe: No! I am fine! I just sometimes cry when I am tired. My story? Ah. My story is simple. I was born in Middle Belt, and I have four brothers. Like many of us, my father died when—

Zee-Zee: Uh. One thing though. My dad is not dead, Efe. He's alive. I just wanted to say that. I need to call him. Are you sure none of you has a phone?

Efe: My father died when I was six. My mother did not have money to care for the rest of us, so she send me to live with her sister, my aunty in a village near Cross River. There, my aunty . . . hmm.

She suffered me, eh. Showed me hot pepper! She said I was always following boys. Yes, I like following boys, but must she beat me? Even a goat cannot take the kind of suffering she suffered me. See. Let me show you my hands. Look at this line crossing this one? My aunty used a hot iron to burned it there on my skin. You see this mark behind my ears like the shape of a bottle-cover? That one, she used hot spoon to press it there, tumbled hot tea over my head because I mistake and put salt inside her tea instead of sugar. Okay. It was not a mistake.

But eh! My whole body is like a map of her suffering. The suffering was so much that one day, I ran away and found myself in another town. There, I met one woman. I call her Madam K. Madam K said she can help me with a job. A housemaid job. I was happy because I was thinking my life is going to be better. Only for me to see that the job is not anything housemaid. The job . . .

Sorry.

I . . . cannot . . . I feel like to rap.

Can I sing or rap instead of telling this stupid story of me?

Zee-Zee: Your story is not . . . It is so not stupid.
Girls, can we, like, clap to encourage her? That's it,
girls! A big clap. More, more! That's it, keep it going!
Go, Efe! You've got this!

Efe: Stop all this clapping please. Thank you. I
am not crying. Crying is for weak people. I am
not weak. I am big superstar. I was talking about
the job.
    The job.
    It was in a big house. Cement building. No
paint. Big compound, farmland at the back. Ten
bedrooms. I think it was a small school before.
    This house was full of girls. About twenty,
twenty-one of us. Some from the age of thirteen.
They—I mean Madam K and her workers—they
locked us girls in a room and every day . . .
    Every day . . . **Chai.** Please can I rap? I want
to sing.

Zee-Zee: Can I hold your hand, Efe? Will that make
it easy to talk? That's it, Efe. Take it one by one.
Don't rush yourself. We are listening.

Efe: It is . . . It is hard to think back to that time.
Give me one minute. No shakings! Leave my hand
alone. I don't need nobody to pity me. I can talk now.
They—I mean Madam K and some other women—or
did I already say that part? They put us in a room.

Every day, different men will come in and force themselves to sleep with us. Every day. Different men. Different smells. Piss. **Ciga.** Gin. The perfume of their wife.

So . . . many.

But me? Efe-the-Superstar? Not me. Me, I fight them all. I bite them and scratch them and kick them until they beat me back and black my eyes.

Sorry. Give me time.

Has this thing happened to you before? You will be thinking of a memory of a wound and the body part starts paining you?

My eyes is paining me a little. Let me . . . close them, rest them small. That is better. I am okay now. No shakings!

Once one of us girls is pregnant, they will take us out of the room and give us to a midwife to keep watching us until when we born our baby.

When the baby is born, they snatch up the baby and sell it to a rich family that is having problem of having babies. That place is a simple marketplace of babies. Only that we, the container of the babies, they promised us that if we born a boy, they will pay us money and release us to go. Plenty millions.

The day I heard that, I relax myself. Millions for a baby boy? No shakings! I stopped fighting the men. I got pregnant.

A boy! I was so happy when they collected the boy and sell it to a rich family.

I was thinking that after this, I can be free to pursue my dream to be actress. I can be free to go. With the money, I will go to acting school, I can travel to audition.

But no. They kept me there. Locked up. They say I have a good body for borning boys. They want me to give birth more and more. They bring more men.

More and more. Coming in. Going out.

Every week, the midwife will do test of pregnant. She will put a cup and stand in front of us and watch us piss, because sometimes the girls that want to run away and escape with their baby will use another girl's piss to lie that they are not pregnant. Other times, the midwife will dig her hand inside of us, to check if we are already carrying baby.

The second time I was pregnant, I vexed and said no! No more using me as baby-machine for no money.

Last month, Madam K sent me to collect antibiotics medicine from the pharmacy in town for one of the girls. I take my chance and escape from there and find my way back to my mother in our village.

I told my mother that I don't know the father of my baby. I told her it is one man or two men or three men. Or five men. I don't know. You ask why I am here? I true-true don't know. My mother said my life is bad, dirty, full of rubbish men touching me, and that I must come for sacrifice in Ikati because my father was from here before he died and that his brother will carry sacrifice for me tonight.

After the sacrifice, my mother wants me to born the baby and leave the child for her. I don't know what will happen after, but I know this. I will never stop pursuing my dream. Not just for me, but for this baby in my stomach, because one day, I will come back to my village and take my baby and give him or her better life. I swear it on my life!

My throat is scratching me please. If I cannot have **ciga**, can I rap another song? Or sing? Who wants to dance?

Zee-Zee: Efe . . . I am so very sorry for what you've been through.

Efe: Sorry for what? Me? Pocket your sorry! All of this is so that I can have a sweet story to tell. After this baby is born, after all this troubles, I become an actress! Every one of you: Look my face. Remember me. Remember me because one day you will turn on your TV and you will see this face on it! I take a bow! CUT!

||||||||||||||||

ON DREAMS
Chasing a dream is like a new-born baby learning to walk.

You will stagger many times and fall down, but
one day, if you don't give up, you will crawl,
walk, run, climb, and maybe even fly.

—THE VERY IMPORTANT SMALL BOOK OF
LIFE'S LITTLE WISDOMS BY ADUNNI

Aha! I remember now.

I was talking about Adunni's **baba agba**. What is English for it? Grandfather? Yes, thank you. You see, he was not like the other mens back then, or even some of the mens now, who see a girl as a shoe you can wear and rough up and change anyhow. He been always wanting to send his **pickin** go to school. Sorry for my not-so-good English. Like Kayus and many of us, we learn small of it in small school. Throw the rest away inside the dustbin of life. The English I know, is Adunni that teached me many of it. She teached me how to read too. Count naira money, do plus and minus.

On the night Idowu was turning **fit-teen** years of

age, a man by the name of Festus Adebiyi, a man full of no shame and no hair, gather all of his fifty years of age with his two smelling legs and bring it come to Idowu's house. Why? Good question.

He bring hisself, along with two baskets of fresh tomato and one basket of yam, to ask for the hand of Idowu in marriage.

I remember that day like yesterday. The time was around thirteen to six. The sundown. Air the color orange-yellow of a ripe mango. Me and Idowu, we hide ourselfs in the back of the paw-paw tree in their compound, watching this man Festus, a rich man (he have a snail farm, and he was building hisself a hut, the second one), tell Idowu's mama and baba that he want to marry her. See, this man with no shame have four wifes already, and he have goats and cows. What he is looking for another wife for?

But Yeye, Idowu's mother, was wanting her **pickin** to marry. This Festus been already ask for Idowu to marry him when she was just around ten years. Her baba say god-forbid it. So that night, Festus put the basket of food down and say that the gift of foods is a final warning. He give them one day to talk their yes or their no—yes for him to marry Idowu.

Me and Idowu, we stand, our back to the paw-paw tree, which was bleeding a white-milky gum down the back of it, and watch how her baba give the baskets of tomatoes a long look before he shoot up his left feet to kick one of the baskets to the side. All of the tomatoes vomit out from the mouth

of the basket, cover the whole ground. Ah. Never
seen Festus so mad. He look the sea of tomato on
the ground, some bursting, painting the ground
red with **jui-ice**, and make a promise to never come
back to ask for Idowu's hand in marriage. He tell
Baba-Idowu to marry his **pickin** hisself.

Us, with our hearts banging together and making
music under that tree, we watch as Festus march off
like a horse, slapping his **fila** on the back of his head
and cursing.

After the sun rest hisself to sleep, we hear Yeye and
Baba fighting. We listen to them fight a big fight.

Yeye, Adunni's granma, she was a angry fire! I
hear her now. Shouting: "Idowu is **fit-teen**!" I hear
her feet slapping the cement floor of their parlor,
knocking down the lantern, the candle, the snuff-
box Baba-Idowu use to sniff up his nose. "Her
age-mates have all marry!" she shout. "All of them.
Idowu is the last. You think her beauty is forever, Baba-Idowu? Eh? Beauty is like a flower-o.
A sunflower that shine in the morning and die at
night. Soon she be old! Soon her menses dry up,
her breast squeeze like orange with no water, her
skin fold like the newspaper I use for my puff-puff.
Soon she be too-too old to marry! What you want
to do with her? Marry her yourself? Tell me! You
know Labake? Her best of friend? She is marrying
Morufu! A young-boy taxi driver!"

Idowu's mother was shouting loud, her voice
stretch-thin from the pull of her angry, her words

flying out of her mouth like a bombs, blowing up Baba's face.

"You already chase off five mens," Yeye say.

Idowu lay stiff beside me—I don't think she know just how many mens been coming and going.

Baba-Idowu answer his wife with his quiet voice, speaking as if he borrow it from somewhere afar. "You want her to do quick and marry. Do quick and born. Do quick and do this and that. All for what? My **pickin** can go to school. She don't have to go back to learn ABCs, but she can learn maybe to write shorthand, type, small English. You know Mrs. Henshaw? She is a Lagos typing teacher from Pitman. She open up a typing school in town. Maybe Idowu can learn typing and go to ministry and become a **sek-ree-tree**?"

I look Idowu: "You want go to school? You want me to beg your Yeye to let you go to school? Or you want marriage?"

Idowu, her mind is like a water under a soft breeze. She shift any which way it blow, dancing left and right. One minute, she say, "Yes, Iya. I don't know what typing mean, but I can paint lipstick and go to office." The next minute, she say, "Or I can marry. I don't mind it, Iya. I don't mind school too. Any which one you give me, I take it."

So, I tell her this, I say, "Marriage is a deep well of love of two peoples. You dig the well with your two hands, pour your loads of life inside the well, drag it about with you. Why you want to drag a load with a man with four wifes? Or with a man you didn't love? You need a friend, Idowu. A man you and him can forever be friending each others, helping each others so that the load of life is easy to carry. That kind love is beautiful. It take time to come. You must know yourself first. Grow in mind and body. For now, use your time to learn typing work. Find a job inside town, a working office-job. Wash your English, make it clean, become a big woman with big money. One day, that type of love will find you. What you think?"

Idowu take my hand and press it flat on the heart of her chest so I can feel the leg of her heart kicking. She say, "I can find that true love you talk of, but will Yeye let me wait for that love? Will Yeye let me learn typing?"

I wait until Idowu is sleeping before I pick myself from the mat and—

Kayus, bring me my **agbo** water from behind my head.

My power to talk is finishing.

❀

Thank you for waiting.

That night.

When Idowu was sleeping very deep, I climb down from the mat, wrap myself in my night-cloth, and on my way to the outside, I see Baba-Idowu sitting in the parlor chair, his two hands holding his head. He was in deep sorrowing, maybe full of regret that he say no to the marriage of Idowu, or maybe just sad that he didn't have money to send Idowu to school. I run to the outside, where the moon was big and round and filling up the whole sky.

It was a cold night, the color of a purple-blue bulb under the white globe of the moon. My whole bones was a shiver and shaking as I find Yeye sitting under the paw-paw tree, on the **apoti**, which is a bench of wood. She was talking to herself, saying angry things about her husband.

Till this day, I wish in my heart of hearts that she don't be rushing to say angry words because I know the Sprits of the Full Moon is always walking up and down to be collecting words a person is saying at night and cause it to happen.

When I reach Yeye, she was breathing fast and hard, looking left and right, slapping her leg. There was a . . . What is **garawa** in English? Bucket? Basin? Yes . . . a basin in between of her legs, a bag of flour beside it. I know she was thinking to mix her flour for puff-puff, so I collect the yeast, the sugar, and a bowl of water from the backyard kitchen and carry it to her, and sit on my bench, and look my friend eyes-to-eyes.

"Yeye? Calm yourself," I say. "And hear your husband."

Yeye snatch a cloth hanging from the hand of the tree, shake it, and spread it on her knees. "It is night," she say. "You must wake up early to sell your leafs. Leave me with my puff-puff."

"Idowu say she will learn typing work," I say as Yeye begins to pour flour on the cloth, shake it up and down. I keep my eyes on the black ants dropping to the ground like shit. I feel the heat of her eyes on me that night. I still feel it now, burning inside the middle of my head.

"Iya," Yeye say, "my Idowu is **fit-teen**! Five mens come and go. Five! Mens with strong blood. My husband send them packing. Which school is she going? For what?" Her words were twisting inside each other, like a singing-song.

"She is a good child," I say. "Your husband have a good mind for her."

Yeye raise her eyes to me as if I stain her white soul with my words. "You mind your family-matter. You hear me? Mind your matter!" She hiss, move the cloth to check the flour. "Give me sugar. Five hand-cups."

I cup the sugar, feel it in my fingers, rough like sand. We stay quiet like that, as she mix the flour and add the yeast and cover it with a cloth, until Baba-Idowu come to stand in front of us, his back to the hills of Ikati.

"Iya, thank you. I hear the words you been telling your friend. Thank—"

"She cannot go to school," Yeye shout, and the rest flour climb up like a cloud in the air. "Where will you find the school fees money for typing school?"

"I sell our chair and tables in the house." Baba was talking to his chest, quiet-quiet. "I sell it all for Idowu to go to school."

"No!" Yeye push up herself to her feet, and her whole basin of flour scatter to the floor. "At what age? Answer me! At what age will Idowu learn typing work? Eh? It is too late! Let her marry. Let. This. Girl. Marry." She shout every word, clapping in the middle of each one.

Baba turn around, and before he reach the door, he look us both, say, "Over my dead body will my only girl marry at the age of **fit-teen**."

When he say that, I think of the spirits in the pocket of the night, catching his words and making it life.

I awake up at sunrise to feed the chickens and pluck my leafs for my medicine, and I find Baba-Idowu on the parlor floor, his eyes stiff like a looking-glass, mouth open, as if he was wanting to shout for help, just before the spirit of dead come and collect his soul.

||||||||||||||

ON SCHOOLING
Sending only boys to school is like
clapping with one hand.
Where is the sense in that?

Hear me this: Every single child is deserve
of a chance to go to school.
When you send a girl to school, her whole
village will eat the fruit of it, especially
including you, the sender.

—THE VERY IMPORTANT SMALL BOOK OF
LIFE'S LITTLE WISDOMS BY ADUNNI

‖‖‖‖‖‖‖

TIA

‖‖‖‖‖‖‖

And so Adunni's grandfather died," I mutter. "Death. Such a bloody bastard."

My eyeballs feel like I've plucked them—frozen solid—out of a deep freezer and smashed them into my eye sockets. It hurts to even think of blinking. There is an anxious tic at the pit of my stomach; a touch of grief for Adunni's grandfather, who died without fulfilling his dreams for his daughter. Clearly, Adunni inherited her grandmother's quick tongue combined with her grandfather's ambition. I exhale, glancing at my watch, as air sails out of my lungs, a cloud of steam over the picture of Idowu's life I'd painted in my mind with Iya's words.

I saw the butcher wandering off a few minutes ago, the dead goat slung across his neck like a giant wooly muffler, its blood dripping down the open gash around its neck. A spider clambers over the silk threads of its web in the corner behind the window, toward a trapped, twitching fly. An outside tap twists open, creaks closed. I stretch my legs out, giving them a shake to get the blood flowing, to ease the pins and needles.

Iya inhales, her abdomen pushing toward her spine. I look away, afraid she might give her last breath. But she's a tough cookie, this woman. I have a feeling this story is a lifeline, a drip bag feeding life back into her, giving her a reason to hold on just a little longer.

"Yes," she says. "Baba-Idowu, he die that night, just like that, a good man gone on his way. He was a man with no fire to fight. They bury him quick, sorrow over him for six months. Is Kayus sleeping?"

I check. The poor darling had slackened beside me, lulled to a near drowsy state by the whirring fan, the rhythm with which Iya told the story of his mother and grandmother. He makes a grunting sound in his throat now, as if to reassure us of his alertness. Poor thing's exhausted—who can blame him? I stretch my legs out, gently guiding his head to the cushion of my lap, flinching at a throbbing in my head, in the small of my back.

"Sleep," I say to Kayus, feeling a fierce and

sudden, familiar protectiveness grip me. He's just a child. "Sleep, okay? You have been very brave today. Your body is tired."

"The drink I give him is to make him sleep so me and you can talk," Iya says as Kayus yawns and shakes his head in protest. His eyes betray him. They flutter closed, open, closed. I bet he'll be asleep in less than five. I bet **I'd** be asleep in less than ten—sedative or not—if my mind weren't in a bloody turmoil.

"After the burying of Idowu's father," Iya continues, "Yeye make it a work to find a husband for Idowu. You see, after Baba die, the people of Dende, they were talking, saying Idowu is a real **emere**. A witch that bring bad luck. For the next one year, Idowu was following her mother up and down, learning how to fry puff-puff and selling. But inside of her, she have a hope that one day she will meet a man that will love her and marry her. Weeks and weeks pass, and no man was coming. Yeye keep going up and down Dende, begging for mens to marry Idowu. But all of them close the door on her face, one by one—"

"Can we, uh, fast-forward to the part where she meets Adunni's father? We need to find him, don't we? Where is he located?" I'd give a kidney to hear the entire story on a good day, but this is so not a good day, and time's ticking along like a bastard.

"You wear the cap of patient," Iya snaps. "I talk in my time."

"How long is this going to take?" I'm speaking in the gentlest tone I can muster, but inside I'm yelling, **Come on, woman!!** "We need to try and get back to Adunni. Can you, uh, skip . . . jump to the, uh, relevant parts?"

Iya purses her lips and starts to chew on air, saying nothing, bloody obstinate in her silence.

"Iya?" I press my hands together. "Please."

"I sense your vexing. The color of it is the black of evil. It cover my thinking. Make it hard to talk. Chase it first. Then I talk."

"Fine," I say, waving my arms manically in the air as if to ward off evil. "There. It's gone. Ready to carry on?"

HAUWA

Transcript of The Zee-Zee Show on Ikati Forest TV

Zee-Zee: I thought I could do this, but our stories are so hard to share! Our dreams even harder to bear. But we cannot give up, right, Adunni? You said so yourself. So, let's smile and clap because our next guest is only twelve years old. Her name is Hauwa. She doesn't speak English, so I'll translate for her. Oh. She's asking for us not to clap. Not to say anything. She wants absolute silence? Can we respect that? Okay? Great. I've got this. Actually, I haven't. I need a moment. A deep breath.

Here we go:

You. Hauwa.

You are twelve years old.

The first daughter of your parents.

You never went to school. You don't even have an interest in education. You love plaiting the hair of your younger sisters.

You love laughing in the evening with your family, bathing in the stream, helping your baba with farming and cattle.

You love food. Frozen milk soaked in sugar is your favorite.

You don't have a TV at home, but you love to watch TV.

Especially YouTube.

You are learning recipes, and so your favorite shows are the cooking shows on YouTube. You sometimes wander off to Barnaba Hair Beauty Salon in the town near your village, to watch the cooking videos on the phone of one of the hairdressers.

You . . .

You had hopes to one day meet a man that would cook for you. In return, you would write him love letters.

You are sometimes lazy, and this makes your mother angry with you. This, you think, is why she agreed for you to come here tonight. You already know your judgment. It is marriage. To a young Ikati chief. A man named Semi. Your father's friend.

A young man who sells in the same market as your father, and who once lent your father money to buy a cow.

One evening, your father sent you on an errand to fetch water from the next village. On your way back, you decided to wander off to town, to watch your favorite YouTube cooking show. You wish you hadn't. But you really wanted to learn how to make Chinese rice! You watched the show for an hour before you realized that the sky was black. You took off, running home, your heart pounding at how late it was.

You bumped into Semi, riding his motorcycle, on his way back from your house. He offered you a lift home, told you it was quicker, safer than walking. You agreed.

But Semi.

He did not take you home.

He turned into a side bush and tore your dress and he . . . raped you.

. . .

Semi raped you.

. . .

He left you to walk home, bleeding from in between your sore legs. At first your father was enraged. He wept and screamed and cursed Semi. He reported to the village council. They summoned Semi from Ikati and agreed to involve the state police. This was a crime, they said! He needed to be arrested. Punished. But Semi was remorseful.

He rolled on the mat and wept and begged for forgiveness. He offered your parents money and asked for your hand in marriage. He reminded them that your father owed him money for cows. He reminded them that no one would marry you. You, who were no longer a virgin, who had been defiled.

Your father, after much thinking, agreed.

Your world shattered.

You, at twelve, were being forced to marry a twenty-nine-year-old chief.

Your father is not happy about it, but he says it will cover your shame. You will have a husband, a crown on your head; his debt will be settled.

Your mother is troubled. She threatened to divorce your father if he allowed this marriage, but you knew she wouldn't because how would she take care of you and your siblings without Baba's contribution?

You have faith. Even if you don't understand why this is happening, you hope God will help you.

But . . .

You confess to me now that you are scared.

You are scared because you think this is going to destroy your family. You are sorry all of this has happened. You don't even understand why this is happening to you. Why your parents have sent you to Ikati tonight to sacrifice for the stain on you for no longer being a virgin, and afterward to be officially judged to become Semi's first wife. In a month's

time, you will move to his house here in Ikati. Away
from your siblings, away from your family.

You . . .
You never wanted much out of life. You didn't even
want to go to school.
All you wanted was to be a girl.
It is so simple.
Yet so hard.

IYA

J a-nu-ary.

Nine-teen . . . nine-ty- . . . something.

Was when Idowu fall inside a deep love with one young man that come visiting his grandmother who was living inside of Ikati. The boy hisself was from Lagos. Don't ask me of his name because I don't tell it until I finish my story. You hear me?

You see, in the one year since Idowu's father was dead, the whole of Dende village carry a bad story about him. Some say he have a accident and fall deep inside the well. Others say he kill hisself because his **pickin** is having a wicked man-killing spirit.

Idowu keep up the work of learning puff-puff. Soon she start to make it. I tell you, Idowu become so good at this puff-puff, mixing it with more sugar, adding fruits—sometimes a slice of orange or mango or paw-paw or a cup of groundnut, coconut milk. Sometimes she fry small stew, mix with onions and crayfish, add a slice of this or that, put it in a paper and sell it. She give her puff-puff a taste, wear a crown on it like a queen, put high-heel shoes on its feets. Soon all the villages begin to talk of Idowu's puff-puff.

In January of the next year, Idowu carry her puff-puff to the market.

A rich woman wearing costly cloth and shoe and driving a new motorcar buy one of Idowu's puff-puff, take a bite of it. She vex and buy the whole of it. She give Idowu three times money for it. She tell Idowu she is from Lagos, vising her mother, who is living in Ikati. That her mother is having eighty-five-years-of-age birthday party in her house in Ikati. Can Idowu fry puff-puff for the party?

Idowu say yes. The woman give Idowu more-more money and tell her she going to send a car to pick her. That night, Idowu was full of happy.

"Iya," she say, clapping her hands, "me cooking for her party!? Me? A rich people's party?"

The day of the party, Idowu wake up before the sun. The rich woman send her new motorcar—a blue 504—the nylon of brand-new still covering the seat of the car. Idowu wear her best dress, put a pink rose flower in her hair, wear her one shoe.

Me and Yeye, we wave and smile with all our

teeths as the rich woman's car carry Idowu go. At this party, one young man come to the backyard where Idowu was frying puff-puff and tell her he want to taste.

"Everybody is raving about it indoors," he say.

I remember it. She say the boy use the word "raving." Till today, I don't know what it mean.

The boy bite her puff-puff, close his eyes, and breathe in deep. When he open his eyes, he smile a wide smile, pick up a chair, and sit down, telling her he never seen a girl so beautiful. The boy can speak Yoruba, so the two of them get to talking and laughing like they been knowing each other for ten years.

This boy was twenty-one to her sixteen. A boy from Lagos. A good boy. For three hours, the boy sit there. Somes-times, he will stop talking, look her eyes, search it deep, and shake his head like he never seen this type of beautiful.

When the time come for Idowu to go home, the boy follow her in the car, and I meet him.

He tall—too tall if you ask me, but you don't ask me. Skin like the brown of a coconut. Smooth. Full of respecting, quick to bending his head to greet us.

Soon he be coming every evening at around six o'clock. He and Idowu, they will go to the mouth of the river and sit down and talk, holding hands, throwing stones in the water, fishing, swimming. Idowu can swim like a fish, so she teach him. He teach her some English, and she teach me too.

Sometimes I follow them, just to sit on a rock watch them afar, fill my own mind my own love with my husband, Akin.

I never seen a boy love a girl-**pickin** like that. Never.

After four weeks of staying in Ikati, the boy make a promise of his love to Idowu. He say he going to marry her and take her to Lagos and send her to school. Give her a good life. He say he going to wait four years for her to learn English, to learn a work like typing or hairdressing so that he too can finish his big un'versty school before they marry.

And Idowu say yes. That she will marry him. So—wait. Is Kayus sleeping deep? Check it for me. He is sleeping? You sure? Good. Because he is too small to hear this part of the story.

So.

My heart was full of so much hope for Idowu. I see the love-eyes the boy always use to look Idowu. I know he mean well for her.

And Yeye? Ah! She was so very happy! She jump up, dance and dance in the small parlor, thanking the spirit of Baba-Idowu. Me and Yeye and Idowu, we dance around the parlor—laughing like we drink too much palm wine. In the early morning, Yeye wake me up. She say she is having feelings to go to the house of the grandmother of the boy. She tell us that the boy's mother, who come visiting with him from Lagos, is also staying inside that house in Ikati. So, Yeye tell me she think it is a good time to meet his mother and even maybe his grandmother, the two both of them. Can I follow her?

I ask why.

She say we must to tell them about the dowry, and all the things they need for the marriage.

Hmm. What a mistake of a thing to do. We didn't know better. If we know, maybe we stay back in our house. Wait for them to come to us. But Yeye did not have a husband. She didn't want them to hear of how her husband die. So, she dress herself up nice, wear the best of **iro** and **buba** from the below of her cupboard. Me, I tie my **gele** and follow her.

Their house is the one on the hill. It stand up straight like a church-hat on the head of old woman. It been lockup since ten years or so back. We reach there, knock the gate, our heart kicking in our chest. When we enter, we stand side by side in a sitting room. Whole place look like the parlor of God. Everything new and gold, wearing the dress of too-much money.

When the mother of the boy see us as we are standing and catching a cold in the air-con, she ask if we want to come and do cleaning work? Or washerwoman, or house girl?

Together we shake our head no.

She eye us up and down. Ask us what we want.

Yeye clear her throat, say, "We are soon become in-laws. One family. Your boy-**pickin** is marrying my girl-**pickin**."

"In-law?" The woman sweep her eyes from the

no-shoes on my feet, to the tearing sandals on Yeye's feet, to her damask **gele** stiff on her head like she starch it and iron it, to the makeups on Yeye's whole face, the line of black on her eyes, the white lipstick on her bottom lip, make her look like she lick chalk for morning-food.

The boy's mother throw her head back and laugh.

At first me and Yeye we laugh too. Thinking she is happy that we are in-laws.

But this woman did not stop her laughing.

She laugh and laugh until we understand that she is not laughing a real laugh. That she is laughing a shock-surprise laugh, the kind of laugh that just come with no power to stop it.

She stop her laugh with a short cry and drag a breath. Look behind her shoulder, eyes on the staircase climbing up, and shout: "Son? Come out here! Some riffraffs are looking for you."

We smile, nod. Say yes. We are the riffraff in-law. We are happy to meet you. You know, we think that "riffraff" is a English word for Something That Travel from Far. We didn't know it was a curse.

The tall boy come out, see us, and bow his head. Soon he and his mama talk in big English. Talk. Talk. Talk.

My mind can never forget the words I catch from her:

"Riffraff."

"**Pour-ver-tee.**"

"**In-sail**" . . . or is it . . . "**in-sain**"?

"Ree-dee-ku-laws."

"Hin-fa-tu-hay-shun."

"Hill-lee-ter-rate."

"Hell is no"? Okay, is it "hell, no"? Thank for telling me correct thing. Now keep shut and let me finish this story.

I remember how the boy's mama face change from surprise to a fire angry.

"You are in love with what?" she shout. "You are just twenty-one! What do you know about love, son? What about Bunmi in Beer-meeng-ham? She is coming home next week. You've got a bright future ahead of you!"

The boy say, "I love Idowu."

"Idowu is a bloody **hill-lee-ter-rate**," the boy-mama say, her voice like the hiss of a snake. "You can't marry a girl like that, son. What's wrong with you?"

"I love her," the boy say, sounding so much like a small **pickin** that wants to cry. "She's wonderful. Beautiful. You said so yourself."

The woman vex so much after that. She march to the telephone sitting on a glass table beside the sofa and pick it up, slap her ears with it. Then she turn around the face of the phone, shout inside of it, and say, "Rex. Rio. Get in here NOW. Come chase these bunch of something-something bastard something the hell out of my mother's house."

I don't know plenty English, but I know "bastard," and I know who born me. My father was hunter. I am poor, but I am not a bastard. **Lai-lai.** Never.

I vex too. Tell her to don't call us bastard. To hear our story. The story of our two **pickins.**

Two giant-men come running inside, wearing red police uniform and holding belt and **kondo**-stick, face strong. They flog us with the belt until we are bleeding and falling on top each other and running for our lives. When we reach home, we meet Idowu at the door.

I tell her what happen because Yeye didn't have the power to talk. She just go inside and put a pot of water on the stove to boil for pressing her swelling, bleeding body.

"They say you don't go to school," I tell Idowu as I put medicine cream on my knees. "That you are too small for their son." As I was talking, the boy enter Idowu's house, tears running down his face. He must been following us behind as we was leaving his house.

He been crying too, full of sorrow.

"I love you and I am marrying you," he say to Idowu. He turn to me, bend his head in a sorry. "I am sorry, ma, about what happened at my house. I love Idowu and I'm marrying her. I'll go back to Lagos tomorrow to speak to my father. I'll come back in less than a month. I want to talk to my father to help. Promise me you will keep Idowu safe for me? Promise?"

I didn't able to promise one word. My mouth was

paining me from the flogging and Yeye was still
crying loud in the room.

I leave Idowu and this boy alone and enter the
room and lie down on the mat and close my eyes
and cry. For how they flog us like a goat, for not
having money. I hear Idowu tell the boy she is going
to kill herself if she didn't marry him. That she will
never love another man. That he is the owner of her
heart, the air inside her chest, the ball of her eyes.

I never seen a love so deep, so true, so sad, like the
love of the two both of them.

My eyes is beginning to see spirits flying outside
of my window. I already cross over, but Idowu, she
send me back, give me this story like a bitter-tasting
food to eat and vomit for you. The spirits been flying around me for one year, calling me come, but
Idowu keep pushing them back, waiting for the day
to tell this story.

Where is my water?

Bring it come-quick.

ELEVEN HOURS TO MIDNIGHT

ZENAB

Transcript of The Zee-Zee Show on Ikati Forest TV

Zee-Zee: What an emotional roller coaster this has been!

Does Lady G want to be interviewed? No? What's she saying, Adunni? That it's not our business? Fair enough. Do your thing, Lady G.

I **do** want to share my own story, so, Adunni, will you interview me? Shall we swap seats? No? All right. You literally sit there, and I'll stay right here, and you'll interview me, and I will interview you, and we can round it out with a dance, maybe a song from Efe?

I almost forgot! Afterward, we'll reveal the special box under your bench? It's a pretend box! I once saw Oprah do this on her show. Every guest had like this uber-special box, a gift under their seats, so I need you all to begin to imagine now that under that wooden bench is a special box. A gift from **The Zee-Zee Show** to the girls of Ikati forest. Okay? Fab! Awesome. This is so great.

Right! Adunni, are you ready? Pass the pretend-pen to Lady G to transcribe? It's the least she can do for us, right, Lady G? Pretty please with a chewy cherry on top? Is that a smile I spot on your face? Fantastic! Thank you, Lady G!

All right! Ladies and . . . ladies! Our final two guests are Adunni, our Wisdom, and myself!

But me first.

And you know I've got to do this the proper way, so I am going to get up and to walk in, and you'll clap for me while I take a bow? Okay? Awesome! Here I go! Adunni, announce my arrival, will you? Perfect! Now come on, girls, clap for me! Thank you!

Adunni: It is good very pleasure of meeting you, Zenab. My English is not like your own, so try and manage my small communications of it.

Zenab: That's perfectly fine! As long as we can communicate!

Adunni: Talk to us the . . . audiences. Why you are here? What village you come from? What is the story of your growing up?

Zenab: Well, I have a slightly different background . . . Scratch that. My background is **majorly** different from you all. My parents met when they were, like, really young. My father, a northerner, was a student teacher in a village secondary school, and my mother was selling, uh, some millet-drink thingy . . . My dad has a local name for it? But I can't for the life of me remember it now? Oh, what did you call it, Lady G? **Kunu**? That's it! Yeah.

Mum sold that **kunu** drink at the school where Dad taught. They met, she got pregnant and had me.

But Dad refused to marry her. He had just been short-listed to train in the Nigerian navy, and his future was, like, sorted. He also wanted an educated wife and all, and so he literally left.

I lived with my mother in her family hut in the north, where I learned to speak Hausa, which is, like, my mother tongue and all that. A week or so after my third birthday, Dad literally came back to get me from my mum. He was worried I would miss out on a quality education? To be fair, my mother still believes that Western education would make me stubborn and strong-headed and all that. So, I, like, lived with my father from the age of three, and he became literally my best friend. Dad refused to marry. He said another woman would probably mess things up between us, but he's had loads of girlfriends! Some are cool, others are just nasty.

Dad's now a high-ranking naval officer, and I don't, like, mean to brag, but I've always attended the best schools in the country, and I play the piano and the violin, and I am a chess champion, a brilliant orator, a prizewinning junior computer scientist.

For my ninth birthday, Dad got me a phone. With it, I taught myself to code. I am insanely good at playing video games. PS4, anyone? No? No one here has heard of Xbox? **Call of Duty**? **Tomb Raider**? Oh, crap! Anyway, so Dad was worried my love for games and stuff would become an addiction, so he decided to get me in on this programming course thing and told me to use that energy to learn to build stuff.

Last year, I built an app! It was a simple puzzle, a bit like **Candy Crush**, but that's not the point. Point is, I could build something with my own hands!

Anyway.

I am now, like, in the process of creating another app, but this time, to make a difference. I am going to help girls track their periods and body changes? Cool, right? I know! I think also that things like sanitary towels should be free for girls who cannot

afford it, so I'm, like, hoping my app would attract
sponsors who'd donate free pads to schools
in communities like this. Cool, right? I know!
Very cool.

I also want to have my own talk show before I
turn twenty-one, a bit like Oprah, and, like, literally
invite people to share their stories and inspire
the world?

Sorry, I need a moment to, like, to breathe?

I rushed all of that out because I am . . . This is
all, like, so strange? No offense to you guys and all,
but it's insane that I am here. Like. I literally don't
belong here.

Adunni: This is all very good but very plenty things.
Can you small your English because I can see
Kike is turning crazy mental with how to make
the exactly transcribing-explanations of your
big English.

Zenab: Oh, right. I'll try to speak a little less
complicatedly? I am sorry. Can I continue?

So, like.

While I lived with Dad, I'd often visit Mum. But
always, **always** with this Shrek-like armed escort
from the Nigerian navy! I hated the fact that my
father did not seem to trust me with my mother by
myself? I absolutely loved my stays with Mum—
her house is all right, I guess? Comfy enough
with a bit more than the basics. She married

this leather-merchant guy, and they live in a nice round house on a hill with their three kids. Now I absolutely adore my brothers and sister. And I love learning how to sculpt clay and sieve corn and all those villagey things some of you girls do! And that feeling of waking up to clean village air at the sound of a cock crowing at dawn? That's literally the most amazing feeling in the world!

But as I got older, Dad got increasingly uncomfortable with my visits to my mum. He felt I sounded a little different when I returned? Like, he felt I was being brainwashed? I mean. Like, he thought my mind was being altered? Sorry, Adunni, not sure how to better explain what "brainwashed" means?

Adunni: Brainwash. Is simple. It means they wash all your brain-sense away with soap and water.

Zenab: Yeah. Whatever. Dad did worry about me being different. Especially when I began to lose interest in finishing my computer projects? I wasn't being brainwashed! I just wanted to explore more creative things! Like, to learn to paint and sculpt and write scripts for my talk show? To weave baskets and learn a traditional dance and paint henna on my hands and all that, right? Fun stuff!

So fast-forward to last year, Mum calls Dad and asks when I'd visit. I hadn't been in like a year, and

Mum was missing me. Dad asked her to come to see me instead. He said he'd put her in a fancy hotel and all. She said she had a husband and three other children to take care of, and he could go eat his fancy hotel? Like.

Two weeks ago, Mum calls again, this time she's literally in tears, begging for me to visit? Dad again says no. I was so done with their crap, and so I called Mum back on my mobile phone and told her I'd come to her. It sounds crazy, but listen, girls, I am fifteen and able to make my own decisions?

I am not, like, proud of this next bit, but I stole cash from Dad and got myself on one of those buses to go see Mum. It was like the most amazing feeling ever? Like I was literally going on an adventure!

When I got there, I called Dad and told him I was so fine! I did not need him to send any escort from the army or naval office or whatever! Dad was pissed off at first, but he reluctantly agreed and said he'd allow me a week with them.

It was, like, literally the coolest thing ever: me on my own with Mum, minus Shrek dude.

Mum and my half siblings were so thrilled! But I noticed that my half sister, Hasina, did not seem so pleased. Actually, she looked quite upset. At me. For coming?! Like? She's one of my favorite people, so I didn't get her being all nasty and all.

I noticed too that Hasina was in, like, a lot of pain? She was literally limping when she crawled

into my room two nights ago to warn me to return
to Abuja.

When I asked why, she told me . . .

Adunni: She told you what, Zenab? Please don't cry.

Zenab: . . .

Adunni: Try, Zenab, try to find the words.

Zenab: Can I, like, take a break? You all sit tight and
think happy things, okay? I'll be right back, thanks!

IYA

A week after the boy go back to Lagos, a man by the name of Akala from Ikati come knocking. He stand in the door wearing a khaki short-knicker on his bowlegs, open wide his scatter-teeth, and ask for the hand of Idowu in marriage. I look this man that day, the hair on his chest gray, the toes on his feet like five fingers on a hand. There was dead in his eyes. Worse of all, he smell of **ogogoro** gin. "No," I say. "You cannot marry Idowu. First of all, you look like you are fifty years. Idowu is just sixteen and a half."

"I am thirty years," he say. "My first wife die three years back. I need a young wife."

I tell him to get out from our front, but Yeye hold up one hand.

"Let him marry Idowu," she say. She didn't for one time even look the man. She keep her head down to her laps, twisting her fingers in and out. "Take her away so I have peace. Her baba is dead. Her brothers have brain-angry problem. I am tired. Take her away before her beauty will dry up, before that rich boy will bring more trouble from Lagos."

And that is how Yeye and this Akala pick a date of marriage for Idowu. They agree everything before Idowu come back from the market.

That night, after Idowu finish baffing and settle on the mat, I tell her she is marrying a man by the name of Akala from Ikati. She wide her eyes, put two hands on her head, and say, "Me, marriage to Akala? Who is Akala? When?"

"Two weeks coming," I say, the most sad of all things I ever say.

I watch her with my heart breaking as Idowu press her two hands on her ears and scream so loud that her voice shake up the waters, the ground, the sky, and the most deep part of my tired soul. That night, something the shape and color of a laugh fall out from the heart of Idowu and die dead by my feet.

|||||||||||||

ON CHOICE
God gives all of us the freedom
to choose our choice.

You can choose to be happy. Or choose
to be kind, or to smile, or to give,
or to be at peace, or to dance.
I say, always choose a good choice.
But first choose common sense.

—THE VERY IMPORTANT SMALL BOOK OF
LIFE'S LITTLE WISDOMS BY ADUNNI

|||||||||||||
TIA
|||||||||||||

There are tears on Iya's cheeks.

Dried tears; a crusty, scaly path along her sunken cheeks. I consider consoling her, saying something nice, but I decide against it, and hobble back to sit after she takes another sip from her nearly empty cup. My back feels brittle, like a thin slab of ice, as I deliberate on Idowu's story. **Sixteen.** Same age I was when I first met Boma. When I knew and felt love. I sigh, wiping my eyes, remembering the devastation after. The stitching back of my soul with the feeble needle and thread of letters to Boma, with ambition, and, later, with the convenience of my marriage to Ken. And how, as the years went by, I watched the jagged seams of my life continue to rip.

I lift Kayus's head from where I'd laid it on the floor and put it back on my lap. He groans, muttering, but carries on sleeping.

I hear scratching behind the wall; the sharp bark of two dogs, followed by a fierce growling and gnarling, as if they'd been tossed some chunky flesh and are fighting over it.

"What happened to the Lagos boy?" I ask. "What's his name? Just tell me his name and surname."

Once she gives me the guy's name, I'll excuse myself, tell her I need to wee, and find a way to a mechanic or an internet café or a hair salon, pay them to charge my phone. All I need is 10 percent and—the gods of network willing—I can look him up on social media, send him an SOS DM, let him know he's needed here ASAP.

Something sounds from within me. A jarring, earsplitting, monophonic tone. I startle, confused, looking out the window, as though it's the cry of some creature. Iya hisses, slapping a hand on the floor. "Pick phone!"

It's Adunni's phone: a number I vaguely recognize. The phone buzzes, humming. My "Hello" is tentative, unsure.

"Tia?"

I exhale. Dad. I cup a hand over the phone speaker and whisper to Iya, "I need to take this call." I step out into the airless corridor.

"Dad?"

"Your husband gave us this number. Your mother

is . . ." He pauses. "She's been restless. Asking for you. She says she has something to tell you."

My heart stops for an instant. When I speak, my words are slow, measured: "Did she tell you what she wants to say?" She couldn't have. She refused to even discuss it two days ago because Dad was around.

"No," he says. "I am just worried. I had to cancel my board meeting because Ken says you won't come. I mean, it's not the first time you've booked a flight and changed your mind. We are used to the disappointment."

I shrink at his accusatory tone. I have **never** changed my mind about flying to Port Harcourt. I've always flown over as promised, but I always stop over at Boma's on my way from the airport. Sometimes, I finish with Boma and head right back to Lagos. Other times, I stay in a hotel and fly back the next day because I can't bear seeing Boma and my mother on the same day.

Time with Boma always disfigures me: with fury for what could have been, with anguish for what we lost, with rage for my mother's part in our destruction.

"But this is different," Dad says. "Eno has never asked for you like this. Ken says you cannot come because of work?"

"I need to . . . attend to something. I'll see you tomorrow morning, I promise. First flight." I sense his hesitation, restraint. "Are you okay, Dad?"

"Your mother is impatient." He hands her the phone before I can ask why.

"Tia." Mum sounds lethargic, drugged. "You said Wednesday."

"I just told Dad . . . not today. I am heading to the airport for a work conference."

"I want to see you today," she repeats as though she didn't hear me the first time. She probably did and, as always, is choosing not to listen. Why does everything have to be according to her demands?

I look down, my shadow lengthening across the floor like a leak. There's the scrape of the phone changing hands. My father comes back a moment later. "Try, Tia. I know you are busy. But try." A cock crows in the distance. Urgent. Throaty.

"What's that?" Dad says. "Are you on a farm?"

"Car radio. Dad, I've got to go. Speak soon."

"Tia?"

"Yes, Dad?"

"I don't know if . . ." He breaks off. Muffled sobbing. It lands on me like the crushing weight of a sudden flood. I've never heard my father cry. My throat swells.

"Dad?" I raise my voice, forcing him to return to the phone.

"Fine. Take your time," he says. "She says you are refusing to see her. That you don't love her. Tia, I want you and your mother . . . to be in a good place before. Before she . . ."

Before she dies.

My father's misery breaks my heart and makes me mad. I want to yell at my mother to stop being selfish for once, to dare her to tell my father why we have become like this, but the words melt in my mouth, morphing into a dense lie and slithering down my tongue:

"We're in a good place! I saw you both a few days back! We bonded when you left us alone, right?" I can almost hear my heart over the whirring of a machine in the distance. I press my palms to the wall, my head thundering. The phone buzzes another warning.

"See you tomorrow?" Dad sounds optimistic, unsure.

"See you both in the morning. Love you."

"Sweetheart, are you sure you cannot come today? There are still flights, right?"

Could I leave Kayus and Iya and find my way to Port Harcourt today?

Something churns in me, an acerbic concoction of extreme feelings. It swirls from the bottom of my stomach and rises, spilling into my heart, into the tears that pour down my cheeks and dissolve into the wrapper.

I. Will not. Leave Adunni.

"Tomorrow morning, Dad," I repeat firmly.

"Your mother loves you," Dad says, as he always does.

Adunni's phone hums and dies, swallowing a response I do not have.

I fumble, unsteady on my feet, back into Iya's room, and fold myself to the floor. "Sorry," I say. "You were about to tell me Adunni's father's name?"

"I tell you his name when I finish my story," she says firmly. "I have his name, his mobile of phone number, his internet-house address. I have everything you need. But hear this proverb: **A ki fi ikanju la obe gbigbona.** You cannot be rushing to use your tongue to lick a very hot soup. If you rush it, it burned you. Be patient. Now are you ready for the final leg of the story?"

"No," I say, my voice dripping with sarcasm, exhaustion. "You take all the time you need. All the **precious** time."

TEN HOURS
TO MIDNIGHT

||||||||||||||
IYA
||||||||||||||

I need rest.

I been talking for how long now? What is time now? Time is going-gone.

I keep talking.

My eyes could not take the pain of seeing Idowu marry a man she didn't love, so I tell Yeye I wish her well, but I cannot watch the pain of the wedding. I find myself a small place in Agan, beg the landlord to let me pay small-small rent. I was living there until around six months back when the no-rains problem chase me come to this Goma.

So.

The night before Idowu will marry, around middle of the night, she knock on my door. I open it, see her standing there, holding a nylon bag of things. She rush inside my house and tell me she cannot marry Akala. That if she marry him, she going to kill herself on her wedding day. So, I say, "What you want to do? You cannot stay here with me in this small room. If you stay, me and your Yeye, we become enemies. And I cannot be letting that to happen. You are like a **pickin** to me, Idowu. Go back and try to love Akala. Try to find something small in your heart to love of him."

She look me with her eyes red, sore from crying, and say, "My heart can force itself to be sad or happy or angry, but my heart cannot force itself to love. I cannot ever love Akala. There is something I can tell only you, Iya. I been calling my Lagos boy from the Ministry of Telephoning Company, the NITEL office. He give me a calling card before he was leaving, some money too. I tell him about my wedding tomorrow, and he promise to come to meet me at the junction this very middle of the night. You know that roundabout of grass just before the river? He will meet me there. Me and him, we will run together to Lagos and start our life there. I want to tell you so you can give my mama comfort in the morning. Tell her to not cry for me. That one day, when my life is better, I come back and find her. Tell her that I forgive her for forcing me to marry Akala. Tell Akala too to not be angry with me. Tell him to find his own true love."

My heart is paining me as I think to that night.

That night, I tell her to think it well. "You are just sixteen, Idowu. This boy say he loves you now, but what happen if he change his mind in Lagos? The mind of a man is always shaking like water. Where you will go if he change his mind about you? Who knows you in Lagos? What will his mother think of him and you running away?"

But she was so sure of herself. She give me a paper—inside of it was the name of the boy, the address of his house in Lagos, the number of telephone. I tell her to bend her head, and I say a prayer for her.

I wait until the afternoon of her wedding—before I rush quick to her house in Dende, thinking I will go and hold Yeye and tell her to not worry, that her **pickin** is alive and well, but when I reach Dende, I see a crowding of people outside in the compound. I see Idowu standing stiff, tears running down her face, as Akala hold her tight as the people were saying, "**Congra-lations!**"

Hmm. The sorrow of that day!

I stand there, watching as Yeye marry off this girl. And then I go back to my house and wait for Idowu to come and tell me what happen to her plan. It take nearly six months—but when she finally come back to me, she come with a bowl of puff-puff and a stomach swelling with her first **pickin**.

She low the bowl of puff-puff to my feet and just start to cry. Oh, how she cry and cry and cry, that after she was leaving me the night before her wedding, she carry herself to the roundabout and wait there for the Lagos boy. She wait and wait. After about two hours of waiting in the deep dark of the night at the mouth of the forest, a car drive up to her. The 504. She was so happy, jumping up and down, thinking it was her Lagos lover. But it was his mama. And she bring her car to a stop and say, "He's not coming. He's on his way abroad as we speak. Find your own riffraff to marry."

"Riffraff." What a word. It always make me think of a tearing paper.

The boy's mama zip up the window of her car and the car drive off, splashing water all over Idowu and her belongings. She say she drag her herself home to marry Akala, how she is sad to be the wife of Akala. How she sometimes think to kill herself. She tell me how Akala don't like to work. I hold her tight as she off-load her sorrow on me and I tell her to manage the life of suffering. The life of many of us womens is a life of no chance at happiness. You see, since we were born as a baby, the world keep telling us women that we are a donkey. We look in a looking-glass and see the skin of a donkey and the long face of a donkey. So, we behave like a donkey. We eat grass and carry heavy load of the world on our shoulders and keep silent, suffering. But nobody tell us ever that under the donkey skin is a cut, a opening. Right there on top our belly button is the door to the true self of us: the lion inside of us.

If you find that cut and tear off the donkey skin, inside you find that lion: strong and full of power to fight. But how many women know that they carry a lion inside them? How many of them even look inside a looking-glass to find the true self of them, hiding in the stomach of the tired donkey?

After that night, me and Idowu, we become so close. More close than before. She begin to bring food to me and the other womens around us once in the month, and we use the time to talk and talk about her Lagos love-boy.

After Born-boy is turning five and a half years of age, she tell me she is no more thinking of her Lagos love-boy. That she is sure he have forget about her since, anyway. So, she ask me to give her the paper of his phone number. She take it from me, and just as she about to tear it to pieces, she change her mind, put it inside of her bra.

"Maybe I call him to greet him Merry Christmas," she say.

When she come back to my house a month after, her eyes was shining. "I call him!" she say, laughing. "We been talking every day since Christmas Day. He find a way to send calling money, and since then, we been speaking every day! Ah, Iya, he send me money! He is coming to Ikati tomorrow! Coming to see me. He didn't forget me. He loves me just like I love him."

I look this girl, just twenty-one years old, and feel

something pity for her. Real pity. "You remember you have a husband?" I say. "You cannot see another man. Did he not marry yet?"

"He didn't marry yet," she say. "Iya, he have a woman that want to marry him, but he tell me he didn't love her. So, he keep pushing the wedding date since five years now. He say he just finish his master education and is coming to marry me. Take care of Born-boy too. He will take us two to Lagos. Iya, promise me you don't tell Yeye?"

I shake my head, tell her to remember that there is a curse in Ikati for women who leave their husband and run away. "You don't want that curse, Idowu. You are with Akala. Manage him."

Idowu look me long and hard and say, "Good night, Iya."

It was that day that I understand that yes, Idowu is quiet, but she have a strong mind.

The very next week, she come visiting with the boy! Ah! This boy come all the way from Lagos and bring me so much food. Yams and beans and rice and plantains and corns and potato. Idowu was just thanking him and thanking him. Again, the boy tell me how much he love her. How he will find a way to marry her even if she is already a wife and a mother. He promise me that he will go back to the Abroad after the end of New Year, and when he come back to take Idowu, he and her will come back again to see me.

Six months pass before I see Idowu again.

This time, when she come, her stomach was swelling with Adunni. I ask her if she ever see the Lagos love-boy, if he ever come back that New Year? But she refuse herself to say one word. She was so sad, so empty, she look like a dirty cup sitting in the sun, with ants and small snakes crawling inside of it, with the owner looking the cup, dying of thirsty. She tell me to forget of her Lagos love-boy. That she don't ever want to talk of him again.

My throat is scratching me. Is Kayus waking up? The tea he drink is very strong. It keep him sleeping for hours. Any more of my water behind of my head?

Bring it, let me drink.

🌸

Thank you.

You are a good person, you know. You been listening for hours, not saying plenty words. Soon I finish my story. Where I stop my talking? Yes. I remember now.

Me and Idowu, we stop talking of the boy. But many times, I catch her kneeling down by the well, crying and calling his name; other times, I catch her looking at baby Adunni, tears running down her face. It worry my heart because I know she love Adunni so much, so why she keep crying when she sometimes looking her?

It take one year or so for the love-boy to come see

me. He tell me that when he come back that New
Year, Idowu say she love him with all her spirit and
mind, but she cannot leave Akala and follow him.
He tell me that him he is still full of love for her,
that I should bring her come to my house, and he
will meet her here and carry her run away to the
Abroad. But I didn't able to do that! Idowu is the
wife of Akala! How I can bring her here to meet her
love-boy to run away? Oh, how he beg me to find
her, to show him the way to her house. So, I give
him a red-eye warning, tell him to not go to Ikati
to find her because he going to put her inside a hot
soup of trouble!

The love-boy keep coming every year, a week
before the festival of the corn, bringing me plenty
food. He keep wanting me to show him Idowu's
house. He keep telling me he still love her. But how
can I tell him Idowu love him so much that she is
punish herself by forcing herself to no more think of
him? That she have already two childrens for Akala?

One evening, I gather my mouth to tell Idowu
that her love-boy been coming here every year since
after that New Year. That he love her still. I can
never forget how Idowu shake her head and close
her eyes as if the love-boy is a knife I press to her
neck. She look me with tears in her eyes and beg me:
"Iya. **Ejo.** Please don't talk of him again. If I hear of
him, it pain my heart! You know I have two childrens now! I want to try to make big my business of
puff-puff, to give my own childrens, especially this

Adunni, a good schooling so that no man will look his nose down on her."

Me and she didn't talk one word about the love-boy for many years.

The last time the love-boy come to visit me, he tell me he will marry his wife since Idowu is refusing to come back to him. He give me money, enough to buy fifty basket of yams, and touch his head to the floor and wish me well.

He give me his number of telephone and inter-net address—a special one for only me—and say if Idowu ever need a thing, she can call him or send him internet message.

Idowu born Kayus.

Adunni grow up and become a strong child with plenty words and love for reading; a child that speak up her mind and shout her thinking with no fear; a child that fill up Idowu with a special kind of fire, a dancing laugh, true-true joy but sometimes a sad-ness of things bury deep.

My mouth is paining me.

I don't think I been able to talk this plenty in a long-long time! The spirits are with you! They want you to hear this story finish. Is your ears sleeping, or it is awake? Awake? Good. I like you, this woman. I already tell you that? You have a good but strong head spirit. What is English for it? Don't tell me! I know it. "Stubborn." That is the word. You have the spirit of stubborn. Strong head. Learn to use it well. And Kayus? He still sleeping?

Good-good. Give me one minutes to two, let me rest my tongue.

Thank you.

A month after Yeye was dead, after my left eye was closing to blindness, Idowu bring me food. Yam and palm oil stew. She put the food down in my front and watch me with her eyes as I was eating.

When I finish eating, I pray for her. Then she start to cry. She tell me she and Labake, her best of friend, are not talking. I ask why. She say because she tell Labake the true story of Adunni's father.

I confuse. "What true story?"

"The true story about Adunni's father," she say. She was so very afraid to look my eyes. "My love-boy is Adunni's father."

"You sure?" I ask. But I wasn't too shock. I been seeing it already in Adunni. She look like that love-boy; she walk like him too, have a sharp mind like him.

Idowu say yes, she is very sure of it. "He come back to me that New Year, and me and him, we . . . make love to ourselfs under a tree. When we finish, I tell him that I cannot follow him to his Abroad. You see, the Idowu of sixteen years old is not the same. I was thinking of my mama, Yeye, what she will think if the whole village start talking about how I run away with a man to Abroad, so I tell my love-boy to go away and leave me be. We cried, and he promise me that he will never forget me. He leave me alone that night, and I try my best to don't think of him. But when my stomach was starting to swell with Adunni, I didn't sure who is the father: Akala or him. After I born Adunni and I look at her and I see that she have a mark behind of her ears, the shape of a crawling crab. It is the same shape of mark of her father. And now, when I look Adunni at ten years of age, the things she say, how she is quick on her feet and thinking, it is just like my love-boy, I am so sure of it. Akala is not her father.

"I tell Labake my fears, thinking she will give me words to keep calm my mind, but she vex so much, she since refuse to talk to me."

"Why you tell Labake?" I ask her. Why?

. . . Wait. Is Kayus waking up?

||||||||||||||

ON HUMBLENESS
A tiny mosquito can bite a whole adult
human being man and cause him to
catch malaria. Meaning what?
Stay humble; a pinch of thing can bring
the whole of all of you down.

—THE VERY IMPORTANT SMALL BOOK OF
LIFE'S LITTLE WISDOMS BY ADUNNI

ZENAB

Zenab: I am sorry. I needed to . . . to just breathe.
I'm good now. I've got this. Where was I?

Adunni: What your small sister was telling you
happen to her?

Zenab: Yeah. She . . . uh . . .
   She told me they cut her in between her legs.
She's only like seven? They circumcised her. And.
That it was my turn. I could not believe it! I had once
given a speech in school, on the International Day of
the Girl Child, about the dangers of female genital
mutilation! I know it is a form of violence. I know
it is illegal, against the law in Nigeria. I know that

over two hundred million girls have gone through
this in different parts of the world. All over the
world? Like. This thing is not about tradition. Or
culture. Or religion. Or whatever you all think. This
is abuse! A blatant oppression of us girls.

I remember asking Mum, as I prepared my
speech as part of research and all, if she believed in
it, and she said no. If she had said yes, I would have
informed her! I would have educated her!

After Hasina left, I found Mum sieving corn
outside. This was like midnight? I asked about what
Hasina said. She said it was true, that a woman was
coming to our family home in the morning, to cut
me. Are you kidding?

I knew I had to get back to Dad, like, ASAP, but it
was so late!

I called Dad and told him, and he asked to speak
to my mum. I literally heard him screaming down
the phone, warning her not to touch me. Heard
him say he'd get her arrested if she did. So, Mum
promised not to allow the cutting and all. She
hung up and refused to hand me my phone. She
ordered my half brothers to lock me up in the
backyard room. They did. I was there for like hours,
crying, hitting the door, begging to be let out. Not
sure of when it was, but it felt like two a.m.? Mum
opened the door and said I was leaving for another
village! I was like, why? She said she didn't want
Dad to meet me in her home and cause trouble.
And that the woman who cuts girls is traveling

through this village to help the chief priest with
some sacrifice prep. She said the woman will cut
me here and she'll explain the importance of the
cutting to my father later. She started crying and
begged me to understand, that this was for my own
good, that she loved me and all and would never
hurt me.

My half brothers tied me up and covered my eyes
with a blindfold and brought me here, and when I
got here and saw that bastard Semi talking about
marrying Hauwa, I began to scream, and they
locked me up and put me in some shitty room.

This whole thing? Feels like I'm stuck in
some nightmare.

I . . .

I am . . . not here for a sacrifice or to beg for
rain or whatever? My mother's village doesn't
even have the weather problems you all have here
in Ikati. I guess I am just dressed like you all to
blend in, and after the woman cuts me, I guess I'll
return to my mother. She's in the market square,
waiting? I am sorry. This isn't a real laugh. This is
me laughing out of, like, shock. I am hoping Dad
will get here before midnight or whenever they
want to cut me, but I also think he's so upset with
me, he won't come? That he'd change his mind?
I don't know. This really sucks. Are you sure no
one has a phone? I need to find a way to tell Dad
where we are? Please? Did anyone smuggle a
phone here?

Adunni: Ms. Tia has a phone. When she comes back, she will call your father. I hope she comes back soon.

Zenab: Just for the record. Lady G? Can you get this on paper? No one is cutting me. If that woman tries to cut me tonight, **walahi**, I will kill her.

But I must say this. You girls. Look at me. It's not your fault there's been no rain! Come on! It's all over the news, this thing called global warming? Dad says countries abroad are mostly responsible for the problems this is causing in Africa. That they emit . . . uh, release stuff called carbon emissions? Like a whole lot more than us here in Africa? I don't get it either, but when I leave this place, I will research it. Dad thinks Africa has always suffered at the hand of the Western world and that this is just another example?

So yeah. This drought and flooding and all? Nothing to do with you girls! Nothing. You all need to educate your chiefs on that. Adunni, listen. Can your Lagos friend help? Did you not say she is interested in things like this? Ikati and the villages need to find a way to, like, tackle and adapt? To fight it? The way the rest of the world is fighting it instead of blaming it on poor girls? Uh. I guess that's me done here. Any more questions for me, Adunni?

Adunni?

Adunni: You say you will kill the woman?

Zenab: Did I say that? Never mind!

Adunni: Oh, Zenab. You have a bright mind! A shining mind. And look, Zenab! Did you see four more women joining us as you were sharing your story? Over there is my friend Enitan, sitting by that tree. It seem like someone is whispering around the village telling them what we are doing! I don't have any more question for you. Can I tell you my story now? Thank you.

Like all of us, I had a dream.

A stubborn mind of having my education.

But when my mother died, my dream died with her, but I keep praying for that things get better for me, but things just keep getting worst for me.

One morning . . .

||||||||||||||||

ON GOD
God is something very mystery.
More than what the box of your mind
can measure.
It takes the eyes of your heart to see the everyday
miracles
wrapped around the sun, the moon, and the
billion-billion of stars.

—THE VERY IMPORTANT SMALL BOOK OF
LIFE'S LITTLE WISDOMS BY ADUNNI

NINE HOURS
TO MIDNIGHT

TIA

Kayus startles awake and stares at me through narrowed, sleepy eyes.

"It's okay, Kayus," I mutter, rubbing his back with my palm in slow, circular motions. "We are still here at Iya's house. You okay, love?"

Kayus wrinkles his nose, shakes his head as if to clear fog from it. "I seen my papa," he says, sitting up straight, shielding his eyes from the sun, and pointing at the window. "I seen Papa cross that road over there, stand under that mango tree and wave bye-bye."

I'm certain it's the herbs Iya gave him. They might have made him hallucinate. "I am sure your papa is fine," I say.

"He is going far away," Iya says, in a distant, croaky voice. "His sadness is a neck-chain. Ah, I hear that he is a spirit now."

"A spirit?" Kayus asks, glancing at me with surprise, fear. "He dead?"

"Ignore her," I whisper to Kayus. "Your father is fine. Listen. Can you take my phone to one of the mechanics or market women, see if they can charge it for me? Please?"

Kayus gives me a blank look, nods.

I pluck my phone out of the pouch around my boobs and hand it over. "They can use any iPhone charger, and I'll pay them when I get my bag back. Promise."

Kayus takes the phone and shuffles out of the room.

I turn to Iya. "Let's get back to Idowu."

Why did Adunni's mother continue to procreate for a man she loathed just to stay married and keep her mother happy? Why did I keep quiet about what happened to me at sixteen, just to make my mother happy?

Iya sighs. "You have a mother still living?"

Her question startles me. Why is she asking?

"You have a angry soul for her," she says. "I sense it."

Anger often blends into a trio of disappointment, desperation, dismay. "A little," I say.

"How many **pickins** she born before or after you?"

"One," I tell Iya. "Me. I am her only child."

Iya slowly nods. "What is causing of your angry soul for her? Only you she born? Only you vexing for her. Why?"

"I . . . Nothing." This woman is crossing the line by wandering into the alcoves of my past.

"You need to free her."

"Thanks," I murmur.

"**Idariji.**"

"Sorry, what?"

"Forgivement," she says. "Forgive your mother. You free her and you free yourself with it."

Forgiveness, I think. "Carry on about Idowu," I urge. "Please."

Iya licks her lips. "Will you forgive your mama for me?"

"I don't owe you jack," I say.

"Jack? From which village?" She's reaching a hand to her ear as if to cup over it, to ask me to speak up. I laugh in spite of myself.

"Listen to me this," she says. "Forgivement is not for the person that wrong you; it is for you. The anger and pain inside your soul is a darkness that block out your light. Remove that block and see the light." She cracks a smile. "You cannot change what happen. But you can gather your heart and say, No more. No more dragging me back and filling me with sorrow."

I sigh. "The story? Please?"

"Ah," she says. "Where I stop it?"

"Idowu told Labake she suspects her lover is Adunni's father?"

There is something about Idowu's love life that resonates deeply within me.

I wonder if Ken has gotten through every letter, what conclusions he's drawn, if he now understands.

June 1999

Dear Boma,

It's been four months, and your absence feels like the ground under my feet: harsh, gritty, everywhere. I can't take it anymore, and so I have decided to visit our village home to surprise you. What's life like out there? When will you leave for uni? What's the plan for your future? So much to discuss! I'll bring along all the letters I've written, and we can read them together and laugh.

There's something I need to tell you!!

It's a secret that has outgrown my mouth and I can't keep it for much longer! I simply MUST see you!!!

I sent Daddy's driver to get me a ticket from the ABC Transport station and I will see you in a week!!!

A thousand kisses,
Tia

IYA

Eh! You have a good memory.

Yes. I ask Idowu why she tell Labake this deep secret, and she say because they are best of friends. Big mistake. Because that very night, Labake tell Akala! There are some things you don't tell even the shadow of your spirit, talk less of a best of friend!

Idowu tell me too that since he is Adunni's father, maybe she can send for him, and he can help pay for Adunni's schooling. "Can you help me find him, Iya? Find him and tell him to come and see me quick-quick."

I tell her he been already marry another woman. I show her the wedding card of her love-boy and his wife, and all the money he been giving me.

Ah! Idowu cry and cry until her eyes was red and big, until she rumple up the wedding card, use it as toilet paper to dry her eyes. She cry for the things her no-educations take from her. For the years she didn't want to hear of him, for how she wish she give him a chance when he come back. There is word for it?

"Regret"?

Yes.

She cry so much regret . . .

Hmm. This life. It don't ever find a balance.

I give her all the money, tell her to use it for Adunni's schooling. Then I tell her to keep her secret with her. To not tell anybody after Labake. I tell her to go home and beg Akala. To be a fool for him if she can manage it. You see, in our world, a woman need a marriage to have respect. Look at me. No husband, no respect. Sometimes, they call me a flying witch. They say I kill my husband, and I tell them yes, I kill him with too much loving.

And in this our village, a wife who sleep with another man will suffer. Not so for the mens. No. The mens can marry maybe two, four, seven wifes. So, I tell Idowu to use the money to send Adunni to school and keep her secret tight to her chest because the village will shame her whole family if they know Akala is not her father.

That day, Idowu look me eyeball to eyeball, and tell me she is dying of a sickness. She been coughing blood since the day Labake tell Akala about her love-boy. Sometimes she tastes sand and salt of blood in her mouth; sometimes it will scratch her throat, twist her stomach. I give her many leafs to help her, tell her to drink it.

She make me promise it that if she ever die, I must keep Adunni alive and only tell Adunni this story when it is a very, very important time in her life. A time when she is inside troubles. But I cannot tell Adunni myself because they are keeping her lock up. I tell you— I tell you because her mother, Idowu, is giving you blessing and thank-you for taking care of Adunni.

Hmm.

That day she tell me of her sickness was the last time this my two eyes touch Idowu. My Idowu, my **pickin**, she die maybe two weeks after that day of a coughing-blood sickness.

Ah, Idowu, may the spirit of my mother keep you in heaven.

Now, you—I keep forget your name? Shift to one side of that stove over there.

Look at the back of it.

Yes. That place.

Can you see a tin of Milo?

Color green?

Bring it.

TIA

Iya flips open the lid of the Milo tin with surprising strength.

She gives it an affirming jiggle, nods to the raucous soundtrack of coins, nails, and whatever else is inside it. She digs a fist in, pulls out wads of naira, pieces of folded papers, a pen, a hard envelope. She lays them down on the floor beside her with a deliberate slowness of movement, as though she's presenting diamonds to a crowd of keen bidders.

"He write a letter to Adunni," she says, her voice slurry, growing weaker. I am concerned for her now, and I want to tell her to slow down, rest. But I can't. Time's ticking and I don't know if we have to search far to locate Adunni's father.

"He did?" I push myself to my knees—partly so I can hear her better, but also to observe her closely. Her face is pasty, a thin trickle of sweat sliding down her forehead. Her drinking cup is empty, the rim stained with a powdery white substance. A housefly hovers, buzzing around it.

"Do you want or need an extra pillow?" There isn't an extra pillow anywhere, but I can fold some of her clothes, slide it under her head, prop her up.

"Some times ago," she says, her voice frail, a whisper, "before Idowu die of sickness, the man, Adunni's father—I call him her father from now, you hear me? He come from afar-Abroad." She pauses to inhale, cough. Her rib cage lengthens, quivering as she tries to pat her chest. I find myself crawling even nearer, sitting on my heels beside her. I start to pat at her chest gently, secretly pleased she doesn't resist or protest, and I remember how I used to rub my grandmother's back with menthol when she had a chest cough. My grandma Oyi, who died when I was ten, whose love for me, however infrequently she showed it due to old age and distance, was a sure, solid thing. She taught me how to crochet, to knit, to make up songs to remember recipes and spellings. She loved to read stories out loud from storybooks with funny voices. My grandmother never once pushed me to chase ambition. She simply wanted to laugh and sing and dance. To live. When she died, I wished my mother could trade places with my grandmother. The night before her funeral, my mother found me sprawled on the floor in my bedroom, sobbing while visitors trooped in and out of our home to sign the condolence register on the grand console table in the marbled hallway.

My mother ordered me to stop crying at once. "Grandma Oyi is gone, but you know who is downstairs? Professor Banugo!" Her voice juddered with awe. "A distinguished professor of literature from University of Ibadan! He came all the way here to see your father, and I've told him you'd recite 'Futility'! You remember the poem, Tia? By Wilfred Owen? 'Move him into the sun— Gently its touch awoke him once!'"

I hear my mother whispering now, her voice cold and hard, as she shoved me out of my bedroom: "Wipe your eyes, Tia! Go down there and show him what you've got up in your brain! Show him you are my daughter! That you inherited a measure of my intelligence! Go! NOW!"

Iya attempts a smile as I massage her chest. "I must to finish this story," she says. "You go and come back in thirty minutes."

"Me?" I stop massaging. "You want me to step out and come back?"

"Not you," she says, turning her head, her unseeing eye, toward the window. "Them. Go, I say! Go and come back. Leave me to finish this story."

I turn to look. Washing flaps gently from the tree

branch. A ripe mango, low-hanging and dangling from one of the weaker stems, shakes loose and falls, landing on the floor with a splat. I look away and think of the last letter I wrote to Boma after my visit to our village. I remember weeping so hard, I could only manage one line:

Dear Boma,

Grief is a crazy animal with jagged teeth.

Tia

"Adunni's father come here to see me," Iya says, and I look up. "He say he seen Adunni years back. She was washing cloth, asking him question upon question. I tell him Adunni is like a tee-vee with no off button. You on it, and it keep talking and talking until she fall asleep off. Then he ask me if Adunni is his **pickin**. I say, 'Why you asking me that?' He say, 'Nothing. Just a hunch.' I don't know what a 'just a hunch' is, but I tell him Adunni is not his **pickin**. He look me, say, 'Iya, you are sure?' He give me his internet address and mobile of telephone number and say, 'Call me if you ever need me.'"

"Why didn't you tell him she was his daughter?"

"Idowu was not dead at that time," Iya says. "She was Akala's wife. A sad wife, but a wife. In our land, a sad wife is better than a happy woman with no husband." She turns her sightless gaze toward my finger, focusing on the mirrored surface of my platinum wedding band through closed, flickering eyelids, as though she can see the warped reflection of the eyes of a sad and unsure woman on it, a woman who must place an unhappy marriage before her physical, mental, or spiritual health.

"I didn't want to cause trouble for Idowu. But long, long after Idowu die, and Adunni was in Lagos, I send one of my boys to call the man for me. To tell him to see me quick. It take him around three months—he was travel afar—but he come here to see me. I tell him that Idowu is no more alive. That Adunni is his daughter. I give him my brother Kola's number of phone. Tell him to call Kola. I was thinking he will save Adunni from Lagos. Give her a happy life. But Kola—God punish him with hot fire—he didn't answer the phone till this day. Or maybe he answer it, and when he hear that Adunni's father want to help her, he cut the phone. He was afraid maybe of police."

I pinch the bridge of my nose, taking this all in. Mr. Kola, that bastard.

"Can I have his name now?" I ask. "You said he wrote her a letter."

She pushes the envelope toward me, sliding it across the floor. "Read it."

The handwriting is neat, tiny, all caps—in a way that doesn't come across as shouty.

My heart races as I read:

Adunni,

First time I saw you, you were sitting under a
tree outside of your home, washing clothes. I
remember thinking there was something special
about you. I felt it at the pit of my stomach—a
tightening hold of conviction that you were my
daughter. I rushed to Iya's house to ask how old
you were, if I could have fathered you. Iya denied I
was your father, but I wasn't convinced.

I don't know if your mother ever told you about
our love—it was the deepest, most special love.
Until her death, I secretly nursed a desperate
hope that we'd one day be together. If life had
gone the way I wanted it, if my parents had
overlooked what they thought your mother lacked
in education and instead saw her beautiful heart
and soul, if they realized that getting an education
is a lifetime pursuit—that which we must
continually seek until we die, and that it is never
too late to pick it up from where you left it—then I
have no doubt we'd have had a very happy family.
Your mother was willing to learn, but my parents
were unwilling to let me let her.

Iya told me so much about you, and it both breaks
my heart and nurses my wound that we have so
much in common: our quick, curious minds, our
thirst for life. Somehow, I feel like I have known you
all my life—that your mother and I started a story
and we now both need you to finish this story.

Iya told me too that you may be working in Lagos.
I cannot imagine what kind of job a fourteen-year-
old girl can do in Lagos. I feel sick just thinking
about it. I thought to inform the police, but I
understand there's stuff involving you and the death
of another woman—and Iya has asked me not to
expose you. She assures me you are safe, in good
hands, but I know better, and I am scared for you
and your future. But I write this hoping that you'll
one day get to read this—actually, I hope you don't. I
hope I get to find you in Lagos and tell you myself.
That I am given a chance to make life worthwhile
and beautiful for you. That you can someday forgive
me for not being there.

I hope you understand that I never deliberately
abandoned you.

And finally, Adunni—and what a beautiful name
you have—I am sorry. For the life you've had to
live. For the pain you and your mother have had to
endure, for all that could have been.

I look forward to making up for the lost years,
and until then, I am going to spend every moment
of every day looking for you.

I love you.
Ade Enahoro

I fold the letter, slide it into the creases in my
wrapper, and put my head in b̶_̶_̶_̶n̶ my knees and

start to cry. In the distance I hear Kayus returning, shouting out words of gratitude in Yoruba at
someone in the backyard. I hear the mournful cry
of some animal, the hacking of a machine against
a hard surface. I hear my tears rumbling in my ear
canal, deep inside the cavity of my chest. I am aware
I am weeping, and I don't want Kayus to see me in
this state, but I cannot stop. My entire body shudders with sobs.

"Why are you weeping sore?" Iya asks. "You know
the man?"

I shake my head, tears sliding down my face. I
don't know him, and I hope Ken can find him, but
that's not why I am crying.

I don't know how to tell Iya that this letter—
written at a different time and place and under very
different circumstances—could have been written
by me. Because Adunni's father has written some
of the exact words—apologies and wishes and
regrets—that I have carried inside of my heart all
these years for the precious baby girl I had at sixteen.

EIGHT HOURS TO MIDNIGHT

ADUNNI

Transcript of The Zee-Zee Show on Ikati Forest TV

Zenab: Wow! Now that was a story, Adunni. You went through hell as a housemaid in Lagos, but I must ask? Why did you come back?

Adunni: I came back because the life in front of me is a dress.

Zenab: Uh . . . sorry, what?

Adunni: The dress of my education. It has pink bows with green shine-shine stones, hanging under

the bright light of Chance and Seasons. I want to
wear this dress, feel the stone grind my skin, the
fabric kiss my back, the bows tangle my feet. I want
every part of me, my hand and leg and neck and
body, to feel myself wearing the dress. I want to
show the world the color and beauty of my dress.
But I cannot wear my dress if people think I am
a killer.

I came back to wash my name clean, but also for
Kayus. I did not want to live my forever with a part
of me missing, stucked inside the box of my past,
never knowing how my family is doing, because
when a baby is ripe to be born from a womb, you
cannot born half a baby. I was a half of a baby
in Lagos, wanting to go to school, but somehow
with one hand and leg and one half of my nostrils
and eye still stucked inside the womb of Ikati. I
came back home, to this land, so that I can be born
full, the whole of me, free to walk away, to live
my life.

Zenab: That is, like, so intensely profound? I've got
all this education and I've always just assumed
everyone had access to it? **Obviously** not on the
same scale as mine, but the bare minimum,
right? Hearing your story is just . . . I don't
know? Humbling?

Adunni: I know I didn't do well by leaving Khadija to
die by the waterside. I true didn't want her to die.

She was my friend. A sister. A mother. But I had to run because I was afraid of this very thing. A wicked judging.

Zenab: So, who killed her? From your story, Bamidele only abandoned her, right? He didn't actually kill her.

Adunni: Can I stand up to answer this question? I want to face the women sitting here—there are fifteen of us here now?

The real true is this: Khadija did not die in the hand of really anybody. Khadija died because we don't have good hospitals in our village. She died because she was marrying too young to born four children. She died because she was borning baby after baby like everyday shit, because Morufu, who was also my own husband, was asking for her to give him boy-children. Khadija died because she was a girl. In our community, many of us girls are a nobody. We are not going to school. My mama didn't go, my mama's mama didn't go. Yes, our people are poor. Yes, many of us girls must help our mama to cook and fetch water. But if we can find a way to allow us all to school, we can stop this poor way of living. Our girls can become teacher, doctor, lawyer, even farmer. We can join hands with the men, our men, to build good schools and good things in our land. Not so?

I see a fire in each of your eyes. It burns me too, your anger. Your tiredness. Since the small rains, many girls been spending hours walking to far places to find water, some of them been suffering from men raping them on the way, and the ones that have a small chance for school are stopping. Our land is bleeding, the world is bleeding, and it is us girls that are suffering the most. Today it is our turn. My turn. Your turn. Next full moon, another girl's turn. How many more girl-children will suffer? When will this nonsense stop? Think about the million-millions of girls that haven't yet born. Think of the girls and women sleeping in their beds all over the world around us, dreaming of big things and a shining-bright tomorrow, not knowing if their village or country will kill their dreams and hopes dead before they wake up? Who will help us if not us for ourselves, by ourselves? Who will help women if not us girls and us women? Tonight I want us to try to fight for ourselves as girls. Tonight I want us to say no to all these wicked things.

Zenab: Yes! Adunni! But listen, we need education beyond the classroom. We need to empower our girls and women on the dangers of some of our practices. Don't get me wrong, not all our tradition is bad! I love our communal living and singing and dancing. I love how we tell stories and learn from each other. I love the respect we give our elders, the beauty of our land and food and culture. But there are harmful parts of our tradition that must stop. And the change can start with us!

But before we end the show, Adunni, can you translate for me? I think Kike is struggling. Thank you. All right! Everyone, I want you all to look under your benches. And if you are sitting on the ground, maybe dig a little into the sand? As if to find something there?

Got it? I'll give you a minute, Lady G. It's right there, keep digging—not literally though!

Are we all done? Perfect!

Now I want you to imagine it's a gift!

Wrapped in a silk cloth. Pink and yellow and orange! A pretty bow on it?

I want you to unwrap it slowly. That's right. Sloo-wly.

Do it! Open it. I want you to imagine you are opening the gift of your future!

Each of you gets what they wish for! Adunni, you get to become a teacher and to save the girls in Ikati! And you, Efe, you get to become an Oscar-winning actress? Right? I literally see you on TV! On fleek everywhere! I see you giving acceptance speeches and people literally queuing up for your autograph and all!

Lady G, you found nothing? Don't you dare shrug at me! There is something for everyone, even you!

Unwrap it again, look again. Keep looking, Lady G, keep looking!

And you, Hauwa, you get to become . . . just a girl? A happy girl!

And Chichi . . . what do you want? I cannot hear you? Oh, you want your husband to get here and take you home? He will! He's nearly here! Dad's nearly here to rescue me! I am going to build apps and transform the world. And even if I don't conquer the world, I'll make a difference in my little corner! And I will launch **The Zee-Zee Show** and invite all of you to it?

No dream is too big to achieve!

The world is a small place, but we are not too small to be big!

Can we all stand up and give a clap for all the guests of **The Zee-Zee Show**?

||||||||||||||||

ON CHANGE

Rich people say the world is a small place.
But that don't mean you can trek all of it.
Meaning what? You can't possible change the world all by yourself. The only thing you can change all by yourself is yourself, and the tiny corner of the world you find yourself.
Start with that. Small by small and corner by corner, soon your goodness will spread all over your world-corner like a blanket.

And know too that you are never too small, or
old, or rich, or poor, or sick to start.
Change begins with you.
As you are.

—THE VERY IMPORTANT SMALL BOOK OF
LIFE'S LITTLE WISDOMS BY ADUNNI

TIA

had a baby."

I blurt out through another sob, and my confession is like a crowning at the entrance of my birth canal, an engulfing ring of fire. "I had a baby," I repeat, a solid, single push, as I touch a juddering hand to my abdomen. Now I've said it, the release of tension comes over me in waves, and I take the moment to send Ken a text with the man's details and with a plea for him to find him.

"A **pickin**?" Iya says.

"Yes," I say, putting Adunni's phone away. "A daughter. A girl."

"Tell me," Iya says softly, gently, leaning over to

touch my lap, a barely-there graze, before she collapses back on the mattress, exhausted. "Tell me."

I tell her my story, but as I speak, I feel like I am telling it to myself, to an audience of one, and I have no care in the world if Iya understands me or not:

❦

"I was sixteen when I met Boma, our house-maid's son.

"She had been working for us for nearly twenty years when he came to stay. Boma was waiting for his university to resume, to start, and his mother thought it'd make sense if he came to stay with us for three months to work on the garden, the neglected pond, whatever he could help with. First time I saw him, I thought he reminded me of a Malteser—it is a ball of hard chocolate with a crunchy core. He had a squashed head, tiny eyes, and sharp teeth, but he had a heart of gold, full of goodness, the sweetness of a honeycomb oozing out of his warm center. I remember the first time we spoke; I had stubbed my right toe on a rock in the garden, and he dropped the shears he was trimming a hedge with and ran to my aid. It was him, not my mother, who wrapped the toe in a bandage and comforted me while I howled in pain. We began to say hello often . . . and then, a few weeks after my toe healed, he saw me sitting at the dining table, struggling with a complicated math problem. He paused, leaned over my shoulder, and explained the equation with a funny mnemonic—a way of remembering things—that made me laugh. And somehow, in that moment, he won my introverted heart over. We soon became best friends and then I fell in love. Hard. He taught me to play the piano; to pull a last card in the game of Whot; to love all things Nigerian, African. He was skilled at making **adire**, creating intricate and dazzling patterns in fabric. His fingers were always tinged indigo; his clothes stained with purple; pink and blue dyes streaked here and there with candle wax. He taught me to write letters, said it was the best way to bare our souls. And after we met, we began this ritual of writing each other every week and spraying the letters with our favorite perfume."

I smile sadly at the memory.

"We tried to hide our love from everyone; we often met at midnight, after everyone had gone to bed, under an oak tree in our garden. We'd talk well until morning. Or exchange letters or sing songs in whispers."

I pause to wipe my tears.

"It was the happiest time of my life, Iya. He was so intelligent, so intense, so intentional. He was scared of my mother and she tried to get him to break up with me, but I begged, pleaded with tears. I told him how much I needed him, how I didn't think I would survive the heartbreak. When I discovered I was pregnant, I was so happy. I was sure I was going to marry Boma. I had figured out that I'd need to halt my education briefly to have the baby, but Boma was going to university too, and although I knew he could not afford to take care of a child at the time, I was certain my dad would support us.

"But I was scared of my mother finding out, and so I hid my pregnancy well, wearing loose clothing and staying in my room for hours—my usual routine unaffected. I didn't tell Boma either. I didn't want to scare him away, and so I thought to wait until I was far along in my pregnancy, but when I was ready, my mother sent him to our village home to do some work. I thought it was strange, that she'd send him and his mother, Ada, away so suddenly."

"So quick?" Iya says.

I nod.

"I kept hoping Boma would return so that we could tell my father together of our plans to never leave each other."

I pause. Exhale. "I began to suspect something was wrong when my mother introduced a new housemaid and gardener barely a month or two after Boma and his mother left. When my stomach bulged and quivered with the first kick, I decided to visit our village home. I got there one afternoon when I was about five months pregnant."

I stop talking again. This part is always the hardest to share. Iya nods to encourage me.

"I found out that Boma and Ada had died in

an accident on the way to our village home. My
mother paid for their funerals and never said a
word to me. In hindsight, looking back, I realize
my father attempted to subtly suggest it to me:
He'd say, 'I hope you know Ada and Boma are in
a better place,' quietly, as he brushed against me
in the kitchen, and I'd nod, thinking he was refer-
ring to our village home! Boma was buried in Port
Harcourt, and I soon began the ritual of visiting
his graveside to talk to him. It was my only way of
making sense of things. I pretended he was away, on
holiday. I promised Boma to raise our baby right, to
give her the best, an abundance of the love I lacked
in my mother and had gained in Boma. I finally
told my mother one evening after I returned from
Boma's graveside.

"'How pregnant are you?' she asked that evening
as I stood trembling in her library, the door shut
solid, sealing the world outside from the cocoon of
books she'd created for herself.

"'I don't know,' I said. 'I missed my period about
five months ago.'

"'Who is the father? How on earth did I miss this?'

"'Boma,' I said.

"'Boma?' My mother nearly spat the word out.
'I knew you both were messing around, but, Tia,
pregnancy?'

"'He was a good man,' I said. 'And now he's dead,
I will take care of our baby.'

"'You are a fool,' my mother said, without looking

up from her books. 'Your admission in England awaits, your career in science beckons! How could you do this to me? We have to give it up for adoption, Tia. That is nonnegotiable.'

"I cradled my stomach, turned away from her, and whispered a furious no. I wanted this child. I would love this child. I had already named her Oyibinga, after my maternal grandmother. Oyi, for short. It means 'I will endure all for this child' or 'This child has taken me to unexpected places.'

"My mother started to cry, to explain how Boma and Ada's family would come for us, demanding money and access to our generational wealth, how she was sure Boma had other children from other girls and how they too could attack me, how I had made a terrible mistake. My heart broke to see her that way, to see how disappointed she was, how I'd failed. I agreed to give the baby up for adoption.

"My mother looked at me. 'Then you will go on to study?' Her eyes shone bright. 'Find a respectable man to marry? A doctor. A lawyer. Something along those lines. But you must promise me this, you will not give up your career for anyone! You become everything you want to be without apology. Is that understood?'

"'Yes, ma'am.' I felt hard balls growing in the pit of my stomach, lodging in my throat. I wanted all of what she was saying, but I wanted Boma's baby first. And I wanted my mother to hold me, to tell me not to be afraid.

"'Tia, I underestimated how smart you can be! This . . . is just a minor inconvenience. Tomorrow morning, we'll go to my sister in Lagos. You will have your child there, away from your father. I'll find something to tell him—a course, a trip abroad, something. He's always traveling anyway; he won't notice a thing!'

"I cried throughout the journey to Lagos—and decided I had no way out of this. Panic spread through me, expanding in my growing abdomen as I convinced myself that because giving up my baby for adoption was what would make my mother happy, it was what I wanted too.

"Oyi arrived, a wailing thing, slithering out of me with a head full of curly hair on a Tuesday afternoon in the year 1999. The pain was like a pair of arrow-pointed claws tearing my belly into two and carving out what was inside of me—my intestines, kidneys, liver, heart—and laying it on a slab of hot iron to sizzle. Every contraction ripped me apart, my screams an earthquake shuddering through the hospital floors. I held her to my chest and kissed her damp, clammy forehead and whispered her name. I saw perfection in her tiny pinch of a mouth, in her tired yawn, the crust around her eyelids, the slick of baby hair, the nearly translucent fingernails, soft and fragile and tinged with blood as they curled around my pinkie. In her, I saw her father, my Boma.

"She had—and I could never forget this—the

largest, most beautiful eyes, like Adunni's. I inhaled her for a precious, beautiful moment, and as I did, as it dawned on me that I did not have to give her up for adoption to please my mother, that she and I could survive together, someone or something yanked her out of my grip. I wanted to shout, to protest, but something was crammed into my mouth, ramming into my words. And I was so tired, I fell asleep.

"When I woke up—several hours later—my mother was looking down at me, and with my body quivering with fear and rage and determination, I told her I wanted my baby. I sobbed and begged. I told her to bring my baby back to me. We did not sign anything official; my little knowledge of law at the time gave me the confidence that I could get my baby back. My mother tried to convince me to forget Oyi and, by extension, Boma. To heal.

"When I saw that she wasn't even willing to listen, I told my mother I'd involve my father. That Daddy would hire top lawyers and find a way to bring my baby back to me.

"I never should have said that.

"Because my mother looked me dead in the eyes and said, 'You gave your baby away—yes—but she didn't even have a chance to live. A few minutes after she was born, the doctors noticed she was suffering from a type of neonatal infection called sepsis. Did you notice how quickly the doctors snatched her out of your grip? They needed to rush her to the

ICU to save her life, but the infection progressed too quickly. Your baby lost her life. Please don't cry. Just . . . take the time you need to heal and then let's focus on your A levels.' She squeezed my hand and left, and I lay there, engulfed in grief, screaming, until a doctor appeared and sedated me. The guilt and grief followed me out of the hospital, and as I boarded a plane barely three weeks later to England. For the first three years I was abroad, I lived in a shell of myself, cocooned with an eternal ache, a throbbing, palpable pain.

"This grief, Iya. This fat, anaconda-sized grief wrapped itself around my neck and squeezed life, hope, desire for anything beyond professional success out of me. Every day, I bled. I bled invisible blood of regret, pain, guilt. And I vowed never to bring a child into this world and fail her the way my mother failed me. At least not until I was ready. And I was okay with never being ready. I never told a soul. Ken did not question my decision. I found it odd that he didn't ask me to use contraception— you know, something to prevent, to stop me from getting pregnant. I just assumed he was leaving the family planning to me, as most men do. And I never stopped writing Boma—it wasn't often, maybe once a year, but I would write to him, and whenever I went to Port Harcourt, I'd stop by his graveside to read the letters to him. Those visits made the guilt of his death easier to bear. If Boma hadn't fallen in love with me, if he hadn't met me or if he'd broken up with me at my mother's insistence, he'd still be alive. My mother sent him away because he was a threat to the future she'd mapped out for me without even consulting me. It's insane."

I laugh, a caustic sound.

"When I met Adunni, she stirred up a yearning inside of me, the grief for my Oyi. She helped me realize that my past did not have to implode my future into this guilt-filled oblivion. This was around the time my mother-in-law, convinced I was cursed with infertility, cajoled . . . forced me to follow her to a river for a spiritual bath.

"You see, I had always vocalized my belief that a woman is valuable and worthy irrespective of if she has children. That who we are inside, the light we carry, the hope we share, the dreams we build, the future we desire and how we shape that future, are some of what defines us. Not children. Not marriage. But who you are, the essence of your goodness.

"Iya, I believe all of this, but it is so, so hard to live it in this society. Life for a woman in Africa is often a barrage of scrutiny and accusations.

"At the bath, I stood, head bent, as those women flogged me, and each whip was a shout of blame. I took everything in dignified silence, fury: It was my punishment for projecting a truth I could not live, for not telling Ken I'd had a child in the past, for not letting him see how badly affected I was by the taunts of childlessness. Afterward, I went to visit my mother with my scars, these marks on my face,

to ask her where my baby girl was buried. I wanted
to see Oyi's birth and death certificates. I wanted to
shove them in Ken's mother's face. To show her I
was not infertile. My husband is . . . He was sick
as a child and he cannot have children. His mother
now knows this, but somehow, she thinks it's still
my fault.

"When my mother refused to give me answers,
I left her bedside and took a walk. Well, I meant
to go buy myself a drink, but I forgot my handbag, and so I turned around and walked back to her
hospital bed, and just before I went in, I overheard
my mother talking on the phone to her sister, my
aunty Beatrice.

"My mother wanted to know if she should tell
me the truth now that she's dying. What was the
truth, you ask? That Oyi isn't dead. She gave Oyi to
a nurse, Iya. A random nurse took my baby and . . .
gosh. I am sorry, Iya, please give me a moment.

"Thank you.

"This . . . this was only last week. I cannot. It's
hard to even process it. I don't know where Oyi is,
or who took her, or what has happened to her. All I
know is she did not die on that day. I need answers!
I was meant to go back to my mother tonight to
find out who adopted Oyi and how to find her, but
those men came for Adunni, and I couldn't . . . I
couldn't leave Adunni by herself.

"You see, when I thought Oyi died, I blamed
myself for failing her, for failing Boma. But knowing

our daughter might be alive, possibly working as a housemaid for a vile woman like Big Madam or living as a child-bride like some of the other girls here, is a different form of torture, punishment.

"Iya, you didn't ask, but I thought to tell you why I came with Adunni to Ikati, why I will stand by her and hold her hand."

"Why?" Iya says.

"Because saving Adunni," I say, "is the only way I know how to say sorry to the precious daughter Boma and I had."

|||||||||||||||||

ON BEING A MAMA
A mama is always there even if she cannot
be there.
A mama is more than just the science of body.
It is the true deepness of heart, the beginning
and end of love,
the true meaning of sacrifice.

—THE VERY IMPORTANT SMALL BOOK OF
LIFE'S LITTLE WISDOMS BY ADUNNI

balanced
||||||||||||
TIA
||||||||||||

A sadness has crawled into the room.
    I've stopped talking, but my tears continue to
speak. Iya has been crying too, breathlessly, silently.
"It remain one more thing," Iya says when she can
speak. "In the story of Idowu I didn't tell you before.
One thing that I didn't able to stop thinking about
since it happen."

    I raise my head. My watch tells me we have less
than eight hours before midnight, but my distress
and urgency about Adunni have been tempered by
my grief. I shouldn't have shared my story with Iya
with little or no time to spare. That was selfish of
me, but the birthing of a child often bypasses permission, planning. It is often indifferent to your

carefully selected birth plans and curated scenarios, leaving the mother unexpectedly bruised and battered, delirious.

"Idowu didn't die of normal sickness," Iya says in between sobs.

"What do you mean?"

"She swallow **majele** . . . erm . . . poison? Yes. My Idowu swallow poison herself and die slow with it."

What? I feel a sudden tightness in my chest. "Adunni's mother killed herself?" Why?

"After Labake was telling Akala the true story-secret of Adunni's father, Idowu was afraid of the shame. Afraid they will drag her to the village chief and stone her and shame Adunni. So, she drink a cup of poison that very night."

"I am . . . Gosh. Sorry. Did Akala threaten divorce? What did he do to Idowu to make her—?"

"Nothing," Iya says, as if this fact still baffles her, years later. "Akala did not do nothing. He just stand up to his two feets, push Idowu from his front, and leave the house. Idowu maybe was thinking he was going to the village chief, to tell them, so she run to her backyard, cut some leafs of poison—the one we use to kill bush-rat—and grind it in a cup, add gin, and drink it up. But Akala did not go to the village chief. He go straight to the beer parlor to drink, and when he return-come home in the middle of the night, he find Idowu holding her stomach, blood pouring from her mouth, the cup of the poison by her feets. He send Born-boy to quick come to me, to collect strong leafs for killing poison. I swear I didn't know it was for Idowu; Born-boy did not tell me. God knows, if maybe he tell me, maybe I make the leafs stronger, maybe I go myself to save her." She sighs. "The leafs stop her pain and save her life that night. But her insides was already full of wound. For the next coming months, she just coughing blood and begging God to mercy for her spirit. And Akala? He keep drinking and drinking and smelling up and down the whole place and dying from the knowing that he is not Adunni's father. He did not say one word to Idowu about her love-boy. But maybe or don't maybe she was afraid of when he will say a word, I don't know. I think she was afraid too, of what happen if the whole village will know, the shame it will bring on Adunni, her small **pickin** who did not ask for all this mess."

I shake my head. Outside, a gentle wind rustles the trees. A farmer whistles a sad song, to the faint clucking of some bird. "That's . . ." What can I say? Heartrendingly tragic does not begin to qualify.

"I swear I did not know all of this until many years after Idowu die," Iya says. "I didn't know until Akala himself tell me—he come finding me one night, months after Adunni was in Lagos. He knock on my door, smelling of drink, to tell me he knows it was me that help Adunni runs away. He just wants to thank me a big thank-you. He tell me to keep her in Lagos, that it is good for her to be there. That night, I ask him why? Why he force

Adunni to marry, why he didn't keep the promise he make to his dead wife? That was when he tell me about the poison. He tell me that every time he see Adunni, he remember everything he lost, the wife he lost, the chance to do anything with his-self except to drink. The shame it bring to him as a man, if the village is knowing she is not his true **pickin**." She blows out a coarse breath. "This secret is in the middle of only me and you. You hear me? Adunni must not never know it that her mother kill herself. She will think she cause it and it run mad her mind. Don't tell her or no anybody. You hear me? Promise it to me now."

"You have my word," I say, touching my chest. "I promise that this remains between you and me. Can I ask you a question, Iya?"

She grunts.

"You never had kids? Didn't you want to remarry after your husband died?"

She rolls her eyeballs underneath her flickering eyelids. "There was a one good man for me, Akin. He gone—but not for long. Soon me and him, we see each other, we carry on our love. I didn't born childrens, but that don't mean I am not a mother. A mother gives a wise word and food and love. A mother is takes care of people. I been doing all that since I been around twenty-three years of old."

She pauses as if to briefly contemplate. "You know, is not too late for you." Her close-eyed gaze is heavy on me.

"Me?"

"Yes, you. You can find your **pickin** and tell her your story with your own mouth so you can try and give her love. She maybe or don't maybe take your love, but you must to try to find her."

Kayus, who must have slipped into the room unnoticed, stands at the doorjamb, lips folded between his teeth. At first, I am scared, wondering if he heard that his mother poisoned herself, but he looks lost, confused. He holds out my phone, the screen twirling with messages. "I manage and charge it small," he says. "Everything okay, Miss Tee-Yah?" He is watching me with the brownest, softest eyes. "You been crying? And Iya too? Have we find the man that is Adunni's father?"

"It's going to be okay," I say, thinking how precious he is. How strong. To have grown up without his mother, not much love from his father, but look how he forges along, how Adunni forges along. There is no anger in him, no bitterness, just hope. It's what many of the kids here hold on to: hope. Because there is no alternative, because hope cannot be stripped away unless you let it go. I hope my Oyi is the same.

My phone rings. Ken. "Hey," I say, sounding like I chewed on rocks and forced the fragments down my throat. "I—"

"I can't get through to Adunni's phone!" he cuts in. I hear cars whizzing in the background, water pelting the glass panes of a window.

I step out of Iya's room and lean on the wall. "Did you get my text about Adunni's father?" I ask. "Can you find him in the next hour? We don't have—"

"Tia!" Ken's voice is wind-whipped, frustrated. "I've sent him a message and called twice. Listen. Even if I find him, how do you expect me to just tell this man he's someone's father? What if he doesn't believe me? What if—"

"He knows!" I yell back, gripping the phone. "He knows and he's expecting a call from Iya! If he's in the country, he will make himself available. Ken. Please don't come to Ikati without him. Hurry!"

"Damn," Ken says. "This is beyond ridiculous! It's starting to rain. It's likely to be heavy."

My heart sinks. Heavy rain in Lagos can bring an assortment of disasters for the traveler: gutters spilling over litter, mud clogging pathways, cars grinding to a halt, potholes becoming puddles.

"I am sorry," I say. "I am tired, Ken. It's been a bloody long night, but if you are going to help us, you need to do this. We have very little time—"

"Hey, hey," he cuts in, tone surprisingly gentle. "It's okay, babe. Is your phone all good now?"

My phone beeps a damning response. I hope it lasts the night.

"Tia?"

"Yes?"

"I am sorry about Boma," he says. "I am sorry I thought you were having an affair."

I press my eyes closed at the cackle of thunder.

"I am most especially sorry about Oyi."

I swipe a tear from my cheek, open my eyes. "So, you've read them all?"

He is silent for a beat. "I stopped reading when I realized they . . ."

"Died?" Now is not the time to tell him Oyi survived. That my baby is out there somewhere.

"I am sorry, Tia," he says. "You've had to endure so much pain. I should have trusted . . . waited until you were ready to share."

"Me too," I say. "I am sorry I hid a significant chunk of my past from you."

Iya croaks as soon as I hang up and return.

"Two years back," Iya says, "Adunni tell me something deep about forgiveness. Something I didn't ever forget."

I wipe my eyes, arch an eyebrow.

"She say forgiveness is like a door to a small corridor inside of your heart where you can find healing. Forgive your mama so you can collect the key to that door of your heart, open it and free yourself from the cage of anger. Don't let her die with the key inside of her hand. Don't keep any anger inside of you. You know something?"

"I know a few things," I say, "even if you don't think so."

She snorts out a weak but sarcastic laugh. "The way you say your mama raise you up with no love, the lie she was telling you about your **pickin**, all those things you say she do to make you sad? Maybe there is a why. You ever ask her, what is her why? We all have a why, even if the why don't make sense to other people."

A fist clenches inside of me and grows into a ball of fury. I hear all Iya has said, but my mother is not Idowu. Idowu wanted to save Adunni from ridicule. Idowu wanted to protect her child. My mother sent Boma and Ada on a journey that ended their lives. She did not cause the accident, but they died because she sent them away. She wanted Boma out of reach, out of my life.

"Your mama has a heart wound." Iya carries on like she and my mum grew up in the same hood. As if they pushed bottle-covers on dusty grounds and played **ten-ten** under mango trees. "I sense it in my spirit," she says. "Her heart wound is the cause of the sickness in her soul. **Ilé ọba tójó ẹwà ló bùsi.** It means 'The house of the king that burn in a fire is only to make it more beautiful.' You understand?"

"Uh, not really?"

She grunts. "If the old house did not burnt up, how can we have a chance to build a new, more fine house?"

"Every cloud has a silver lining, right?"

"Right," Iya says, mimicking me. "If you didn't lost your child, Oyi, your eyes will not be open to see Adunni. And who knows, maybe Oyi is happy! With a good person like you. Maybe she is going to school and learning well and full of life."

Maybe. Oyi might be thriving. But I am not.

Not until I know for sure that she's safe. Alive. In good hands.

I bite my bottom lip cluelessly, exhausted. It is truly a tragedy to know so much and understand so little.

"Ah," Iya says. "My peoples, they are here. See my Akin." She cracks a smile. "He don't grow old one day since twenty years. Look all of them on the window, shining bright and calling me come. Is so beautiful. So beautiful. You, I forget your name? Tell Adunni for me to climb on top the world and sit on the forehead of it. Tell her I am watching her from the sky, clapping for her, saying well done! Well done!"

She's getting delirious now, exhausted. She needs to sleep. I turn to Kayus. "Iya needs her sleep. Let's go."

I will return to give her some money, get her to see a doctor, pay someone to tidy up her room, and if she refuses all of that, I'll just sit with her and listen to her talk.

Kayus gives a feeble smile. "So Adunni have a father in Lagos?" A cheeky grin. "Thank you, Miss Tee-Yah!"

"Don't thank me yet, pet," I say, pulling him close and rubbing his head. "But let's thank Iya," I say just as we step out of her tiny room. "For the gift of her time. For helping us." For holding my hand as I pushed, birthed.

"Thank you, Iya," Kayus says in Yoruba. "**Ese ma.**"

Iya doesn't respond. Tears continue to cascade

down her cheeks, around the tiny arch of her sadly smiling face and into the rumple and folds of her gently rising and falling chest.

May 2014

Dear Boma,

I met a fourteen-year-old, semi-illiterate girl who works as a housemaid for Florence Adeoti, my neighbor. (Remember her? The deranged woman who cannot keep her nose out of my business re: kids, and who wants me to join her meaningless group? That's her.)

The girl's name is Adunni, and last week, we became friends.

There's so much more to tell you about her: the laugh that tumbles out of her mouth as a song; her acute observations and witty aphorisms, which make me regard her almost as a child-sage, discerning and well reasoned, but also naïve, gullible, childlike.

I could share examples, but I have only ten minutes before Ken gets back from the gym. And I really need to tell you that Adunni unlocked the strangest sensation in me today.

It felt like a surge of memory from my past, an unleashing of a previously forbidden desire to wade into a tangled mesh of loss; isolation and

pain awakened, incensed. I can only articulate
it as a want. A strong desire to permit myself to
love and be loved in return. To, and it breaks my
heart to even tell you this: consider the possibility
of becoming a mother to another baby girl to
replace our Oyi, to fill this cavernous hole in
my soul, to free me from becoming wretchedly
trapped in our unfinished story. But it's not as
simple as that: There's also this shameful desire
to have a baby because I want to prove a point to
the world that I am not an empty barrel.

That's what I overheard a woman call me at the
last event I attended: an empty barrel. As if that's all
there is to being a woman: a container of flesh and
blood created solely to reproduce flesh and blood.

I know all of these might not be the right reasons
and I'll think about it, but I wanted to write to share
this with you, and to especially say sorry I am
doing this without you, that I have carried on living,
acquiring a degree and getting married and moving
from England to Lagos. I have had the gift of
troubles and joy, of changing my wants and desires
and hopes and dreams. I have had the selfish
choice to keep writing you, knowing you can't reply.
You can't have the benefit of pain or joy anymore
because your life was tragically cut short.

Because of me.

I blamed my mother for your death, but I also
blamed myself for so long.

I held on to you so tightly for so long because you were the first to show me what unconditional love is, because I needed you to help me navigate the unfathomable pain that consumed me in the wake of Oyi's tragic death so soon after birth. You became my anchor in an ocean of desolation, my solace, but I realize now that it's time for me to accept that you aren't coming back, to let you go.

I'll bring all these letters to your graveside when next I am in Port Harcourt, and I'll bury them next to you.

Thank you for listening. For always listening.

Rest in peace, Bow.

Much love,
Tie

‖‖‖‖‖‖‖‖‖‖‖‖

ON FORGIVENESS
Forgiveness is the door to that tiny passage of
your heart where healing lives.
And the key to open the door of it is
to say yes to a sorry
you may not ever get.

—THE VERY IMPORTANT SMALL BOOK OF
LIFE'S LITTLE WISDOMS BY ADUNNI

SEVEN HOURS
TO MIDNIGHT

TIA

The sky is awash with streaks of brown and orange as the sun descends, giving way to dusk. Kayus is silent, contemplative, on the ride back on Bala's canoe, and I am grateful for the time to gather my thoughts.

"We don't take the water side," Kayus says as we alight from the canoe. "I am tired, and I cannot help you to swim if you fall inside."

And so, we walk.

Past fields covered with weary animals who lie flat in the sun, writhing from thirst, beside farmers sitting under the canopy of trees, eyes closed, unable to do anything else. Past acres of sparse land covered with tree stumps, grass the color of hay, as

Kayus tells me the land was once forest, and I am broken by the devastation, the emptiness.

We walk past women sitting with arms on knees, in the blazing heat, staring at three-mile-long queues of empty buckets under dry community taps. My feet are numb, swollen from all the walking, but I take photos. It is the only way to take my mind off Adunni, the anxiety of not knowing if Ken will find Ade.

❦

I hide behind a tree at the entrance to the chief priest's house while Kayus tiptoes toward the shrine. It takes a few minutes, but he emerges with Kike.

"You come back," Kike says, and the joy on her face melts my heart. "You find her blood father?"

"Yes," I say, "but he is in Lagos. My husband, Ken, will try and bring him before midnight. Where is Adunni?"

She presses her hands together. "In the Circle of Forest." She points at the forest behind her husband's house. "I come and go and keep eye on them."

"Can you take me to her?"

She firmly shakes her head.

"Please."

"No!" She sounds panicked. "It cannot work, Miss Tee-Yah. This too danger for you. Circle of Forest is for us womens of Ikati and the sacrifice girls."

"Please."

She sighs. Wipes her eyes. She's exhausted, the poor thing. "You sit down here, wait. I take you when other womens be there. Now they are telling story. Happy story."

I feel sudden tears at that. The girls are telling stories. It's typical of Adunni to want to do that. To make good out of nothing.

Kike looks at Kayus. "Something . . . happen to your papa." A pause. "He was trying to find Bamidele, and they enter a big fight. Bamidele knife him here—" She touches her chest area. "Your papa is . . ."

Kayus nods, tears streaming down his face. I pull him into my arms and let him sob quietly into my chest, through me. Kike watches us for a moment with her head angled before she gently disentangles Kayus from my grip. "Eh. Stop this tears! Be a man!"

"It's okay for men to cry," I whisper as I let go. "It's okay, sweetheart. It's okay. Kike . . . please. Let me see Adunni. I just want to . . . tell her to be strong. For tonight."

Kike gives me a long look and rests her hand on her bump.

"Go, Kayus," Kike says. "Go to your house and wait. Miss Tee-Yah, follow me. I take you." She holds up her ten fingers. "Ten minutes."

"Wait!" I say as Kayus swivels. "Here. Take Adunni's phone. Keep it with you, charge it if you can. If it rings, press here. Listen and tell them where we are. Okay? Hopefully see you later."

He nods.

"And, Kayus?"

He looks at me, eyes wide, pools of anguish, despair.

"Thank you for everything. You are a wonderful and brave boy." I press a kiss to his forehead and jog behind Kike toward the yawning mouth of the Circle of Forest.

|||||||||||||||

ON LEARNING

As long as you are alive, there will always be
things to learn
because learning is like food.
Once of it is never enough for
the rest of your life.
So, keep feeding your hunger for learning
and keep humble your heart to learn the wisdom
of those who learned before you.
Even if you are more old than they are.

—THE VERY IMPORTANT SMALL BOOK OF
LIFE'S LITTLE WISDOMS BY ADUNNI

ADUNNI

I run to Ms. Tia, my spirit full of joy.

"You are safe! You came back! Did you catch our Zee-Zee Show?"

Ms. Tia says sorry, hello, hi, to the girls, waving her fingers left and right, using the light from the dying sun to try to search each their faces as if she is finding something in their eyes, but not all of them seem to mind her.

"Are all these girls from around here?" Ms. Tia asks, after I sit, and she holds my hand, her curve of shoulder pressed against my own, skin to skin, making me feel almost like a new-born baby, naked against the warm breast of my mama.

"All the girls are from here," I say. "But, why you keep asking me where the girls are from? Why it matters so much to you?"

Ms. Tia shakes her head and throws another look back at the girls. "So you are saying"—she turns to face me—"that none of them were maybe born in Lagos?"

Why is she keep asking and asking where they born the girls? Why too was she searching each their faces with a sad look in her eyes? "I don't think so," I say. "We tell each our story, and nobody say she was born in Lagos. Why you keep asking?"

"It's just . . . Never mind. I have only ten minutes here. How are you holding up?"

"I am fine," I say. "Is Kayus . . . Did he hear about Papa?"

"Kike told him. I am sorry, Adunni."

I drop my head. "He was not my really real papa. Strange to think it."

"Who told you?"

"I really want to cry for him," I say. "But how do you cry for somebody you didn't ever know?"

"I haven't cried for my mother," Ms. Tia says. "Not even after I got news she wouldn't get better from her sickness."

"But your mother didn't do you bad," I say to Ms. Tia. She keep saying her mother did this and that, but to me, her mother didn't do her any wickedness. She just didn't close to her, that's all. Which is not a bad thing. Rich people always like to find trouble when there is no trouble.

"My mother hurt me," Ms. Tia says. "In ways I cannot begin to explain."

"Tell me?"

She sighs. "She . . . lied to me about something very important and took things away from me, but forget about me for a moment. Where—" She stops talking at the sound of a beating gong from the village afar. **Ko-ko-ko.** Is so loud, I hear it inside my chest. "What's that?" Ms. Tia asks.

"The warning," I say, picking up my clay pot and tipping it to my mouth to drink some water. I set the pot down, wipe my mouth with the edge of my wrapper. "It is for the women to begin to settle themselves so they can gather for the sacrifice tonight."

Ms. Tia makes a loud exhale.

"Who is my real father?" I am whispering my words now, keeping it between me and her so the rest girls cannot hear us.

"I've asked Ken to try and get him here to help us."

"He knows about me?" This is a shock. I was thinking he didn't know of me. "Why did he abandoned me all my life?"

"He didn't," Ms. Tia says, voice whisper-strong. "There's a story behind it all. He wrote you a letter. I think you should see it?" She picks out a letter from inside her bra, and I smile a little that Ms. Tia is hiding things in her bra like us village girls. I take the letter from her and keep in my own bra, but I shake my head no.

"No?"

"No." I don't know this man, and he don't know me. What if he doesn't make it here on time? What if I never meet him? Then I will carry the punishment of knowing him in the letter he wrote, in the story Ms. Tia tells me. A heart can only carry so much pain. I rest my head on Ms. Tia's shoulder.

Zenab comes out from the bush and runs to Ms. Tia as if she's been knowing her all her life. She don't even wait for me to make introduction, she just comes, waves, and says, "Hi, I am guessing you are Adunni's friend from Lagos? Could I like borrow your phone this minute? Please?"

Ms. Tia looks at her like something wonder. "Who are you?"

"Name's Zenab," I say, with a side smile. "Zenab, this is my friend, and name's Ms. Tia."

Zenab holds out her hand for a shake of hand. She don't always climb to her knees like us village girls to greet people hello. "Hi, Ms. Tia? It's very nice to meet you. Please can I call my dad? With your phone?"

"Of course you can," Ms. Tia says, "but the reception here is terrible. Here. Type the number in."

Zenab punches a number and presses the phone to her ears. "There is, like, literally no reception up

AND SO I ROAR

here," she says. "Can you please go call him and tell him we are here? He's a naval officer, and if he's at my mother's village, then he's only a few hours from here? I am sure he's upset with me, but he'll help us! Please!"

"Of course," Ms. Tia says. "I need Kike to take me out of here. While I wait for her, can you walk around? Hold the phone up in the air, see if you can get a signal."

Zenab runs off, waving the phone at the sun.

"What's she doing here?" Ms. Tia asks, and I quick tell her the story just as Zenab is coming back.

She shakes her head, mutters "No signal" to Ms. Tia.

"Adunni just told me what happened," Ms. Tia says, looking like she wants to vomit. She keeps strong her face, maybe because I warned her before to don't keep her ears closed to the suffering of us girls. "I am so sorry. I feel so useless. Adunni, can you maybe hurry Kike up so she can lead me out of here? I need to call Zenab's father. Zenab, you keep trying for now, okay?"

I nod, climb to my feet, and run to Kike, run back to Ms. Tia.

"She say give her five minutes." I sit. "I am sorry my stubborn head caused us trouble today," I say after a moment of looking at Zenab holding the phone up and walking up and down the circle, turning it this way and that. "If I listened to you, stayed back in Lagos, and hide myself, then all of this didn't happen. You know, I been wondering if these people, our chiefs, just need a understanding. If someone can make explanation to them that girls is not the problem. That is your work, Ms. Tia? Maybe if you, we . . . can show the chiefs that . . ."

I sigh. No point in trying to find a way from all this mess. I am already deep inside it. I grip Ms. Tia's hand tight. "If they lock me this night, will you take care of Kayus for me? I don't want him to be all alone by himself with no mama, no papa . . . no Adunni. Born-boy, our big brother, I hear he is in another far village. Can you promise me that you will take care of Kayus?"

"I won't promise," she says, a crack of a whisper, "because I know you are going to make it and take care of him yourself. Adunni, your biological father's name is Ade Enahoro. He wants to meet you. I am sure he's finding a way to get here on time. I want you to believe that, Adunni. You need to trust that you'll get out of here tonight. Don't you want to go to school? Your scholarship is still there. You have always been strong. Now is the time to gather all your strength and fight. Do you understand me? Do you—"

"Ms. Tia?"

"Huh?" She sounds confused.

"Tell me something I can think of as I am waiting for judgment. What can make me happy."

"What. What do you want to know?"

"So much," I say after a moment. "Like, what it feels like to fly on an airplane?"

"A what?" She coughs out a shock of laugh. "Seriously?"

"Seriously—seriously," I say, wiping my tears. "I want to know what it feels like to fall inside a deep love. Tell me. What it feels like to enter secondary school and university and learn books? What it feels like, Ms. Tia, to work a real job and live in a nice house? Tell me so that I can carry the picture of it in my heart. Tell me so that, through you, I can say I tasted the edge of good life."

The girls around me slowly stop what they are doing. They become very silent; seem like they been listening to us.

"No," Zenab says as she comes back and gives to Ms. Tia the phone. "There's still no reception. But please don't tell just her. Tell **us**. Tell us all what it feels like to be free of the shackles of harmful beliefs, despite your education?"

"Or what it be like to be free to pursue your dream with no shakings," Efe says.

"Or to be strong to wait for your husband who is coming very soon?" Chichi whispers.

"Or to find the strength to reveal the father of your children to your people." Lady G starts to cry, and I am full of wonder because this is the first time she is giving a sign to what is bothering her, and I want to ask her to tell me more, but Chichi joins Lady G in crying, and soon all of us are asking many questions and Ms. Tia stays silent, her shoulders shaking, saying nothing. Maybe the heat of the questions has melted her answers.

And so, I imagine that an airplane feels like sitting on the back of a giant bird, swimming in the clear sky on its spread-out shine-shine wings. Deep love feels, maybe, like the licking of a sweet ice cream on a very hot day and laughing with no end. A nice house is like a warm embrace from Love itself. And university? Like stepping into a world covered with the carpet of every possible thing.

Finally, Kike says it is time for Ms. Tia to leave us.

Ms. Tia stands, kissing the middle of my head. "I won't leave you. I'll be waiting and watching. And, Zenab, I'll call your father as soon as I can." She comes closer, presses her mouth into my ears: "Your father might not have known you, but he loved you, regardless. And I love you. Think about that and let that guide you tonight as you fight for yourself and for these girls. Okay?"

I sniff, nod, but I cannot say okay. "Here, Ms. Tia." I give her my papers, my tiny book.

"What's that?"

"A paper-book. I want to give Enitan to take it to printer. Can you do that for me? Tell her to print it of many copies and share with all the girls in our village. Make it sure they can all read it one day."

"Oh, Adunni," Ms. Tia says, shaking her head and pressing the papers back into my hands. "You'll give it to Enitan yourself. And one day, the girls will read it and teach others to read it too.

"Iya told me something," she says as I put my book down on the floor. "That some women are made to believe they are donkeys until they look inside of them to find the lion hiding in their stomach, waiting to burst out of the seams. There is a lion inside you, Adunni. And what does a lion do, babe?"

"I don't know. It can like to eat up everybody?"

She smiles a little. "It roars."

"Like a shout?"

"Like that. But often driven by anger, by a want and a need. A lion's roar will travel far and cause the jungle to tremble, to be afraid. All its power is in that roar. It's what it uses to defeat the enemy. You are a lion, baby girl. You've always known that, right? Right?"

I raise my head to nod a nod, but it stay stiff in the air, not able to come back down.

"All I am saying is, don't lose hope," Ms. Tia says as she walks backward. "Remember what you told me this morning? You said, 'The only thing that makes a difference is you. You fighting back, you speaking up, you taking action!' Where is that strong, courageous Adunni? Find her. And tell her to not give up. I'll see you all soon."

||||||||||||||||||||

ON FAITH
Faith is the knowing that somehow,
tomorrow will be better than today.
Even if today doesn't make much sense.

—THE VERY IMPORTANT SMALL BOOK OF
LIFE'S LITTLE WISDOMS BY ADUNNI

TIA

Kike and four silently observing women lead me to a hedge of wilting trumpet-shaped flowers that faces Baba Ogun's compound and ask me to hide on a concealed patch of grass beside it. I try to ignore the ragged breathing raging through my lungs, the urge to crumble, to rest my head between my knees and close my eyes.

"I tell them you are one of us for this night," Kike explains, pressing a hand to the small of her back, and I marvel at her strength, her ability to walk for miles without resting. "But you stay here. You hide. My mama will bring you something to drink . . ." She stops speaking as a faint scream impales the night, a sound that is swallowed by the screeching of an animal. "I think is the girls. They afraid."

I glance at my phone. There are now three network bars. I need to call Zenab's father. I need him here before it's too late. I need Kike to get out of here so I can make the call, but I need to understand just how long we have.

"The cutting is bad," I hear myself saying. "So bad! When exactly is it happening to Zenab? Before or after the bath?"

"After." She narrows her eyes at me. "We don't do cutting-of-girls in Ikati. Cutting is bad. A wicked, God-forbid bad thing. The woman who is cutting Zenab? She is not from here. She only help to cut Zenab. No sacrifice for Zenab. You wait there. Soon my mama bring you something to drink for strong."

"How long do you think all of this will take?"

She shrugs and slowly rolls herself away.

I am left alone; the surrounding village is eerily quiet until a local dog with a protruding rib cage ambles across, a swarm of night insects buzzing around its scarred left ear. It pauses to regard me for a moment before stretching itself and lying on the ground and closing its eyes as though completely exhausted.

SIX HOURS
TO MIDNIGHT

ADUNNI

The show is long over, and now our joy is missing its teeth.

No amount of clapping and singing and **The Zee-Zee Show** can change that. We are stuffed full of its rising light, shining on the fear that trembles in our bones. Ms. Tia and the rest women have gone. Labake is now setting a fire, stacking up of firewood on top each other, watching as the flame is slowly burning. She uses a stick with a sharp end like a nail to shift the charcoal, to fire up the fire, waving it in the air, maybe to chase away mosquitoes or make a sign that we are still here.

Zenab is sitting by herself in a corner now, biting her nails. Hauwa is beside her, resting her tiny

head on Zenab's shoulder. Efe is lying down on the
ground, humming a song, her hand folded under
her head, eyes closed. Lady G is picking a stone
from the floor and throwing it to the space in front
of her, back and front, like a game. Chichi is talking to herself, her arms curling around the fold of
her knees, calling her husband's name: "Zuke . . .
Zuke . . . Zuke."

Where is her husband? Why is she here? The fire
makes a cracking sound like a plastic breaking into
two, as it flies up and dances, painting the trees a
beautiful gold. The air smells of smoke, ashes that
sting my eyes. I have a pressing to piss, so I carry
myself to behind one of the trees and pull up my
wrapper. When I finish, I crawl to Kike, who is just
coming back from taking Ms. Tia to the village. I
meet her at the entry place and sit beside her.

"Chichi," I say to Kike, speaking quietly, not
wanting to disturb the rest girls, "she keeps calling her husband's name. When is her husband coming for her?"

Kike looks at me, a patch of firelight stretching
over her face. "He dead," she whispers in a voice
that seems to scrape her chest.

"Dead?" I look at Chichi, her shoulders bent, her
mouth moving, and I feel a forever sorrow for her.
"When?"

"He fall down last week from a motorcycle. He
was going to buy meat pie for her. But he fall down
and break his head and die dead. Now his family

say she kill him, so she is here to carry a sacrifice for killing him. After that, she maybe marry her husband's brother."

The sudden bursting of gunshot in the air traps the words I want to say. I jump as Labake drops her firewood stick. Kike looks up, eyes on the back of the forest. The other girls push forward too, looking up in the sky.

Kike climbs slowly to her feet. "Soon each you pick your clay pot. You put it on your head and wait for us. It is time for me to rest my back. Soon I come back with the small-chief that wants to greet his coming-soon wife, Hauwa, and with Shaki. Don't forget," she adds in Yoruba, "there is only one way to enter the forest and go out of it. Shaki is at the entering place holding her gun. You cannot run far!"

Kike and Labake walk through a curtain of trees and disappear into the afar.

There is a long drag of silence after, and then the whisper of hurrying feet.

I smell him before I see him. Semi. This is the second time he is coming to this Circle of Forest by himself. I know Kike said she was going to bring him to come, so why he is here again without no Kike? Has he been hiding, watching us, waiting for Kike and Labake to leave us by ourselves?

He is looking even more handsome this evening, skin blazing under the fire. He nods at me, but his eyes is on Hauwa. This time, Zenab stands and goes to him. She puts her hands on her hips and asks him a question in her language, her voice low but still commanding. The man makes his response in their language, but from the way he is looking at Zenab, and from the story Zenab was telling us, I imagine it that he is saying: **You this girl, again? Mind your business and bring me my wife!**

The man takes a step toward a shaking Hauwa, but Zenab jumps in front of him again and shouts "No!" in English. I stand up, heart beating fast. The man throws Zenab to nearly the ground and cuts across the circle and pinches Hauwa, who is rolling up herself like a ball and trying to hide at the back of Efe's wide body, and pulls her up to her feet and drags her skinny hand and tiny screaming self out of the Circle of Forest.

ADUNNI

Zenab picks up the firewood stick, pulls up her wrapper to her knees, and runs after Semi and Hauwa.

I follow behind, using the dying sun as a torchlight, calling for her to wait for me as the ground is rising to slap my face, my heart twisting with fear and worry from the hooting and shrilling noise of animals.

Zenab is a very fast runner.

She seems like the wind of anger is making her fly; I don't see her legs touching the ground; I just see her moving, like she is floating and panting, snapping the tree branches from her face with the firewood in her hand, shouting for the man to stop, until Semi reaches another space of land with a embrace of trees snapped up into two, with thick rocks growing out from the earth like extra hands, with the saw and other machines of woodcutters gathered to one side of one of the rocks.

Behind the rocks, a street of cleared bush, a piling to the top of wood logs.

I bend myself behind one of the half trees, looking at the man who has put his hand around the neck of Hauwa; at Zenab, who is standing in front of them, panting. Her scarf is no longer on her head, and all her hair is pouring around her shoulders like shining cloth of black satin.

The man spits to the floor, shakes Hauwa to stop her crying, but she cries even more until he slaps silence into her mouth with the back of his hand.

"Leave her alone!" Zenab shouts in English, her voice making an echo all over the forest. "You are a pig!"

"She is my wife!" he shouts back in English. "After this night, I marry her!"

"In one month, you bastard!" Zenab says, panting, holding up her firewood. "One month! **Haba!** Not tonight! She's going to be judged to marry you tonight. After that, she'll have a month to prepare! Is that not the plan?" She shouts something in her language to Hauwa, and Hauwa says something back, her voice tight and full of tears and fear and sorrow.

"One month for who?" the man shouts back.

"Me?" He laughs a wicked laugh and says something in his language in a sound like an angry dog. His head flings to the left, near where I am hiding, and I bend more low, heart pounding.

He is now looking at the stack-up of machines, the tree-cutting knives, his eyes growing bigger, full of something hot. I listen to my heart, rising and falling like a sea wave crashing against my chest. Should I come out and let them see me? Should I stay hiding? Or run back to find the rest girls?

"You cannot do that!" Zenab speaks through a dragging of her breath. "She's not yet your wife!"

"I want to have her!" he shouts again. "This night! Since you are here, you watch me. And after I finish with her, I take you—and you too!" He turns and points at me.

"Adunni!" Zenab makes a gasp. "Come!"

I feel a coldness rise under my skin as I come out from the hiding place and run to hide behind her, breathing hard, my feet burning.

The man drags Hauwa to where the axe is and picks it up by the handle of wood and waves it at me and Zenab like a flag. "You come to near me, **walahi**, I butcher three of you!"

The man rakes Hauwa's legs with his own so that she crashes to the floor and lands on her back with a sharp, short sound, but I feel the earth under me tremble as if it was a big rock and not a small girl that fell.

The man climbs to his knees, puts down the axe to one side, and pushes apart Hauwa's legs, pinning her left leg down with the load of his knee. Hauwa does not cry; she just lies there, stiff, and in her wide-open eyes, I see the gold of dying sun.

Zenab stops panting, her hand hanging down to her side, limp like a wet rope. I think she is too much shock of what is about to happen. I put a hand on her shoulder, air hissing from my throat.

The man throws off his cap and pulls his **buba** over his neck and, at the same time, struggles to remove the rope of his trousers. I watch his back view, and under the silver light of the moon, he looks like he is bending down to dig inside his stomach and pluck out all his organs and throw them in the air. The **buba** and cap fly, landing on top of a short bush.

The memory rushes at me: Of how Big Daddy wanted to do this to me. How I fought.

Fight. That was the word I heard in my spirit. **Fight.**

The man's trouser drops to his bended knees, his buttocks as black as tires. Any moment now, he will climb on Hauwa. Zenab makes a sound like an animal who been wounded in the throat, but she does not move. She cannot move. The firewood stick drops out of her hand, and she falls to the floor beside it, crying.

After that, the whole earth seem to slow down as

I feel myself rushing forward and jumping on his back and digging my teeth into his neck and tasting the salt of his sweat and bitter of his perfume and the smoke of the forest.

Semi groans when I land on him. He elbows my ribs as he throws me to the ground. I groan. Semi spits into my eyes, blinding me for one moment. He packs a handful of sand as I start to climb back up, to stretch my hands to scratch his face. He pushes the sand into my mouth down my throat and jumps on me.

I begin to cough.

He squeezes my neck, pressing my cough back into my throat until my eyes grow thin and the circle of sky above us grow smaller and smaller until it is a dot of light. Through that dot, I see the sweat on his forehead shining like oil. Now the dot is exploding, and it is full of shapes of light that scatter and come together, and then it mix up and blend, forming the picture of my mama laughing; of Papa standing in a sea of white clouds, tears running down his face; and of Khadija, dressed in a gown of golden net, her pregnant stomach hard, her skin smooth. Hot air scrapes my throat and so I stop fighting to breathe. I hear feet behind me, running, faint. As if the feet is in another world, the feet of welcoming angels. The man is pressing the whole of his weight on the hands on my neck now. I feel my eyes closing, the drag of sweet sleep.

There is a sudden whoosh of air, a **swiiiii** sound, a **whack**. It shifts him off me, and he looks around, dazed, as his head swings to the left at another whack. He touches a hand to his head, blinks at the blood staining his fingers.

He staggers to his feet. Another whack paralyze him down, back to his knees. I drag myself from under him, coughing, drawing air, pressing my hands to my chest, but still watching as his head is turning left to collect another whack, and right again for another whack, like a game of table tennis so that his head is the bat, the stick is the ball.

Whack. Whack. Whack. Until the man falls with a groan.

Hauwa shifts with her buttocks back-back, until she is safe away from the lump of his body, pulling her wrapper to wrap up herself, to curl up beside a rock, to cry.

I climb to my trembling knees. The man is lying on his back, eyes wide open with no blink. There is a wound on the side of his head, a snap of a piece of stick coming out of his ear like a knife in a cake, blood pouring slowly into the foam of spit bubbling from his open mouth and forming a pool behind his head. His manhood lies like a bent finger along the flesh of his thigh, the rag of his trousers a puddle of cloth around his feet.

Then I see Zenab.

Standing over him, breathing hard, holding her

blood-covered firewood stick, with tears running down her face. She swipes the back of her hand on her cheeks, drops the stick on his stomach, and without looking at me, she says, "Can we burn him before the bath?"

FIVE HOURS TO MIDNIGHT

I've been calling Zenab's father, but the phone appears disconnected.

I send him four messages in succession: a quick introduction to who I am, info about my location, info about Zenab's situation and how urgent it is that he get here now, how important it is for him to call me back.

I sit, back numb, twirling my phone in my hands, feeling useless, helpless, the grass around me glowing silver, until my legs begin to ache.

The air has a strong scent of roasted chicken flesh, of smoke, shea, fried palm oil, despair. A distant singing is gradually accompanied by clapping, the clashing of metals, beaded feet slapping the ground to create a rhythm. My soul feels full on the fat of desolation, apprehension, anticipation. I am tempted to go and look, to see what's going on, but I am also terrified of getting caught. And where is Kayus? I wish I could hold his hands and lead him through his grief and loss. I wish I could crawl into a hole of nothingness and shut the door against myself.

Ken calls. I pick up, feeling unraveled, turned inside out with anguish. "Please tell me you found Ade and you guys are on your way."

"Are you crying?" He sounds like he's trapped in the center of a cyclone.

I sniff, wiping my eyes. "Did you find Adunni's father?"

"He replied to my text just as he was leaving his office. He says he's been waiting for this day for years. He's driving up to meet me. We'll probably ditch his car and take mine—"

"Oh, God." The land around me swirls on the tide of pure relief. I let out a strangled cry. "Thank God, Ken. If you speed and—"

"Listen," Ken says. "We can't get there on time."

I tense, gripping the phone with sweaty palms, eyes on a bony black goat gnawing at weeds at the base of the well and sneezing from its fragrance, so that the wandering brown-necked and speckled chickens, which were busy scratching their feet around goat pellets, are forced to disperse in haste. "Why?"

"A combination of woes," Ken says. "Rain.

Traffic. I hear there's been a major blockage on the express that leads us to Ikati. I hear whispers that the son of some rich dude was kidnapped by bandits or something. The police are slowing cars down to check the kid's not in it."

"For goodness' sake!" I yell. "Does the world have to come to a bloody standstill because someone's precious son was kidnapped? I mean, I feel for them, but there's Adunni and the girls who need help and no one cares?! This is the problem with the world! Rich privilege! Male privilege!"

Ken exhales. "I've been on the same spot for nearly two hours, and I've still got to wait for Ade to catch up."

I swallow a lump, looking down at my feet: brown, mud-caked, my toenails crescents of black glue. A tear drops from my eye, splattering my scaly skin. I've been through too much to give up now. "That's fine, Ken. You just keep coming?"

"Tia, come on. You need to really figure out how to get out of there before midnight. I don't want you—"

"No, Ken." I growl out the words. "You need to listen. You focus on getting here with Ade Enahoro. I am not moving an inch out of this village until Adunni is safe."

"Tia." He sounds helpless. "Please."

"Focus, Ken," I snap without meaning to. The pressure has broken me. "Please. Thank you." I hang up and let out a wobbly breath.

My father sends pictures, messages. I click open the first one: It's an image of my mother on the bed, eyes closed, a slope of a smile on her face. My father has added a caption: **She's waiting to see you. Tomorrow? Confirm.**

I reply: **Confirmed.**

A moment later: **Mum okay. Smiling. See you soon.**

Tomorrow I'll hear her out. I'll listen to her side of the story. Because we all have a story. Ade has his for Adunni. I have mine for Oyi, and I'd love for her to give me a chance to tell it. My mother deserves an opportunity to tell hers, to be forgiven. And maybe, maybe we can be friends before she dies. Maybe we can salvage the scraps of our relationship. Give it meaning, no matter how short the time is.

I smile through my tears for the first time, thinking of my mother.

I climb to my knees and look over the hedge: A queue of about four men—their chests naked and hairy, red wrappers tied around their waists—has formed behind the shrine. I crouch low before one of them notices me, my back against a carpet of thorns. I hardly feel the thorns graze my back; I hardly smell the stench of chickenshit and blood; I hardly see the chaos and poverty around me. That's the disgusting reality about the human ability to adapt. At first the shock, the repulsion, is all in 3D—sights and sounds and smells. You recoil and gag and wish for a bath and cry at the devastation. Time passes. You live in it. You spend time in it.

You blend, and everything fizzles to normalcy, and that which once repulsed slowly becomes natural, acceptable if you do nothing.

That, I realize, is what culture is: doing things a certain way until you get used to it.

My phone rings.

Zenab's father.

AND SO I ROAR

ADUNNI

My heart is running after my breath, but it cannot catch it.

I cannot breathe as I look at the body of the dead man with a hope that he will somehow magic and answer us with ideas of how to burn his body.

Zenab drops to her knees and bends her ears to near the man's mouth as if she wants him to lick her ears with his swollen-up tongue peeping from the trap of his white teeth. "He's a hundred percent gone," she says, pushing herself back up. "Adunni, how far away is this part of the forest from the village?"

I want to tell her we are not far from the curve of the hills behind Baba Ogun's house, that we cannot burn him with no matches or fire, that a fire will pour smoke out of the nose of the forest and color the night air with the guilty of our sins, but my words are stucked inside the man's dead eyes. I try, but I cannot drag myself from the trap of him, and so I bend my neck, looking at him, his swollen-up head, the edge of it like a mash-up cake of flesh. Did I kill a man? Or did I help Zenab kill a man? Or did we kill him together? Is he really dead?

His neck is bend too, a little to the left as if he was looking at a sideways photo that baffle him and was thinking deep about it before he just collected a blow and die dead. There is a dot-dot line of dried blood around his swollen-up neck that makes me think of a chain of thick red beads. And somehow, he looks like a child. Innocent. A baby-man with wet eyes open to a lost-forever world. How is it that I came back to wash my name clean, but I end up soaking my whole future in the blood of another dead man? How will I ever be free?

"Not your fault," Zenab says, as if she can hear my thinking. "None of this is anyone's fault. He's a rapist. A monster, and he literally came at us? He would have killed us!" Her voice is shaking like she is catching a cold, her teeth clapping with each word. She's now walking back and front from Semi's head to his toes, tapping her forehead with her fingers, **tap-tap-tap**. "So quit the guilt and let's, like, I don't know? Keep it quiet and find a way out of this mess? I need Dad. I need Dad. I need Dad."

Zenab stops walking a moment to make a noise like she wants to vomit, pressing a hand over her stomach and pushing herself back up. "I need Dad. I need Dad. I need Dad."

I make a cross sign, touch my finger to my forehead and chest and left and right shoulder, and pray for God to forgive me, to see my heart, and don't let this make things worse for me. I wipe my tears, pick up his **buba** from near Hauwa, the smell of gin and men's perfume still strong on it, and cover his body, the window of his judging eye with it.

"Oh, I know!" Zenab sudden picks up a stick and breaks it into two, the light from the climbing moon shining on the fear in her eyes. "We'll create a fire with sticks. I've done this in camping! I was a Girl Scout in primary school, and we'll, like, basically create a fire by just—" She grunts, trying to rub the end of the two sticks together while talking and breathing fast with the sticks making a scratch-scratch noise as she rubs back and front, back and front. "If the sticks are dry enough, we'll . . . Hauwa, think you can stop, like, crying for a moment and let me think? Please? Right, Adunni, don't just stand there, pick up two sticks and let's do this."

"Maybe we go back and find help?" I climb to my feet, still looking at her: the fold of her bottom lip tight between her teeth as if to make a hole in the flesh of it, her eye growing bigger as she keeps rubbing the stick and rubbing it until it breaks with a soft **ka** sound.

Zenab drops the broken sticks and wipes her forehead with the back of her hand. "It was way easier at summer camp." She looks up at me. "Can we maybe dig and bury him?" She's looking around before I can find my words, eyes jumping from wood log to wood log, to the machines of the woodcutter. "We could drag him there?" She points afar, to somewhere behind my head. "Or there? Anywhere really? And, like, bury him between two trees? We only need like three feet? Just enough to hide his body until I can get out of here and get my dad to help? My dad will never let me get arrested, Adunni. Okay? We'll get out of this. We just need to be strong. Be strong. Repeat after me: I am strong?"

"I am strong?" I say.

"We've got this?" Zenab says.

"We've got this?" I say.

"You good, Adunni?"

"You good, Adunni?" I repeat with a nod, and the pain in my neck rolls all over my body. Zenab blows out a laugh from her mouth. A laugh like she cannot understand why she is laughing.

"You are nuts," she says, standing and dropping her wrapper so that she is in just her pant and bra. She wraps her wrapper around the man's feet and his ankles.

"No fingerprints," she says as she begins to drag the man over the dirt of the floor and the sand to near where she said we should bury him. "While I do this, can you find a makeshift shovel for you and

Hauwa?" She moves left and right from the heavy
of his body, her mouth filling with air that she
blows out with each word: "We. Need. Something.
Flat. Curved. Check one of those machines. Hurry.
Argh. Please."

I set about looking around me, scattering the
earth with my fingers, peeping behind wood logs
and trees and finding nothing but one iron stick
and the axe. The rest machines are too big and will
make too much noise.

Hauwa keeps her head in the middle of her knees
and shakes her head no, no, no, so I leave her and
her sad singing-cry and run to meet Zenab, where I
find her collapsed of herself next to the man behind
one big log of wood, her chest climbing and falling,
her face shining black with night sweat. She points.
"The ground. Is. Soft. Over there. Start. We need.
Hauwa."

"She is too shocked to move," I say to Zenab. "She
will slow us too down."

"Fine," Zenab says with a hiss that feels like a
rope tight around my neck, and Hauwa's soft crying from afar is a lock around the rope to tight it
even more.

"We'll do this for her, right?" Zenab says. "No
matter what happens, we protect her? We protect
each other. Come on, Adunni, let's do this."

Zenab picks up the axe and slaps the face of the
ground with the edge of it and begins to dig, her
hands moving up and down, the axe slicing the air

one moment, the blade of the axe cupping sand the next minute. I join her, scratching the ground with my hands, with the iron stick, with anything I find. Soon there is a mix of scratching and grunting and swishing swoosh and spitting noise in the silence as we dig and dig, growing the hill of sand, carving a bowl in the earth.

Zenab does not stop for one seconds to even rest. Her black skin is shining with sweat as she bends and cups and stands and pours, and I steal a peep at her many times, full of shock at how she doesn't slow down, how she doesn't even make one complain of the hard work of digging.

After what feel like plenty minutes of time, Zenab drops the axe, breathing fast. She puts her hand on her knees. "We need an extra hand," she says. "We can't. We are too slow."

I slap the sand from my hand and nod. We have already dig up a hole that is like a sink of kitchen in the ground, but not enough to cover the whole of Semi's body. If we bury him like this, his head and knees will peep from the top of the sand.

"I bring Hauwa," I say. "You rest five minutes."

Zenab shakes her head no, picks up the axe, and continues to dig.

The sound of digging follows me until I find Hauwa looking at the night sky, eyes wide. "You cannot sit there and be looking," I say. "Come and help us."

She blinks at me. I am not sure if she didn't

understand my English or if she is too daze.
"Quick!" I whisper-shout. "We need your help to
dig! Time is nearly reaching for the bath!"

Hauwa wipes her mouth with the back of her
hand, a slow dragging across her lips. She raises up
her head, as if finding something over the fence of
my shoulders. Slowly, she climbs to her feet and
begins to follow me. Just as we reach Zenab, a
gunshot burst in the air, making an echo on the
whole forest.

Hauwa and I, we freeze. Zenab drops the axe
on the ground, and the blade of it nearly slice off
Semi's right ear. The three of us turn toward the
sound as if it is a giant thing walking toward us and
the dead body.

Then Zenab says, "Run!"

FOUR HOURS
TO MIDNIGHT

TIA

The conversation with Zenab's father was brief, frenzied: He is on his way and wants me to keep him informed on how the girls are doing. At one point, his voice broke as he begged me to keep his daughter safe, to keep my phone free. There is a sudden wind ripping through the air and whirling the dust. Someone's coming. I hide my phone, thinking of Kayus and missing his guidance, the brilliant hope that sparkles in his eyes as though everything were an adventure.

The person emerges.

A woman—older, weathered face, a long wrapper tied around her chest. Did I not see her in the Circle of Forest, trying to start a fire?

"Madam?" she whispers, looking over her shoulder. "Me. Labake. The mother of Kike." She holds out a metal cup filled with a dark liquid. "Drink."

Kike's mother. Idowu's bigmouthed former best friend. I accept the cup and take a sip, tasting weed and salt. It almost immediately calms my nerves and makes me feel full. Rational. I whisper my gratitude, knocking the rest back, pressing the cup into her hands.

"Where is the man. Her papa? True. One?" Her words and phrases are wedged with pauses, as if each word is a special offering that ought to be arranged on her tongue before it is uttered.

"On his way," I say.

A shriek from a nocturnal animal pierces the air. "If the man. He didn't come on time. Bad. For Adunni." Labake talks more to herself than to me. She's clutching the cup in her wrapper as if trying to suppress her agitation into its hollow center.

"Listen, Labake. We need to—" I push myself up on my knees, sticks and twigs cracking from the suddenness of my rise, falling off the fabric of my wrapper. "We need to talk to the chiefs."

"You talk to chiefs? No. You woman, you don't. Even my Kike. She don't." She lets out a solemn hiss. "Lagos peoples. You come. You think to change the-this and the-that. Speak with big-big English. Wear jeans-trouser."

"I just . . . Listen, I, uh, have money." I should be ashamed of touting a bribe, but what choice have I got? "I have money to give the people. To help your village."

"You give to us. Rain?" she says, eyeing me warily. "The big problem? No rain here. Rain there. Animal dying. Flooding killing. Everything. Suffer-suffer."

"I know how—" I trail off as a thought takes root. I pluck out my phone and start to record a voice note to my boss on WhatsApp. Labake watches, a stunned and irritated expression on her face.

"Mr. Mike, it's Tia Dada. I'm sorry I haven't checked my email today—I had a family emergency . . . I am in the village of Ikati," I breathe into the phone. "The epicenter of a perfect candidate for the Green Education Funding. It's a rural remote village, hours from Lagos. At midnight today, that's in . . . a few hours, six girls will be judged and maybe punished—for various offenses. What bothers me is that these girls are being blamed indirectly for reduced rainfall in the land. What terrifies me is that this will continue—until someone stops it. I know one of the girls, Adunni. She's accused of—"

I swipe up—deliberately breaking off mid-sentence—to send. No point exposing Adunni in that manner.

I resume recording.

"It's pretty obvious to me, that this . . . drought and flooding is not unique to Ikati and its surrounding villages. Ikati has a unique landscape. It is surrounded by mountains and hills and forests and waterfalls and rivers—it is spectacular, but a potential major melting point for disaster. I have seen firsthand how their people have cut down thousands of trees to sell to parts of Asia and the West, illegally and indiscriminately, with zero intention to replant, thereby probably obliterating an entire carbon sink. It's not an immediate solution, but can we find a way for the farmers to learn how to cultivate their soil with drought-tolerant seeds and all that good stuff the food team can help with? The women can be educated on how to rely less on farming as a major source of income and figure out other ways to help their community. But I need your help . . . to somehow make these people see this, buy into this vision. This is important, sir. We may be able to save many lives from hardship and death. I will be in touch in the morning."

I swipe up the second time. "Listen, Labake," I say, tucking my phone into my wrapper. Excitement and dread rise in my throat like vomit. "I respect your . . . beliefs and all, but I have an idea that might help your people. My company in Lagos, we . . . we help with—" I scramble for how best to explain our partnership with the Nigerian environmental agency. "There are ways to make things better. A little by little. Please let me speak to the chiefs. Help me, Labake. Please."

"No," she insists, eyeing me like I've got some viral disease. "Women. They don't. They don't supposed to talk." She narrows her eyes and heaves a sigh that appears to ride the tide of her rising and falling bosom. "I try. Ask—" Gunshot cracks the air, cutting her off. She glances around as if to locate the sound in the evening wind. "I think. Is nearing time. For baff."

I won't panic. I won't.

"She tell you?" Labake glances down at me and puts her arms on her hips. "She tell you? Say it is me. I cause all problems for Idowu?"

I shrug, remembering my promise to Iya.

"Me? Not bad person," Labake continues, her voice wobbly with tears. "I true-true didn't know. Idowu swallow . . . **majele**."

"Poison? I understand. It's sad."

She's unraveling her wrapper from under her armpit and wiping her eyes with the edge of the fabric, a motion that fills the air with the scent of onions, sweat. "My angry? It is boiling. Hot. Idowu tell me of man-friend. Me? Very angry. Angry too, because Adunni. She marry my Morufu. So, I think . . . mother bad, **pickin** bad."

"When did you find out Idowu killed herself?"

"After Adunni. Run aways, go to Lagos." Her chin quakes. "I feel. Sorry. Plenty sorry."

"Idowu was your friend," I say. "She trusted you. You should not have told her husband about her affair. You knew she was meant to have married Ade—she never loved Akala. And Adunni was a child. Your husband married a child, Labake. And somehow you think it's Adunni's fault?" A breeze blows over us. Part of me wants to talk to her about this, the unrealistic and harsh expectations of women in this part of our world.

"I didn't know Idowu. She killed herself," she says.

"Adunni cannot know," I say. "It would break her heart and she might blame herself forever. Can you please not tell her or your daughter, Kike?"

Labake points to the sky. "If I tell her, then the thunder? It fire me dead."

"We need to support each other, Labake," I say, softening my voice. "Idowu made a mistake. And you never gave her a chance to make it right, to tell her husband herself. She's dead, and Adunni has suffered because of her death."

"I go now. You stay this place. Me? I try. I help Adunni. Helping Adunni is way for me. To say sorry for break of rope that tie me and Idowu. The rope of friends."

I understand. I've tried to say sorry to Oyi by being here tonight with Adunni, but I am not sure that is ever going to be enough.

|||||||||||||||||||||||||||||||
ADUNNI
|||||||||||||||||||||||||||||||

We run.
   Me and Hauwa and Zenab, we run toward the gunshot and the rest girls, stumbling in our wrapper, panting hard.

My throat feels like it is full of cuttings of wood, but still, I try to talk to Zenab to make a plan. "What do we do?"

My chest burns as Zenab shouts, "We'll go back and bury him!"

"We cannot go back! We don't have time!" I shout back, stammering my words, over the snapping of branches under our feet.

"We'll burn him! I'll grab the matchbox Labake used and set him on fire."

"We cannot set a fire!" I scream. "Everybody will see it burning!" I slow down to catch my breathing, to draw in air. "You know the girls saw him two times? Kike too said he was coming! They will be looking for him."

"We can tell them we saw him and chased him away!" Zenab says, slowing down too. "Listen, Adunni. We have to finish burying him together, or I find a way to burn him. If we burn him and they ever find his corpse, they won't be able to identify him! I watch it all the time on **Crime TV**. I doubt Ikati has the forensic technology to identify bodies with dental records!"

I stop running, and crumple like an empty sack to the ground. "Are you having madness in your head? This is not a Technology TV!" I am crying now. "This is true life! We kill a man!"

Zenab stops running.

She walks back and bends, pressing her hands on her knees. "I killed a man," she says, touching her chest, her fingers black and dirty with sand. She doesn't look afraid or worried. Just calm. As if she been planning this since she was born. "I literally just killed a man and tried to bury him, okay? **Me.** Not you. Now is not the time to be stupid and take the blame. Now get up and let's get back before anyone suspects." She points to an opening to our left. "I dropped my scarf when I was running so we'd find our way back. I see it flapping over there. Come on up."

She holds out her hand and I take it. She pulls me up, says something in her language, and hugs Hauwa tight as she continues to cry.

"I told her to be strong and pretend she didn't see a thing."

I am empty of my words, tears. What will I say to Ms. Tia? To Kayus? What kind of day is this? Why did I come back from Lagos?

"Listen," Zenab says. "We haven't dug enough to bury him, but we have to hide his body. So, let's go back to the circle thing. I assume that gunshot was a warning for us to get ready for the bath, right?"

I try to nod, but my head is shaking.

"Perfect," Zenab says, touching a hand to my trembling shoulder. "I was going to fight the woman cutting me, but now I think I'll let her cut me, right? So that after, when the rest of you are going to the village for your sacrifice, I can go back and burn him. People will think the smoke and stuff is all part of tonight's sacrifice. No one will find him. We'll be fine."

Then, from nowhere, a voice: "Where did you people go?!"

Efe.

She appeared sudden and is now standing in front of us. Looking confused. Afraid. "You people? Ha! Where have you been?"

I hold my breath, heart beating fast in my chest.

"We hear screaming all over the forest!" Efe keeps talking. "Loud! We thought it was animals,

no shakings, but you people did not come back!
For almost one and half hour! Now Kike and all of
them is here! It is time for us to dance back. Where
are you coming from? What happened to you?" She
takes a step close to Zenab, squinting her eyes as if
the moon light is too very bright.

"You kill one animal?" She bends her neck, and
I see what she is looking at: blood. A swipe of it on
Zenab's wrapper; drops of it on her skin, her chest,
her shoulders, like tiny black, shining beads.

I quick check the rest of us: Hauwa's wrapper is
full of dirty, Zenab's scarf is full of tearing holes
from when she hang it on a tree and try to tangle
it free, and my wrapper is painted everywhere with
mud and leaves.

But no blood on me or Hauwa. Only Zenab.

"Yeah," Zenab says. Her voice is hard. "I killed
an animal."

"Which animal?" Efe asks. "Where?

"A bird," I say, talking too fast, acting like something is wrong with my head. "Up in the sky, flying,
flying!" I flap my hands like a wing. "Then sudden
it fall!" I slap my hand down on my thighs. "Land
on a tree, cut itself, **slash**! Fall on Zenab chest, **twai**!
Blood! Everywhere! Blood! Spray of it!"

I wave my arms in the air until Zenab knocks me
in the rib with her elbow and says, "Shut up."

Efe twists her mouth, the light of the moon dancing a happy dance on her yellow hair. "Where is
the man?"

I look at Zenab, the calm on her face as she picks up her walking, my heart a swelling thing in my chest.

"Because Kike was finding him?" Efe says, running to block Zenab, to stop her walking. "She says she was looking for him to bring him to Hauwa, and I told her all of you chased him away."

"Yep," Zenab says. "We chased him away, okay? I need like a moment to catch my breath, so please no further questions."

I feel a fire burning me, the fire of fear. "Where is Kike now?"

"In the circle. Shaki fired a gun for us to get ready. Why did it take you so long?"

"BECAUSE!" Zenab says, voice sharp.

Efe folds her arms, not moving.

"We thought to find some corn to roast," Zenab says. "That's why it took us ages to come back. Now please. Get out of my way."

"Where is the corn?" Efe asks, and I want to head-butt her for that stupid question.

"In the land of No Shakings," Zenab says.

"But the man—" The cry of an animal pinches the rest of Efe's question.

"Come on!" Zenab shouts at the sky, and her voice bounces on the trees. She wipes her chest with her hands, and as we start walking, she leans close and whispers: "We protect each other, okay?"

By the time we reach the circle, the girls are already preparing to carry their pots. Kike gives me a long look, but she doesn't ask where we are coming from, not even when Hauwa starts to cry.

I am still trembling as I fold myself pick up my pot of water, eyes on Zenab, who is crawling toward the fire with her pot, saying, "I'm cold? I just need to warm up for, like, a minute?" I keep watching her, wondering how she is not afraid, how her body is not shaking, as she crawls to near the fire and with one hand feeling the ground and the other hand holding her pot, until she finds the box of matches and quick hides it in her wrapper and nods at me.

Finally, we form a line. Shaki fires another gunshot. **Pow!**

Kike, in front, starts to sing.

We join her. Singing and dancing all the way to the edge of the cliff.

THREE HOURS
TO MIDNIGHT

TIA

The expanse is slowly starting to sizzle with the frenzy of dancing women, their figures captured in moonlight.

They are wearing wrappers and dresses and headscarves, with braided hair and beaded twists and combed-out afros. There is chatter, excitement, an undercurrent of fear as the music swells and falls. The drummers, a group of three men dressed in cropped **agbadas**, sit on the ground with legs spread apart, hourglass-shaped batá drums trapped between their thighs. Their frowns are intense, menacing as they slap coarse palms against the goatskin surface of the drums, and produce a barrage of harmonized beats that ricochet from the hill to the cliff to the ground.

I sag against a tree, feeling dizzy as more women troop into the chief priest's compound. The women whisper, some raising their arms toward the sky, others looking up at the forest behind, the rocky edge of the cliff to its left, as if anticipating the return of the girls from the bath.

Through the spinning haze, I notice Labake approach a woman with an oval face and a neck adorned with a string of beads. She sits on a log of timber, next to three other women dressed like her, her back stiff, narrowed eyes scanning the crowd. Labake whispers into her ear and points vaguely in my direction. The chief's wife shakes her head, spits to the floor by her side, and glares at me with venom-laced eyes.

I take that as a colossal no.

Labake slithers away, defeated.

I exhale, trying to control the panic fluttering in my belly, eyes raking from one luminous face to the other. There is a woman set far apart from the rest, as if to willfully isolate herself. She is hunched over a rosewood log, pressing her hands together as if to pray, her cheeks glistening with tears. I watch her until she lifts her head and stares at me, as if the pressure of my gaze beckoned. At first, I think it is Zenab: She has the same angled cheekbones, the same stunning features. Her mother? The woman's weathered face contorts, as though crushed by the singing. She looks away, anxiously glancing toward the forest to our right.

I call Ken, Zenab's father, Ken, Zenab's father. No one picks up. I try again and again, my fingers growing stiff from the pressure on the dial pad until I am forced to turn my phone off to preserve battery. I try to calm myself down, but my body quivers like a dying flame. And so, I press a hand to my chest and breathe in and out, slowly, and each breath feels like the ticking hand of a clock, slowly traveling through my body.

ADUNNI

We are by the edge of a cliff behind Ikati forest, under the big-white watching eye of the full-up moon, which is turning to the white of a bone, a ticking clock pointing to midnight.

Kike's husband is at the front of the line, looking like a broomstick-man with bone-joining-bone on his no-flesh body. A curl of gray hair snakes down to the middle of his left eye, a cowrie hanging at the tip of it. His eyes are the blade of a knife, a slant of two shining metals inside his forehead.

This man, who wrap himself up with a red cloth, with cowries and small horns dancing around the fabric, with the skull of a goat hanging from a string of beads on his neck, has been washing all of us one by one with the dead chicken in his hand; around and around, the thing stinking of shit and blood, under our armpit, between our legs, the back of our heads, around our feet. I watched myself, thinking of the dead man in the forest, the man Zenab killed, as Baba Ogun lifted up his blade, said one or two incantations and sliced the flesh open of my right elbow, my blood drop-drop-dropping into the calabash in his hand. I made a cup with my hands to collect the water from my clay pot to wash myself hard, as if to wash off the memory of the dead man, the **thwack** of the stick sounding in my head every time I nod or breathe.

After, I wrapped myself in the white wrapper and lined up and waited.

Now, with water drying from my body, I stand shivering as Kike calls for Zenab to kneel down in front of the chief priest. The sky looks darker, a blue-black with not one single star shining. Even the moon seems to be hiding behind the curtain of the sky. Like he did for us, he turns the chicken around Zenab's head as if to draw a circle, the blood from the neck of it dripping to her hair and shoulder.

His wife Shaki, who has been standing beside her husband since all this while, is now nodding yes even when nobody is talking to her. She has been holding a tray with a calabash on top of it, a razor blade, bottles of something dark.

"What happens next?" Lady G asks.

"I think they cut Zenab," I say. "After, we go for the sacrifice." **And then Zenab will go and try to burn the dead man.** But won't she feel pain from the cutting? Why she wants to make herself suffer all that pain just to help us? What if she just runs to hide and waits for her papa to reach us? But what if her papa cannot reach us on time? Even if Zenab is able to hide the man, I don't know how I can keep quiet about it and not tell Ms. Tia.

My mind will not let me have peace if I don't tell her.

The air is whistling soft, blowing a warm wind. Mosquitoes are flying about, buzzing inside the room of our ears. I slap one or two, and as I am rubbing my hands together, I feel my book making a crunch under my wrapper.

The old man spits in Zenab's eyes, rubs it with his fingers. She snatch her head back, and gives him a look of anger. My heart makes a thunder in my chest. I am afraid she will push him or wound him. I pray she just stays quiet and don't fight. He shouts some words in the same language Zenab and Hauwa been speaking—I didn't know he can speak another language.

Zenab shakes her head no.

The old man sudden pulls off her wrapper and exposes her naked. Zenab cries and falls forward, slamming her head on a mud-stone, the sound like a slap on the face of the rock.

Efe shouts: "No!"

Lady G covers her wide-open mouth with her hand and shakes and shakes her head, as if to remove it from her body, send it rolling off the cliff.

Chichi starts to cry.

Zenab, be strong, I shout at her with my eyes. **Stand up and be strong.**

The old man shouts at Zenab again, giving her a kick that I feel the thud of it at the bottom of my brain. He looks behind, to the fence of forest trees. "Where is the woman? Where is she?"

Shaki points to the trees and makes a strange noise in her throat.

"What?" Lady G whispers, shivering beside me. "What's happening?"

The air grows hotter as we wait.

A woman comes walking out from behind the trees. Never seen her before in my life. Her skin is the black of night, her head shaped like a question mark, as if the back is growing a small extra head. A cloth is covering her right eye—and I wonder if she is the woman that will cut Zenab?

She don't wear one single cloth: naked from head to feet, each her two breasts like a long stretching letter U hanging from the flat of her chest. I know for sure that she is not from this village. The air screams inside my ears as we watch her, all of us shaking with fear and burning with heat, as she plucks a razor blade from the tray, holds it up.

I taste something rough, like salty sand, in the back of my throat.

The woman wants to do this? In front of all of us? No!

The old woman folds her waist like a cloth, climb to her knees. She slaps Zenab two times, a sound that causes a bird to take off in the afar, its wings sounding like the blade of a ceiling fan.

"I cannot watch this," Lady G says, turning her head around to look in my eyes. "I can't."

Zenab's body is breathing in and out, a line of blood is crawling out from behind her head, tracing a curve under a wet rock with a frog hiding behind it. Slowly she turns herself around and opens wide her two legs. The old woman holds up the blade and shouts some words.

One by one, every of us girls bend our head. We want to give Zenab the respect, to not look when such a wicked thing is happening to her. I put my head in the middle of my knees and close my eyes.

I hear her kicking, fighting, and a force pushes forward my knees, lifting up my arms, pushing me to break free, to drag her away from that woman, but a hand, Lady G's, touches my shoulder, gentle.

"Don't call attention to yourself, Adunni," she whispers. "Zenab will be fine. We will all be fine."

"Who is Attention?" I whisper-shout.

"Just . . . don't do anything. Don't make this worse for Zenab," Lady G says.

And so, I stay there, with my head trapped in my knees with blood booming in my ears, with fire burning my lungs, liver, and heart.

I wait for the scream of pain from Zenab. For the cutting.

But someone is running. The panting voice of a man. "Semi is dead!" the man shouts in Yoruba. "His body is inside the forest, near a new grave!"

I open my eyes and turn around, a hammer banging inside my head.

The man is from Ikati, and he stiffs his back when he sees Zenab lying on the ground. He turns himself around and bows his head. His name comes to me: Dauda. One of the servants of the chiefs. There is a stick in his hand. The firewood? I peep more close, see the sharp tip of his stick is covered with dried blood, the edges along of it shattered. I feel a sudden pressing to piss, for the ground to open its mouth and cover me and Hauwa and Zenab.

"This is what killed him!" Dauda says, still speaking Yoruba, holding up the stick. "Somebody killed him and was digging a grave to bury him!"

There is a low murmur from all the girls, a cry of shock. There is something else in his hand, a ball of a cloth, but I cannot see what it is because the naked old woman is covering Zenab's legs with her white cloth and standing up. Zenab sits up after, her eyes widening wide as she looks around, maybe trying to catch my face, Hauwa's face.

"Which Semi?" the chief priest asks. "The young chief of Ikati?"

"The man!" Efe whispers, covering her mouth with her hand. "The man that came to meet us in the circle is dead? Did you people kill him? I knew you people—"

"Keep quiet!" I say, whisper-shouting. My head is banging, the world swimming around and around.

"We find this," Dauda says, "not far from the body of Semi. Can I turn, to look your face, Chief Priest?"

"Turn!" the chief priest screams.

Dauda turns, still holding up his hand. Inside it is a tearing of Zenab's scarf, the shape of a half a square with a rough edge that dances in the stiff wind. "Who owns this scarf? We know it is one of you! Nobody this night entered the Circle of Forest, only the women and you girls!"

My legs make a buckle. Hauwa cries a sharp cry.

"Who owns this scarf?" the chief priest asks, his voice shaking with anger. "Who among of you kill a young chief in Ikati?"

Hauwa takes a step forward. She starts to put up her hand, inch by inch, but Zenab jumps to her feet, says, "No, Hauwa. Stay back. This was me! All me."

I want to move, to join her, to say it was me too, that I was there, but my legs is a root planted in the soil of the rocks under me, and I feel so afraid, ashamed of myself.

"I did it," Zenab says before Hauwa can say another word. There is a small smile on Zenab's face, a curve like a comma. She sounds so calm, like she is about to sleep. "I killed him because he wanted to rape Hauwa. The first time he did it, he was offered the girl as a wife? That's just . . . It's unfair! She's a little girl! I have a little sister! Why couldn't Semi wait for one month to marry her? He wanted to . . . to defile her again!" She spits to the floor. "He deserved to die." Then she raises her voice up, a shout: "And you all deserve to rot in hell for what you do to us girls! Every single one of you!"

"She kill a chief?" the chief priest shouts, his voice so full of anger. "Semi, the son of our fathers? Dauda, take her and lock her up!"

I press my hand to my lips and begin to beg the chief priest for Zenab. "Please, sir. It was accident. Semi had accident." The killing of a young chief is very, very bad in Ikati. I was having a hope before, that Zenab will burn Semi and be safe in Abuja with her papa before they find the body of Semi, but now they already find him, I don't know how she will escape plenty suffering.

Zenab spins herself and begins to run, her wrapper flapping in the wind, the box of matches dropping from under her as she runs to near the mouth of the rocks.

"Where is she going?" Lady G whispers. Her words are breaking, her teeth clapping. "Does she know how quick that edge drops down?"

I want to go to her, to warn her, but Shaki pushes up her gun and points it to us, as if to shoot if we make to move.

"Adunni, does she know what she is doing?"

Lady G's question is like drilling noise in my ears. "Someone has to stop her!"

We all watch her, my stomach pressing full of piss, every one of us shivering, holding our breath as Zenab wears the dark like a cloth, her hair bouncing on her bare back, until she reaches almost to the very edge of the cliff's teeth. Behind her, Dauda is running. Any moment now, he will reach her.

"Zenab?" I whisper, afraid that if I shout, my voice will push her over. Why is she so close on the edge of the cliff? Why is she falling to her knees?

"Think of **The Zee-Zee Show**, Zenab! Think of your transcript, your book of it! Think, Zenab, of your daddy! Your computer-app things. Of the future!"

Hauwa wails with each whisper, and Efe starts to cry too.

"She's going to meet Zuke," Chichi says. I hear a smile in her voice.

"Turn around and come back," Lady G says. "Zenab, please. You are too close to the edge! Come back!"

The rest girls behind cover their mouths, the fear on their faces brighter than the moon.

Kike too starts walking toward her, her pregnant stomach leading her. She sings a slow song as she walks, a song of calming, tears sliding down her face. I hope the song will make Zenab turn around and come back.

Zenab is spreading out her arms now. Dauda, who was almost reaching her, sudden stops running, and stands not too afar, panting, as if afraid that if he is too close, she will pull him down the cliff.

I scream her name.

She turns around. Shouts: "Kike, tell your husband this was all me. Not Hauwa, not Adunni. It was me. Adunni, tell my father I am sorry I stole from him? That I did not listen?" She shouts another something to Hauwa, words I cannot understand.

Shaki fires her gun in the air, to maybe stop Zenab, but it only makes Zenab shock and fall over so that she rolls on her wrapper, more down to the very near the edge of the cliff. I stop breathing. I am afraid now that anything, a small wind, a finger-push, my breath . . . will push Zenab off.

"Am I going to fall?" she asks, her voice so tiny, as if she knows that if she speaks more loud, the force of it can push her down. We all stand stiff, watching her body tilting close to the edge. **I must help her. I must.** My heart is banging so hard I feel it in my throat.

"I am going to come to you," I say, quiet. "Don't move. I come. I will make a rope with my wrapper, give to you. You hold it and I pull you. Okay?"

"Okay, Adunni," Zenab says, crying softly. "I don't know what I was thinking? I just wanted to run away? Please help me, Adunni."

"**Quiet!**" I say, starting to walk on tip of my toe toward her. "Just stay there, Zenab. Don't move one minute. Close your eyes, think of your daddy coming."

"Okay," Zenab says. "I am thinking of my daddy."

I am a few feet away from the slide of rock when Shaki fires another gun. I freeze.

Zenab rolls.

Falls.

She does not scream. She does not say one word. She falls, silent, like a bubble of spit floating out from an open mouth.

I freeze.

Her body bumps and crashes down the staircase of rocks behind, down and down, into a dip that I know will lead to the Agan river. I freeze. At the screaming from the girls slicing the air.

I freeze. Even though I am thinking, **I can still save her. I can get to the edge and save her. I can jump off the cliff to save her.** I freeze, but I see myself tearing off my wrapper and running, near naked, the twisting of my wrapper weaving between my legs and nearly falling me down. Then I gather myself and begin to run, screaming and screaming her name.

"ZENAB?" I stop close to the mouth of the cliff, swaying in the night wind. "Zenab?!" I am crying and filling my mouth with something that is choking me, and my tears is becoming an ocean on my face, flooding all around me.

I hear Efe shouting: "Wisdom! Come back!"

Hauwa is wailing. Kike, who is near me, is still singing her song of sorrow.

But I don't hear Zenab, and I don't see her. I call for her. I call her name. I beg her. I beg and tell her to come back for **The Zee-Zee Show**. I tell her I am sorry. Sorry that I did not transcript the show on real paper. That I caused her to kill Semi, that I did not say it was me.

But she does not come back.

I stand there, my eyes searching the dark of everywhere, running mad with looking for Zenab, for my brilliant-mind Zenab, the most beautiful of all girls I ever seen, but all I see is a sink of darkness and trees and forests, and the silver face of a small circle of water down below.

TWO HOURS
TO MIDNIGHT

ADUNNI

A part of me fell down the cliff and died with Zenab.

The other alive part cannot speak as we begin the slow march away from the cliff through the dark that takes us out of the forest. I don't hear what anybody says because I am too busy feeling.

Feeling that thing, the thing I swallowed at the edge of the cliff, tearing me up from inside, twisting the pit of my stomach. It is becoming a hard thing in my mouth. A hot thing. It burns as it grows and takes the shape of our sorrow-singing. It becomes the clapping of our hands and the drumming of drums and the **ko-ko-ko** of the town-crier afar. It fills me and holds me tight and fits into my throat. It is hard to breathe.

We walk.

Our feet feels like cement to the floor, hard to move, to shift, the chief priest in front, holding a big lantern, his wife Shaki behind him, shaking the **shekere**. Kike is behind her; the naked old woman who was cutting Zenab, and who has wrapped herself up with a wrapper, behind Kike.

We reach the compound of the chief priest. There, the colors of the night fill the air, red of lanterns and orange of candles and the shining of beads and neckchains and purple and blue shine-shine wrappers of some of the women standing in a circle around the chiefs. They are our mothers, sisters, friends, aunties. They see us, and line up with hands pressing their chests, shaking their heads. I see Enitan crying into her mother's chest, and all the girls I growed up with, some of them seeing me for the first time since I ran to Lagos. I see Labake running behind one of the chiefs to come to me, to whisper something into my ears about Ms. Tia and her work. I see Ms. Tia stretching her neck, her eyes growing wide as she looks at the line of us. The drumming picks up again.

We come to a stop.

The women dance.

They dance like they have no bones. Like the

flesh of their arms is made up of elastic, with arms and legs stretching and bending and turning and twisting to the beating of the batá drum. These women, the women I will grow up into one day, they dance, while a girl like me cries for Zenab.

These women killed her. Her mother killed her. I killed her. The chief priest, the chiefs, every one of us, we killed her. Why did these women answer yes when they called them? If nobody came here this night, will they gather around? What is the worst they would have done?

The thing in me grows more and more big. It fills my chest. It set itself on fire. It burns.

Kike leans on the first tree she sees, swaying herself left and right. Her face shines with the salt of her dried tears.

A woman who was kneeling near the mouth of the forest stands up as we finish lining up. She rushes to us, shouting, "Zenab, Zenab!"

She starts to touch our shoulders, to search our faces, cupping each our chin in her brown painted hands, the same paint on Zenab's hands, speaking her language. Her eyes move around our faces, back and front, until another woman comes and drags her to where Kike is. I watch as Kike says something to her. She pulls off her headscarf and folds herself to the floor, her mouth open in a scream that is swallowed by the sound of the happy drumming.

ONE HOUR
TO MIDNIGHT

||||||||||
TIA
||||||||||

The singing and dancing and music and spontaneous gunfire from the depth of the forest mercifully halt.

Silence.

The chief priest, a scrawny old man with a bent back, steps forward and makes a pronouncement, words that have no meaning to me. But his voice is an unexpected baritone that balloons in the air. There is a collective gasp from the crowd as he speaks, the distant wail of a woman weeping. A man behind one of the chiefs stands, his anger blazing in his stride as he turns and runs into the forest, shouting, "Semi! Semi!"

Who is Semi? Why are some women crying? Why

do the other chiefs look stunned? I glance around, confused. What's happening?

The woman beside me flinches, muttering to herself. She has a chubby face that would have been friendly under different circumstances, her keen eyes darting around the arena. I lean toward her. "Hello. I am a mother. Of one of the girls. Do you . . . Do you speak English?"

She gives me a long look, nods.

I breathe out my relief. "Can you translate? Please. Explain in English for me? I am not from Ikati."

"I try," she says.

"What's happening now?" There is a patch of pressure in my abdomen, growing warm.

"Sacrifice. Baba Ogun is calling the father of Chichi to come begin."

"But how can they start now? It's not yet midnight, is it??"

"They start now before midnight," the woman explains. "Because the chief priest just say it now that someone die in the forest. A young chief by the name of Semi."

And where is Zenab? I scan the crowd frantically, searching. I noticed she was missing from the queue the moment the girls arrived, but I assumed she was lagging behind. And who is the young chief who died? What does that have to do with anything?

"But there is still a girl missing," I say, pushing myself up to recount the girls. The woman I assumed was Zenab's mother is approaching them now. She is touching each girl on her shoulders, tracing her henna-tinged fingertips along the jaw-line of each face, cupping each chin, flattening her palm on each cheek, as though each skin is covered with raised dots containing hidden code, like braille. What is wrong with her? And where is Zenab? I notice the woman who appears and tows her away. I follow her with my gaze, heart convulsing as she is led to Kike. She nods, too quickly, too many times, as if the effort is out of her control, as if her head has become unfettered, unshackled by what Kike is say-ing. Now she throws her headscarf off and screams to the sound of another set of rhythmic drumming.

My stomach tumbles. Drops. My hands clench into fists by my sides.

"Has he mentioned Zenab?" I ask my translator. "She was with the girls!"

My translator shrugs.

The drumming halts.

I check my phone: Zenab's father hasn't called back. I call him. It rings off. I curse, slapping the phone against my thigh. Ken's line does not even connect. I draw in breaths to keep my lungs from collapsing. I tell myself that Zenab is fine. That she's lost amid the women, watching the girls from a corner somewhere. Did Adunni not say she wasn't exactly part of the sac-rifice? Did she say that, or did I imagine it?

I turn on my camera, hit the record button, slide the phone into the center gore of my bra so that it stays anchored, capturing everything.

The chief priest speaks again.

The chubby woman translates: "He is calling the father of Chichi. They want to make his own quick so he can go back to his village."

A tiny man pushes through the crowd now. He is dressed in a white lace top, the sleeves dangling over his arms like the collapsed wings of a dying bird. He is cradling a calabash to his chest, a small wooden pot with steam curling out of it into the sky. I assume it's filled with the chicken concoction. He presents it toward the chiefs, who punch the air twice in acknowledgment, and toward the women, who clap and cheer.

The man starts to speak in a high-pitched voice when the crowd goes silent. Thankfully, he speaks in English and a man next to him translates for the crowd. He explains how his father, Chichi's grand-father, is a landowner in Ikati, and how he is pleased that, even after he has moved far from Ikati, the communities can make collective atonement for the sins of their sisters and daughters, and of how he hopes the spirits will release rain and bless his own land and make a way for his daughter to be free of the curse that killed her husband. He says that his daughter is sorry for the death of her husband and thanks this community for supporting him on what is the first leg in her purification process.

He puts the calabash on a red stone on the ground and bows three times before it.

Chichi utters a cry and throws herself to the

ground and starts to weep and roll and call the name Zuke, until a woman grabs her by her left ankle and drags her through the crowd and away.

There are now four in the queue: a young woman, older than the others; a girl of about twelve, who I recall seemed so close to Zenab in the forest; Adunni; and a girl with low-cut hair dyed copper and defiant eyes. Was she the one who asked about chasing her dreams?

Zenab is still missing. Where is she?

The chief priest puts the megaphone to his mouth and calls a name: "Hauwa." The girl of about twelve reacts, a jerk, but her head remains bent, shoulders slouched.

The chief priest beckons. He shouts out something.

A muttering weaves through the crowd, a thrumming of murmured questions, comments, quiet expressions of shock.

The woman beside me translates: "He say this girl is the wife of the young chief from Ikati. The Semi that die this night. They want to judge her for him dying."

What? Why? I jerk my head at the girl. She's stepping out of the line and forward, but Adunni is lurching toward her and grabbing her arm and pulling her back.

What the hell's happening?

I pitch myself forward to look, be sure. It is Adunni.

What . . . is she doing?

ADUNNI

I have been thinking.

Back to when I was wanting to have a louding voice.

I still want it with all my heart, but I am understanding that a louding voice starts as a seed. You pluck it, you plant it in a soil, you feed it water, and you keep it under the sun, growing until it takes root, shoots up a flower of pink and red and green, a flower with a branch for birds and bees to perch on . . . until it borns a fruit you can eat of it. And then you plant another and another. It has no end and can never be silent and lives on after you have gone from this earth.

What I need this very now-now is something

quick. Sharp-urgent as the chief priest is telling everybody that Semi is dead; that one of us girls—he did not say which one of us—killed him. That Hauwa, his coming-soon wife, must still collect a judging. What is the judging? Will they find her another young chief as a husband?

No, I think. **No.**

I need something that can cause everybody to stop this madness and bend their ears, to listen.

But I don't know what that thing is.

Hauwa is crying soft, praying quiet in her language. I shiver, pimples climbing up and down my arms, my back, behind my neck. Hauwa takes one step forward, stilling herself beside me; her hand, cold and shaking, grabbing my own.

"Adunni . . . help."

That is the first word of English she is speaking to me. The only word she ever speak to me since the Circle of Forest and since the time in the other place with Zenab. One word. A thousand meanings of it: **Help.**

My stomach twists tight.

But how can I help her? I did not able to help Khadija. Or Zenab. Or myself.

What can I do?

Roar.

I hear in my head, Ms. Tia's voice, like the roaring of a lion in the deep in the forest. I hear Zenab's voice, her laugh. I hear Khadija, my mama, Iya. I hear the mountains cracking at the bottom of my feet as I gather all of myself, as the thing that been growing and growing in me explodes into a ball of fire that blinds my eyes and causes me to see nothing.

Even if I die fighting. These girls will know it was for them. That I tried.

If I die fighting, in my next life, I promise I will come back as a lion. With a roaring thunder in my voice and a blazing fire in my eyes. I'll come back and scatter this madness in our land, that which makes them think us girls are nothing. Or maybe I'll come back as me. As Adunni, the Girl with the Louding Voice. I will live my life so that I can change the world in the small way I can. Whatever happens, I will not, never be just an ordinary girl.

I pray a quick prayer for courage, push Hauwa to one side, and snatch the microphone speaker from Baba Ogun.

Then I look at the crowd left and right, press the speaker to my lips, and open my mouth wide . . . and so I roar.

MIDNIGHT

‖‖‖‖‖‖‖‖
TIA
‖‖‖‖‖‖‖‖

Adunni seizes the megaphone from the frail chief priest, causing him to teeter toward the chiefs.

A woman rushes forward, perhaps to accost her, pull her back into the queue, where she belongs, but Adunni snatches her hand away and juts the woman in the stomach with her elbow. A gasp ripples through the crowd.

I exhale, my heart fluttering in my chest. "Adunni?" I whisper. **What are you doing?** Adunni presses the megaphone to her mouth, her feet planted wide apart, her eyes glistening. She stands still for a long moment before she starts to scream. It's a full-throated, splintered scream, a sound that causes everyone to stop whispering and focus on her. There is no elegance or grace to the guttural sound she makes; she is an angry spirit, a wounded soul, a broken girl intent to make her throat collapse, for her soul to die with the hurtling out of that sound. She screams like it is both a curse and a prayer, a promise, an oath, a plea for mercy, justice. She screams until the woman in front of me presses her palms against her ears and breaks away from the crowd and saunters off.

She screams until a chief's wife throws her hand in the air, demanding silence.

Until a chief rises and stabs the earth with his mace.

She stops.

Falls to her knees and touches her head, the megaphone to the ground. She stays there, affixed, like a clay sculpture, until a cloud crosses the moon, covering the earth with a brief darkness, slipping away to spill a brilliant spot of moonlight against Adunni's bowed head. It feels like a divine crowning, an anointing. Finally, she elevates her head and looks at me, terror in her eyes, as if she is unsure of what to say now, what next to do. Without standing, she starts to creep toward the queue of waiting girls, crawling to her place, conquered, crushed.

She cannot do that.

No.

"No, Adunni!" I holler, my voice a bellow exploding from my gut. I do not want her crawling back into a hole and giving up. She must do something to buy herself more time.

A chief glares and points his mace at me. "She is not from our land!" he bellows. "Take her and—"

"My elders." It's Adunni, snatching attention off me and the chief, and turning it on herself. The man who translated for Chichi's father translates for Adunni, but with his back turned to her as if she's not worth the gift of his contemplation.

"I greet you this night." Her voice is at first shaky, a reverberating sound through the night, slicing hearts and minds. "Please forgive me for causing trouble," Adunni says. "For making so much noise. Please—" She glances around the crowd and stands. "Zenab is dead. Even if—"

A woman lets out a piercing wail from somewhere to my right—I glance at her, Zenab's mother. She is bent in half by grief, sorrow.

My heart slips out of me. I sob into my hands. **Zenab. Oh, Zenab.**

"Zenab is dead!" Adunni repeats, her voice trapped in the cave of her agony, her tears. "She was a computer science girl! A beautiful girl. She was my friend!" She slaps a hand on her chest, a sound amplified by the megaphone. "How many more of my friends will we kill? How many more of our daughters and mothers and sisters in future must die?"

The crowd buzzes. The women beside me lean in, some translating Adunni's English to their own native languages, others questioning what she means.

"Zenab died because Semi wanted to . . . He wanted to rape Hauwa again! He cannot even wait for one month for her, a tiny girl, to be his wife! Even if Zenab didn't die tonight," Adunni says, "she would have died when that woman cut her—" She jerks an accusing finger at a bald old woman, who lowers her head and shrivels away, into the crowd.

"Why are we cutting girls? Why are—" Adunni pauses to weep, wobbling her head as if this isn't quite where she wanted to start from, as if she's traumatized by this and must find the strength to deliver her message. "Please give me . . . just five minutes to talk my mind. To tell you what is caus- ing the no-rains in our land."

One of the chiefs, eyes blazing, shifts forward on his throne-like chair, and beckons for her to carry on.

"When I was in Lagos, which is the big city with shining lights, I met a friend, a woman doing a very important work around why the earth is fighting all of us. Her name is Ms. Tia, and she is here with us today, standing under that paw-paw tree."

The crowd turns toward me. I stand frozen, unable to react, my veins throbbing in my temples.

"Our cows and goats and chickens have been slowly dying." Adunni hurls out her words. "Our farmers have been crying because the land is become deaf. All of us, not just girls, is suffering it." She pauses, nods. "My friend Ms. Tia, she has ideas of how we can get big money to help us learn how to fight it."

The crowd cheers as Adunni nods at me.

Who told her about the funds?

Labake. Labake overheard my voice note and told Adunni, and Adunni, being incredibly smart, knows that a financial incentive would at least buy her the time she needs to speak and for Ken and Mr. Ade to get here. A sob wheezes out of me.

"Ms. Tia is doing very good work of helping a village like our own become better," Adunni says. "I will tell you small of what she thinks, and maybe after all of this, you can give me and her chance to talk our mind."

She clenches the megaphone. "You see, the whole wide world is suffering what we are suffering. The countries in the Abroad are the big cause of most of this problem—but we in Ikati, we suffer it the more. Why? Because of where our land is sitting. We have mountains and hills and forest and plenty sun. We have oil. But we keep cutting our trees and collecting our oil and selling it to the Abroad with no care for it. We are dirtying our land with non-sense rubbish, using firewood to be cooking every day, bleeding the blood of our land. Now the earth is very vexing and shouting. The land is blowing hot and cold. We must think how to help ourselves. Look behind you—look!"

She pauses, panting heavily. The women turn to

face the forest—the void in the land, a dusty val-
ley surrounded by embracing trees, the desiccated
red earth, the Circle of Forest. They watch it for a
moment, train their eyes back on Adunni.

"See how there is a big hole in that forest? That
is the Circle of Forest. Where us girls were waiting.
That hole was one time the home of trees and birds
and animals and the medicine leaves we drink to
help ourselves. But we killed it all. We burned it
with fire and cut it like we are a blind devil-barber
barbing stubborn hair."

There is a collective hiss, stamping of feet.
Someone yells what sounds like a curse word in her
native language. It's a woman. She charges toward
Adunni, yelling Khadija's name, until someone
pulls her back and drags her away.

Adunni sighs into the speakers. "I didn't want
Khadija to die. She was my friend. A sister. A
mother." Adunni breaks off and wipes her eyes. "I
did not kill her."

"Who killed her?" someone yells.

A few women snigger, but Adunni's face is stoic,
her eyes roving through the crowd. She waits for
calm, carries on.

"Khadija, like Zenab, died because she was a girl."
Adunni raises her head, eyes blazing. She appears
to have left herself, separated body from soul, sus-
pended above the crowd, and I am mesmerized by
how magnificent she looks, by the luminescence
that trails the outline of her jaw, her shoulders. She's

an irradiated sunflower, an ethereal goddess, standing there in the middle of the compound, under the
beam of moonlight, with her back to the forest.

"Our land is bleeding, the world is bleeding, and
it is the girls that are suffering the most." She pauses
again, to weep, to smear her face with her hands.

"Yes!" a handful of women bellow, and I notice
the chief's wife is nodding, wiping her eyes.

"My mothers and sisters—" She turns toward the
women, her voice rising, a roar thundering through
the gathering. "Are you not tired of carrying the
heavy load of suffering? Don't you want to be free?
For your girls to grow up and become somebody
important? Don't you want them to go to school or
learn a work and buy you cars and wig and makeup
paint? Who tells you that girls are supposed to be a
servant? Look at yourself, you are so full of power!
So great! We need to understand the power we are
having, and if our world is not a letting us climb
high, if they are removing the ladder for us to climb,
let we women bend our backs on top of each other
and make a ladder for ourselves, by ourselves!"

The crowd cheers.

Empowered, Adunni smiles through her misery.
"If you suffer and kill us girls for nothing, know
this, today will be the beginning of many more sad
days for our land."

"Adunni, tell them! Tell them!" It is Enitan,
Adunni's best friend. "Tell them we can help our
land, we can be—!" Her mother deals her a slap

that cuts off the rest of her words. Enitan covers
her cheek with a hand, gives her mother a stunned,
pained look, continues to shout, "We all of us can!
We can! Adunni, tell them!"

"We. Can," Labake shouts from beside Kike. She
searches the crowd, catches my gaze, gives me a
nod. "We. Can!"

"We can!" I cry, my voice broken.

The chanting soon becomes a frenzy, with clapping and yelling, the women throwing their arms
up. I feel a flurry of emotions rising to the surface.
It pours out of me, and I start to clap. Slowly at first
and then louder. The women join me, and in the
thunder of the applause, Adunni falls to her knees
and drops the megaphone and holds up her arms in
surrender, as if to say, **I am done. Finished.**

We remain standing, clapping, crying.

Until, finally, quiet.

The chief rises. His gaze searches the multitude
until he finds me. He looks directly at me, eyes
like black pebbles in the rain. "You. See me after."
He turns to the row of men behind him. "Where
is Bamidele!"

There is a general undercurrent of unease as a
man is led, spine curved and head bowed, to the
center. He is shirtless and bleeding from thick
gashes in his head, his chest. His arms are bound
behind him with a thick rope, his bare feet kicking
up dust as he twitches and turns as if to free himself
but recognizes his effort will be futile. Behind him,

the eager eyes of the crowd sparkle with a certain light, hope, as they watch him. They hope he will tell us what happened the night Khadija died. That he will give evidence that would help Adunni.

Bamidele falls to his knees before the crowd. His left eye is swollen shut, his jaw nearly misaligned and bruised—aftermath from the fight with Akala? A knot of rage threads his expression as he lifts his head and looks around until he finds the object of his fury: Adunni.

"Bamidele. Did Adunni kill Khadija?" the chief asks. "Tell the truth to the gods!"

Bamidele nods.

"What happened that night?" the chief asks, stabbing his mace to the ground. "Tell us!"

"Khadija was pregnant, true," Bamidele says, his voice dipping. "Adunni bring her to me, and I tell them two that they should go to the stream and wait for me. But Adunni, she did not take Khadija to the correct stream. She took her too far and maybe the trouble of the journey make Khadija tired. I find Khadija dying dead by herself. I try very hard to save her." He glares at Adunni. "Adunni leave her to die by herself. She was jealous of not having a boy-child!"

"No way!" I gasp, desperate to charge toward him, but afraid of making things worse for Adunni. "He's lying! Adunni doesn't want a son! She's a child herself!"

There is a hand on my shoulder now, my translator's. "Calm," she whispers. "Calm yourself."

"Bamidele!" Adunni whimpers. She is curved almost into her chest, a figure burdened by grief, despair. "Bamidele, tell them the truth!" She lifts her head, reenergized, determined. "I left Khadija after she was dead! I came to your house to knock on your door, and you didn't come out!"

"Enough!" the chief bellows. He nods for one of the servant men to take Bamidele away. "Lock him up for killing Akala!" he calls as Bamidele is scooped up and shuffled away in shackles.

"Now—" He turns to the chief priest, and my translator is nearly breathless as she explains what is happening. "Baba Ogun, who will make a sacrifice for this girl? WHERE IS THE MAN IN HER FAMILY? HER BLOOD?" He points his mace at the crowd. "Who will carry a sacrifice for this girl?"

A chill slaps against my shoulder. The crowd remains quiet; the women at first appear contrite and then they defiantly push their heads up, shoulders high, saying nothing.

"Where is the man of her blood?"

Kike's husband, the chief priest, steps forward. "The time is twenty minutes after the midnight," he cries in a croaky voice, his words soaked in spit bubbles. "There is no man in her blood. Bamidele say he seen Khadija that day, but say he leave her with Adunni. I cannot give her a judging to go free because there is no sacrifice." He bows and steps back.

The chief grunts, stabs the earth twice with his

mace. "Kike, the wife of the chief priest, the mother of mothers, come forward!" he declares. "Bring the rope of blood."

My translator's voice breaks as she explains in a low voice that once the rope of blood is tied around Adunni and she's locked up, she might not survive.

It hurts to breathe.

Kike waddles to the center and comes to a stop beside Adunni. There is a blood-soaked rope dangling from her left hand. She shakes her head as if to say no. Shaki pushes Adunni, causing her to fall flat on her face, smashing her cheek against the pebbly ground. She groans as another woman—one of the chief's wives—kicks her twice in the shin.

"Tie her!" someone says from across the square. "Tie her!"

Kike lifts up an unsteady arm. A mutter of disbelief throbs in the air.

"Kike . . . don't," I plead under my breath. **Don't seal her fate. Don't tie Adunni.**

Adunni crosses herself and looks down, her lips moving as if in prayer.

I can't watch this. I can't. But I find myself unable to stop looking at Kike, to stop pleading with my eyes. I brace myself as the air around me expands, solidifies.

Kike slowly goes on her knees beside Adunni. "Adunni didn't kill Khadija. I know it, and we all know it." She presses her body into Adunni's, her pregnant stomach a fleshy barrier.

"Tie me first," Kike says, holding up the rope toward her husband. "Tie me with the rope of blood! Put me inside lockup with Adunni! Kill me too! Kill me with Adunni! With Zenab! Kill everyone, all of us together!"

Kike is the chief priest's wife. She's carrying his child. No one is going to touch her.

Fierce optimism pulses through me as I stop recording and attach the video and send it to Ken. I hope it gets delivered, that he sees it and understands how critical it is that he gets here right this minute. I look around as heads and bodies begin to lower as if in unison, a planned reverse ovation.

"Tie all of us!" The women crumble to the ground, chanting in English and in their native languages. About five of them crawl toward Adunni to form a fence of humans—women—around Adunni and Kike.

The fathers of each of the girls follow, kneeling, some taking off their caps and dropping them to the floor as if in reverence for Adunni, for Kike.

For Zenab.

I fall to my knees, humbled, awed, fractured.

Only the three chiefs remain standing. There is a shocked gasp as the chief who was at my house this morning lowers himself and hangs his head as if in shame, as if he knows and expects to be punished for what he's done tonight.

I feel a hand pressing my shoulder, a voice, breathless, gasping my name. "Miss Tee-Yah."

Kayus?

I turn around and squint in the indigo-colored night. The face staring back at me is partially veiled, a pink scarf covering half. I notice the unnaturally molded breasts, like twin cement cones, jutting out of the chest. It **is** Kayus. As a young boy, he's forbidden to be here tonight, and so he's disguised himself to look like a woman.

"They lost, Miss Tee-Yah," he says, tears garbling his voice. "Adunni's real papa and Mr. Ken, they call me! They lost! They cannot reach here—"

His words are snatched by the sound of feet thundering through the crowd, a boisterous clamor. It is a row of soldiers. Army men. Naval officers. Policemen. A blend of forces. About twenty of them, brandishing guns, rifles, charging into the cluster of humans, marching through gaps, bellowing orders, threatening to shoot if anyone moves or tries to escape.

The crowd cowers in fear, terror. Someone starts to cry. Another moans.

Gunshots raid the night sky.

Everyone freezes.

But no one falls dead.

The air tremors in a convulsive hush.

My ears ring.

Kayus grips my hand, his eyes wide.

A man pushes forward. Dark. All muscle and height, an unnerving presence of strength, furious and resplendent in his naval uniform.

"Where is Zenab?" he booms. "Where is my daughter?"

"She dead!" someone yells.

The crowd gasps.

The man whips his head left and right, scanning the crowd, looking for his daughter.

"She's dead, sir," Adunni says, weeping on her knees, with her head still bent. "She said to tell you she sorry she did not listen to you."

The man at first jerks, arching his back as if struck in the spine with a missile; then he keels over as if his heart is a weighted stone sitting in his stomach. For a long moment, he remains bowled over, heaving, a wolfish, feral sound coursing out of him.

When he wrenches himself up, tears glimmer in his tortured, burning eyes.

He points toward the row of chiefs, their wives, and lets out an instruction tucked into a terrible moan, an anguished cry: "Arrest them. Every one of these bastards! And bring me Zenab's mother!"

The soldiers power through the gathering, yanking men to their feet, slapping cuffs onto wrists, barking commands and warnings. I try to stand, to wade through the fury and dread and fear, to get to Adunni and hug her close, but a wave sweeps over my head, and then everything goes black.

THURSDAY

||||||||||||
TIA
||||||||||||
Predawn

The air is humid with the stench of old leather. I open my eyes to Ken fanning my face with a bunch of folded papers, his face glowing with sweat. My head throbs as my eyes sweep to a throne-like chair with ornately carved wooden handles to my left, a leather footstool on the floor in front of it, a set of wooden benches on either side. There is a sofa behind me with a tattered cushion back, a square of ankara covering torn parts of the chair, two turquoise pillows nestled in the cracks between the wood. A static ceiling fan with rusty blades dangles from a rope above; a lantern sits on a side table, a low flickering flame dancing in its stained-glass orb. There are paintings on either side of the wall in black and white, of human skulls, eggs, a peacock in full display of feathers. Shabby magnificence.

I hear voices, hushed whispers, the occasional cry filtering in from outside.

"One of the chief's deserted palaces," Ken says to a yet unasked question. "This wrapper looks good on you." There is a teasing smile in his voice.

The mat is brittle, hard on my back. I lick my lips, tasting something bitter. "What happened to me?"

"You passed out. Exhaustion. Some woman— Labake, I think was her name—she brought you here and forced you to drink some concoction to rehydrate you. How are you feeling?"

"The chiefs?" I manage.

"They've all been arrested. The chiefs, their wives and guards, the village council, the women who supported them. It was chaos when we arrived. Never seen so many army and naval trucks in my life." He pauses. "I am sorry we got here so late."

I wave his apology away.

"Your video is trending," he says. "Alongside the news of the raid."

"What video?"

"Your video of Adunni's speech. I got it while we were heading here, and I sent it to a lawyer friend who posted it online. It's trending. Too bad you aren't on social media, Tia, but NGOs and human rights activists and lawyers are tearing down the walls and demanding justice. And now I hear the chiefs and women in neighboring villages are terrified of arrest." He glances behind him, lowers his voice. "I've got your clothes. Do you want to get changed so we can hit the road?"

I close my eyes, relieved, scared. "Where is Adunni—"

"Outside with Ade. We got here just as the chiefs were taken away, so there's no sacrifice to carry. The other girls have been released." He sighs. "A girl died. Did you know her? A Zenab? Tuns out she was the reason why the roads were blocked. Her father wasn't sure where her mother took her, so he used his connections to get support from the army and police and ordered for all the cars on the express to be searched. They only stopped searching after you called him, I think."

But my call came too late.

"I met . . . Zenab. For ten minutes." My voice is throaty. "She was . . . It's tragic . . ." I trail off, exhausted, thinking of her heartbroken father, of how I judged him for using his resources to find his precious daughter, knowing I would do the same for Oyi. "We are taking Adunni back to Lagos," I say to Ken. It is not a question.

He nods. "She's so brave." Then softly adds: "I can see why you love her, Tia."

I close my eyes. "She's going to need a lot of professional help to overcome the trauma. I don't think it has sunk in yet."

"You will also need help, Tia," he says. "Hey, take my arm and sit up." He holds a cup to my lips as I straighten and take a sip, tasting something fruity, sweet. I tip my head back. Somehow, I feel deflated, emptied of the adrenaline rush from the last twelve hours. It's a feeling of purposelessness; it's how I imagine a tennis ball wandering in a football field at midnight would feel. And there's the stabbing grief of Zenab's loss.

Ken draws a breath. "I am sorry for all we've had to go through. But we must get out of here ASAP. You've got a nine o'clock flight—think you can make it? To see your mum?"

"I **need** to see my mum," I say, climbing to my knees. The room swivels, and I grip Ken's shoulder for support. He holds his hand out to help me up, but I shake my head and let myself sag back to the floor. I was going to wait until I discussed with my mum, but I might as well tell him now. Leave all of the secrets behind in Ikati.

"When last did you eat?" he asks as he presses another kiss, warm and solid, on my forehead.

"No idea. Ken?"

"Yeah, babe?"

"Can we get Adunni on the same flight to PH? With me?"

"I can try . . . Why?"

"She's never been on a plane."

"That can be arranged. Has she got a form of ID? To fly?"

"Student ID? Would that work? Listen, Ken."
I touch his arm. "There is—something I need to
tell you."

I suck in air and tell him that Oyi might still
be alive.

ADUNNI

After the police people came and take away the chiefs and the woman who very nearly cut Zenab, everybody was scattering everywhere and the whole village was in plenty commotions until just maybe thirty minutes ago.

Now we are gather around the good doctor's car in the market square under the mango tree, with some of the women touching the front boot as if it is magic, and saying thank you, thank you for opening our eyes, for telling us that we can do it, that we can help our land, our future.

Others stay back, eyeing me with bad eye from afar and cursing me because of the police and navy and army men that bundled up the chief priest and chiefs and their wives and take them away. They are calling me bringer of bad luck and are not wanting to come near me. I don't mind the cursing. I am just happy that Hauwa is safe. That all the girls are free to go. I hear that Chichi's papa is afraid for her to suffer any more for her husband dying. I hear that the woman who was wanting to cut Zenab is under special lock and key of arrest. That Zenab's mother is in the police station. That all the other communities around us are now so afraid of arrest, of harming the girls, of doing anything sacrifice or judging.

I look around now, looking for Hauwa, and I see her walking across the square with Efe and Lady G. I wave, calling them to come. Lady G waves to me, but she stands back for Hauwa and Efe to talk to me.

Hauwa presses her hands to her lips and bows her head when she reaches me, tears shining in her eyes. "You. Help," she says. "You. Zenab." She looks up to the sky, then back at me. "Thank. You."

I nod, pressing my hands to my lips too. "Now you," I say, keeping my voice very serious. "You **must** go to school. School first. Then YouTube watching after. You hear?"

She throws her small head back and laughs, so that I have a small concern that she didn't understand me. She is still laughing and crying when she steps aside to make a way for Efe, who snatches me off the floor and embraces me so tight, she nearly squeezes out all my kidney.

"Wisdom!" Efe says when she sets me down. "Take five!"

"I take five of what?" I blink, breathing fast, feeling to vomit from the squeeze.

"High five!" She holds out up her five fingers. "You don't know it?" And then she snatches my palm and force slaps it on her own. "That's how we greet on TV!" She sweeps her wrapper with her hands, as if to remove dirty from it. "I am going back to our village to birth my baby; then after, I will go to Lagos or Asaba to find acting job." Her voice drops, becomes sad. "I promise I will do this for Zenab. Then, when I become big, win Oscar, I tell everybody on TV about Zenab and you, Wisdom. Remember this face, Wisdom! Don't ever forget me!"

I swallow at the mention of Zenab. "Even if I forget your face," I say, "I don't think I will ever forget how you nearly cut off my breathing just now." I smile a sad smile. "Bye-bye, Efe!"

"Because of Zenab, you **will** see me onstage!" she shouts, walking away in a stagger like she drunk. "No shakings!?"

"No shakings," I whisper, watching her snap her fingers in the air as she crosses the square and disappears between the paths that leads to the village.

I watch the rest women for another moment, not believing that this is me, Adunni, with my blood father—who is standing beside me, folding his arms across his chest, with tears shining in his eyes. He says he will give me time to finish with my friends before he talks to me, but I see him looking, just looking at me with a little wonder. It is a bit hard to allow the thinking of it, that this man is my father.

One by one, my friends embrace me and say their bye-byes. When it gets to Enitan's turn, I press my book of papers into her hands and say, "I wrote it for you. Print it one day, give it to all the girls in our village." Enitan collects the papers and holds me tight.

"You will come back for us?" she asks.

"Very soon," I say, promising it with my whole heart. I cannot leave Kayus here by himself. How will he eat, live? Become somebody? My heart is a sack full of stones as Enitan nods her head, crying as she turns away to allow Kike and Labake to say bye-bye.

"The police, they take my husband gone," Kike says, rubbing her stomach, her eyes red. "But I am not sad. He is not a bad man, but he is not good for me. For us girls. I hope they give **him** a good judging." She smiles a little. "When my baby born, I give her your name. If it is a boy, still I give him your name. Adunni."

I laugh because I never in my life hear of a boy by the name of Adunni.

"I just seen Efe and Hauwa, and Lady G is there. But where is Chichi?"

"She gone," Kike says. "She keep crying too much for Zuke, so her papa take her gone. Zenab . . ." She starts to cry, and I give Kike a side embrace and tell her not to cry, even though me, I am crying inside of myself too. Then I turn to Labake and bend my knees. "Thank you for helping me and Ms. Tia. They say you take her to the chief house to sleep and give her medicine to rest. My mama is saying thank you too. Please, ma, can you take care of Kayus for me until I can come back to visit?"

Labake touches my head and turns away with not one word of answer. I don't know why she didn't answer, but I don't think she is angry with me. I hope she will help me take care of my brother. I look around for Kayus. I want his own bye-bye to be a special one. I want to tell him to keep my phone, to find a way to call me on Ms. Tia's number so that I can plan how to be seeing him every so often.

Lady G waits until I am alone before she walks to me, and as she nears, I see the fear in her eyes. "I wanted us to be alone because . . . you've given me courage to . . . speak up."

"To roar," I say. "Because sometimes speak up alone is not enough. You roar. Like a lion."

She gives a shaky smile. "When you were talking about your time in Lagos, in the circle, some of the things you said . . . Can I ask you this between me and you? Was your former madam called Big Madam? Mrs. Florence, the wife of Chief Adeoti?"

I nod. "How did you know?"

Lady G twists the edge of her wrapper. "Me too,

I worked there. She was wicked to me, but it didn't matter. I was managing her to save up and finish my schooling."

"Why you leave?"

She looks at me, and it seems like she is struggling to find the words at first, but then she talks, speaking so fast, I am nearly not catching all she's saying: "I got pregnant. I had to run. For my life. I couldn't tell anyone who their father is. I mean the twins. My sons. That's why I am here for the sacrifice. Because my people think my children are a bastard children who will bring a curse to our family line. It's time to tell them the truth. Goodbye, Adunni. Thank you."

Lady G squeezes me a quick embrace, and before I can ask what she means by "tell them the truth," she runs off, her beads clapping to the dance of her feet. I watch her, feeling confused, until something in the clapping beads slaps my brain with a hot slap of memory: I seen those beads before! Are they not the same of the Rebecca's beads that I brought back from Lagos? The one in my bag? Is Lady G the same Rebecca that worked for Big Madam? That was pregnant for Big Madam's husband and was missing? Are her twins children for Big Daddy?

I lift my voice to shout, **Rebecca, WAIT!**—but she's already gone, taking the truth of her life with her and melting into the crowd of darkness. My heart sighs. Rebecca. I been looking for her all my time in Lagos, and she was right there in the Circle of Forest with me, and I did not know? Will I ever see her again?

A tall man with a big stomach is walking to come meet me, a slow limp in his legs. When the light shifts, I see his face, the long **fila** on his head. Morufu. The man I married. He gives me a long, long look when he reaches my front, the colors of the night shining on the shock in his eyes.

I wait, heart slamming itself on the floor of my stomach. Will he cause troubles for me again? But when he speaks, there is no anger or sorrow or fear or anything in his voice. Just tiredness. The tiredness of a man tired of fighting a stubborn mind.

"Adunni . . . I hear of how . . ." He pauses to spit, to wipe his mouth with the back of his hand. "I hear of how you talk to all the womens to be more strong. To fight."

I nod my head yes. Don't say one word.

"You are not for me." He takes my hand, pressing something folded, rough, inside of it. "Go well," he says. "Find a strong-head like yourself to marry." He turns around. Then stops. "Adunni?"

I don't answer. I wait for him to talk his mind.

"If the police peoples. They come back? Don't mention my name. Don't tell them me and you we ever marry. I did not do you bad. Please. I don't want to go to prison." Then he walks off fast, as if I bite him in his buttocks, crossing in front of Ms. Tia and Dr. Ken.

I check my hand. It is money, squeezed up like used toilet paper. What is the money for? My bride price? He paid it again? In Ikati, if a man pays the bride price two times, the first time is to marry the girl; the second time, he will pay half the money to forever say bye-bye. He is freeing his wife to go bye-bye forever, and he will never take care of the girl or her family again. Also, if he pays the second bride price, then the girl cannot marry any man in Ikati again, which is very okay for me because plenty of the men in Ikati are having ice-block for a brain.

Morufu must be very afraid too, like all the other men here, of the police coming back. Of Zenab's father. Zenab did that, I think. Zenab will live forever as a fear in the heart of the wicked in Ikati. I allow a sad smile, making a beckon to Enitan, pressing the money into her hand. "Use it to buy food for Kayus, and to buy more makeup for your business. Use it to maybe print the book, maybe even buy a nice dress for the baby of Kike, when she born it, okay. Use it to—"

We both laugh, sadly, because we know the money cannot travel so far to buy so much plenty things. I wipe my eyes as Enitan turns a corner, waving me bye-bye one last time.

"We've discussed," the good doctor says when they reach us. "And Tia and I thought we'd take Kayus along with us. Someone has sent for him. Is that all right with you? Where is he?"

I wide my eyes, jumping up and down with a clap and laugh. "Kayus can come? True? Ms. Tia?"

"Come here." Ms. Tia holds me tight. "You did it. You cleared your name, and you are going to school—this time, nothing holding you back. And yes, Kayus can come with us."

"I come with you!" I hear Kayus saying in a happy voice, running up to meet us, holding a small nylon bag of his things. The boy is so quick to think! When did he already run to pack his belongings? My Kayus. My boy is coming with me. Forever and ever, we be together. He will go to school too! My heart swells as he jumps up and down and gives me a big, tight embrace, so that me and him and Ms. Tia, we hold each other for a long time, the three of us becoming one.

I start to cry then, thinking of it all, of Zenab, of every fight I fought, not for myself but for Kayus, and now that the world is knowing of Ikati, that because the chiefs are inside arrest, the girls here will be free. There will be fear to treat them bad for a very long time.

Mr. Ade comes to stand beside us and touches a hand to my shoulder. "You've done something incredible here tonight, Adunni." His voice is so soft, so cream, like warm milk in my ears. "You have maybe changed the hearts and minds of the women and girls in your village. You've given them hope. That's remarkable, and I am so proud of you."

"We really do have to go now," the good doctor

says, pressing his car key so that it makes a **peen** sound and the door claps open. "I hear there are newsmen around the corner. Unless you want to be interviewed?"

"No," I say. "Let's go."

One by one, we climb inside the Jeep car. First the good doctor in front of the steering wheel, then Ms. Tia beside of him. Kayus climbs in and rests his head on my chest. Mr. Ade sits beside me.

The Jeep makes a vroom and speeds off.

We drive past the town-center, past all the houses and shops, past the quiet farms with the animals sleeping hungry around the trees, past the sign saying **GOODBYE TO IKATI**.

"You might be coming with me to Port Harcourt in the morning, Adunni," Ms. Tia says, waving at some of the women outside, who came to wish us bye-bye. "So, get some sleep because you may be going on an airplane."

"Kayus, you hear that? You hear that?" I kick Kayus, but he is already falling asleeping.

"And . . ." Ms. Tia says. "Apart from the arrest of the chiefs and their wives, Ken says some . . . agencies . . . uh, big government people also saw your speech, Adunni. It's gone viral and . . . it's likely they'd want to interview you at some point. Not this morning, but soon."

"What a wowing wow . . ." I whisper. Because I don't fully understand what she means by "gone virus" and all of that, but it sound like a very big

thing. And then I am sad again, thinking Zenab
would have know what it means. Zenab would been
too happy to give interview to these virus people
and tell them, **Oh, I know this, and I know that!**

Me and Zenab, we could been forever friends
after today. We are so alike, only she is having more
brave and more chance at things in life because she
was born to a family that have what I don't have.

Before we join the express, I look back at the cliffs
where she died, and I whisper my bye-bye to her,
and to the part of me that died with her in the wind.

The good doctor puts on a soft piano music. Soon
Ms. Tia starts to snore.

I kiss the top of my brother's head.

"You are quiet, Adunni," Mr. Ade says. "What are
you thinking?"

I think I am thinking many things. Of Zenab
and **The Zee-Zee Show** that was born and died in
the forest of Ikati. Of how her good life and education and good father did not escape her from the
suffering of girls. I am thinking of the other girls,
Hauwa and Efe and Chichi and Lady G; of my uniform and cap and shoes, waiting folded for me on
Ms. Tia's bed with not one wrinkle on the skin of it.
I am thinking, with hope in my heart, that rain will
fall very soon and water our land; that the world
will be okay and that the earth will be taken care
of by all of us; that I must read the letter from my
father, which is folded inside my bra, so that I can

start to know this strange milk-voice man who is my father.

I am thinking of Papa, hoping he will find a little peace now because he helped me find Bamidele, and of my sweet mama, who maybe had to die to make a way for Ms. Tia to come into my life because death must always born life; it is the circle of things to somehow make sense.

This, I think, is one more for my book, but I don't have a pen or paper, so I write it in the paper of my heart:

> Be full of thank-you that things did not always
> work out the way you are wanting them.
> Because sometimes the one No you get
> is the door to open a thousand Yeses.

But.

All of this is maybe too much to tell Mr. Ade all at once, so I sigh soft, give the man an easy smile, and tell him I am thinking of tomorrow.

‖‖‖‖‖‖‖‖
TIA
‖‖‖‖‖‖‖‖
PORT HARCOURT
Morning

S he's gone."
My father turns around and walks to the hospital window. He's not talking about her going to the Shoprite supermarket or to the Anglican Church of the Ascension or to her home library. He's saying she's gone. Dead. My mother died an hour before we got here.

Still, I glance at her empty bed, the brown rubber mattress glistening with a wet sheen from disinfectant spray, the folded white bedsheet at its foot, her flask and glasses and leather handbag sitting on the pile, her Adidas travel bag under the bed.

She's gone.

When it sinks in, a sound roars out of my broken core, the center of my soul. I drop to my knees and crawl to Aunty Beatrice, who is sitting in the visitor's chair, weeping. My father lags, leaning against the window overlooking the hospital grounds. His head is in his arms, and his shoulders heave. He's crying. We all are, but my tears are for Oyi.

"Did she tell you?" I ask my aunty. "Did she tell you where Oyi went? My daughter, Oyi? Did she tell you which family took her? Aunty, please, I beg you. Tell me."

My aunty stops weeping abruptly, as if a switch went off inside of her. Her eyes search mine, with anguish and pain twisting, tying a knot around her features. "Tiana . . ." She glances at my father, lowers her voice. "Now is not the time to—"

"Where is my daughter?" I shriek, grabbing the legs of her chair. I know my voice might attract Adunni's attention (she's watching TV in the waiting room next to my mother's ward), but I don't care.

"Where is Oyi?" I shout.

My father gathers me in his arms and weeps, not with me but for my mother. "It's okay, baby. Mummy is gone, and I know it hurts and it's making you imagine—"

I tear myself out of his arms. "No, Dad! I know what I am talking about. I had a child. A baby girl. I was sixteen." I pound my fists against his chest. "Dad, you remember Ada? Our housemaid? Her son, Boma, is the father of my child."

Dad nods, gripping my arms to stop me from delivering a deathly blow to his chest, from killing him. But he doesn't believe me. I can see it in the compassion in his eyes. He thinks I am crazy. Imagining things.

"Aunty, please tell Dad I am telling the truth. Tell him Mummy took my baby from me—" I stop talking as hysteria, a force I cannot control, seizes me. I fall against my father and wail.

"Brother, it is true-o," Aunty Beatrice finally says. "My sister, Eno, did not want Tiana to suffer how she suffered."

"Eno never suffered," my father growls. "Never. I loved her with my very soul and took care of her."

My father is right. Theirs was pure, enviable love.

"Brother, you were a good husband," Aunty Beatrice says. "A good man. But your wife wanted more than that. She wanted to be herself, to find her destiny, to make a name for herself. When she gave birth to Tiana, what did you tell her?"

"Tell her?"

"You told her to stop working and look after your baby girl. She had to give up opportunities for promotion at work, a chance to go and lecture at a top university. My sister had a PhD, brother. You met her as a scientist. But you—" She nods at my dad. "You got your oil job and were always traveling— today Warri, tomorrow Aberdeen, next week Qatar. You asked her to stay at home. She **kuku** did. She made the sacrifice we women make. She stayed home and watched the child. My Eno—the professor of the family, the brilliant mind and brilliant spirit—she killed her soul for you to live your own good dreams. A life without good dreams is a nightmare life. She eventually dragged herself out of the house after seven years, to become a librarian at the local university. A job that depressed her. She wanted more, brother! She wanted to travel, to fly up and down around the world, breaking boundaries, inventing things. Do you know why she used to lock herself up in that big library you built in your house? To teach the books. Yes-o, my sister began to teach books and lecture them. It was inside that library that she began to run mad small-small, the kind of madness that smiles a happy smile and wears lipstick and high-heel shoes. A madness that ties **gele** at parties and serves pounded yam at functions to guests. My sister"—Aunty Beatrice coughs out a laugh that sounds like a cry—"became depressed. A depression she denied and refused to get treated for because she didn't want her good man, her husband, you, to feel bad." She grunts, yanking the neckline of her **bou-bou** to adjust it. "When will the world see us women with our own hopes and dreams? When will society stop dictating what we can or cannot do with our lives, our careers, our everything?"

My father stares at my aunt as if stunned. "But

Eno did not mind staying at home, Beatrice. **Haba.**
You know my job was demanding, we needed someone to take care of Tia."

"Did you ever ask her if she was happy giving up
her career, a crucial part of her identity, to raise your
daughter? Did you discuss? Communicate? Did you
check in with her, as you rose up the ladder, if she
was still happy with this choice?"

"Did I?" My father spreads his palms, shrugs.
"There was nothing to discuss, Beatrice. A mother
is responsible for— **Kai!** Bea, what kind of question
are you asking me? I was a good husband. Eno just
died, and you are here accusing me of what?"

"You were a good . . . a providing and kind husband, yes," Aunty Beatrice says in a more subdued
tone. "But you were blind to your wife's depression
and silent resentment. She hid it from you because
she loved you. And you were blind to it because
society offers you that blindfold, that thick cloth of
entitlement, patriarchy, at birth."

"No such thing," my father mutters. "We had a
good marriage! No such thing."

"Maybe Mummy suffered," I whisper, "silently."

My dad shakes his head. He will never accept
this, and I can understand why. Dad thought he
made sure Mum lacked nothing. But how do you
define what's lacking when there isn't an understanding of what is needed?

"My sister," my aunty says, "did not want Tia's
future tampered with, the way she thought hers was

tampered with. In a way, she blamed Tia for the death of her dreams, and in another way, Tia was a path to resurrect those dead dreams. Eno focused on only one thing: for Tia to be a sky flyer, to achieve all she wasn't able to."

Everyone has a story.

I wish my mother had told me this. I wish she hadn't pretended to be okay with giving up her dreams to raise me, because she did not even raise me! She resented me! I wish I hadn't agreed to giving Oyi up for adoption, that she hadn't lied to me.

I wish we had a chance to speak, to make amends, before she died.

But I don't for one moment regret being with Adunni when she needed me.

"I could have been all those things," I say, feeling a strange sense of relief as a seismic wave of fresh grief for my mother rocks through me. "I can be all those things! Why did she lie to me?"

"Because, number one"—Aunty Beatrice leans forward, anchoring her hands on her knees—"you were too young to understand what motherhood demands; and two, you can be all those things, yes, but not at the same time. You would have had to sacrifice to raise your child, and that is okay if you understand what you are doing, if you understand that life is in compartments built around the demands of time and season."

My aunty leans back. "Your mother did what she thought was best for you at the time."

"Was the baby adopted?" my father asks. "A girl, right? Can we check the medical records at the hospital?"

"No," Aunty Beatrice says, mournfully. "Eno arranged with a nurse at the hospital to take the baby away. I don't even know the name of the nurse—my sister made sure the baby would not be traced. And the hospital was pulled down five years ago. There is a hotel there now. Hotel Magnifique or something. Sorry, Tiana. You will have another child-o. Forget about this one. Another one will come. You have been married for how long now? I am surprised another one has not come. It's the emptiness that is worrying your mind. Please-o, Tia, forget that one and look ahead."

Forget that one—like Oyi is an umbrella, an object one often forgets to take along on a journey. **Forget that one . . . that one.**

Oh, Oyi. I am sorry. So sorry.

My father gently lets go of me and stands. "I need to attend to the doctors . . ." He gives a clipped nod and lumbers to the door. My aunty utters something indiscernible and rises out of the chair and gathers her **bou-bou** around her, and with the sequins and stones at the helm crinkling as if to announce her intention to exit, she limps out of the room after my father.

A WEEK LATER

ADUNNI

LAGOS
Morning

The time is fifteen to six in the morning, and I cannot sleep because today I am going to school. I been awake since middle of the night, afraid to close the window of my eyes, of hearing a bitter banging cracking noise on the gate, of the chiefs or somebody coming back for me. But there was only the breathing soft of Kayus sleeping beside me all night and the quiet muffle of Ms. Tia and Dr. Ken talking and talking in their room until Dr. Ken leaved the house before sun rise to run catch a flight to Port Harcourt.

Hard to believe all the so much that been happening to me in the last four days since we come back from the Port Harcourt. (It was a very wonderful thing to fly up-up in the air and see the bed of the clouds, but nobody warned me the airplane is a very crazy noisemaking machine that nearly deaf your both ears as it is climbing back down or that it keeps you all lock and belt up so that you don't even get a small chance to walk a little on the street of the sky.)

My real father been coming here to Ms. Tia's house at nine o'clock in every morning to take me to visit one doctor they are calling doctor child **terra-pist**.

This doctor child **terra-pist** of a woman, who is not working a real hospital like a normal doctor and who look nothing like a child with her short gray hair and windscreen glasses and purple lipstick, is having a nice office with a window that is facing the beach in Lekki so that you can sometimes hear the crashing waves from the outside and it calm your mind.

But there are too many books and flowers and different color paintings of the brain of a child in her office. There is also a bright yellow sofa-chair for me to sit or sleep on, a photo of her and her white dog with plenty hairs in his eyes and plenty biscuit and drinking-tea.

The first two times I seen her, she don't say much except to blink-slow at me and ask me questions with that voice that sound like she half dead. But I like her smile and how she likes for me to talk and talk and talk about all the things that happened to me because she say talking can help me be all okay inside my head when I have a bad screaming dream of Zenab falling or Mama and Khadija and Semi dying. My real father told me that the doctor will help me. "It's a gradual process, Adunni."

Just yesterday, he said too that Kayus will visit doctor **terra-pist** to help him "overcome the traumatic events that have happened." I tell him me and Kayus didn't suffer any traumatic. We are just children who find ourselves in the hard of life and who are fighting with hope, but rich people always see everything as a traumatic, so I say okay.

I like my real father.

I like the letter he wrote to me. I keep it with me always, inside my mama's Bible. He is a kind man, I think, with a quiet laugh and eyes that hook you deep with questions. He says he is a **pro-fesor** of something in one or two schools of business in this Lagos. He is also working another job to help the Nigeria president think sense about how to spend money. **Eco-monic adviser**, I think, was what he called the job to me. He has a wife too, my real father, a woman who lives with him inside one place they are calling campus, and the two both have one very "beautiful son with special needs," by the name of Ife. He showed me a video of Ife on his phone, a happy smiling boy with happy smiling eyes, and I tell him I am sure me and Ife will be friends one day. My father said too that his wife at home is "not ready to meet you just yet, Adunni. It's a lot for her to take in."

Is okay, I understand. It is hard to one day wake up and know your husband been having a child somewhere for so long, to open the door of your heart to that child.

But my father make a promise that he will not stop coming to visit me in Ms. Tia's house and in school every time he has a chance. He promise to be a part of my life forever, to one day bring Ife with him, and to spend the rest of his life "making up for lost times." I am happy we have the rest of our life to be knowing each other small by small.

The alarm makes a **shree-shree** noise. Six o'clock!

I jump out from the bed. Kayus is deep asleep still, snoring softly, spit climbing down from his open mouth into the towel he wrap his whole head with. He never sleep inside cold air-con before, so he bury himself deep in the blanket and wrap up a towel around his head to keep him from catching cold. I shake him by the shoulder now and peel the towel from around his head.

"Wake up, Kayus!"

Kayus pinches open one eye, looks at me, and smiles a smile that crowds my heart with joy. Then he sits up and stretches his mouth in a long yawn.

"I am going to school," I say. "You be good to Ms. Tia. Sweep the floor, clean the toilet like I taught you, and make it everywhere shining."

He nods his head okay, then throws the rope of his thin arms around my neck and starts to cry.

Ms. Tia been already found a primary school near her house for Kayus, but she said she must also find a lawyer-somebody to make it sure she can take care of Kayus without no problem from Papa's family or from the school or the **gov-ment**, but I tell her Papa didn't have any family with sense. Maybe just a small sister in one afar place who stoned the back of his head with her high-heel shoe the last time he visited her because Papa borrowed money from her and didn't pay back.

"When you will come back from the school?" Kayus asks. "What if another something bad is happens to you?"

"Middle of term." I tear his arm from my neck before he will squeeze my neck and kill me dead on the day I am finally going to school. "Nothing bad will happen. I am safe in school. And Ms. Tia can bring you before then, okay? And you, make sure you learn your ABCs and 123s, and when you start school, be the best boy for your teachers, you hear?" I clap a happy clap. "Now come! Get up and let us prepare for today!"

He is still crying soft when we climb downstairs, me in my uniform and Kayus in the new short-knicker and t-shirt and good-shoes the good doctor bought for him. The good doctor took him to barb his hair too, so that his head now look shrink, like a dot on his thin neck that make the whole of him look like the small letter **i**, but I know Ms. Tia will fat him up before he is starting school.

We find Ms. Tia in the parlor, all dressed in her t-shirt and jeans-trousers, her luggage box beside of her feet. Her eyes are red, sore-looking, her nose swelling from blowing too much of it inside a tissue because her mama died. Honest, Ms. Tia been in so much deep sorrow, I been wondering if maybe she is sorrowing for more than just her mama. Because she seem too-too sad, and yesternight, after evening-food, I seen her wiping her eyes as she was looking her computer machine, and when I peep it, I seen she was checking the internet of the Google for:

How to locate records of a demolished Hospital in Surulere, Lagos 2010 + Hotel Magnifique

It doesn't make sense to me. Why is the demol-ished of a hospital plus or minus a hotel make her so sorrow?

After she and Mr. Ade is dropping me in school this morning, she is going to see her papa so they can plan the burial, and I hope maybe she become more happy after that. Maybe.

I make a salute before I kneel to greet her because I must always make a salute when I am wearing my school cap.

"Good morning, Ms. . . ." I low my head. I been wanting to ask Ms. Tia one very important question since we came back from Port Harcourt, but I am afraid she will say no.

"Adunni?"

I lift my head. "I have a question to ask of you," I say, looking at my black school shoe, trying to find the words. "Can I . . ."

She pushes up her eyebrow. "Go on, Adunni. What would you like? Something to eat? I've packed us some tuna sandwiches and a drink and—"

"Can I call you Mama, Ms. Tia?"

She makes a gasp, covering her mouth, her eyes filling with tears. "Oh, my love . . . of course you can. I was your mother in my heart long before you asked."

"And Kayus?" I pull Kayus close. "He too needs a mama? We have our first mama in heaven who suffered much for us and is watching us every day, but please, Ms. Tia, we need for you to be our mama on this very earth. We promise to be very good children and be every day eating everything organic."

Mama laughs her ringing bell laugh and wipes her cheek, pulling me and Kayus close. "You are both so precious to me." She pauses to draw a breath, as if to think back to how a journey that started one evening when she agreed to teach me English so that I can find my louding voice ended with her getting the gift of two children from Ikati. Is it not a mystery, how kindness is a circle that somehow ends its curving journey right back where it started from?

Mama rubs a hand on Kayus's head, her voice

sounding like she pinch her nose tight to talk. "No more tears, Kayus. I know you'll miss Adunni, but we'll see her next weekend when we pick her up for therapy."

"I feeling afraid," Kayus whispers, twisting his shirt around his finger. "I feeling afraid of something bad to happen to all of us again. I didn't want us to go to anywhere."

Mama lows herself to her knees and takes Kayus's hands. "I am afraid too," she says, looking into his eyes, her voice shaking with tears. "I am scared of so many things about the future, but when I am scared, I think of what you told me at the edge of the river. Do you remember?"

Kayus nods, sniffs.

I look at the two both of them, confused about what is this secret they share.

"What did you tell me?" Mama asks.

I watch my brother, a smile traveling slowly around the road of his whole face and lighting up his eyes. He lifts up his left leg and stamps his feet on the floor, then says: "When you afraid, you think of something that angry you so much you want to just crush it." He lifts up his right leg, stamps it up and down. "You think of your fear like that." His voice is more strong with each stamp. "Like the head of your fear is under your feets! Then you stamp it! Stamp it! Then you run—quick!—and you don't look back!"

Mama laughs a happy laugh, stands. "That's

exactly what we are going to do. Come on, kids, Mr. Ade is waiting outside. Let's crush our fear about the future under our feet and let's go!"

Together, we begin to stamp our feet left, right, left in a happy march to the song of our laughter, all the way to the outside to where my real father is waiting in the car, waiting to finally, **finally** take me to school.

||||||||||||
TIA
||||||||||||
PORT HARCOURT

I could locate Boma's grave with my eyes closed: a concrete slab at the end of a row of soil mounds along a jagged path littered with moss and rotting rose petals, a gray stone marker inscribed with his name and the dates **1978–1999**.

He was buried next to his mother, both graves underneath an aging tree with gnarled roots and a crumbling bark that sheds its leaves on his mother's headstone so that it looks almost like an oblong dwarf tree. I tried to keep the area clean over the years, paying for the maintenance of the site, but after I got married, my visits became less regular, the time spent with Boma stolen from the time I was meant to spend visiting my mother.

I smell wet grass and damp leaves now as I sit on the edge of the cool stone grave and clear away the decomposing rose petals with a shaky hand and lean with my head tilted to one side as I often do, as if to listen to the whisper of his laugh from beyond the grave. We both had so much love to give each other, and had he lived, I think we would have had a great relationship. But that's the thing: I may think that, but I will never know. We might have broken up along the way. We might have split over the burden of raising Oyi. I will never know, and it's unfair to keep holding on to him as though I am certain of the future we'd have had. I pull the envelope of letters from my bag and slowly tear each one to pieces that float around me, settling on the earth, my feet.

Minute balls of egg-shaped light glide in the line of my vision as I spread myself on his grave, inhaling the soil and moss, my cheeks prickling against the cold, hard ground, tears sliding toward my left ear. I tell him I am sorry I refused when he asked for us to break up after my mother told him to leave me alone. If I had, he might have survived. I tell him about Adunni and Kayus and the girls I met in Ikati. About Ken, our fragile relationship, the unsure future of our marriage; about my mother, her story, and how forgiving her has felt like the release of a pent-up breath.

Finally, I tell him about Oyi. That I hope she's alive. That I will search for her with everything in me.

The sun winks through the canopy of trees as I gather the pieces of my torn letters and bury them beside his grave, and when I turn to walk away, I am surprised to find my father standing behind a fresh hole in the ground, his head bowed.

"I am sorry," he says when I walk up to him. He's aged since Mum died, his features crumpled, dejected. "About Boma. I am sorry I never paid attention to your mother, that she took it out on you. I was just . . ."

"She told Aunty Bea you didn't let her work."

"It wasn't a case of not letting her do anything," he says, tipping his cap back and pinching the bridge of his nose. "There was no conversation over the matter. My job was to give her a comfortable life. I did. Once, she complained of boredom, and I suggested she become a librarian. I thought it was enough to keep her busy." He's still baffled by this, by my mother's deep dissatisfaction with what he offered her.

"She was extremely brilliant," I say. "She wanted more." **She could have earned more recognition, fame, than you**, I think, but don't say. I wonder though, watching him, if he knew this, if he was silently threatened by what could have been a hugely successful career.

We begin the slow walk toward the wrought iron gate leading out of the cemetery.

"She never told me," Dad repeats. "She only said

she wanted to bury herself in books, and I built her a library."

I pause to look at him. "If she had told you, would you have stayed home to watch me? Or maybe, I don't know, taken a career break in turns? You had Ada to help out, right?"

He pauses beside the granite bust of a bald man in round glasses and observes the sculpture as if searching the rocky eyes for clues as to how to respond, then shakes his head. "I don't know, Tia. In my time, no man stayed at home. We did not take career breaks and I could not let Ada raise you alone. You are my daughter. Eno was my wife. My job was to provide. It was, still is, a thing of honor and pride for me." He touches his chest, his fingers knobbly. "I have no regrets for providing for my family. I worked for forty years. I gave you both my definition of the best."

I nod.

"I am deeply sorry for how everything affected you," he says, eyes glassy with tears that stain his gray lashes. "That my Eno suffered in the way she did. I made costly assumptions and I . . ." He jabs his hands into his pockets, sighs. "I will live with that pain for the rest of my life. The pain of not taking a moment to just ask my wife if this was what she wanted, if she was coping with it all. I might have . . . I don't know, retired sooner? Found a way to encourage her to ease back into the field she loved? I don't know." He gives a dejected shrug. "I never asked if **you** were okay. I could see the cracks in your relationship with her, but I kept on hoping, riding on a false enthusiasm, making stupid assumptions that you both would outgrow it, that it was a mother's job to keep her child happy. I was a financial success but an emotional failure. I failed you both."

I surprise myself by hugging him. He clings to me tightly, sobbing. "I am sorry," he says. Then he lets go and grabs my shoulder. "I've made that mistake, and you've suffered, but you can make amends for yourself, Tia. For you and Ken. Be open. Communicate. Make choices you can live with, choices you both understand and accept so that you can look back at your life one day and have no regrets."

He nods at someone behind my shoulder, and I turn to look. It's Ken, leaning on the hood of the taxi across the road from the cemetery, waiting for me.

"I'll meet you at the house," my dad says. He presses a kiss to my forehead. "Go to your husband. And, Tia?"

"Yes, Dad?"

"When we've said . . . goodbye to Mum, let's find your daughter together?"

I whisper my thanks, jog up the hilly graveside, and cross the road, to where Ken gathers me in his arms and lets me weep into his shoulders. There is so much uncertainty about our future together, but what matters right now is him holding me so I don't crumble. When he gently releases me and wipes my face with a crumpled tissue, he peers at me, concern in his eyes. "You okay?"

I nod. "Dad will meet us at home. We'll plan Mum's funeral, bury her, get it all over and done with." I have forgiven her, but I don't know how to love a woman I never knew, and this, I think, is easier to bear than when I had to find a way to pretend to mourn her. I won't mourn my mother, but I will mourn the relationship we might have had, what could have been, the memories we might have made.

"And then what?" He's asking about the After. It's not the first time he's asking, but it's the first time I have a definite answer.

"Two things," I say. "First, I am going back to Ikati. Hang on. Hear me out. Adunni roared for the freedom of the girls in her village, and I witnessed it. I now carry the resonant vibrations of her voice in my belly, this burning invitation to do more. I think often of the women and girls I met; of Kike, Enitan, Iya, Labake. Of Zenab, who died there; of little Hauwa, who isn't too far away. I must go back to Ikati, but this time with my office and the NGOs that have shown interest from the viral video. We are going to implement programs to empower those women and girls and basically transform lives. It's kind of a new life mission."

He nods. "Fair enough. And?"

"I'll continue my search for Oyi," I say. "Dad has promised to help. I stopped by Hotel Magnifique on my way to the airport, but the owner is out of town and—"

"Tia."

"Please," I say, tearing myself out of his grip. "Don't ask me to give up on my daughter, because I can't. I won't look back at my life with regrets. I—"

"What about us?" he cuts in, twisting and turning the platinum wedding band around his finger. "Where do we go from here?" He lifts his eyes, and I see despair, countered by a tinge of hope.

My chest is laden with intricate, convoluted thoughts. Do I love Ken? Yes. Do we have what it takes to continue to build a life together? I don't know. Is it fair to want a life with Adunni and Kayus and a chance to find and reconcile with Oyi and impose all of this on Ken?

I think of his mother then, of her intrusions into our lives and marriage, the questions she continues to probe us with, the suggestions to keep trying for children she knows her son cannot biologically produce.

"We want different things," I finally manage. "I love you, Ken, but you don't want kids. And now that Adunni—"

"And I love you," he says, plainly, simply, reaching for my wrist and slowly weaving his fingers into mine. "I don't know if love is enough to navigate the labyrinthian maze that is our marriage, but I know that because I love you, I am willing to try. I'll stumble through the dark and knock into things, but I'll find my way if you are by my side. I want you. Tia. I want what you want. And yes, I know I can't"—his voice breaks—"have kids of my own. But I have grown so fond of Kayus and Adunni . . . and now the thought of life with them, of making a positive difference in their lives, fills me with so much joy. I think it will be one of my greatest privileges." He gives me a shaky smile. "It won't be easy, but it'd be worth every moment. Can we start afresh? In truth? And if we decide to walk away from this, can we do so knowing we both gave it our best shot? We both deserve a fresh start, Tia. Please."

A fresh start. With Ken. And with Adunni and Kayus. And possibly Oyi. My heart beats with the words I struggle to utter: **I want this. I want all of this.**

A car whizzes past with the force of a breeze that ruffles the trees. I feel the seconds ticking by as he waits for my response. I am afraid but hopeful, comforted by his admission that our future together will be an honest and gradual exploration of where life takes us, and so, finally, I nod, tears in my eyes. "It won't be easy," I whisper. "But I think it'd be worth it."

"Thank you," Ken says, pressing a warm-lipped kiss to my forehead. "About Oyi," he says, when he takes a step back. "I'll help you find her, Tia, if that's what you want." He thumbs the tears on my cheek. "But can you pause to acknowledge how far you've come and enjoy this moment? I am awed by your strength, by what you've done for Adunni. You made all the difference in her and little Kayus's lives, and now you, we . . . will always have each other." His lips curve in a sad, shaky smile. "That's got to be something, right?"

I lift my head and look behind his shoulder, the sun casting hazy light in the horizon, soaking the world in copper dust. I think I hear the euphoric yet somewhat mournful cry of a baby far away, like a newborn acquiescing to its arrival into the world, and I wonder if it's the sign of what is to come, the voice of strength I'll need to live my world in parallels of motherhood, forever mourning Oyi, the daughter I birthed and lost and will never stop searching for, and raising Adunni and now Kayus, the children I was gifted with, the children I love. But Ken's wrong, I think, because what Adunni and Kayus and I have is a lot more than something.

It is the beginning of everything . . . of which there is no end.

||||||||||||||||||||||||||||||||||
EPILOGUE
||||||||||||||||||||||||||||||||||

THE DAILY TRIBUNE: 25 NOVEMBER 2015

The Nigerian army on Tuesday raided a baby factory in Eastern-Sheffi local government area and rescued ten pregnant teenagers and two babies. A midwife identified as Nurse Rose was also arrested. The facility, known as Beauty Charity Home, is said to have been operated by one Mrs. Katherine Ochu, popularly known as Madam K, who was apprehended a few meters from the scene while attempting escape. Troops raided the baby factory following an intelligence report from a girl identified as Efe.

The **Daily Tribune** recently reported that three village chiefs and ten other suspects were arrested in Ikati community in connection with various offenses relating to child abuse, child marriage, and female genital mutilation, which tragically resulted in the death of a promising young girl. It is believed that last night's raid on the baby factory is connected to the arrests in Ikati community. The commissioner for women's affairs told journalists on Saturday that a total of thirteen people were arrested in Ikati, including the mother of the deceased girl.

The minister said that this complex case, involving several states and several crimes, has been transferred to the criminal investigation department for each state, and that the suspects remain in custody.

"We continue to appreciate those who tendered evidence to help our case. Commendation once again to Adunni, the young girl whose passionate speech condemning such practices continues to trend. The timing of her speech allowed the officers to reach the scene in time to capture the perpetrators in action."

The police, in collaboration with nongovernmental organizations, will continue to work in Ikati and the surrounding communities to fish out additional offenders and ensure there is safety and stability for the girls from that region. A representative of the Lagos Environmental Consultancy, in partnership with the Africa Bank, has also begun a series of training sessions. These sessions aim to educate the newly installed community chiefs specifically on effective land-use practices and sustainable land management techniques.

The **Daily Tribune** has reached out to Adunni via her guardian for comment.

Efe, on the other hand, has requested that her contact details be printed alongside this story, and has expressly requested further interviews from TV stations and movie producers keen on adapting her story for the big screen.

ACKNOWLEDGMENTS

I'm immensely grateful to: God, the precious Holy Spirit, my ever-present help and companion, for this gift and for more to come.

I am thankful to every reader and advocate of my debut novel, **The Girl with the Louding Voice**. Its impact has surpassed my wildest dreams, resonating across borders and touching hearts in ways I never anticipated, from intimate book clubs in small towns to discussions at the highest echelons of government, to esteemed platforms and institutions that have graciously welcomed me to share insights from the book.

Writing this novel was a tough journey to an unknown destination. First, I suffered the devastating loss of my beloved sister-in-law, Elaine

Olutoyin Daré, followed shortly by my mother-in-law. Navigating grief, everything I wrote felt inadequate, half-baked; and this book is a testament to the collective effort of many hands and hearts that tirelessly supported me: Felicity Blunt, my indefatigable agent, who is wonderful in ways beyond what words can express, and who somehow never got (gets) tired of saying "Abi, you can do this." You possess such graceful wisdom and honesty, and "thank you" has always felt like a feeble attempt to convey the depths of my gratitude. Jen Joel (my US agent), Rosie Pierce, Flo Sandelson, and everyone at Curtis Brown and CAA, for your wisdom and guidance, for cheering me on, and for ceaselessly pushing my books into hearts and minds. Isn't it wonderful that we get to do this again? Lindsey Rose: Getting that first, wonderful email in response to **And So I Roar** made me cry. Thank you to you and the entire team at Dutton for believing in me and in the women and girls whose stories I've been compelled to tell. Fede Andorino: for your wisdom and invaluable insights; I am so excited and honored to work with you, Louise Court, Holly Knox, and everyone at Sceptre.

To my beloved family: Segs, who has loved me and let me be; unshackled, unfettered, unapologetically me. And who has somehow kept up with my spontaneous bursts of inspiration for two decades. The girls, A & D, you are both my heartbeat and my beating heart. Professor Teju Somorin, my dearest mum—who hadn't read a word of fiction in thirty years—read **The Girl with the Louding Voice** and called me rather annoyed at how it ended, demanding a sequel. I am sorry I couldn't fit Adunni's twenty-year plan for conquering the world into this book, but I hope this gives you a bit of respite. Thank you for being my best friend, from picking my outfits to wear to events to going over my keynote addresses and giving your (very often painfully academic) insights. Yemi, my sounding board, my biggest cheerleader. Mrs. Busola Awofuwa, my dearest mama. Olusco, Aunty Joke (for the puff-puffs that make sense when nothing else will), and the girls: You know.

The Tearfund team, particularly Jasmine Flagg for orchestrating that crucial meeting with Oscar Fwangmun Danladi at the Nigerian Jos Green Centre, who patiently discussed the effects of climate change on rural communities and women with me. Your impactful work continually inspires me. The passing of my father during the editing of this novel brought forth a profound realization: Our subconscious is always preparing us for what lies ahead. Beyond the struggle and resilience depicted in the women and girls I write about lies a contemplation on life's fragility, the balance between life and death, and the significance of making an impact versus mere existence. Adunni, your voice remains a cherished gift, inspiring me to continue being a voice for the voiceless. Thank you for the stark reminder that there is still much work to be done, and for showing me, even at a greater depth, that the injustices you and millions of girls face are not isolated incidents but symptoms of larger systemic issues that persist worldwide. I think you'd be pleased to know that the heart-wrenching exploration of your fictional life has led me to a new life's mission: to educate and empower women and girls in underserved communities in Nigeria through the establishment of my nonprofit, the Louding Voice Education and Empowerment Foundation. This is perhaps why you roared.

I apologize if I've inadvertently omitted anyone who played a significant role in my journey. Your support is invaluable, and I am grateful for each and every one of you.

ABOUT THE AUTHOR

Abi Daré is the author of **The Girl with the Louding Voice**, which was a **New York Times** bestseller, a **Today** show #ReadWithJenna book club pick, and an Indie Next pick. She grew up in Lagos, Nigeria, went on to study law at the University of Wolverhampton, and has an MSc in international project management from Glasgow Caledonian University, as well as an MA in creative writing from Birkbeck, University of London. Abi lives in Essex with her husband and two daughters, who inspired her to write her debut novel.